Malcolm Brabant is a veteran fore
had assignments in over ninety coun
olutions, earthquakes, refugee crises, and the tethered parrot who picked up a parking ticket in Southern Greece. He travels across Europe, shooting and editing his own films for America's *PBS Newshour*, and has a gong or five. He co-wrote the international bestseller, *The Daughter of Auschwitz*, which is the biography of Tova Friedman, one of the youngest survivors of the extermination camp. He is four inches shorter than Trine Villemann and ahem, a tad heavier. Well, more than a tad. At home in Sussex, the family golden retriever identifies him as Bacon Man. Any similarities with Bacon Man in *Dogsplaining* are purely in the reader's imagination.

Trine Villemann is best known in her native Denmark as a journalist with impeccable sources and a knack for breaking exclusive stories. She's the author of *1015 Copenhagen K*, a bestselling book regarded as the definitive guide to Denmark's Royal Family. Villemann is also the author of the *Queen of Deception*, a novel about the scandal ridden royal family of a small unnamed Nordic country. She met Malcolm Brabant in Sarajevo during the siege, and only gave him a second glance because he made her laugh. They married in Santorini in 1996. *Dogsplaining* is Villemann's idea. She wanted it to be a cute and cuddly dog book. But for once in their long, happy marriage, her husband didn't do as he was told.

First published in February 2025.

Copyright © 2025 Malcolm Brabant and Trine Villemann
The moral right of Malcolm Brabant and Trine Villemann to be identified as the authors of this book has been asserted in accordance with the Copyright, Designs and Patents Act, 1988. All rights reserved. No part of this publication may be reproduced or transmitted in any form, or any means, electronic or mechanical, including photocopying, recording, or any information storage and retrieval system without permission in writing from the authors.

BRABANTPRODUCTIONS@GMAIL.COM

DISCLAIMER

This is a work of fiction. Names, characters, businesses, organizations, places, and incidents either are the product of the author's imagination or are used fictitiously. Any resemblance to actual persons, living or dead, events, or locales is entirely coincidental.

DOGSPLAINING

DOGSPLAINING

A COMIC NOVEL

Malcolm Brabant
&
Trine Villemann

INSPIRED BY A REAL DOG

Praise for *Dogsplaining*.

Dogsplaining is an indispensable guide to canine thinking and recommended for all humans with animals in their lives. It's inventive, intriguing, and hilarious.
Ken Bruce. Broadcaster

I read *Dogsplaining* in one sitting. It's brilliant, very funny and honest. I was howling with laughter. Finally, I've discovered the origins of the phrase "all fur coat and no knickers." As *Dogsplaining* proves, not all heroes wear capes, but they do carry poo bags. You'd be barking mad not to read this book.
Beverley Cuddy. Editor, Dogs Today.

Dogsplaining is wickedly funny. It's a highly original take on human relationships through the eyes of the world's most observant golden retriever. Some of the scenes are so outrageous that I almost inhaled my morning coffee laughing.
Caroline Wyatt, Radio Four.

Dogsplaining is not the obvious follow up to an international bestseller about the Holocaust. But it's a welcome antidote to the global misery of the 21st century. A very clever novel where the gags just keep coming. The committee scene in which Morgan and Daisy battle their island nemesis Maurice Oxford is a hilarious satirical portrait of Brexit Britain. A must read.
Martin Brunt, Sky News.

A riotous and ribald helping of trenchantly witty marital dysfunction as observed by a dog. Just what the vet ordered.
Johnny Maitland. Playwright and broadcaster.

Bjørn isn't just any golden retriever. He's a Barry White fan, a joy-riding poseur, and a shrewd observer of family life. Comic set pieces involve family dinners residents' meetings, PR conferences and operatically accident-prone sex. Throughout, absurd situations are used to illustrate underlying truths. But Brabant and Villemann's critique of morality in modern Britain is applied with a light touch. They skewer curtain-twitching prurience and committee-room bullying, and examine free speech, for example, through the prism of a veteran rock singer who risks being cancelled because his lyrics haven't aged as well as he has. But the novel sidesteps earnest disapproval in favour of celebrating the sort of quirkiness that is not only exuberant but redemptive. *Dogsplaining* is an entertaining romp, the human reader's equivalent of a bracing game of fetch on the daily canine constitutional.
Kevin Sullivan. Novelist.

Hilarious. A joy to read. We dog lovers believe we understand what makes our pets tick. But *Dogsplaining* turns that perception on its head. In fact, our little darlings notice every embarrassing human moment and are brutally honest in their judgements. I'll never look at my pooch in the same light.
John Jason. Broadcaster.

Dogsplaining is very funny. Hilarious in fact, although rather low brow for literary agents who fancy themselves as being elevated. But it should be a wild success because the dog loving public will adore it.
Laura Trevelyan, Journalist and dog-lover.

DOGOLOGUE	11
BACON MAN	17
DOGNAPPED	26
MISSING DAISY	35
ALMOST ROADKILL	37
SNOOP DOG	47
TICKETY-BOO	52
IT'S COMPLICATED	61
LED ZEPPELIN SNORING	66
THE PIGEON FANCIER	74
SLUT	81
BADGERS AND BACON SANDWICHES	91
THE HYDRO-DONG	105
GUERILLA MARMALADE	122
PURPLE HEARTS AND BODY BAGS	141

STAR WARS 158

THE FAT MAN'S KAMA SUTRA 174

A WORD TO THE WISE. 208

PENALTY SHOOT OUT 215

LENTIL MAN. 233

LIQUORICE MICHELIN MAN 246

MIRROR, MIRROR 255

THE OTHER WOMAN 269

NO MERCY SHAGS 291

ROUND TWO. 300

TWATS. 316

BACK IN THE SACK 331

BACON MAN DOWN 342

THE RECKONING 355

GOOD GOLLY MISS MOLLY 365

CHAPTER ONE

DOGOLOGUE

The more I think about that news item on Good Morning Britain, the more outraged I become. The reporter was trumpeting the "findings" of one Professor Stanley Coren, a psychologist at the University of British Columbia in Vancouver, who specialises in studying the intelligence and mental ability of dogs.

After analysing data collected by obedience judges at dog shows, Professor Coren claimed that golden retrievers can understand about a hundred and sixty-five words. He concluded that we have the same linguistic ability as a two-year-old child.

What an insult. A hundred and sixty-five words? Anyone would think we're monosyllabic.

"Sit! Stay! Lie down! Dinner time! Leave the cat alone! Look! Squirrel! Better luck next time."

Let me assure you that our vocabulary and comprehension are a squillion times more sophisticated than that.

Where's the Prof's empirical evidence for this contemptuous slur? Has he been peer reviewed? How does he have the nerve to call himself an expert? The only thing that irritates me more is the ginger cat at Number 23.

Trust me, I'm not hurling my squeaky toys out of my

basket just because sheepdogs, poodles, and German Shepherds have been gifted the first three places in Coren's Pantheon of Canine Cleverness. I'm being Zen because all my golden retriever instincts are screaming that his conclusion is bollocks. And definitely not the dog's bollocks.

The only vaguely credible element of the Professor's "research" is that Afghan hounds are the most stupid dogs on the planet. Given the Taliban's attitude to education, that's hardly surprising.

Allow me to introduce myself. My name is Bjørn. My head is resting on a throw cushion, my paws are hanging over the edge of the big cream sofa in the sitting room and I'm basking in a sunbeam. My lungs are full of cool, fresh air because the balcony door is open. Outside, Old Father Thames keeps rolling along, down to the mighty sea.

I live in a gated community called Galahad Island. I'm not sure of the precise coordinates and that's only because I haven't mastered Google Maps. Give me time and I'll succeed, and maybe I'll pin it for you with my dew claw. But I'm certain the island is west of London, on the way to Henley. Together with boisterous wildlife, flowing water is the soundtrack to my new existence as head of this household.

I'm not yet fully grown, but I'm already running rings around my humans, or owners as they like to call themselves. They do my bidding. Not the other way round because I'm super smart.

From my vantage point in the sitting room, I've been binge-watching television recently. My people have the box on in the background much of the time. Back in their day, they were top newshounds, and old habits die hard.

Often, there's nothing that troubles my brain cells.

For example, that show Prime Minister's Questions is nothing more than an outlet for narcissists with small dog syndrome to bark at each other. Really!

Nevertheless, if you cherry pick, television can be highly informative. My young brain is like a sponge. My ability to absorb knowledge has improved exponentially since I manipulated my paw to change channels with the remote, or as my humans call it, the doovalacky. Which, just in case you didn't know, is Australian slang for an item whose name you've forgotten.

Thank goodness not all TV producers are dumbing down to the lowest common denominator and some professionals still adhere to the most important pillar of Lord John Reith's broadcasting principles. And what's that, people? To educate, of course.

You humans are barking up the wrong dog urinal if you think we're just dumb animals. You completely underestimate us. Our potential is huge, if only we could smash the doggist glass ceiling holding us back.

Face facts, people. Men are making a complete Horlicks of this wonderful planet of ours. Need I say more than Ukraine, the Middle East, theocracies with nuclear weapons?

Where are the peacemakers?

The United Nations?

Pah.

If that's your yardstick, then put the Pope in charge of world population control.

Isn't it about time you gave women a crack? But if you're not willing to give the female of your species a chance to rule the world, then provide golden retrievers with the tools to do the job.

And I don't mean the type available at your local gender reassignment centre.

The only reason one of our representatives doesn't have a permanent seat on the United Nations Security Council is that we lack the mechanical means to articulate our thoughts. If life was a level playing field, the UN Secretary-General would certainly be a golden retriever.

Of all the mammals on earth, we are the most suitable and qualified. I'm not suggesting for one minute that we're cognitively superior to dolphins, whales or octopi.

Yes, I know an octopus isn't a mammal, but grant me a little literary latitude, will you? I'm fully aware it's a marine mollusc, and a cephalopod, which is a compound Greek word meaning head-foot.

But when was the last time you saw an octopus going for walkies? You can't achieve your daily target of ten thousand steps with a creature best served grilled, and accompanied by a carafe of ouzo in a taverna on the island of Serifos.

So, don't be swayed by the aquatic lobby. Whales will sink your boat. Swim with dolphins, and they'll try to slip you one. It doesn't matter how you identify, whether you wear budgie-smugglers, a bikini or even a burkini, any hole's a goal as far as Flipper is concerned.

I do admit that some of my breed will occasionally dry hump your leg. But trust me, it's nothing more than a K9 version of the Haka. It's harmless retriever banter. Get over it.

Golden retrievers are friends with absolutely anybody and everybody. We do not discriminate, and we are the least aggressive dogs on earth.

If I could compare us to one historical personification of peace, it would be Mahatma Gandhi. Except we've got bigger appetites, and we're not vegetarians.

Have you ever listened to a golden retriever? We don't just bark, we make other distinctive sounds, like woooohooooo, especially in the morning. We're trying to have a sophisticated conversation with you, but for some reason, our voice boxes are still operating Version 1.0 and have never been upgraded.

Now, if one of your Artificial Intelligence specialists or neuroscientists would be kind enough to resolve that issue and help us transform yapping into mellifluous speech, then perhaps we could put an end to wars, world hunger and climate change.

Stephen Hawking got a squawk box. So why can't we? Just don't make us sound so tinny. Give us the rich baritone we deserve. And there's one thing I must insist upon. When you eventually get around to mastering the operation, I don't want to emerge from the anaesthetic haze speaking with a Brummie accent or sounding like Jamie Carragher. I want to hold conversations with people. Not spit at them.

While I'm loath to play the victim card as so many humans do, I do think the brain boxes running MENSA need to undergo a period of bio-diversity re-education. Perhaps then, their institution might see fit to establish a canine chapter. It may be hard for you to grasp, but with my IQ, it's probable that I'm a puppy prodigy. The better educated among your species will easily identify a handful of child prodigies. Just in case you're having a brain freeze, permit me to enlighten you.

Wolfgang Amadeus Mozart could play the harpsichord at three-years-old. Two years later, Wolfie gave a piano concert at the University of Salzburg. He wrote his first composition at the age of six.

Here's a more contemporary reference for those of you who believe the Second World War belongs to the realms of Ancient History.

Stevie Wonder went blind as a baby after being given too much oxygen in an incubator. But he demonstrated his genius by teaching himself to play numerous instruments by the age of ten. One year later, Motown Records signed Little Stevie Wonder as an artist, and the rest is pop music history. Signed. Sealed. Delivered.

So, if it's possible for humans to be intellectually advanced at a tender age, then I'm living proof that it can also happen in golden retrievers. You're seeking intelligent life in outer space. But you're looking in all the wrong places. It's right here in front of you. Lounging on your sofas, dog-spreading. Licking our balls. Because we can.

Here endeth the dogologue.

Except to say, I can't believe how far I've come since I moved here. But that's genius for you.

CHAPTER TWO

BACON MAN

"What the hell is that?"

Damn. I've just peed over The Blonde's jacket. But unruffled, she keeps holding on to me as she calmly turns towards the man's deep voice.

"This," she says, "is a present to myself. He's a golden retriever. He's eight-weeks-old and you just made him piss all over me."

I twist around and set sight on a rotund man standing in a doorway.

"Very funny. Just don't forget to hand it back when you've had your fun," he says.

I'm offended. My personal pronoun is him, not it.

"I didn't borrow him. He's mine and his name is Bjørn," retorts The Blonde.

"You can call him Vlad the Impaler for all I care," he says. "I know you, and you don't want a dog."

The man is shorter than The Blonde but much heavier, and his oversized shirt barely covers a stomach that's more planet than paunch. The buttons look primed to shoot into orbit at any minute.

"Then you don't know me at all," says The Blonde. "Yes, I do want a dog. He's going to bring so much joy into my life."

"I want some joy too," he says. "Fat chance of that happening if we're his prisoners for the next ten to fifteen years."

The fat guy is bald, and his eyes resemble angry shards of flint. For some reason, I'm drawn to a long single grey hair protruding from his left nostril. What's odd is that although it's winter, he's wearing shorts. Red ones. Is he trying to draw attention to himself? Or is he just an overgrown schoolboy? On the plus side, his feet are encased in fat squirrels.

They can wait. My priority is to protect The Blonde, my new Mama. I take a deep breath, reach down for the most terrifying bark in my repertoire, and let rip.

The fat guy is not the slightest bit perturbed, and I know why. I was aiming for rottweiler, but the bark comes out all poodley.

"Are you completely out of your mind? We're not having a dog."

My bladder goes weak again.

"Look. Now it's pissing on the floor. What the hell were you thinking?"

"Stop shouting, *Skatter*. You're scaring him," she says.

"How much did you pay for it?"

"Two and a half thousand," replies The Blonde.

"You're kidding," he groans.

"No. That's the going rate. I'm lucky I didn't have to pay three."

"How could you?"

"Because I want a dog."

I'm stuck in The Blonde's arms and getting dizzy. My head is going backwards and forwards as I try to keep up with them shouting at each other. How long is this going to last?

"Please take him back. Please," pleads the fat guy, breathing hard.

"No, I won't."

"Jesus, Daisy. You're impossible."

Aha. He called her Daisy. That must be The Blonde's name. See, I'm a fast learner.

Skatter disappears into the next room. I start wriggling. Daisy sets me down on the floor and I scamper after the fat squirrels. I fling myself at the one on the left and tear off a lump of fur with my teeth. Bugger. There's no meat attached.

"Now it's going for my slippers. Get that dog out of here."

"Oh calm down, will you?"

Daisy snarls like my siblings did when we wrestled at the breeder's place. She's trying to grab me. But I'm engrossed in the squirrel game. I've torn several clumps of fur that are now scattered across the floor.

"Get off."

Skatter shakes his foot, catching me by surprise and I slide halfway across the room. What fun. I lunge at his right foot, and this time he flicks more vigorously, slamming me into a table leg. I'm winded and yelp. But I'm not giving up. I sprint back and find myself lifted into the air.

"Okay, that's enough. It's too rough," says Daisy. "Let's take it easy."

She sits down on a sofa, and I gauge the change in mood. I'd better calm down. The fat squirrels aren't going anywhere. I'll try again later.

"What on earth were you thinking, Daisy?" asks the fat guy, sinking into the sofa opposite.

"Look at him. Isn't he adorable?"

Daisy's talking about *me*. I give her my best golden retriever smile. Lips back, teeth half showing, tongue fully extended, although I'm panting harder than usual because of my exertions. Daisy smiles back. I'm convinced she likes me a lot.

Maybe my charm will win over *Skatter*. I smile at him with my most open face and try to catch his eye. But he blanks me.

"That's not the point," he replies. "All puppies are adorable and then they grow up."

Aha. There's a chink in *Skatter's* armour. He's admitted that I'm adorable.

"What's happening here, Daisy? Are you having a midlife crisis?" asks the fat guy, in an almost compassionate tone.

"I wouldn't have minded if you'd bought a sports car. But a dog?"

"I'm not having a mid-life crisis," replies Daisy, equably.

"But I'm desperate for a companion to share the small pleasures in life."

"If you want a pet, why not get a cat."

Now I'm really offended.

"Cats are more independent. They get put out at night and if you're lucky, they don't come back."

"I'm not a cat person," replies Daisy.

Her approval ratings keep climbing.

"But I need someone to share my life with, especially since the kids left home."

"Go the whole hog then," smirks the fat guy.

"Divorce me and marry the bloody thing. It should be possible these days. You'll just have to identify as a golden retriever. Find a trendy Church of England vicar and Bob's your uncle. Or Spot the dog is."

"Don't be ridiculous," replies Daisy.

"My point is you never want to come walking with me."

"Yes, I do," he protests.

"I've seen snails move faster than you," says Daisy, curling her upper lip.

"You can't keep up with me. I love walking by the Thames, but you keep making excuses not to come because you get out of breath so quickly."

The tone of the conversation is not so civilised now.

"You're making me out to be an invalid, I mean an ambulatorily challenged person."

"That's the elephant in the room isn't it," says Daisy.

"Thanks for the elephant analogy. Stop nagging, will you?"

"I stopped nagging when you reached a hundred and twenty kilos. What do you weigh now? A hundred and fifty? You're not far off the upper limit for a mobility scooter. If you get any bigger, you'll need police outriders to go to Tesco."

Daisy is breathing fast. I start looking for a place to hide when *Skatter* loses it.

"All you ever do is drone on about my weight. It's so tiresome. You just can't resist it, can you? I've had enough of you."

With some difficulty, he prises himself off the sofa and storms out. I hear banging and slamming.

"Whatever happened to the man I married?" she shouts.

"The award-winning war reporter who could tie his own shoelaces without passing out."

Daisy bends down and scratches me behind my ear. I love it and don't want her to stop. But I can tell she's distracted, so instead of rolling onto my back for a serious tummy scrub, I lie still.

"Let's go and talk some sense into that old fart in the kitchen, shall we?"

She sighs and looks me in the eyes with a mixture of pessimism and determination. I can tell she's used to winning battles. I wouldn't want to get on her wrong side. I follow her into the next room and am overwhelmed by a sensational aroma. A strand of drool appears from nowhere and hangs from my jaw to the floor.

"Yes. Before you say anything, I plead guilty to having a bacon sandwich," says *Skatter*.

He's sitting down at a wooden table and talking with his mouth full.

"I skipped lunch because I thought we were going shopping together and eating afterwards."

The smell coming from his plate is irresistible. I try to climb up his outstretched leg to get at the food.

"Get down Big Guy," commands Daisy. "There's a good boy. Leave Bacon Man alone."

So, *Skatter* has another name. Bacon Man. It suits him perfectly.

Bacon Man shakes his leg and I fall off. Back on the ground, I realise that he must be a serially untidy cook. There are crumbs all over the floor which I hoover up as quickly as possible. I can taste traces of meat. I'm not interested in grated carrot, avocado peel, or any vegan muck. No wonder Bacon Man likes it out here. I hope he won't mind sharing.

"It's no good hiding in the kitchen," says Daisy. "And why are you eating a bacon sandwich so close to suppertime?"

She's lost me there. What's wrong with a bacon sandwich before a meal?

"Because I fancy one, okay?"

Bacon Man looks like he'd defend that sandwich with his life. I'm with you, brother.

"Darling, you've got type two diabetes," she says.

"Don't call me darling, it's patronising," he snaps back.

"You're on statins for high cholesterol, on top of the diabetes medication. You're getting fatter and fatter and refusing to do anything about it. You're a prime candidate for a heart attack. Don't you realise that one of these days you're just going to drop dead?"

"Stop being hysterical. Of course, I'm not."

"You're delusional, *Skatter*."

Daisy sounds genuinely concerned. She hammers her hand into the kitchen counter and makes me jump.

"Have you seen the size of your calves? The cuts on your shins aren't healing. Your right big toe is discoloured and swollen. You may not die straight away, but you could end up with your extremities being amputated. How are you going to eat a bacon sandwich with no hands?"

I have a suggestion. Just bend down and use your mouth.

A sliver of bacon tumbles from Bacon Man's sandwich onto the floor. I dive on it and swallow it whole. Ouch. It's hot. I get a brief taste before it plunges down my gullet. Wow. Bacon! Now that is the dog's bollocks. The first hit blows my mind. I'm going to be chasing the bacon dragon for the rest of my life. Suddenly the bacon comes rushing back up again. I sample it a second time before it's projected onto the floor.

"Look, he just threw up. Don't feed him. You are making him sick," shouts Daisy.

Although the bacon is now lying in a puddle of drool, garnished by other ingredients from my stomach, it still smells divine. Daisy tears off some kitchen roll and heads for the vomit. Maybe she also fancies that piece of bacon in the middle. Who wouldn't? Daisy may be lovely, but I'm not sharing. I bend down and swallow it before she can steal my prize.

"No. Stop," she shouts. "Oh, that's disgusting."

Bacon Man chuckles.

"So, Daisy, how do you think you're doing? He's running rings around you."

"Don't change the subject. Feel free to eat yourself into an early grave but you're not going to feed him. Understood? He's *my* dog. I feed him."

She's being a tad unfair here. What's wrong with Bacon Man feeding me too?

"Suit yourself," he snarls.

Bacon Man grabs a plate with two thick bacon sandwiches and leaves the kitchen. I follow him into a room containing a long white wooden table. Ignoring the fat squirrels, I sit next to his feet and wag my tail. I catch him peering at me out of the corner of an eye, but he looks away and takes a big bite of the sandwich.

The smell is intoxicating. I try to spring onto his lap but

fail miserably. I land painfully and yelp. Something falls from Bacon Man's fingers. Christ. What a messy eater he is. If I was human, I couldn't bear to look at him at chow time. But from a dog's perspective, he's total box office.

I need to hurry because here comes Daisy with the kitchen paper.

"Are you feeding him?"

"No, I'm not feeding the bloody dog."

I pounce on the morsel. It contains a slithery piece of bacon fat attached to a decent chunk of the rasher, and it's stuck to a piece of bread, moist with grease. Pure nectar.

"I assume you won't be hungry later?" says Daisy.

It doesn't sound like a question.

"So, there won't be supper tonight. And drop any notion of having secret cheese sandwiches to compensate. I found the cheddar you'd hidden in the larder. It's in the bin. And just in case you think about salvaging it, I've wrapped it in the kitchen roll I used to mop up the dog's piss."

"You really are something else," he groans.

"You're always going on about how much food we waste, and yet you're chucking out good quality stuff. Cheese is protein and good for you."

"Not in the amounts that you eat it."

I'm suddenly exhausted. I can't stop yawning. The bread is laying heavily in my stomach. I've got a fantastic after taste in my mouth. They're arguing again, but the sound is becoming fainter and fainter and fainter and ……….

CHAPTER THREE
DOGNAPPED

I WAKE UP ON THE floor outside Daisy's room. It's dark outside and the house is almost completely silent. I can hear Daisy breathing deeply and Bacon Man moving about. For someone that size, he's surprisingly stealthy. I'd say he's had plenty of practice sneaking out of bedrooms. As we meet on the landing, I roll over and invite a tummy scrub. But he ignores me and closes Daisy's door with the faintest of clicks.

"Shhhh," he whispers as he picks me up.

Perhaps he's changed his mind and likes me after all. I lick his cheek and he chuckles quietly. He tiptoes downstairs into my favourite room, the kitchen. Hurray.

Then he takes a key off a hook, and we go outside into the darkness. All of this has been achieved with minimal noise. The experience has been so intriguing, I've forgotten to bark. The air is freezing. It feels like I'm inhaling particles of ice. Ah, I recognise the silver thing. It's the car. Bacon Man inserts the key into the door. There's no beep or flashing orange lights as there were when Daisy collected me from the breeder.

Bacon Man deposits me in the box which Daisy used to bring me home. The engine fires up quietly and we start moving slowly and smoothly. I look up and see big metal gates swinging open. The car speeds up and Bacon Man's phone starts talking to him.

"At the T-junction, turn right and head towards the roundabout. At the roundabout, take the third exit and follow signs for the M4 motorway."

Bacon Man looks at ease behind the wheel. This seems like his natural habitat. He glances down starts talking to me in a far more urbane manner than the hostile tone of yesterday.

"Well, young fella, I've traced the farm where Daisy bought you. And I'm taking you back."

I thought I was set for life at Daisy's house. I'm so bewildered, the bark gets stuck in my throat.

"I'm sure you're hungry. Don't worry. I'm starving as well."

The car brakes gently. Bacon Man's window slides down, and he stops next to a brightly illuminated machine covered in pictures of food.

"Could I have a sausage breakfast muffin, two bacon breakfast muffins, a cinnamon roll and a cappuccino please?"

Just a light breakfast then. The car moves forward to a bright window and delicious smelling paper parcels are handed over. Bacon Man drives a short distance, turns off the engine and gets down to the serious business of eating.

I smell bacon and drool starts building in my mouth. The aroma distracts me from my current predicament of being dognapped and returned to sender.

Bacon Man goes for the steaming sausage muffin first. It's gone within three bites.

"Hey, Mister. What about sharing?" I bark. "Hey, what about me?"

"That hit the spot," he says..

He unwraps another parcel, takes the top off and puts a piece of bacon between his fingers, blows on it and holds it outside in the cold air.

"Come on, you're teasing me. Give me some," I bark.

It seems an eternity before he turns my way.

"There you go. Breakfast time."

I snaffle the bacon in one go. It burns my mouth, but cluster bombs my taste buds. Terrific. It doesn't have the same succulence as yesterday's bacon. This seems cheaper, less well cured, possibly unsmoked. Nevertheless, I'm in a state of bliss. And now he's offering me the bottom half of the muffin.

"I bet you haven't had an egg before," he says. "Well, you can eat that later, when it's cooled down."

With that, Bacon Man unwraps his bacon muffin and it disappears faster than the sausage one. No surprise there.

He turns the ignition, and we ease away from the drive-thru, accelerating smoothly as we hit the open road. It's all I can do to maintain my balance and keep my food down.

"Take the M4 for twenty miles to junction eleven for the Basingstoke turning,." instructs the voice inside the phone.

With his hunger banished, Bacon Man is even more laid back, steering with one hand, and quaffing coffee. And he's smiling at me. Maybe having a full stomach will persuade him to do a U-turn.

"How was breakfast so far? Did you enjoy it? You can have the egg part in a minute. Do you know what? You're a lovely little fella and ordinarily, you and I would be great friends but it's just the wrong time. I was gobsmacked when Daisy brought you home yesterday. We had a cast-iron agreement that we wouldn't have a dog again. We used to have a labrador called Dash. He was wonderful. Such a great temperament. He used to love playing football and swimming in the river. But he got bad arthritis, and he could barely move."

"Shortly before his tenth birthday he had a massive heart attack and dropped dead. We don't think he suffered. But it was extremely painful for us."

I don't believe it. Beneath that gruff exterior, Bacon Man has a soft spot for dogs. Golden retrievers aren't so different from labradors. So, why aren't I cute enough for him?

"Anyway, you couldn't possibly understand this, but we've not been getting on well for some time."

Let me tell you, pal, it's about to get even worse if you don't turn around.

"We used to have a very happy marriage. We had such a romantic start. But it's just drifted over the years and now we're little more than friends, if that. I dream about turning the clock back and trying to rekindle the spark."

I don't really know what love is, but I think I got a taste of it yesterday when Daisy picked me up. But I fully understand the concept of happiness. A good stick. And my new discovery. Bacon. And Daisy, of course. She's made me very happy. I wonder if Bacon Man realises just how unkind he's being.

Oh, he's off again.

"I've been looking forward to travelling abroad again and taking Daisy to places on her bucket list, in the hope that we can fall in love again. But every time I try to plan something, life gets in the way. And that's it. We can't just nip off for long weekends to Budapest or Riga if we have a dog. I've been looking at cruises to Greenland, which is top of her list. But it wouldn't be fair to leave you in kennels for two weeks, while we're off spotting icebergs and polar bears."

"Here. The egg half of the muffin has cooled off, you can eat it now."

He drops the food into my box. Is that really an egg? Has he made a mistake and got some plant-based mush? I doubt it's even seen a hen's butt. But it has had a fleeting relationship with the bacon half of the muffin, so there's a smoky frisson as it slithers down my throat.

"The other thing is, I hate what I do for a living. I've lost all self-respect."

What is this? Confession time? I know I'm wearing a dog collar, but do I look like a priest?

"I never used to feel this bad in a war zone."

He's going to need a flak jacket if we don't turn back soon.

"I know I've turned into this grumpy old git. But that's only because my reporting career ended so badly. The irony is we make a good living. But I've sold my soul. I've joined the dark side. I can't begin to tell you how much I hate corporate work."

Suddenly the phone vibrates.

"Oh bugger. You weren't supposed to get up this early, Daisy," exclaims Bacon Man as he hits the red button.

Moments later, the phone vibrates again. This time Bacon Man is faster on the trigger.

"In three hundred yards, take the slipway to the left at junction eleven and follow the signs to Basingstoke."

Again, the phone rings.

"Damn, I'll have to call her back," says Bacon Man, looking flustered.

Every time he hits the red button, the phone lights up immediately. Shortly after leaving the motorway, he pulls over and stops. Bacon Man swipes the phone attached to the fresh air grill. He opens his mouth and is silenced by Daisy raging at full volume.

"I know exactly where you are. I'm tracking you on Find My iPhone. You've just turned off the M4 onto the Basingstoke road. I guess you're in a lay-by near that hospital outside Reading. I hope you've still got the dog with you, otherwise you're in deep shit."

"Yes, he's with me."

"I assume you're heading to the kennels in Wiltshire."

"Er yes."

Bacon Man is stuttering.

"You had no right to buy him, Daisy. It's not fair on me. I'm taking him back. It's for the best."

"You listen to me. If you don't bring him back home within an hour. I'm going to divorce you."

I told you she'd be on the warpath.

"Oh, you don't mean that. Stop trying to blackmail me."

"I have never been more serious in my life. If you want to spend your old age alone, then go ahead and take him back to the kennels."

"You're kidding."

"No, *Skatter*, let me assure you I'm not. I'm being deadly

serious. You bring him back here right now. Do you understand?"

"Look Daisy. I'll bend over backwards to make you happy."

"You can't bend at all."

"Daisy, I'll do anything to make it up to you."

"Good. Put the hammer down on the way home, and we'll forget this episode ever happened."

"You can have anything you want within reason. How about a second honeymoon?"

"A second honeymoon, *Skatter*? What planet are you on?"

"Well, whatever you want? A personal trainer. You can even have a toy boy, and I'll turn a blind eye if it makes you happy."

"I wouldn't know what to do with a toy boy. We'd have nothing to talk about."

"Isn't that the whole point? How about a toy girl then? As long as I can watch."

Bacon Man has got a strange grin on his face. There's silence on the other end, but then Daisy comes back.

"Do you really expect me to indulge your fantasies. Anyway, I tried that girl-on-girl action once. It wasn't for me. I'm a Deliveroo girl."

"What do you mean?"

"I'm not that keen on eating out."

Bacon Man roars with laughter. I hope this is the turning point and that Daisy has won the argument.

"Great one liner, Daisy, but joking aside, I can't think of a single good reason to keep the dog."

"You just identified one compelling reason. Think about it.

He'll be the perfect personal trainer for both of us. He could save your life. That's what I'm trying to do."

"Daisy, think practically for a minute. If we keep the puppy, he'll seriously impact the business."

"It'll be fine," she replies. "We'll manage, we always do."

"Hang on a minute," says Bacon Man. "You haven't thought this through."

"Yes I have," she retorts.

"Will you just listen to me for a minute," says Bacon Man. "You're being completely unreasonable. Stop shutting me down and let me explain."

"Go on then."

"Crisis management is our biggest earner. Do you really think a corporation is going to say, 'Take your time. Our share price is falling off a cliff, we're about to go bankrupt, but we'll hang on until you can find your puppy a kennel?' Get a grip, Daisy."

"We'll manage."

"That's not a solution, Daisy."

"You never used to fear change. Having a dog scares you because it's upsetting your complacent existence."

"I'm not scared of change. But I am bothered about not being able to earn a living because we can't get a dog sitter. What pisses me off more than anything else is the way you're trying to impose this on me without any consideration whatsoever."

"Oh dear. For once, I've done something for me. After more than twenty-five years, I've finally put myself first instead of playing second fiddle to you and the children."

"You just aren't listening, Daisy. There's no point in arguing with you. I'm going to put the phone down and take the dog back."

Oh no. I'd have bet the farm on Daisy winning this argument. But Bacon Man possesses more steel than I thought.

"If you take the dog back, believe me, you'll suffer the consequences."

Daisy's voice gives me the chills. The fur on my neck is standing up. I hope I'm not transitioning into a cat.

"I don't believe you, Daisy. This is just another of your empty threats. You do it all the time whenever we have an argument. You can call all you want. I'm not going to answer."

CHAPTER FOUR
MISSING DAISY

WHAT HAVE I DONE TO deserve this? Tasting freedom for a day, and then having it snatched away. I've never felt more alone. I can't begin to tell you how much I miss Daisy. My heart feels as though it's weighed down by rocks. I feel even more bereaved than when my birth Mama was led away.

The breeder looked distinctly unhappy when Bacon Man said he was returning me. But you should have seen her face light up when he said he didn't want his money back.

I tried to catch Bacon Man's eyes as he walked away, to appeal to his better nature. I wanted him to know that not only was he being unkind to me, but he was also hurting his wife, maybe even breaking her heart.

I think Bacon Man is a coward. He turned on his heel after handing me over and didn't glance back. I didn't get a chance to look him in the eye and riddle him with guilt.

I have no idea what the future holds for me. At least I now know the procedure. The breeder will try to sell me to someone else. I just hope that whoever buys me is as sweet as Daisy.

I wonder if I'll ever have bacon again. The breeder certainly hasn't rolled out the welcome mat by dropping a few rashers in my plastic container.

I've heard her ringing around and offering me for sale. It's so degrading. I'm not a goldfish. I'm a sentient being with a warm heart and emotions.

Right now, the breeder is outside the shed or barn or wherever it is she's holding me.

"Yes, I have an eight-week-old puppy. But I suspect he'll be gone by the end of the day. There's a high demand at the moment. I've got three different people coming to see him before lunchtime."

I strained to hear what the person at the other end of the phone was saying. But it was impossible. I could only hear the breeder.

"Well, I'll need a bank transfer for the full amount. Ok."

What does that mean? I'm tired. The drive here exhausted me, as has all the sobbing.

I'll just lie down for a minute.

I open my eyes and my heart sinks as I realise that I haven't moved from the cage. I may have slept but I'm not rested. I had a nightmare about being chased by a pack of black, muscular dogs with huge square heads, sinister eyes and teeth that could scythe through metal. They were just about to catch me when I woke up.

Oh, no, here comes the breeder.

My senses are confusing me. My head is telling me she's going to give me to a stranger. But my nose is telling me something else. I recognise that smell.

"Hello big guy. I've missed you so much. Come on. We're going home. This time for good."

CHAPTER FIVE
ALMOST ROADKILL

I'm back in the cardboard box, padded with a blanket, sitting in the front seat next to Daisy. We seem to be moving fast, but I can't work out where we're going. Daisy pushes a button to the left of the steering wheel and suddenly my balls start tingling like crazy.

"*You're the first, my last, my everything, the answer to all my dreams.*"

Crumbs, that guy has got a lascivious voice. Testosterone by the bucketload. I want whatever he's got. I wonder what his pipes do to Daisy's balls.

"Do you like the music, Big Guy? It's Barry White. The soundtrack of my youth. When I was almost as gorgeous as you."

I'm not too sure about the music, although I love the sensation in my balls.

"Barry White's voice goes straight to my lady bits. But it's been a while since there's been any real sensation down there."

I wonder if Daisy's car's entertainment system incorporates one of those remote vibrators I once heard the breeder discussing. This version is reverberating in Sensurround. If so, cars are clearly designed with more than transportation in mind. They must also be pleasure wagons. How on earth do people concentrate on driving? The death toll on the roads must be epic.

"As far as I'm concerned, the world ended when Barry popped his clogs. But you're going to make it a whole lot better, aren't you?"

Daisy starts singing along.

"*You're my sun, my moon, my guiding star. My kind of wonderful, that's what you are.*"

For some reason, the impact on my balls isn't the same. She's not hitting the same notes as this Barry White guy. I don't have perfect pitch, but I'd say she was way off tune. However, I like the words. I think she's singing to me. It ill-behoves me to criticise so quickly. I should endeavour to be more charitable.

The car is pitching from side to side as Daisy feeds the wheel through her hands. I can't see where we're going, and my limited horizon keeps changing. I start to feel queasy and lie down. I don't want to disgrace myself.

Daisy seems to perceive my discomfort. Maybe like me, she has a sixth sense. She stops singing and pets my stomach. That's exactly what I wanted. She strokes my tummy gently with her thumb, while looking straight ahead and holding the wheel with the other hand. The pressure starts to ease. I sit up and lick her hand. I wonder if she knows I'm showing my appreciation.

"Do you know what the name Bjørn means? It's Danish

for bear. You're my little bear, but I wonder what you're really like?"

It sounds like one of those rapid-fire quizzes.

Beef or chicken?

Both.

Cat or dog?

Well, it's not a cat, is it? Duh!

Ball or stick?

Ball. Stick. Stick. Ball.

I'd like to tell Daisy that I whimper in my dreams, my poo is runny more often than not, and the breeder told other humans that I suffer from something called separation anxiety. I haven't a clue what that means, but my fear of being alone is off the charts.

* * *

Suddenly, creaking hinges hurt my ears. I'm a bit woozy. I must have woken up during my what's it called? REM? Rapid Eye Movement. Oooh. Hello. We're back. I recognise the sounds and the smells through Daisy's open window. The creaking must have been the gates of Galahad Island opening. As she parks the car, I hear a familiar voice.

"Thank God, Daisy. Where have you been?"

"Out."

"I know that. You've been gone for hours."

"And?"

"I've been ringing and ringing. But you didn't pick up."

"Now you know what it's like."

"I was terrified you'd had an accident, or that you'd left me."

"Well, I'm back. But leaving you is still an option if you keep on shouting."

"I'm not shouting."

"Hello, Maurice."

Daisy addresses a man in a cap. I catch a brief glimpse as he passes by. He's walking a dog. I can smell it. Daisy continues talking through gritted teeth and a fake smile.

"Keep your voice down, dear. You don't want the neighbours to hear how aggressive you can sound."

"I'm not aggressive. I'm just relieved you're back. Oh no."

Bacon Man has just seen me. Daisy picks me up, opens the car door and swings her leg out. Bacon Man blocks her way.

"You didn't?"

"I did."

"You didn't pay for him again, did you?"

"I did."

"You're having me on."

"I'm not."

"So, he's cost us five thousand quid?"

"Yup."

"Fuck me, Daisy. How could you do this?"

I jump with fright as he raises his voice. Daisy loses her grip on me. I bounce out of the car and land badly, twisting my front legs and hurting my tummy as I hit the concrete. I panic and start running. But I've only got a few yards when all the air is squeezed out of me. I'm locked in Bacon Man's hands. He's sprawled next to me, wheezing, and I catch the tail end of Daisy's scream. I also hear a thump.

"Oh my God, *Skatter*," gasps Daisy. "Are you hurt?"

"It's ok," says Bacon Man as he tries to lever himself off the tarmac.

"I'm fine. And are you ok, little fella? Are you still breathing?" I look in Bacon Man's eyes and see genuine concern. Actually, they're grey-green and in daylight I can see they're not hard at all. They're kind and open.

"Have you got a death wish?"

A third person has joined the conversation, a man in his mid-forties, wearing a smart double-breasted jacket with four gold rings on either arm.

"That was the most incompetent suicide attempt I've ever seen."

"You need to get your eyes tested, pal," says Bacon Man, passing me to Daisy and hauling himself to his feet.

"Oh, I didn't see the puppy," says the pilot.

"Here's a suggestion," snarls Bacon Man. "Take the puppy with you and train him to be your guide dog."

The pilot returns to his car, muttering.

"Wanker."

"This is your Captain speaking," says Bacon Man. "Has anyone seen my white stick? Doors to manual."

"I don't know what to say, *Skatter*," says Daisy, as the pilot drives off.

"He could have gone under the wheels."

"I don't think so, it's only a sports car. He'd have got away with it."

"Stop being so modest, *Skatter*. You saved him. Thank you. You're my hero."

And she flashes him a huge smile.

"Well, it's been a while since you've said that, Daisy."

"It's true. What made you do it?"

"Well, Daisy, it's bad enough paying five grand for a puppy, but five grand for roadkill, that would be beyond the pale."

Daisy giggles.

"I have to say, you got down there pretty quickly."

"Yes, I'm still fast over two yards. But then I run out of steam."

Daisy chuckles again. And so, does Bacon Man. What a surprise.

"Pull your shorts up, *Skatter*," says Daisy. "It looks like a giant slot machine down there. We don't want the neighbours trying for a jackpot."

"We couldn't pay out," replies Bacon Man, pointing at me. "You've wiped us out with Muttley here."

They both giggle again. Well, that went a squillion times better than I expected. Perhaps getting run over was a blessing in disguise. As we drove home, Daisy told me she was expecting Bacon Man to go ballistic. I'm learning that human beings are not as straightforward as I imagined.

Bacon Man is limping slightly by the time we get to the house. It's no surprise he goes straight to the kitchen. He pushes a couple of buttons on a silver and black machine and a smoky aroma fills the room.

"Two shots or three?"

"Two please," says Daisy. "And make sure the milk is hot."

"You never fail to surprise me," says Bacon Man in a reasonable tone.

"Are you going to divorce me then?" asks Daisy.

"Of course not."

"We don't have to go to court. You can do it the Arabic way. Just say it three times, and I'll be off. All I want is the puppy."

"Don't be daft. You're exasperating beyond words, but I'm never going to divorce you."

"It was an expensive lesson. And you deserved it."

"That's unfair. Make no mistake, I'm pissed off. Two and a half grand would have bought us flights to Athens and a week at that nice hotel in Angistri. What's it called? The Kekrifalia?"

Then Bacon Man smiles. If I read him correctly, there's a gentle soul beneath all that blubber.

"Personally, I'd rather spend five grand on reliving our honeymoon in Santorini. But what just happened puts everything in perspective."

"What do you mean?"

"Well for a start, the puppy could have been paralysed or badly hurt. We'd have had to put him down and you'd have been distraught. In the end it's only money. It's not as if you copied the stunt pulled by the wife of one of my old friends."

"What did she do?"

"She forged his signature while he was abroad reporting on some God-forsaken war and used it to get a crippling mortgage on a house he couldn't afford. Now that's grounds for divorce. In fact, they split up soon afterwards."

"Are you saying that I'm forgiven?"

"I'll always forgive you. You know that."

"So does that mean you're going to be nice to my puppy?"

"Of course. What do you take me for? But I'm not going to mop up after him, that's your responsibility."

"Fair enough."

"Seriously though Daisy, the puppy's going to be a real burden. And one of the reasons I took him back to the breeder is that I'm fed up with being the least important thing in your life. I know this might sound pathetic, but I felt as though I was at the bottom of the pile while the kids were around."

Oh man up for heaven's sake.

"The last thing I want to be is the third wheel in your relationship with the bloody dog."

"Do you want to know the main reason why I bought him?"

"Go on."

"Because I'm really worried you're not going to be around for much longer. And I'll need something to love when you've gone."

"Here we go again. The same old tune about my weight. Give it a rest, please."

"OK. For the sake of peace and quiet, I will. But as we're being frank, I might as well tell you that for the past year I've been thinking about leaving you."

"I thought you were just being distant. But that explains it. Jesus."

"I've been weighing up the pros and cons without being able to make up my mind. I've also contemplated getting a lover."

"Contemplated, or have taken a lover?"

"Contemplated."

"Are you sure?"

"Yes, I swear."

"Have you been tempted?"

"Well, it would be nice to have some sex once in a while."

"Yes, I'd like some too," says Bacon Man.

"Stop interrupting," says Daisy. "But it's not just about sex. I think I'm emotionally lonely. I'm hankering for the man I fell in love with."

I'm lying on the floor, wondering how this is going to play out. My eyes are flickering this way and that, as I follow the conversation. Daisy has a plaintive expression on her face. I think she's being honest with her husband.

"I want to give our marriage a chance. I admit that getting a dog is a pretty desperate way of trying to rescue *us*. But if the dog can inject some joy into my life, I'll hopefully be distracted by him and I'll find it easier to accept you as you are now, with all your flaws."

"Well, that's not very encouraging, is it? What you're basically saying is that if the dog cheers you up, you'll tolerate all my shit. In that case, I'll definitely be the third wheel in this relationship."

"No, it doesn't sound great when you put it like that does it?"

"I'm glad we've cleared the air, and from what you say, I think there's only one solution?"

"What's that?"

"I'd better shape up."

A grimace flashes across Bacon Man's face, and he writhes in pain.

"What's the matter?" asks Daisy.

"I'm getting a pain in the arse. And for once it's not you."

Daisy chuckles.

"I think I'm now feeling the effect of the car bumper."

"Let me have a look."

Bacon Man drops his shorts and stands up. Suddenly the kitchen seems darker. It's like an eclipse of the sun.

"Wow, that's some bruise there. It's gone black already and seems to be spreading," says Daisy.

"Well, hopefully it'll boost my chances."

They both giggle at a private joke. I haven't a clue what they're talking about.

"But Daisy, let me just ram home the point. I won't try to take the puppy back. I promise. You can keep him. And that's only because we can't afford to shell out two and a half grand every other day. But I will have absolutely nothing to do with him."

"I can live with that."

CHAPTER SIX
SNOOP DOG

I OPEN MY EYES AND relish the relative silence. I yawn, stretch, roll on to my other side and just listen. The sound of the river is punctured by cawing, honking, and quacking. That's what a human would notice.

I discern so much more. You might be able to follow a whispered conversation from twenty feet away. But I can pick it up, crystal clear, from a distance of one hundred feet. My aural abilities are like a spy satellite in comparison to yours. I'm not just shooting the breeze. Let me give you the science, and I'll try to explain it in simple terms.

Nature has given dogs an incredible armoury. Our ears are formidable early warning systems. Our hearing is at least five times more powerful than that of humans. But, if for example, you're a fugitive and trying to get away from a dog, the device that places you in greatest peril is the wet, twitching, harmless looking snout.

There are a billion sensors in a dog's nostrils, sending smells to the brain. The olfactory bulb which makes sense of all this information is thirty times larger than its human counterpart, enabling our noses to map territory all around us, to identify buildings, obstacles and trees, and track creatures whose perspiration emits the pungent fear of capture. What I'm saying is that I've got the same equipment as a German Shepherd or a beagle. But as a golden retriever, the only reason I'd try to catch you is to give you a big, wet, tongue kiss.

Let me explain a little more about my superpowers. There's an abundance of wildlife in the undergrowth nearby.

Gnawing.
Clawing.
Digging.
Slithering.
Sliding.
Stalking.
Fighting.
Moaning.
Dying.

I overheard Daisy telling the breeder she lived near the River Thames. It sounds so gentle. But trust me, it's jungle warfare out there, an exotic ever changing all-you-can-eat buffet, if only I can get to it.

The background babble of running water is soothing. Right now, I feel rested and at home and ready to explore.

I wander into an open space dominated by two cream sofas. I'll claim those for sleeping and chilling later. I'm bursting for a pee. I don't want to do it inside the house, but the gurgling river is playing mind games with me. I can't help myself. I squat and let it all out.

That's better. The pool spreads across the floorboards and

is partially absorbed by low hanging fabric of a sofa, which is now irredeemably marked as mine.

I pad around the room, checking for potential toys or things to eat. Small tables are stationed next to the sofa's arm rests. I nibble a table leg. Despite being sharp, my baby teeth fail to make much of an impression.

I stand back and spot multiple images resembling Daisy and Bacon Man, randomly placed around the room. I say resembling because they both look different to the way they are now. For a start, there are fewer love handles in these pictures. In his case, I'd say about forty percent less.

Don't run away with the notion that Bacon Man once presented as a chiseled Adonis. Think Sunday morning pub footballer going to seed, yet some way from the unappetising figure he cuts today. Without all those chins and with a smattering of hair, I concede the younger Bacon Man might have appealed to the odd female, but only when she was in heat and wearing beer goggles. Even then I'm not sure how much of a stud fee he would have commanded.

He's next to Daisy in almost all these images. She's not classically beautiful, in that her bone structure isn't perfect like mine, yet she possesses a powerful magnetism. Her best features are long blonde hair, reaching midway between her shoulders and her waist, and piercing blue eyes that are simultaneously alluring, passionate and mischievous. She's not averse to showing a glimpse of chest. From my perspective, it'd be more attractive sprouting curly tufts of blonde hair. But each to their own.

In most of the pictures, the couple are wearing fewer

clothes than they do in this house. In fact, I can see their naked feet. There's no apparent need for fat squirrels. Neither of them is as pale as they are in the flesh. In one image, where they're standing on black sand, next to a turquoise sea, holding glasses of bubbly water, she's darker skinned, the shade of a light-coloured dachshund. He has rivulets running down his cheeks and the liquid is clamping what's left of his hair to his forehead. He's also redder than she is, especially in the face. Just like a Rhodesian Ridgeback.

What's striking is that in almost all these photographs, Daisy is the same height as Bacon Man. But I'm sure that's a fake perspective. I know she's several inches taller than he is. I suspect she's stooping to make him feel bigger than he really is.

It's also evident just how close they are. They're either kissing or hugging, smiling, and laughing. Studying their eyes, I sense just how much love and tenderness they're radiating. You don't have to be a guide dog to recognise that she adores him and that he worships her. They look like perfect playmates. Where did it all go so wrong?

The sofas are complemented by two simple, elegant chests of drawers. One carries a display of two young people I don't recognise. Both are tall and distinctive with blonde hair and blue eyes. This must be the couple's litter, Alex and Sarah. Neither seems to have inherited any of Bacon Man's physical attributes, if that's the right word. It's clear to me who possesses the dominant genes in this house and who's got the runty ones.

Now that's interesting. On one of the walls, there's a big picture of a labrador. He's lying down and turning around as if someone has just called him. He's getting on in years, and his eyes indicate he's in some pain. I can tell he's a kind old boy. I sniff the air, but there's no scent of a dog. That must be Dash the labrador.

"Daiseeeeeeeeee!"

Oh no, it's Bacon Man. I didn't hear him enter the room.

"Come and see what the little fucker has done now."

CHAPTER SEVEN
TICKETY-BOO

"So, what's he done?" asks Daisy.

"Look over there. He's pissed on the sofa."

Oh no, Bacon Man has grassed me up, the snitch. Daisy is going to be so cross.

"Oh, that's nothing. I'll strip off the cover and bung it in the washing machine."

Phew. What a wonderful woman.

"Nothing? You're joking. If he carries on like this, the house will soon smell like a third-rate care home."

"It'll be perfect for you then, won't it? If you're not careful, you'll end up in a care home sooner than you think."

"What are you on about?"

"You're a prime candidate for a stroke, if you don't lose weight."

"Oh, give it a rest, Daisy. I'm not going to have a stroke."

"Trust me, I'm not going to be your nurse when you're a vegetable, dribbling into your puréed parsnips."

"Don't you ever stop? It's becoming so tedious."

"If only you realised it, I'm trying to save your life. Now stop raising your voice. The puppy's quivering in the corner. Your shouting scares him."

You're right, Daisy. I am frightened. Bacon Man may look harmless. He's no warrior that's for certain. But there's so much anger in his voice. He sounds capable of anything. If he shouts, my bladder might let me down again.

"OK. I won't shout if you promise to do something about his toilet habits," says Bacon Man in a much calmer voice.

Daisy picks me up and clutches me against her chest. I smile and give her neck an extra moist lick. I think a truce has been declared. They're talking to each other in a civilised manner.

"Seriously, Daisy," says Bacon Man. "Heaven forbid I ever get to the stage where I'm a vegetable in a care home. But if it happens, you have permission to shoot me."

"Deal. I feel the same way," she says." Although I'd prefer sleeping tablets washed down by a bottle of Prosecco. Come on, Bubsie, let's get you some supper."

"I thought his name was Bjørn."

"Bubsie's just a term of affection."

"Why don't you call him Wayne instead? Or Wazza for short? Because that's what he does. He wazzes everywhere."

"Admit it. You can't pronounce his name properly."

"Byoorn."

"Close. You almost sound like a Swede."

"Well, we can't have that can we? If I start sounding Swedish, people will assume I don't have a sense of humour."

Daisy giggles, turns to me and smiles.

"Come on, Bjørn. It's dinner time. Let's go into the kitchen."

"While you feed him. I am just going to nip out for some fresh air," says Bacon Man.

Daisy seems not to notice as I trot behind her to my favourite room. I'm on my best behaviour.

"Who's a good boy?" she says, fixing me directly in the eye and smiling.

She reaches into a cupboard, finds a heavy paper bag and places it on a work surface.

"I've been hiding this for a few days," she says. "It's organic kibble, top of the range."

My heart sinks. Kibble. The unappetising, synthetic bilge served up by the breeder. I was expecting a succulent steak, or at least some free-range chicken.

"It contains sweet potato, beetroot, pumpkin, lentils, peas, dried seaweed, and rice. The perfect balance of protein and carbohydrates to promote muscle growth."

Dried seaweed? I'd rather chew my leg off.

Now she's using a kitchen scale to measure it and is removing pieces. Not only is the food crap, but she's also mean with it.

"Here you go, Bjørn."

She puts the kibble down, next to a bowl of water. I might as well eat cat litter. Doesn't Daisy realise where I stand in the food chain? I'm a carnivore. I turn up my nose and walk away.

"What's the matter? Don't you like it? I'm afraid that's all there is. Take it or leave it."

I give Daisy a meaningful look which says I'll leave it, if it's all the same to you. I am hungry, but I can last a little longer before I go light-headed. Hopefully she'll feel sorry for me and will give me something more appetising. I walk away like I mean it. Then I turn around and see that she's not moving.

Uh oh. I recognise a Mexican stand-off when I see one. She's just staring me down and there's steel in her eyes.

"Ok, Bjørn. If you're not going to eat, let's go for a stroll."

Daisy reaches into a kitchen drawer and pulls out a thin blue collar and matching lead.

"I've been hiding these as well," she says.

The collar looks tastier than the kibble, so I bite it and we wrestle for control. It's no contest. I lose hands down, and before I know it, I'm wearing the collar and being led out of the house.

"Let's go and look at the boats, shall we?"

The lightness in her voice tells me this is going to be fun. My snout is assailed by an array of intriguing new smells. I want to run off and explore. But she tugs on the lead and pulls me back. I'll tolerate this arrangement while I suss out the situation. But in the long term, the lead will be made redundant. Believe me. I want my freedom.

I keep my nose to the ground and suddenly I pick up an interesting scent. All my senses tell me that creature is very close. I look up and there it is squatting on a low wall outside Number 23. A ginger cat with white trimmings, squatting on its haunches. Somehow, it's made its fur stand on end, as if it's the love child of a pufferfish and a porcupine.

We look each other in the eye. I'm about twice its size. I can't believe it's just sitting there, and not running for its life.

I start barking my head off and straining at the leash.

"Be quiet," commands Daisy, as she easily manages to hold me back.

It won't always be that way.

"You're so lucky I'm on a lead, Ginge. One of these days, you'll be as bald as a coot by the time I've finished with you."

"You and whose army?" hisses the cat.

"Does the name Kurt Zouma mean anything to you?"

That shut him up.

"Come on, Bjørn," says Daisy, pulling me in the direction of the river.

"This is the marina that belongs to the island. Everyone who lives here has a berth. But we can't afford a boat, so ours is empty."

We walk to the water's edge and step on to pontoons that gently rise and fall as we progress. What a splendid view. A barge chugs from left to right. Two toned young women scull in the opposite direction in a razor thin rowing boat. A couple of imperious swans glide by silently. One of them catches my eye and hisses. I look elsewhere to avoid his gaze. Open fields on the other riverbank extend as far as the eye can see and melt into a heavily wooded area about a mile distant.

"The island where we live is very strict, Bjørn. If we had a cabin cruiser, it couldn't be longer than twenty-five feet. Twenty-four foot eleven inches would be fine. But twenty-five foot two inches would be *Verboten*. We'd have to park it somewhere else. Ooh look. Here's the man with the measuring tape."

"Evening, Astrid," says a stooping, elderly gentleman with thick glasses and a bushy grey moustache.

Beneath his brown golfing cap is a downturned face. He possesses an air of permanent disapproval. I recognise him from my brush with death.

"Alright?"

It's the briefest of greetings, yet it sounds like a whine. As I try to take the man's measure, I've got another puzzle to solve. He just called her Astrid. I thought her name was Daisy. Do all humans have more than one name?

"Hello, Maurice, how are you?"

"I'm fine, thanks. How's your husband?"

"He's fine. Why do you ask?"

"Didn't he trip up and fall in front of a car."

"Nothing passes you by, Maurice, does it?"

"I keep my eyes open. I like to make sure everything's tickety-boo."

"Don't worry about my husband. He's tickety-boo too. He didn't trip. He leapt in front of the car to save Bjørn here."

"Oooh."

"Yes, we just got him."

"How old is he?"

"Eight weeks."

"Look at those paws. He's going to be huge."

What's this Maurice geezer talking about? My paws are perfect.

"His father is from Belgium where they breed golden retrievers to be more muscular."

"Ah Belgium, that's where you're from, isn't it?"

"No, Maurice. I'm Danish."

"Oh yes, that's right. I think you told me that before. We've got some lovely Dutch friends. You're all so tall, aren't you?"

"No, that's Holland you're thinking of."

"Well, it's all in Europe, isn't it? Anyway, I'm just letting you know that you can't take your puppy on the pontoons."

I've only known her a short while, but I can tell Daisy is exasperated. The signs are imperceptible to humans. But I spotted them. I heard her heart beat a tad faster, and her breathing rate increased a fraction. Her fingers also twitched as though she was about to clench a fist. Although Daisy can't hide her mood change from me, she manages to disguise her true feelings from Maurice, as she looks him in the eye.

"I didn't see any signs. Where does it say no dogs?" she asks.

"If you'd read the sub-section on pets in the island residents' handbook, you'd have seen that dogs aren't allowed onto the pontoons, unless they're being taken on board their owner's boat. And as you don't have a boat, your dog is banned."

"So, isn't he allowed on our section of the pontoon?"

"Surely you know, Astrid, that your berth is on the land side of the marina, not on the pontoon, so he won't be in breach of the rules there. I'll tell you what I'll do. I'll photocopy the relevant subsection when I get home, highlight it, and pop it through the letterbox."

Maurice exudes an aura of self-importance. He's seriously grating on me. I look at Daisy's eyes, to try to gauge her reaction to him, and I can't read them. That's a useful skill, because if I can't tell from her eyes what she's thinking, then Maurice certainly can't either.

Yet I know from Daisy's heart rate and breathing that Maurice is having an impact on her. He's trying to interpret her body language and I'm a hundred percent sure that he's completely baffled. Maurice is used to people yielding to whatever status or power he possesses on this island and beyond.

But Daisy doesn't do deference. She's completely beyond the range of his experience.

"Can I ask you a question about boats, because we've got our eyes on one?" asks Daisy in the most innocent of tones.

"I'm all ears."

"Well, it's eight metres long."

"Oooh, I'm afraid that's totally unacceptable."

"Is that because it's metric?"

"Well, Astrid, we do prefer Imperial measurements, especially as we're now an independent nation once again. But metric measurements are acceptable until the law changes. Soon, I hope."

"So, what's your objection?"

"Eight metres is almost exactly twenty-six feet and three inches, give or take a small fraction. And that's more than a foot over our limit."

"That's extraordinary. Did you just do that calculation in your head?"

"As a matter of fact, I did."

"Were you a professor of mathematics or something similar before you retired?"

Daisy had just the slightest inflection in her voice. Any dog worth his or her salt would have sniffed sarcasm. If Maurice did, he didn't bite.

"No, just a humble accountant."

"I would never have guessed."

That's enough. I can't stand it anymore. My teeth are on edge. I dive on to his left brown shoe, get a grip on a lace and pull.

"Oi, stop that," shouts Maurice.

"Come on, Bjørn, that's enough," says Daisy, tugging on the lead.

She tries to pick me up but I'm not letting go of the shoelace.

"I must warn you, Astrid, that another part of the pet subsection stipulates that the Residents' Committee has the legal authority to enforce the removal of any animal deemed to be anti-social. So, you need to improve his behaviour."

"Oh, for heaven's sake, Maurice, calm down. He's just a puppy. He'll grow out of it."

"I hope so. For his sake."

Maurice turns around and heads home.

"Have a wonderful evening, Maurice," says Daisy.

I wonder if he realises she doesn't mean it.

"Well, that was fun, Bjørn. As I said, we can't afford a boat. I was just pulling his leg. Come on, let's get off the pontoon before you do a poo, and we all get sent to jail."

She picks me up as we step back onto dry land. I reach up, lick her neck and make her giggle. Her laughter is enchanting and replete with naughtiness. It's the sound of a free spirit and a gateway to her soul.

Daisy, I really love you.

CHAPTER EIGHT

IT'S COMPLICATED

As soon as Daisy opens the door, she removes the collar and lead and I scamper into the kitchen. Thank goodness the kibble is still there. I nosedive in and all too soon the bowl is empty. I'm still hungry and push it around as I lick off every crumb.

"So, you like the kibble then? That's great."

Bugger. That was not the impression I wanted to create.

"I'll make a bulk order from Amazon. But first, I need to eat. I'm going to warm up some Greek beans to go with a salad, Bjørn. It's a reminder of better times."

I curl up in a ball in the corner of the kitchen and gaze up at her as she talks to me.

"I don't know if it's the same for dogs, but certain foods stimulate memories in humans. When we got married in Santorini all those years ago, we lived on grilled fish, fruit, and Greek salad. We didn't need anything else. It was the happiest time of my life."

The sound of her voice is comforting. I'm feeling heavier,

but I try to pay attention as she chops up the ingredients of her meal and describes them to me.

"Olive oil, tomatoes, salt, cucumber, yellow pepper, red onion, chunks of feta cheese, and the best olives in the world, from Kalamata. You can taste the sunshine, unlike British supermarket tomatoes, which are completely anaemic. I doubt they've seen the sun at all. Finally, a twist of oregano."

The herb's aroma is powerful. My nose twitches involuntarily. My salivary glands are clearly unimpressed because my mouth is bone dry. The kitchen is a much better place when Bacon Man is on deck. The olives remind me of rabbit droppings. The only ingredient that piques my interest is the feta cheeszzzzzzzzz

* * *

I snap awake at the sound of a key being turned in a lock and the front door opens.

"There's no need to be quiet, *Skatter*," Daisy says. "I haven't gone to bed yet. Where did you go? Actually, no need to tell me. I can guess. You didn't get past the Jaipur Palace curry house in the High Street."

"How do you know?" asks Bacon Man.

"Have you hidden a tracker on me?"

"Why would I put a tracker on you? I don't need to and anyway, it wouldn't tell me that you had chicken tikka masala, pilau rice, some spinach dish, and poppadoms."

"How the hell do you know that? Did I arse dial you while I was ordering?"

"No."

"Come on, tell me. Have you got some spying shit going on, Daisy?"

Bacon Man is exasperated, and his voice is getting louder. Maybe I should hide under the sofa before she has another blast at him. But I smell something tasty worth investigating, so I stick around.

"No, the evidence is on your t-shirt. Your gut acts like a baby's bib."

"Shit. I hate it when that happens," he sighs. "And I know what you're going to say. That's the trouble when you eat your food so quickly."

"How many pints did you have?"

"Just the one," he says.

"You know I never go above the limit. Besides, if I'd had two pints I would never have got home. There were no spaces in the High Street, so I left the Merc in the sports centre car park. When I got back, it was squeezed between two massive SUVs. I couldn't get in through either the driver's or passenger's side. So, I had to open the rear hatch. I couldn't get over the back seat until I removed the headrests. In all it took me ten minutes to get behind the wheel. I was exhausted by the time I was able to drive. It was worse than an assault course."

Daisy chuckles. It's a relief to see them talking reasonably.

"Well, you know what you have to do, don't you?" she says, smiling and raising her eyebrows.

"I know, I know, but let's not talk about my weight again. Anyway, what have you been up to?"

"Changing the subject as usual. Well, I bumped into Maurice Oxford when I was down at the marina. He was out on patrol. He told me off for taking Bjørn on to the pontoons. He said I was in breach of the island's rules on pets."

"Sometimes this place drives me nuts," says Bacon Man. "I adore being right on the river. I sleep brilliantly because the sound is so hypnotic. But the restrictions are too extreme."

"I agree," says Daisy. "One of the things that's really starting to bug me is the colour scheme. When we bought the house, I didn't think it would be an issue. But it's becoming one. The bricks are dark, and the paint is horrible. It would be so much more in keeping with the surroundings if we could paint the houses white or pastel shades."

"What's also extraordinary," says Bacon Man, "is the total inflexibility of Maurice and his cronies. It's self-defeating. They're all concerned about money, and I'm sure the house prices would shoot up if the colour scheme was more attractive."

"Absolutely," says Daisy.

Bacon Man nods. They're singing from the same hymn sheet. He grins. I think this is a signal he's going to make a joke. "It's true. What made you do it?"

"I'm amazed we didn't have to sign a pledge of allegiance to the Residents' Committee in blood before we exchanged contracts."

Daisy giggles.

"It's times like this," Daisy says, "that I regret moving here. We'd never have bought this place if we'd known what the people were like."

"True. Besides a structural survey, you should also get a

psychological profile of the neighbours, listing their flaws so you can make a proper decision."

"Do you want to move?" she asks.

"No. I'm happy to stay for now. Moving is such a hassle. Besides, we could never get anything on the river that's as cheap as this."

"Right," says Daisy, "I'm going to take Bjørn out for a final pee and then I'm going to bed. I'm exhausted."

"Where are you going to take him?"

"I thought we'd go down to the communal lawn to the left of the gates. It's dark there. Most of the grey helmets have probably been in bed for hours, so I doubt anyone will see us."

"Be careful," says Bacon Man.

"You know what this place is like. They've got more curtain twitchers than the Stasi. I'm going up now. I'll see you in the morning."

"Good night," says Daisy. "I love you."

"I love you too."

Well, that's thrown me completely. Earlier today they were talking about divorce. This is complicated.

CHAPTER NINE
LED ZEPPELIN SNORING

"Shhhhhhh."

Daisy shushes me as we enter the house. We've returned from doing my business. I'm just rewinding what happened. As we walked around the island, I had a couple of nice little squirts to lay down a marker that this is Bjørn's turf. When we got to some grass, I let rip. Sooo satisfying. I almost managed to cock my leg and then I had a very luxurious poo. In terms of solidity, on a scale of one to ten, I'd say it was a seven. Maybe it was the kibble effect. Then something weird happened. Daisy put on a high pitched, almost babyish voice and said,

"Who's a good boy? Who's Mama's clever boy?"

Anyone would think I'd found the cure for cancer. But if having a dump makes her happy, who am I to complain? I can poo on cue if she likes.

Millions of years ago we were just wolves. But thanks to the interaction with cavemen and their descendants, we became domesticated and friends with humans. For thousands of years, we were your servants. Now the roles have been reversed. You are here to serve us. You clean up our shit in those little green plastic bags that are almost impossible to open. There couldn't be a clearer manifestation of the arc of evolution. Dogs are masters of the universe.

Daisy must be a turd nerd because she switched on the light of her phone to take a closer look. After she examined the consistency, she put it in the bag. Such an eye for detail.

Something else caught Daisy's eye. She turned off the light and exclaimed,

"There's Maurice Oxford in his window."

She picked me up, we scuttled back to the house, and headed upstairs to the top floor and that's where we are now.

Christ, it's noisy. It's as if someone has mic'd up a farmyard and is playing it back through Led Zeppelin's sound system. Bacon Man is snorting and wheezing like a pig giving birth to triplets.

"Shhhh," says Daisy again. "He's fast asleep. We don't want to disturb him."

Surely, it's the other way around. He's disturbing us. Then she puts on that babyish voice again.

"It's beddie time. We're all going to sleep now, Bjørn. Be a good boy for Mama."

Daisy closes the door quietly and puts me down. I try to jump onto her king-sized bed, but it's too high and I bounce off.

"Get down, Bjørn, there's a good boy. Mama's just going to make you a nice beddie. I still haven't had time to buy a basket, so you're going to sleep on some blankets with a pillow."

She takes off her clothes and then gets dressed again. What's the point of that?

Now she's wearing dark baggy trousers and a matching

loose top covered in stars. Then she puts some thick socks on her feet and carries me over to the pile of fabric on the floor.

"Go to sleep, Big Guy, there's a good boy."

Well, I have to say it's not easy to sleep in this room. Even though the door is closed, the noise coming through the wall is off the scale. No wonder the river is alive with the sound of birdsong. The wildlife around here must suffer from insomnia because of Bacon Man's snoring. He's a prime candidate for one of those, what are they called? ASBOs. Anti-Social Behaviour Orders. Heaven help him if the Environmental Health people descend with their decibel meters.

Anyway, I'm not in the mood to sleep. Something's not right. Before my sisters were taken away, we all used to sleep cuddled up to each other. The combination of body heat, heartbeats and easy breathing ensured it was lights out almost immediately. My internal sleep app tells me I used to have the best zeds ever. The family that sleeps together stays together. Unless of course you're a golden retriever family and trafficked individually by a breeder.

I'm suddenly feeling all alone. I think it's that separation anxiety thing kicking in. Bacon Man and Daisy shouldn't be in different rooms. It's not right, after all they're husband and wife. We should all be together. I need to tell them this very minute and start barking.

"Be quiet, Bjørn," hisses Daisy.

It wasn't a request. Her vehemence speaks straight to my bladder and once again I'm paddling in a warm puddle.

"Oh, Bjørn, we've just been out."

I bark again and look up at her quizzically. Daisy raises an eyebrow, smiles, and turns on her heel. I follow her into a small bathroom and watch as she peels off some paper from a roll at the level of a human's waist. She leaves some paper dangling. If I jump, I might be able to get my teeth around it.

Success! As I fall back down, I see the paper unravelling. Maybe Daisy needs some more of this stuff, and I bounce back into the bedroom with a trail of paper wrapped around my hind paws.

"That's very helpful, Bjørn," Daisy chuckles. "Thank you."

I bark back. I like it when she talks to me. Maybe she'll understand that she needs to go and get Bacon Man so we can all sleep together.

She's talking to me in a calm voice and my bladder isn't suffering from the jitters anymore. After mopping up my accident, she picks me up and returns me to the nest she's created on the floor. I love the physical contact, but it's just not enough.

"Go and get Bacon Man," I bark.

Daisy just doesn't seem to understand. She climbs into bed, switches off the side light, snuggles under the duvet and then her face goes blue. She's looking at a big version of her mobile.

I'm not at all tired. I go to the closed door, stand on my hind legs, scratch the wood and start barking again.

"Shhhhh." hisses Daisy.

She swings out of bed and carries me back to the beddie. But I refuse to lie down. I go back to the door, making as much noise as I can. It's a battle of wills with Daisy returning me to beddie, and me getting up and scratching the door. I'm enjoying the game. I've lost count of the times we've been back and forth. But I detect that Daisy is losing patience.

"What do you want, Bjørn?" she asks.

And she opens the door.

At last. The penny's dropped. That's exactly what I want. I rush to Bacon Man's door. He's no longer doing abattoir impressions.

"Oh, for heaven's sake," he groans.

The door opens and out he stumbles looking dishevelled and more than a little grumpy. A few strands of grey hair are sticking out at random angles. His curry-stained t-shirt fails to cover his gut. I can't see his face. A roll of hanging, crinkled fat is blocking my view. Not very attractive. I've seen better looking pigs' trotters. He's wearing multi-coloured shorts with an opening in the middle. I think I spy a sausage. What are they called? Chipolatas?

"Thanks a bunch for waking me up," complains Bacon Man. "That's exactly why I didn't want a dog."

"I'm sorry," Daisy replies. "I was trying to get him to sleep."

"It's like having a bloody baby in the house. It's impossible to sleep. I need a pee."

"Use my bathroom," she says. "No need to go downstairs."

"Ooooh thank you, soooo much," he replies. "It used to be *our* bathroom."

"And it can be our bathroom again, if you lose forty kilos and stop snoring for England."

"Jesus. Don't you ever stop? It's stupid o'clock and you're still going on about my weight."

I've only partially succeeded. I've got them out of bed and we're all together, but the atmosphere isn't exactly harmonious. I need to get the situation under control so we can all sleep together. Daisy picks me up and takes me back to her room. Bacon Man has finished his business and brushes past us.

"Now let's all try to get some sleep and we'll discuss this in the morning."

I jump out of Daisy's arms and follow him. He closes the door behind him and I'm too slow. The door bangs me in the snout, and I yelp.

"Did you just kick the puppy?" Daisy yells.

"How dare you? You're about fifty times his size."

She storms into Bacon Man's room. My goodness, she's confrontational and scary with it.

"No, of course I didn't. He must have got caught by the door. I didn't mean to hurt him. Sorry."

"Are you sure about that?"

"Yes, of course, I'm sure. Now you owe me an apology."

"Ok, I apologise."

"Can we try to get some sleep now? I'm exhausted."

"Good night," says Daisy.

She closes Bacon Man's door and moves to pick me up. But I run off. I head towards the staircase. Ooooh, that's steep. I could break my neck if I fell down those stairs.

"I can see that's going to be a problem," says Daisy.

She lifts me up and takes me into another room, switches on the light and picks up a box on four wheels.

"I should have done this last night. That looks like it might fit. It's not puppy proof, but the suitcase can act as a temporary barricade, until we come up with a more permanent solution."

As she manoeuvres the case into position, she puts me down, and I rush back to Bacon Man's door and start barking.

"Hey. Come out. Come and sleep in Daisy's room with her and me."

It works. He emerges several degrees grumpier.

"For fuck's sake, Daisy, it's like trying to sleep in a pet shop. If you don't control him, I'll take him down to the river and give him a free diving lesson."

"Look, I'm really sorry. But it's early days. He needs to settle. Heaven knows why, but he clearly wants to be close to you."

"That's because I saved his life."

"Yes, and I'm eternally grateful. Why don't we try an experiment? Let's keep our doors open so he can wander in and out at will. And maybe that will tire him out. And we can all get some sleep."

"I've got a better idea. Come on, Trouble."

"I thought you said you didn't want anything to with him."

"Wait and see."

"I don't like the look of this."

"Trust me. Now go to sleep."

Bacon Man picks me up and carries me downstairs to the kitchen.

"Don't think I'm going to make a habit of this," he says, as brusquely, he drops me on the floor.

I lie down and watch Bacon Man glide around the kitchen. Poetry in motion.

A puddle of drool forms on the kitchen floor as I wait for the rasher of bacon to cool down. Just as Bacon Man is about to hand me my treat, Daisy bursts through the door.

"I thought I heard the frying pan. What do you think you're

doing? Stop feeding him for heaven's sake. Bjørn! Beddie time! Leave Bacon Man alone."

Suddenly I find myself siding with Bacon Man. He's right, you know. Daisy can be a real tyrant.

CHAPTER TEN
THE PIGEON FANCIER

What a beautiful crisp morning. And what a surprise. Bacon Man has joined Daisy and me for my morning ablutions. He could be under duress. Alternatively, this might be a sign that he's weakening. I'm not sure.

We're heading down towards the river. And I'm pulling on the lead so I can bury my nose in all the new scents. Daisy calls it reading my newspaper.

"Look," says Bacon Man. "There's an ambulance outside Number 64."

"That's Lillian's house," says Daisy. "I hope she's alright".

I glance up and see two stocky crew members in dark green overalls arguing with a bright-eyed woman crowned by a bob of neon-pink hair, who's sitting in the back of the ambulance. She glances in my direction, and I see she's as old as Methuselah. She doesn't have lines on her face. She has crevasses, bisected by a slash of red paint around her mouth.

"I don't want to go in the wheelchair," complains the woman.

Despite her age, she has a commanding aura.

"Come on, Mrs. Tremonti," says the female crew member. "It's safer and easier if we take you in the wheelchair, we don't want you to fall."

"Don't give me all that health and safety tish-tosh, young lady. Once you get in a wheelchair, you never get out again. Now give me my sticks."

We draw level with the old woman as she hobbles towards her house.

"Good morning, Lillian. Are you okay?" inquires Bacon Man. "What's been happening?"

"I can't hear you," she replies. "Talk into my left ear, the good one."

Bacon Man walks around to her good side.

"What's been happening, Lillian?"

He then points to the ambulance and speaks louder than usual.

"These aren't your normal wheels. You never go anywhere unless it's in the Jag."

I'm not too sure what a Jag is, but I assume it's that long, slim, sleek car parked in Lillian's driveway with silver wire wheels and painted the same colour as her lippy. The woman raises her pencil thin eyebrows and exhales.

"I'm afraid my E-type days are over. After this latest stint in hospital, they've taken my licence away."

Good job too. Her right foot's twitching. Isn't that the one you use for the accelerator? Imagine the potential for havoc on the M4 if she played Barry White on her in-car vibrator.

"Why were you in hospital, Lillian?" asks Daisy.

"Heart problems. They put a pacemaker in. At my age. Ridiculous."

"That's a good thing, Lillian. It proves the doctors think you've got lots of life left in you."

"Yes, I suppose so."

Finally, Lillian notices me. Maybe poor eyesight is another of her ailments.

"Oh, what a beautiful puppy. I'd love to stroke him, but I can't reach. Why don't you bring him inside, and I'll give him a biscuit."

Now you're talking.

"Why don't you get settled back home first, Lillian. We just need to take Bjørn for a toilet trip, and on the way back, we'll pop in, and make you some tea."

"I'll leave the door on the latch, just walk in when you're ready."

So, after a quick wazz, and a luxurious number two, here I am, on my best behaviour, sitting next to the old lady who's propped up in a wing chair and feeding me from a packet of sweet crunchy kibble. The brand name is Hobnobs. How wonderfully decadent. It's not even ten o'clock in the morning.

Bacon Man is examining faded black and white photographs on a chest of drawers in Lillian's sitting room, which has a splendid view of the river. I can't quite see the pictures he's admiring, but I think they contain some old-fashioned aircraft.

Ooh. Something has grabbed Bacon Man's attention. He's picked up a glass case containing what resembles a circular dog-tag, attached to a purple and white striped ribbon.

"Is this what I think it is, Lillian?" asks Bacon Man.

Now I've got a clearer view, it looks more like a medal from a dog show.

"What, dear?" asks Lillian.

Maybe there's a human Crufts and she got best in breed.

"A Distinguished Flying Cross," says Bacon Man, with a sense of awe in his voice.

Or perhaps she kept pigeons.

"Yes, it is, dear."

I knew it. She's a pigeon fancier.

"Wow. You're a dark horse. I had no idea we had a war heroine as a neighbour."

"I wasn't a hero," replies Lillian modestly. "I was just doing my bit."

"And what was that, Lillian?" asks Daisy.

"Flying Spitfires to frontline airfields."

Lillian pauses as a memory floods back. Then she sighs, frowns, and sets her jaw.

"Russian women were allowed to go on combat missions. They were amazing night-fighter pilots who terrified the Germans. But Winston was too squeamish to let us have some fun."

Probably didn't want to lose his no claims bonus. But that's the insurance business for you. Risk averse.

"So," continues Lillian, "we were little more than taxi drivers, delivering planes."

"But you must have done something special to win the DFC?" says Bacon Man.

She'd have been a proper legend if she'd come home with a party bucket from KFC without being asked.

"I had a very brief dogfight over the Solent. I got bounced by a couple of Messerschmitts after I left the factory in Southampton on the way to Manston."

"But Lillian, I didn't think planes flown by the Air Transport Auxiliary were armed," says Bacon Man with a quizzical look on his face.

"They weren't supposed to be," says Lillian as a smile spreads across her face.

"Officially on delivery flights, the Spits' guns were empty. But the factory's armourer always left a few rounds up the spout, just in case. I did a split S to try to get away. One of the 109s overshot me. So, I gave him a quick squirt and down he went. But the other...."

"Fokker," smirks Bacon Man.

Lillian's eyes twinkle and she chuckles.

"Precisely! I couldn't shake off the other fucker, who hit my left wing and the engine with a long burst. I had to bail out. I flipped the Spit over and came down facing the Isle of Wight. Bloody parachute nearly drowned me. But an MTB got there in the nick of time."

"What's an MTB?" asks Daisy.

"A motor torpedo boat," replies Bacon Man.

"Lillian, you've just made a friend for life," says Daisy. "Morgan loves war stories."

"Well, it's going to be a very short friendship," snorts Lillian.

"Of course not," says Bacon Man. "You've got a pacemaker. You could keep going till you're a hundred and fifty."

"I never thought of it that way. My heart could keep beating even after I'm dead. How dreadful," replies Lillian.

"But what a life you've had," says Daisy. "You must find life on Galahad Island very tame after all those adventures?"

"Oh, I've had some battles here, I can tell you."

"Like what, Lillian?" asks Bacon Man.

"I got some carpenters to put up a fence at the end of the garden so that my grandchildren wouldn't fall in the river when they came to visit. Do you know what? The bloody residents committee told me to take it down because it was against the covenant."

"How incredibly petty," says Daisy with a frown.

"I agree. I fought them tooth and nail, and eventually we reached a compromise. The fence posts could stay, but the fence panels could only be put in place when the children came to play."

"That's not very neighbourly," says Bacon Man.

"You're telling me," splutters Lillian into her teacup. "Some neighbours. Always minding other people's business."

"We've got to go now, Lillian. But we'll bring Bjørn around to see you again soon," says Bacon Man.

"I'll write down my mobile phone number, just in case you feel poorly and need help," says Daisy. "Call me anytime. Day or Night."

"Thank you dear. That's very kind. Oh yes, and don't breathe a word about the DFC. It's still a state secret."

"Your secret's safe with us," says Bacon Man.

After closing Lillian's door, Bacon Man looks around to

determine whether anyone is listening and talks in a conspiratorial tone.

"God, that story about the fence is outrageous. How could they do that to a war hero, of all people?"

"I know," says Daisy. "Dreadful, isn't it?"

"I think a rebellion is called for."

"What do you mean?"

"A little asymmetric warfare."

Daisy giggles, and it makes me smile.

"I've got an idea for a wind-up. It'll do Maurice Oxford's head in."

CHAPTER ELEVEN

SLUT

All that talk of Messerschmitts, Fokkers, and Spitfires has unleashed Bacon Man's inner patriot. As soon as we got home, he started cooking what he called the Full English. You should see his plate. Four sausages, three rashers of bacon, two slices of black pudding, two fried eggs, baked beans, brown sauce. His only concession to Daisy is a grilled tomato. Awful things tomatoes.

Bacon Man should set up an Only Fans site streaming his breakfasts. He'd make a fortune. But Daisy isn't impressed.

"Just wait a minute. Before you eat, let me call Lillian's ambulance, and I'll have it standing by for your heart attack."

"Oh, give over, Daisy. This is all pure protein."

Far better than Daisy's breakfast. What is that? Sawdust?

"It's part of the Keto diet," says Bacon Man. "No carbs."

"Keto diet, my arse. Your plate is big enough to feed Kyoto. Portion control!"

"It keeps me going all day, and I don't feel the need to snack."

"You won't need to eat again until Easter," says Daisy.

I reach up and put my front paws on Bacon Man's thighs. He looks into my eyes and gets the message. He throws down half a slice of black pudding. It looks like a fossilised dog turd but tastes divine.

"Stop feeding the dog," snarls Daisy.

"I was just exercising portion control."

"I despair. You're such an intelligent guy. And yet you're so stupid with your health. You're committing slow suicide with your diet. That's enough."

"Daisy. Don't."

Bacon Man's protests are in vain. She grabs the plate as he's cutting a sausage in half and sweeps two thirds of the meal straight into the bin. Nothing falls on the floor. Bacon Man's right. It's a terrible waste of food. Daisy needs four sheets of kitchen roll to mop up the drool hanging from my chops.

I brace myself for another outbreak of domestic hostilities, but the washing machine beeps, and the tension evaporates instantly. After being at each other's gullets, I sense they have suddenly morphed into a being that is greater than one. The transformation is as rapid as it is extraordinary. My radar senses that the bond between them has become indivisible. You couldn't slip a prophylactic between them. I can't put my paw on it, but maybe their union solidifies when trouble appears on the horizon, or when, as in this case, they stir it up. I make a mental note to watch out for this phenomenon in the future.

"The sofa covers are ready," says Daisy.

"I'll fix the washing line," says Bacon Man.

He reaches into a kitchen drawer, finds a long plastic rope, heads to the balcony, and attaches it to the wooden balustrades. Daisy follows with a washing rack, which she unfolds and places in the sunshine. She drapes the sofa covers across the rack and then pegs seven pairs of extra-large comfortable waist-high knickers into specific clusters. From a distance, the white knickers look like dots, and black ones resemble dashes. The south facing balcony, overlooking both the creek behind the house, and the gated entrance to Galahad Island, has mutated and, not in a good way.

It isn't long before their handiwork attracts attention. Three female grey helmets embarking on their morning constitutional pass by the balcony and lower their voices. Humans wouldn't be able to pick up what they're saying, but with my augmented hearing ability, for me, it's a piece of cake. Or maybe a Hobnob.

"Look at that. She's got her washing out."

"That's against the rules. I'll call Maurice when I get home."

"No need, he's just behind us. I'm sure he'll spot it as well."

"You can take the girl out of the council estate."

"She's not British, she's from Holland."

"I thought she was the Polish maid."

"Look, she's got her knickers on the line."

"I knew she had a big arse, but now there's proof."

The three women all giggle as they leave the island through the pedestrian gate. Then I hear a faint male voice, maybe seventy-five yards distant. I turn round to try to get eyes on and spot a rotund gentleman with a full whiskery beard and moustache holding a brass telescope to his right eye. His voice is low in my ears, almost on the limit of my range, but I can just make out what he's saying.

"Clemmie, that looks like Morse code to me."

He pauses, as if working out something in his head.

"It's a short message. FU."

He pauses, twists his head to one side, and then bellows. I can't determine whether his emotion is one of fury or amusement.

"Good grief, that Dutch woman is giving us the fuck finger." Right on cue, I pick up a familiar nasal West Midlands' whine.

"Now, that's just taking the mickey."

Sure enough, Maurice Oxford hoves into view with his dog in an absurd padded jacket. What's the point of having fur if you don't make the most of it?

"I'll put a stop to that. Come on, Jock, walk on."

I head back into the kitchen to see whether the *agents provocateurs* have realised that their would-be nemesis has taken down their particulars, as it were. A quick glance confirms the answer to that question. No.

Bacon Man drains his coffee cup and picks up a couple of shopping bags.

"I'm just heading into town to pick up some printer ink."

"No second breakfasts. I'll be checking the bank app."

"Don't you ever stop?"

I trot out onto the balcony again to watch Bacon Man. I've only spent a short time in his orbit, and I recognise that my fascination is more than just spectator sport. It borders on obsession and that's simply because disaster only ever seems to be seconds away. I'm a rubbernecker, I confess. But that doesn't infer I'm mean-spirited. I'm rooting for him to be cool. Bacon Man looks askance at the rear window of the Mercedes.

"Hey, Daisy," he shouts. "Look at this. Someone has been creative on our back window. Hang on, I'll send you a picture."

Moments later Daisy's phone pings. Her giggle is so infectious, I feel my mouth break into a broad retriever grin.

"They've written SLUT, in capital letters," she says. "That demands a response."

She sweeps me into her arms, jogs up the stairs to her bedroom, and reaches into a chest of drawers.

"I bought these for our twentieth wedding anniversary," she says, bundling some garments in one hand, picking me up with the other and heading straight downstairs again.

I follow her onto the balcony as she slowly and deliberately decorates the washing line with a 44FF leopard skin quarter-cup bra, leopard skin suspender belt, black lace and pearl thong and two black stockings.

Daisy goes back inside, but I remain on guard, looking out through the balcony's glass walls. A few minutes later, I spy the three grey helmets coming back through the pedestrian gate at the end of their regular morning walk.

One of them points to the underwear. I can just about catch what they were saying.

"Look at that. The cheek of the woman."

"She really has no shame."

"But look on the bright side, it's more evidence against them for the Residents' Committee."

"Do you remember Angela who lived at 69 before them?"

"The one who skinny-dipped in the marina after getting sloshed at the Queen's Birthday barbecue and seduced Gerald at Number 45?"

"Yes. Well, maybe our Dutch neighbour is also in the market for some action on the side."

"You couldn't blame her, could you? I mean, look at the state of her husband. It'd be like trying to have sex with a Space Hopper."

I follow them with my eyes as, giggling, they walk around the corner, but the river drowns out the rest of their conversation. I turn to catch the sun and spot Maurice Oxford with his Scottish terrier, about two hundred yards behind the women.

Maurice's double-take almost causes his glasses to fall off and I hear him muttering to no one in particular.

"Good grief."

Then he leers.

"But it's a vast improvement on the control pants."

Ah, Maurice. You're human after all. Perhaps you can be reasoned with.

Oooh, I've just realised that there's some warmth in that low winter sun. I think I'll just lie down and try to work out the dynamics of what has just taken place and what the potential consequences could be. This is all beyond my experience. Ah, I hear the Mercedes coming down the lane.

Yes, it's Bacon Man. He parks in the driveway and looks up at the balcony. I haven't seen his eyes light up like that before. Good grief, he's almost running. If I could, I'd Tweet.

I use my snout to prise open the door, and enter the sitting room, where Daisy is taking time out after her daily exertions, hoovering up the hair I keep shedding. I look around and there's Bacon Man, slightly breathless. I must say, that's a personal best for climbing the stairs.

"I see you've taken winding up the neighbours to the next level," he smirks.

"Yes, well I couldn't let them get away with calling me a slut, could I? I had to have the last word."

Those two. They can't resist a drama.

"OK, you've had your fun. So why don't we have some? Any chance of you putting that kit on and we fool around upstairs?"

"You must be joking."

"Oh, go on, Daisy, be a sport."

"No way."

"I don't want to beg, but how about a-thanks-for-letting-me-keep-the-dog-shag?"

"Thanks for the opportunity. But the uncomfortable truth is, you couldn't fuck me if your life depended on it."

"That's a bit harsh, Daisy. I admit I could do with some visual encouragement. The leopard skin really does it for me. And you haven't worn it for years."

"The last time you performed half-decently was about thirty kilos ago. Your stomach is enormous. I can barely feel you, so what's the point? There's nothing in it for me."

"Really? That's brutal, Daisy."

"But it's the truth."

"We could always buy one of those sex swings."

"The only way I'm getting onto a sex swing with you is if you transition into Idris Elba."

"OK. How about a deal? If you let me buy a sex swing, you can invite Idris Elba over. But only if I can watch and film it."

That's a typical Bacon Man tactic. Trying to joke his way to success. Or maybe he's being serious.

"That's a fair trade. I'm not shy, *Skatter*. But, believe me, I would never indulge your fantasies. It's too dangerous. You wouldn't like it. It's never going to happen."

"In that case, I could go and buy some Viagra from the High Street. You know you can get it over the counter from any pharmacy these days."

"There's no way I'm letting you do that. In your condition? You're morbidly obese, your BMI is at least 40. You're on anti-cholesterol medication. You're a prime candidate for a heart attack. If you add Viagra to the mix, your blood pressure would sky-rocket and you could drop dead."

"Well, there are worse ways to die."

"Dream on. I'm trying to save your life. Don't you realise that?"

"Look Daisy, I read an article on longevity the other day that said sex can prolong your life."

"Maybe I'd prefer to die young."

"But it's exercise."

"I don't like weight-lifting."

"You're unbelievable. D'you know, Daisy. I really miss you physically. I miss the touch of your skin. I miss the tenderness."

"Lose at least thirty kilos then, and I'll think about it. But if you want instant affection, start being nicer to the dog. He's got tons of unconditional love to give."

Never a truer word spoken.

"You're so unreasonable, Daisy. I bend over backwards to accommodate you, and you never even try to meet me half-way."

"If you want sex, go out and pay for it, or find it elsewhere. I don't care. My only caveat is that I don't want to know about it. I don't want to be humiliated and just make sure you don't bring back any horrible diseases."

"Daisy, my womanizing days ended when I met you. I don't want sex with anyone else. Besides, who's going to fancy me in this state? You're the only woman I want to make love to. It used to be so exciting, and I still fancy you like crazy after all these years."

"Stop confusing lust with love. You're just winding yourself up. Sex can be purely mechanical. If you've got an itch, scratch it."

"I'm not going to start whoring around now, Daisy. You're the only woman I've been faithful to. I'm really proud that I've abided by our marriage vows. I've got no intention of breaking them. Ever."

"Well, it's not happening. It's been ages since I've felt anything in that department. I had loads of great sex when I was younger, and if it's all over now, then so be it."

"I can't believe you said that. We've got so little time left. I can't accept that it's all over. That's so negative and defeatist."

"You're just hankering after your youth. But it's gone. You can't get it back. Be realistic for heaven's sake. Do you know what I think? That's rather sad. Maybe even pathetic. Why can't you accept getting older? Have some dignity."

"I might as well find you a care home now, with that attitude. Whatever happened to the party girl I married?"

"Whatever happened to the war reporter I married? The one who could sprint across Sniper Alley?"

Bacon Man doesn't respond to that snipe and continues his offensive.

"You used to be so glamorous. But you've totally given up. You just slob around in leggings and a baggy sweatshirt."

Bacon Man has a point. That does seem to be her uniform. And it's clearly an issue with him. But he hardly qualifies as the fashion police.

"When was the last time you wore a dress? And you wonder why I'm as big as I am? I eat because it's the only pleasure I have left."

I hear you brother.

"How dare you put the blame on me for your weight?" snarls Daisy. "The only person at fault is you."

I wonder whether that's really fair? Maybe Bacon Man has got bad genes and is programmed to be obese? Or perhaps, over the years, he's had too many pre-cooked meals and ultra-processed food, that taste great but are loaded with false calories and tons of sugar?

"Look, you're incredibly disciplined in some areas of your life, like work. You develop tunnel vision. I've never known anyone to have such determination. But you have no willpower when it comes to food. Every bad decision you make regarding your health has the potential to turn my life into an even worse shit-show."

"I think you're being unreasonable, Daisy. I really do. It's a good job that I'm going away for a few days. I hope the dog makes you happy. Because you've made it perfectly clear that I don't."

CHAPTER TWELVE
BADGERS AND BACON SANDWICHES

Daisy and I are having a *hygge* on the big sofa. I'm lying on my stomach with my chin resting on one of her Sepp Piontek thighs, named after the Polish-German full-back who once managed the Danish football team. Daisy spent half an hour gently stroking my head. I was in raptures, and I'm still infused with a warm glow from a transaction in which I sensed her heartbeat slowing down and stress leaving her body. Don't imagine that I was the sole beneficiary of Daisy's tenderness. Let me assure you that just by being there, I provided a gift in return. Now, she's fast asleep with her head thrown back, her mouth wide open and she's gently snoring.

The sound comforts me. It's nothing like the violent gasping from Bacon Man's room while his lungs fight to suck oxygen down his lardy airways. I can tell that Daisy is truly peaceful. Both her mind and body need it. She's exhausted and I know that I'm mainly responsible, because of all the extra work I've generated. I'm grateful that I can share this *hygge* with her, by way of compensation.

Allow me to explain what a *hygge* is. For Danes, it's a way of life, whose main purpose is to mitigate the cloak of depressing Scandinavian winters. Danes create a temporary state of serenity, coziness, comfort and happiness by appreciating the simpler things of life. These are just some of the ingredients that work individually, or all together. Tea candles, a log fire, snuggling beneath a duvet, cupping your hands around a mug of hot chocolate or sipping a glass of mulled wine, spending time with true friends or taking a moment to do nothing while caressing a golden retriever's ears.

Having a *hygge* may be a Nordic concept, but it comes naturally to me and most other dogs. It's the anthem of my life. I relish every single thing I do. My water bowl is always half-full. For me, a *hygge* is taking a snooze when I'm short of entertainment, or lying on the grass, stripping bark from a stick. Or savouring the generosity of a Sepp Piontek thigh in the dark, as the river murmurs a lullaby. I genuinely feel that my soul is entwined with Daisy's right now.

Oh, I nearly forgot. Daisy has got a vicious shiner. Her right eye is a deep shade of purple. and closed tighter than a superglued mussel. She looks as though she took a swing at Tyson Fury and came off second best. The gossips on Galahad Island, and that means every single resident, are having a field day. Being stopped every few yards during our toilet trips has been disconcerting. The men of the island are far too uptight to inquire, but without exception the women have been probing.

"Oooh, you've been in the wars. Are you alright dear?"

"Don't worry, it isn't what it looks like," replied Daisy jauntily.

"I tripped in the dark while carrying Bjørn down the stairs

to have the final pee of the night. Luckily, I didn't fall on him, I could have crushed him to death."

"Ooh that's terrible. Are you sure you're alright? Is there anything I can do? Is there anyone you'd like me to call?"

They'd tilt their heads, raise their eyebrows, go on their way, and start whispering.

I'm sure Daisy couldn't catch what they were saying, but with my augmented hearing abilities, every word was crystal clear.

"Fell down the stairs carrying the dog? I don't believe it. It sounds like a classic case of domestic violence. She's either in denial, or trying to protect him? Do you think we should call the police?"

"Good Lord no. On this island, we always mind our own business."

Ha. Daisy is telling the truth. I was there and lived to tell the tale. She was trying to protect me as she fell. Daisy stumbled on the last step and crashed headfirst into the post at the end of the bannister as she put out an arm to cushion her fall. Bacon Man's reputation is being traduced and I feel impotent. I wish I could defend his honour. They're such hypocrites. As Lillian the Spitfire pilot so rightly observed, our neighbours love nothing more than minding other people's business.

And if truth were told, so do I. Over the past few days, I've been contemplating Daisy's relationship with Bacon Man. The peaceful atmosphere at home allowed me to take a long, cold, hard look at my benefactors. They both thrive on trouble. Conflict unites and galvanises them. Their marriage vows certainly didn't demand obedience on Daisy's part, of that, I'm sure. Maybe instead, on their wedding day in Santorini Town Hall, they pledged that until their dying day, it would be the pair of them against the world.

Given my good fortune, it seems churlish to be critical, but the episode with the big knickers suddenly made me wonder why the pair of them seek to provoke discord. Like me, they have nothing much to worry about. They might not be as prosperous as they'd like, but they're certainly not struggling. Why can't they just live in harmony with their surroundings and their neighbours? My conclusion is that they see themselves as eternal outsiders, or maybe they're just bored. It's almost as if upsetting people is a sport to them and they don't realise or don't care about the damage they sometimes inflict.

They look aghast at most of the residents of Galahad Island. I suspect they share a deep-rooted fear that old age is a contagious disease, which will infect them. They're raging against the dying of the light by winding up the wrinklies. You might think that's pathetic, and you might be right. But Daisy and Bacon Man are my humans, and I love them. I'll defend them to the death. Preferably of the ginger cat.

Ahhhh. A familiar sound in the distance tells me the *hygge* is coming to an end. Through the background hum of distant traffic, I can isolate the bass frequencies of a twelve-year-old, three litre Mercedes diesel engine, ticking over at low revs, as Bacon Man obeys the speed limit of the country lane leading to Galahad Island.

I lift my head and cock my ears. On cue, I register a click, as the electronic gates unlock. The iron groans as they swing open and the Merc purrs forward. Daisy's radar hasn't alerted her to Bacon Man's imminent arrival. Every second of deep sleep is precious, and I don't want to be the one to disturb her. I'll leave that to Bacon Man. I'm intrigued to see how they'll greet each other after they parted so badly.

As the latch goes, I can tell that Bacon Man is straining to be quiet and considerate, but the heavy turd-coloured wooden front door betrays him. It always creaks. His scent gets stronger as he tiptoes up the stairs in bare feet. My snout never lets me down. He's not angry anymore. He's happy to be home.

"Hello, Bacon Man," I bark.

I can't help myself.

"Shhh, Bjørn," he whispers. "You'll wake Daisy up."

"Too late, I'm awake," says Daisy as she comes to. "What's the time?"

"Just after ten. Do you mind if I turn the light on?"

"If you must."

I jump down and nibble the cuffs of Bacon Man's trousers as he heads for the light switch.

"Bloody Hell, Daisy. What happened? Were you attacked?"

"No. I tripped down the stairs carrying Bjørn."

"When?"

"Two days ago."

"Why didn't you tell me? I'd have come home straight away."

"You were busy with that presentation in Cornwall, and it wouldn't have been fair to disturb you. Besides, the only thing that hurts is my pride."

"Ah, now I realise why you didn't use video on FaceTime. I bet the neighbours have had a field day."

"Oh yes. I've had more conversations over the past two days than in all the time we've lived here. They don't believe it was an accident. You wait and see how they react to you. It's not going to be pleasant."

"I don't care what they think. But I do care about you. Is there anything I can do? You look shattered."

"I am. The dog has worn me out. You were right. It's like having a baby in the house. Oh, I'd better take him out for a pee before bedtime."

"No need. I'll do it. I'm dressed. You're still half asleep."

"Are you sure?"

"Yup, of course. Before I go, did anything else happen while I was away?"

"We've made the front page of the Resident's Committee Newsletter. It's on the coffee table."

Bacon Man picks up the paper and grins as he starts reading aloud.

"Residents are reminded that IT IS ABSOLUTELY FORBIDDEN to dry clothes or any other articles in outside areas on the island. Persistent offenders can face legal action, and under the relevant articles of the, the Residents' Committee has the power to compel owners to sell their properties and/or to require landlords to evict miscreant tenants."

"They don't like civil disobedience, do they?" says Daisy.

"No."

"But maybe someone does."

"Who?"

"I don't know what his name is. Our neighbour. The Silver Fox, the one with the dipsomaniac wife?"

"Yes, him. You should have seen the lecherous look on his face. I produce less drool when I get a marrow bone."

"You mean the couple who have cocktails on the patio in the summer at precisely six o'clock?" asks Bacon Man.

"Yes, the Silver Fox. He never normally surfaces before ten o'clock, but the day after I hung out the lingerie, he accidentally on purpose bumped into us as we went for Bjørn's early morning constitutional. We've never spoken before, but this time he said, 'What a lovely day. Interesting art installation on your balcony last night.'"

"So, I said, 'what are you talking about?' And he replied, 'oh come on. You know what I'm talking about. You really must come for a sundowner on the boat when it gets a little warmer.'"

"What did you say?" asks Bacon Man.

"I don't have sea legs I'm afraid. But my husband just adores the river. I'll pass on your kind offer to him. Thanks very much. Have a great day."

"Brilliant," says Bacon Man, laughing.

And it was. The Silver Fox stopped dead in his tracks with a rictus grin on his face trying to work out what had just happened.

"You should have seen his face," smiles Daisy. "It was a picture."

Bacon Man chuckles and looks at his wife with a sense of pride.

"Somehow, I don't think I'll be going cruising on the river.

Right, come on, Bjørn. Walkies. Go to bed, Daisy. Don't wait up for us. You need your sleep."

"Yes, I do. Thanks. Good night. I love you."

Blimey. Is this really happening? Are Bacon Man's motives honourable, or am I about to go swimming with the Thames Brown Trout? After the dognapping episode I'm not sure. He seems friendly enough. But then so do some psychopaths, as I've learned from *Happy Valley* on the BBC iPlayer.

"Come on, Bjørn, let's go for a stroll."

The frigid air goes straight to my bladder. No sooner are we outside than I need a wazz. Bacon Man waits patiently for me as I drain every last drop.

"Let's go and look at the boats, shall we?"

I trot along at a reasonable pace, occasionally darting into a bush to scope out a new smell. Daisy says I'm reading my newspaper. I don't know what she means. But I'm trying to work out what's new in my manor.

We've only gone a few yards and I realise that Bacon Man is wheezing and breathing deeply. Good Lord, he's unfit. It's going to be a very short walk at this rate. We reach the edge of the marina. Bacon Man suddenly sits down on a low wall. He's appreciating the music of the river and looking at the stars.

"Sit, Bjørn, there's a good boy."

I know exactly what he means, but there's no way I'm going to sit. I haven't come out to laze around while there are scents to explore.

"Come on, Bacon Man," I bark. "Get up, let's see what else is out there."

"Keep it down, Bjørn, there's a good chap, otherwise they'll be manning the watchtowers and turning on the searchlights. Speaking of which, Maurice Oxford is first out of the traps in the curtain twitching Olympics. Come on Bubsie, let's go."

Did Bacon Man just call me Bubsie? Yes, he did. If I'm not mistaken, that's a subtle British display of affection. Crumbs. I wonder if that's an indication of a paradigm shift or just a brain fart.

We turn left and head into a darker part of the estate, where there are fewer streetlamps, and strong trails of nocturnal creatures seeking the shadows. I spot the silhouette of a hedgehog and spy a mole coming up like a periscope and diving straight back down when he realises we're on a collision course.

Then it's my turn to slam on the brakes. There's a fucking badger and he's not shifting.

I know what you're thinking. That puppy has got a seriously potty mouth. I never used to bark this way. But if you spent any time with Daisy and Bacon Man, your language would also be saltier than Long John Silver's.

I thought badgers were easily intimidated by humans. But this one's clearly a hard case. He's not the slightest bit concerned about Bacon Man and is standing his ground. It'd be different if Daisy was out here. He'd be off like a shot.

"Oi, you," I bark. "Hop it. This is private property. You're not allowed here. If you don't leave. I'll get angrier and bark even louder."

The badger just hisses at me and digs his claws into the grass. They look lethal. I really must keep my distance, otherwise he could shiv me.

"Come on, do yourself a favour," I bark. "Back off, or I'll go to DEFCON2 and report you to the Island Residents' Committee. They know how to deal with trespassers."

At last, Bacon Man is galvanized into action. He stomps his foot as hard as he can. Either the vibrations or Bacon Man's wheezing surprise the badger, and he slinks off. I can tell that this isn't a one-off encounter. We're going to meet again and there's going to be more aggro.

Oh no. I've just had a delayed reaction to the encounter with the badger. It's a very wet fart and I've followed through. Even though it's dark, I know what the colour of adrenaline is. The same as our front door.

"Thanks a bunch, Bjørn, That's a stinker."

Bacon Man reaches for his phone and switches on the torch.

"Much as though I'd love to ignore that, I can't."

With some difficulty, he kneels. It gives me a chance to show my appreciation and I jump up to lick his face.

"Stop it, Bjørn, I need to clear this up."

He uses four plastic bags and realises he's reached the end of the reel. There's still some stuck to the grass.

"Oh, that's the best I can do. Hopefully, there'll be some dew or rain overnight and it'll wash away. Otherwise, there'll be trouble."

I was expecting Bacon Man to stand straight up. But he can't. He seems to be stuck on his knees. Somehow, by putting his hands on the ground in front of him, he manages to lever himself up. But in doing so, he tugs hard on my lead. I yelp.

"Sorry, Bjørn, I didn't mean to do that."

I pick up the medium range frequencies of two voices about forty yards away, cutting through the sound of the river. The voices are muffled because they're coming from behind glass, although they're reflected off an open window.

"Did you hear that?"

"Yes, that man is such a brute."

Bacon Man and I head back to the house. Somehow, he manages to open the door without it creaking. I feel a tad woozy after the adrenaline surge. Bacon Man stands at the bottom of the stairs and listens intently. The house is silent. But I can detect Daisy's shallow breathing in her bedroom on the second floor. She's fast asleep.

Bacon Man carries me into the kitchen and closes the door.

"Sssshhhhh, Bjørn. If you're good, you can have a treat."

He washes his hands vigorously and goes to the fridge. My snout is hit by a kaleidoscope of smells. Things are about to get interesting.

"I'm going to have a snack before going to bed. I'm starving after the long drive. But you must be quiet. We don't want to wake Daisy up."

He smiles at me with honest eyes. He's not as commanding in stature as Daisy, but he has a kind face, and the timbre of his voice demands attention.

"Sit. There's a good boy."

This time I comply without complaint and smile back.

"Good boy. Now just wait quietly while I cook."

The kitchen seems to be just as much Bacon Man's natural habitat as the Mercedes. There's a lightness about him as he switches on the grill in the upper part of the double-oven cooker, finds scissors to open the sealed pack of bacon, and lays out several thick back rashers on a sheet of silver foil.

"Normally, I'd fry the bacon in a little Greek olive oil," he whispers, "but the sound might wake her up and we don't want that do we? So, I'm going to grill it."

He finds a sharp knife and saws through a crusty loaf.

"The good thing, Bubsie, is that Daisy has lost her sense of smell. As long as she's asleep, we're in the clear. Not too sure what caused it. She used to be partial to the old Bolivian Marching Powder before she met me. So, it could be the long-term effects of that, or it might be the menopause, or a combination of the two. I don't know."

What the hell is the Bolivian Marching Powder? He's talking in riddles.

"I tried coke once at a party near Ipswich when I was twenty, yonks ago."

Ah, now I know what he's talking about. I've seen the adverts. Things go better with coke.

"A disc jockey from Radio Caroline cut up a couple of lines for me. I was just as clumsy then as I am now, and I sneezed Charlie all over the place."

Who's Charlie? Was that one of his friends? Was he lightweight? Like a snowflake?

While he was talking, Bacon Man was putting the bread in the toaster, checking the progress of the bacon, holding the toaster button to ensure it didn't catapult out and make a noise, turning over the bacon, laying out the toast on a big plate, smearing it with an aromatic brown sauce, brewing a cup of tea in a china cup, using tongs to extract the bacon, turning off the grill, adding a splash of milk to the tea. Mesmerising. Four strands of drool dripped from my mouth to the floor.

"Aww, Bubsie, let me clean you up."

He called me Bubsie again. Maybe it wasn't a brain fart after all.

I know what's going on. Bacon Man and I are having a hygge. He sits down at the kitchen table and puts the plate in front of him. There are two big bacon sandwiches cut in half. Bacon Man peels back a slice of toast and places a piece of bacon on top

"Here you go, Bubsie. Midnight snack."

Oh my. That was delicious, perhaps even better than the first hit three weeks ago.

"Was that good, Bubsie? Do you want some more?"

What a daft question. Of course, I do. But wait a minute, I think I know what you're doing, Bacon Man. You're trying to buy my affections. Ok, just one more piece. Yes. The big one. That one over there. Lovely. Thanks a lot.

I watch Bacon Man as he eats his sandwich. He's not bolting his food. He's chewing slowly with his mouth closed. He's dabbing the corners of his mouth with a kitchen roll. When not forced to be surreptitious, his dining etiquette is immaculate. Maybe I've misjudged him.

There's half a sandwich left. Bacon Man splits it in two, takes half a bite and offers me the rest

"There you go, Bubsie, that's it. I'm going to clean up and then we're going to bed."

After five minutes, all the evidence of our midnight feast is gone. A crime scene specialist would be hard pressed to find any traces. We head upstairs and Bacon Man gently puts me down in No Man's Land on the landing between his room and Daisy's.

"Good night, Bubsie. See you in the morning."

He called me Bubsie again. I trot into Daisy's room and clamber into my beddie. But I can't settle. I lie awake for half an hour. Bacon Man hasn't started snoring yet. I think I'll go and keep him company.

CHAPTER THIRTEEN

THE HYDRO-DONG

So here we are, back where we started. I'm lying on the big sofa in a sunbeam, enjoying the sound of the river.

For weeks, my attempts to leap onto the cushions ended in failure. Whenever I cheated, using the foot stool, I was instantly dumped back on the floor by either Daisy or Bacon Man.

But this week I must have had a growth spurt. My legs feel longer and there's much more power in my rear thighs. A couple of days ago, I managed to gain sufficient traction on the cushions and hauled myself up. The sofa is much more comfortable than the floorboards or the foam-padded dog beddie in Daisy's room.

Although I say so myself, my strategy for occupying the sofa was a masterclass in the understanding of human behaviour. The first time I managed to climb up unassisted, I felt like barking my face off in celebration. But I didn't want to draw attention to myself. So, I lay with my head on the armrest, radiating an image of unadulterated innocence. I flicked my fluffy right ear over my eye in vintage Hollywood peek-a-boo style. I deliberately chose not to display the stereotypical golden retriever grin used to elicit dog treats. Instead, I manufactured a mysterious Mona Lisa smile suggesting I was lost in some inner rhapsody and couldn't be disturbed. Just in case that forensic description has flown over your head, what I mean is, I was hiding in plain sight.

I closed my eyes and occasionally snuck open an eyelid to observe how the humans were reacting. Believe me, I had to suppress the desire to paw pump when I heard Daisy alert Bacon Man.

"Awwwwww. Come and look at this. He looks sooo sweet, doesn't he?"

"I thought you were going to strictly enforce the rules, Daisy? Beds and sofas were supposed to be off limits. Zero tolerance. I'll get him off."

"Oh, don't disturb him. He's fast asleep. Let him be. He's so comfortable. He really feels at home."

"You're unbelievable, Daisy. If only you were half as nice to me as you are to that bloody dog, my life would be so much better."

"Oh, stop complaining will you?"

Allow me to share the methodology behind my fieldcraft. The key to victory was confidence. The sofa was off limits and my presence wasn't part of the landscape. I had to make it look as though I fitted into the scenery. If I had displayed nerves, Daisy and Bacon Man would have picked up on my uncertainty and kicked me off again. But I lay down as if it was my dog-given right. They accepted the suggestion that I was entitled to be there. And so, I was allowed to stay. I've been doing it several times a day, every day since. Once you've created a precedent, it's hard to roll back. That sofa is now mine. I own it. Confirmation was provided the moment Daisy put a blue cover on the sofa to protect it from my dirty paws. I hope you can learn from me. Ignore that tired old trope about it being impossible to teach new tricks to an old human.

Daisy and Bacon Man of all people, ought to be aware of the brilliance of the golden retriever "community." Like the rest of the world's pet owners, my people are living under the delusion that they are top rate ethologists. Don't worry, there's no need to reach for Google. I'll be your search engine. An ethologist is a scientist who studies animal behaviour.

Perhaps the smarter among you will recognise this incontrovertible truth. We are, in fact, studying YOU. Every minute of every day, you are under observation. Your every move is being measured and evaluated. We see every foible, every flaw. And believe me, my pet humans are riddled with them. But, unlike you, we are non-judgmental, and unless we become the victims of cruelty or neglect, our love for you is constant.

Look into the eyes of your dog, hold that gaze for as long as you can without wavering, and you'll see that I'm right.

Oh, here comes Daisy with some new gear for some adventures in the wide world beyond Galahad Island.

The thick turquoise harness is supposed to be more puppy friendly than a collar and lead, so that my body, not my neck, takes the strain when she pulls on the lead. I hate it. I like being naked and feeling the wind through my fur.

I've had some injections, designed to protect me from other animals and vice-versa. They're the passport to expanding my horizons. I now can socialise, whatever that means. Perhaps the odd al fresco appetiser, an occasional barbecue, and some serious butt sniffing. Earlier today, I was chauffeur-driven to the vets to get vaxxed. I'm clearly a babe magnet. All the nurses were cooing over me and calling me the most handsome puppy ever. Considering they see scores of dogs every day, that's some compliment. I couldn't give them my autograph, obviously, so I peed on their rose bushes instead. They rewarded me with meaty tasting biscuits for not complaining about the needles. The vet called me a brave soldier. But I'm not so sure.

I was talking a good game beforehand, when I said it was a jungle out there and I was just itching to get stuck into the all-you-can-eat buffet. If I'm being honest, that was bravado, and I fear I'll be hoisted by my own petard. My snout tells me I'm entering a truly hostile environment.

I smell foxes and, worse, badgers; not to mention all manner of other creatures I've never encountered before. Thank goodness Daisy is my protector. Her bearing, and the aloofness she projects beyond her closest circle, act as a deterrent. In military terms, Daisy is a one-woman armoured brigade. The Catering Corps is back at the house, no doubt filling his face. I'd prefer to be back there with Bacon Man than being here, out of my comfort zone.

A barred gate creaks as Daisy pushes it open then it springs back, almost hitting me. We're on a rough pathway squeezed between a fence on the right and trees to the left. As the track narrows, it darkens. I can barely see the sky, and I don't like the vibe on the left. I'm sure there's a sett of badgers hunkered down close by. My nostrils are overwhelmed by a plethora of musk trails. All my instincts tell me to keep moving. But I feel jittery. My back legs give way and I sit down.

Daisy registers that I've stopped, so she does too.

"Come on, Bjørn, off we go."

I know what she wants me to do but I'm overwhelmed by the enormity of the world and its smells. I remain rooted to the spot. I hear myself whimpering.

"Daisy, Daisy, please pick me up."

"Come on, Bjørn, let's go. Come on, Bubba."

To her credit, she doesn't tug on the lead. She's waiting for me to move of my own volition. I don't. I stay still and cry out again.

"OK, Bjørn, let's do it your way. But not for long."

Daisy bends down and lifts me up, which is just what I want. Daisy's actions are further proof that her fluency in golden retriever is constantly improving.

"We must get a move on. There's so much more to explore."

She carries me along the path for a while and puts me down again. I raise my nose in the air and check the breeze. The badger scent has receded. I feel a tad safer and trot next to Daisy while hugging the fence and using her as a shield from hidden threats in the undergrowth and silver birches.

We've barely gone ten yards, when my ears are assaulted by an almighty squawk as a chubby bird with a brown body, green head, and red eye shadow crashes through the foliage in a clumsy, low trajectory take off.

"Look at the pheasant, Bjørn,"

I've clocked him, Daisy. As a result, my backside is having a suspected spoonerism, a pheasant pucker. I need to sit down again. The countryside is not as quiet as I imagined. It's wilder than a Brighton hen night.

Shell-shocked, I hear myself snivelling. I'm not deliberately crying out for attention. It just happened involuntarily.

"Did the pheasant scare you, Bjørn?" asks Daisy.

"He made me jump a bit. But you're supposed to have some gun dog genes in you. I hope I haven't bought a duff golden retriever. You're not a Monday model, are you?"

I remain sitting down. My brain is scrambled. That remark really hurt. She's talking about me as if I'm a duff car, or refrigerator. I'm flesh and blood. I've got a soul. You've got no idea just how smart I am, Daisy. And above all, I'm the best friend you'll ever have.

Having said my piece, I stop howling.

"That's better," she says. "No need to cry. We're just exploring. It must all be a little frightening. But you'll get used to it. Come on, let's go, there's a good boy."

She looks at me and smiles. That's all the encouragement I need. I get up and start jogging, pulling Daisy along behind me. There are some fascinating scents all around me. If I can keep my cool and overcome my nerves, I'd get a much clearer picture of what's going on in my world. I just have to keep my nose to the ground. Daisy's partially right when she says I'm reading my newspaper. It's also an intelligence briefing. Some of the scents don't tell the whole story, but they give you a clue as to what's happening, so you can make an informed decision.

Hang on, what's that? I smell a rabbit, not very far away. I inhale again and realise there's two of them. I stop, look around and spot them through the hedgerow. They're going at it like rabbits. I can tell she's not into him at all. He's giving it his best shot and she's just chewing on a leaf. Terrible table manners.

Now what's that cheeky, heady aroma coming from the middle of the path? There it is. Small, dark pointed pellets, with fragments of feathers and bones protruding. Irresistible. I dive headfirst and do a full 360-degree roll. Without looking, I can tell that the fur on top of my head now has the perfect quiff. Very Elvis. Very rock n'roll. The best hair gel in the business.

"Oh, Bjørn. That's disgusting. I'm never going to get that out. And it smells disgusting. You're going to need a bath when we get home."

Fox poo. You can't beat it.

Daisy spoils my fun and drags me further along the path. Resistance is futile. She's much stronger than me, so I pick up the pace again. Through her legs, I spy something sinister, and apply the brakes.

The path we've been taking has been gloomy, but directly ahead is what appears to be the entrance to Hades. On closer examination, I can see it's just a brick walled tunnel. Yet alarm bells are going off in my head. Before she was taken away, Mama taught us that our sixth sense could save our lives.

I sit down hard. Daisy can pull all she wants, but there's no way I'm going in there. I'd rather endure a French Bulldog butt wax with my local dogscaping groomer.

The brickwork acts as an echo chamber for my olfactory senses and amplifies the scent of all the humans and wildlife that have used it as a pissoir and worse. I'm overwhelmed by the intensity of testosterone excretions, both old and fresh, not to mention the lingering whiff of decomposition, as if there's been a fight to the death in there.

Despite my intellectual prowess, I'm still only a puppy. I want to go home.

Daisy bends down and looks me in the eye. I tilt my head to accentuate my vulnerability and whimper.

"Ok, Bjørn. You win. I can see you don't want to go any further. We're just taking baby steps. We'll try again later, so let's go back to Bacon Man. I was hoping to stretch my legs and follow the path to the river. Maybe that's going to take longer than I thought."

We turn back and I scamper ahead, along the way we came. I'm no longer hesitating, and Daisy increases her stride to match the pace I'm setting. As we approach a bend, I spot a dog I've observed from the balcony but have never met. It's the Scottie, and he's still wearing that daft padded coat, even though spring is on its way.

"Hello, Maurice. Just the man. I was hoping to find an opportunity to talk to you," says Daisy with steel in her voice.

Maurice Oxford is somewhat taken aback. He raises his eyebrows ever so slightly. The tic tells me that he wasn't expecting to be confronted. Mr. Oxford is used to initiating conversations not reacting to them. He's on the back foot. I hope for his sake he's wearing control pants.

"So, what do you want to discuss, Astrid?" he inquires, four semitones higher than usual.

Time to inspect the Scottie's tackle. My snout puckers a triplet of rapid-fire sniffs. Not a lot of testosterone down there. I step back and take in the bigger picture. Just meat. No two veg. I've seen enough. Or is that eunuch? Listening to Daisy and Maurice Oxford is going to be far more interesting.

"Don't worry, Maurice, it's nothing sinister, nothing that will upset our peaceful island existence. It's the laundry situation."

"Ah, yes."

Maurice takes a deep breath, but Daisy doesn't give him a chance to speak. She adjusts her feet, so she's facing him head on, like a boxer, looking him right in the eye.

"For the life of me, I can't understand why aesthetics are more important than trying to save the planet, Maurice. Why do you insist that I have to put laundry in the tumble dryer when I have access to energy-free, carbon-neutral fresh air on my balconies?"

"Astrid, as you well know, the covenant states very clearly that the island has to be enjoyed by everybody. You can protest all you like, but your laundry spoils that enjoyment."

"Come off it, Maurice. Surely, bed sheets and clothes don't diminish people's enjoyment of the wonderful nature all around us. The covenant is ridiculous."

"Then why did you move here, Astrid? Your solicitor must have been aware of the small print when you bought the place. If you weren't aware of the rules, then take it up with your solicitor or move somewhere else?"

. "It's not as if we put out washing all the time. Why can't people just ignore it or turn a blind eye?"

"Well, that's a bit difficult when your balcony overlooks the island entrance. Everybody sees it as they come in. Besides,

Astrid, as you are well aware, the committee has had complaints. I know you probably do things differently in Belgium, but…"

"Maurice, I'm from Denmark," Daisy snaps. "And in my country the environment matters to us."

"Oh, everything's better in Denmark, isn't it?"

"When it comes to being green, Maurice, yes it is. We're more than doing our bit to make this world a better place."

Daisy seems to be tiring of the conversation, and I'm bored with the Scottie. He's less entertaining than the island Covenant. I try to pull Daisy away.

Maurice tries to manoeuvre around us on the narrow path, but she's not finished yet.

"Aren't you at all interested in leaving a planet for your grandchildren, Maurice? Where people can actually breathe? Or do you really not care?"

"That's unfair, Astrid. If you must know, my wife often dries our laundry by hanging it across doors and chairs inside our house. Now, I must be going."

"Oh dear, Maurice. I'm sorry to hear that. All the moisture from the clothes means you must have mould in your house. That can knock thousands off the value of your property. Enjoy your walk. Come on, Bjørn."

Classic Daisy. She always has the last word and twists the knife whenever possible.

We walk back to the island without further incident. Daisy stops outside the pedestrian gate, pulls out her mobile and pushes a short cut.

"It's me," she says. "I'm locked out. What's the code for the pedestrian gate please? I normally drive in and can't remember it. I know it's a significant date in British history, but the number escapes me."

"1966," replies Bacon Man through the speaker. "The year when England won the World Cup, and the residents of Galahad Island entered a time warp and sealed it shut. They think it's all over. It is now."

Daisy chuckles.

"Thanks. Could you put the kettle on please? I'm dying for a cup of tea."

We walk over the bridge that crosses the creek at the back of the house, and when we get to the other side, I hear a bird going glock, glock. I look down the slope and see two swans. One of them fixes me with the evil eye and hisses. Good grief, everyone round here is trying to pick a fight. Give it a rest. This is the Thames Valley. Not Millwall.

As we approach the house, a white delivery van draws up. The driver recognizes Daisy and slides open his door.

"Number 69?"

"Yes, that's me."

"Got a parcel for you."

He hands over a small brown package.

"I wasn't expecting anything today," says Daisy. "Oh, but it's for my husband, I'll take it. Thanks a lot. Have a good day."

As soon as the door opens, Bacon Man shouts out cheerily.

"Your tea's ready. It's in the kitchen."

Daisy removes my lead and I bound though the house to greet Bacon Man and see if he's got any scraps for me. He's working on his laptop at the kitchen table and looks up with a smile as Daisy enters the room. I've never seen a smile disappear so quickly.

"Got a package for you. Bit of a surprise, I didn't order anything, and I didn't see any purchase popping up on the business account. What is it?"

"Just a gadget I need for my camera," replies Bacon Man.

"Show me."

"Honestly, it's just a specialist piece of gear."

"If it was for your camera, you'd have paid for it with the business card, so we could deduct it when we do the books. Open it."

"No, I won't open it. Just trust me, Daisy."

"Well, if you won't open it, I will. What is it you always say? We have no secrets."

Daisy reaches into a kitchen drawer, takes a sharp knife, slices through thick brown tape and pulls out the contents.

"So how exactly is a Hydro-dong Seven going to help improve your pictures? Has it got anything to do with the focal length? What the hell is this?"

"Er, er, are you sure that's mine? I haven't a clue what it is. Check the address. You were probably given the wrong parcel. It must be something one of the neighbours ordered."

"Don't treat me like an idiot. It was addressed to you. Come on, fess up."

"What do you think it is?"

"Well, I can tell it's not a flower vase, although that's probably all it's good for. Come on, what is it? Spit it out."

"This is excruciating. Er, er. It's a penis pump."

Daisy giggles. It's that contagious laugh that always makes me smile.

"Oh, I wondered why I was suddenly getting adverts in the Mail Online and on Facebook for penis extensions and other male sex aids. Now that explains it. How much did you pay for it?"

"There was a forty percent discount."

"How much?"

"Ninety quid."

"What a waste of money. We're not rolling in it, you know."

"Really? Our parlous financial state must have slipped your mind when you blew five grand on the dog."

"Yes, but the puppy is worth every penny. He's brought joy to my life."

"And aren't I entitled to a little joy? This has got the potential to change my life."

"Don't be daft."

"There are tons of blokes on the website saying they managed to grow an extra two inches and that the growth is permanent."

"Have you completely lost your faculties? You, more than anyone, should know that if something looks too good to be true, it probably is."

"The Hydro-dong has got great five-star reviews on Trust-Pilot."

"Those aren't genuine reviews. The manufacturers have used bots or paid an agency to write them."

"It uses the suction of bathwater to stretch the penis and is more effective than traditional models."

"You've been conned. Why on earth did you decide to buy a penis pump?"

"OK, I'm being completely honest here, Daisy. So, hear me out."

"I'm all ears. But stop whispering. I can't hear you. Pump up the volume."

"Very funny. It was after the conversation we had about sex, and you said you couldn't feel me."

"And you think that contraption is going to make me change my mind? You must be joking. You can pump away till your heart's content, but it's not going to make the slightest bit of difference."

"Do you want the truth, Daisy, or not?"

"Yes. But I'm not sure I'm going to get it. For a start, how did you pay for it? Have you got a secret bank account? I didn't see any transactions on our joint accounts."

"You know we've got a PayPal account. When I sold that old mountain bike on Gumtree, the money went to PayPal. It's been sitting there for a couple of years, and I only just remembered we had it."

"Ok, I accept that. So, why blow it on a penis pump."

"In all honesty, I feel that it's shrunk in the past few years. It used to be longer and thicker. The penis is like a muscle."

"Not in your case."

"Stop it."

"But if it is a muscle, have you thought about using steroids, like bodybuilders do?"

"No, of course not."

"If it was like Arnold Schwarzenegger's forearm, then perhaps I'd be open to persuasion."

"Be serious. My point is that as the penis is like a muscle, if you don't use it, you lose it."

"Are you blaming me for that?"

"Well, you're not exactly putting out, are you?"

"The only reason I can't feel you is because of your gut."

"I thought the pump could help me get it back to its previous size. Before I met you, I bought a pump once, and at full stretch, it measured seven inches."

"Well, someone on the planet has to bring the average size down."

Daisy snorts at her own joke. But Bacon Man goes red in the face and looks genuinely upset

"Is it any wonder I feel inadequate and short of confidence in the bedroom department these days."

"Where's that famous British sense of humour? You dish it out, but you just can't take it."

"No, Daisy, it's not funny. It's remarks like that which make me wonder whether you ever enjoyed having sex with me, or whether you were just faking it."

"Stop. You know I never fake anything. If you want me to start feeling you, then lose some weight. Is that so much to ask? Now take your diabetes tablets. And why don't you throw that thing in the recycling."

"I'm not going to. I want to give it a try."

"It's your life. Do whatever floats your boat. Just make sure it doesn't get too big to fit into the marina. And disinfect the bath once you've finished."

***

Bacon Man is taking his time in the bathroom, which is completely out of character. Ever since I moved here, he has always showered, and has never fully immersed himself in the tub, largely, I suspect, because he might need the Fire Brigade to get him out. He's also locked the door, which he never normally does.

I'm lying outside on the landing because his secretive behaviour intrigues me. I must say there's a lot of grunting and splashing and squelching. It's almost as if there are waves in the bathtub itself. It sounds like an episode of Blue Planet in there, the one in which Sammy the seal gets whacked by a killer whale. All I'm missing is commentary by David Attenborough.

"Daisee. Quick," screams Bacon Man.

Crumbs, it sounds like he's in excruciating pain. Daisy is in the sitting room. But she's clearly heard the commotion and has gone to the bottom of the stairs.

"What is it?"

"Come up here, please."

Bacon Man is pleading. This sounds serious.

"Only if it's worth my while," says Daisy, grinning from ear to ear.

"Stop messing about. Owwwww."

"If it's under seven inches, I'm not interested."

"I can't see the gauge."

"That's probably because your gut's in the way," says Daisy, climbing the stairs.

"It's stuck tight, and the safety valve won't work."

"Well, if the suction's that good, make the most of it."

"I'm in agony."

"Typical, I bet you didn't read the instructions."

"It's a pump, not the bloody Space Shuttle."

Daisy reaches the top of the stairs and tries to open the bathroom door.

"You've locked it. I can't get in."

"Oh God," yells Bacon Man. "Get a coin, or a screwdriver."

"Hang on, I've got a coin in my purse."

"Hurry up, I'm in agony."

I scratch at the door, while Daisy heads in search of a coin. I know she never uses cash, so it could be a while. Ah, that was fast. And she's in.

Daisy's holding me back, so I can't see precisely what's going on. But she's leaning forward and there's the sound of air being expelled. Not just from the contraption but from Bacon Man. It's a clear sigh of relief.

"Thank God," he says. "I thought it was going to explode."

"It's a good job it didn't." says Daisy.

"You're telling me," replies Bacon Man.

"Can you imagine the 999 call? My husband has blown up his own dick. We'd have the anti-terrorist squad here faster than you could say Islamic State."

As Daisy laughs at her own joke, Bacon Man puts the contraption on the bathroom table beside him. It looks like an interesting toy. I must check it out. Damn. My left front fang has gone straight through the rubber bellows at the end. It's stuck.

"Ooh look," says Daisy. "You seem to have a puncture. Hang on, I'll call AA roadside assistance."

CHAPTER FOURTEEN
GUERILLA MARMALADE

SPRING IS HERE AT LAST. Thank goodness the crushing black dog of British winter has embarked on his annual ramble and the memory is being supplanted by freshness, light and the colours of the rainbow.

The number of new smells that assail me has exploded exponentially. Flowers and blossoms dominate the sniffosphere and suppress the scent of the animal kingdom. But on my excursions, that now go deeper into the countryside, I can tell predators are still out in force, marking their territory with extra vigour to break through the pollen. I'm happy to report that although there are foxes and badgers out there, the more I grow, the less menacing they become.

I'm glad winter has retreated because my humans are more content. With every passing day, as the sun sets later and later, I sense deep-rooted tension seeping from their bodies. Feel free to accuse me of braggadocio, but the longer days are only partly responsible for this improvement. I'm convinced that my very presence has generated a seismic improvement in their lives. I thought I needed to devise a complicated peace plan to bring them closer together. But I'm seeing positive results just by being here.

    I can assure you I'm not boasting without cause. Bacon Man is perpetuating the charade of indifference. Yet he's forever taking photographs of me and posting them on Facebook and Instagram. He's not content just to snap away. He's fastidious about his composition. Every frame must be a Rembrandt. I know instinctively when he's about to push the shutter button and so I move a nano-second beforehand, ruining his shot. Pictures of goldens are clickbait on social media. It's a cheap way of attracting likes and loves and wows. But I'm not giving up my image rights just so Bacon Man can become some kind of low-grade influencer. He's better than that. Besides, I enjoy teasing him.

    Although my little wheeze frustrates Bacon Man, I can tell he's more cheerful than when I first arrived on Galahad Island. I'm sure Daisy is also accumulating the contentment she was seeking. Lying on the floor, or on my sofa, I've witnessed their faces transforming. Their frown lines are less furrowed because they smile more. The house reverberates to their laughter. I've invented a new word to describe their condition. They're both puppymatic. It's the antonym of dogmatic, in that it means they're less stubborn and argumentative.

    If my humans are happy, I'm even happier. I'm convinced the number of arguments has declined. Despite my sunny disposition, I am affected by their mood swings. I wish I wasn't overcome by anxiety when their voices become expressive during animated conversations. But I can't help myself. I'm always afraid ordinary disagreements are a precursor to one of those fights when they start ripping shreds off each other. I intervene by barking or trying to distract them by fetching a toy and demanding they entertain me.

The characteristics of the seasons and their weather patterns don't bother me, though. I'm completely adaptable and flexible. Be it, rain, sleet, sun, wind or just meh, I don't mind. I'm happy so long as I get my exercise. On the dot. Give or take five minutes. I don't object to being walked early. But if I'm delayed, I get angsty. I've got a very precise internal clock which is more accurate than the Apple Watch that Daisy wears to count the steps she does every day.

I'm lying on the landing, midway between Daisy and Bacon Man's rooms. I can tell by their breathing that they're both hovering between sleep and consciousness. Ordinarily, I would start harassing them at this time. My stomach is rumbling and that's normally the cue to sound reveille. But this morning I'm enchanted by the chorus of birdsong borne on fresh river air through an open window.

I'm not hesitating out of consideration. In truth, I'm conflicted about who I want to get up first. Daisy doesn't sleep so well and always looks exhausted when she surfaces. No matter how tired she is, though, she's always delighted to see me, greets me with a cheery hello and chats in an animated fashion, while sitting on her throne with those big garments from the washing line stretched around her ankles.

She's very Scandinavian about her body. She doesn't care who sees it. Any part of it. The door to her bathroom never closes. If Maurice Oxford were to enter the house when she was squatting there, the door would remain wide open. She'd just sit there, arguing her corner, baring those Sepp Pionteks, daring him to glance at the confluence. Outsiders might think she's an exhibitionist. But as a member of her family, having observed her at close quarters for a couple of months now, I'm convinced that Daisy must be one of the most secure women in the world. She's completely at ease in her own skin. Nothing, nobody, intimidates her.

But if I must identify one fault, it's that she always measures my food. Really! Daisy complains that Maurice is pedantic about the length of the islanders' cabin cruisers, but you should see her with the kibble and the kitchen scales. It's a hundred grams on the nose, not a single pellet more. She needs to look in the mirror and give herself a good talking to.

That's why I'm hedging my bets this morning. Bacon Man is mercurial and difficult to predict. He doesn't share Daisy's habit of adopting a childlike voice when we chat. There's no shift in his tone. He addresses me just as he would a farmer, a dustman, (or should I say, waste disposal specialist) a prince, or a pauper. I appreciate the equanimity.

Above all, I relish his generosity in the kitchen. Bacon Man never measures anything when he's cooking for himself and Daisy or dishing out my breakfast on the occasions that he's on deck. Like any talented chef, he guesstimates ingredients. His eyes are bigger than his stomach, which takes some doing. Consequently, his portions are always more filling and there's usually the bonus of a treat being tossed my way, so long as Daisy is out of range.

I'll have a taste of whatever he can get away with. I've sampled black pudding, haggis, smoked salmon, kedgeree, and courgettes when Bacon Man fancies himself as a stand-up comedian. They came straight back up. Vegetables are only acceptable if drizzled with gravy or acting as extras in a meaty dish. Believe me, there's nothing remotely amusing about crudités, Bacon Man.

Speak of the Devil. He's up. I wonder what breakfast treat is in store.

"Morning, Bubsie," he whispers. "Shhh. Daisy needs a lie in. Wait a minute while I close her door."

Bacon Man reaches down to stroke my ears and I hear him wheezing. If I had eyebrows, I'd raise them. Much as though I benefit from Bacon Man's culinary expertise, I'm now convinced that Daisy is justified in trying to persuade him to address his weight. I do feel sorry for him, though. Poor Bacon Man. He only has to peruse a menu and he shoots up a trouser size.

"Ok, Bubsie, you go first."

Good. Bacon Man's in an equable mood. When he calls me Bjørn, I'm in trouble.

We're at the top of the stairs. They removed the suitcase a week or so ago. Going up is not a problem. I'm as sure footed as a mountain goat. Descending, however, is a different kettle *de poissons*. I lack confidence and stumble down with my legs frozen in front of me like a baby deer. Bambi on ice. That's me. More than once, I've slipped a few stairs at a time and head butted the floorboards.

Bacon Man closes the kitchen door behind us. I know what that means. He doesn't want Daisy to hear what he's doing. I catch his eye and smile at him. And he smiles back. That's progress. I wonder if he felt what just happened. I did. I sensed my levels of oxytocin rising. Oxytocin is better known as the love hormone. It surges in both animals and humans when they interact. At the very least it makes us feel better, by reducing blood pressure and stress. In women it boosts the ability to breastfeed. I can tell by looking at Bacon Man's t-shirt that his moobs aren't lactating, but I wonder if the strain on his heart decreased just a little during that smile.

Thank goodness I'm not on hard rations this morning. By which I mean the canine equivalent of the army's Meals Ready to Eat. MRE's. In other words. Kibble. A hundred grams of it. Not ninety-nine, not a hundred and one. One hundred.

Hurray, it's leftovers from the humans' supper. One of my favourites. Coq au vin, Bacon Man's trademark dish. He sweated the onions and browned the chicken thighs in a combination of olive oil and streaky bacon. Joy of joys, I spy some of those being spooned into my dog bowl. The chicken is a darker shade of pink than usual. Bacon Man must have used an Argentinian Malbec instead of a Burgundy. What's the herb? Ah tarragon. And there are some new potatoes, speckled with parsley, coarse pink Himalayan rock salt, and congealed butter. Which will be salted and from Normandy if I'm not mistaken.

Bacon Man puts breakfast down and I accelerate into the corner faster than Max Verstappen. The meal might have improved if it had been taken out of the fridge half an hour earlier. Nevertheless, the chicken is succulent and perfectly seasoned. The potatoes provide some comforting ballast. I'm so lucky to live in the best taverna in the Thames Valley.

Although the decibel level is rising as I push morsels

around the metal bowl, I'm conscious of Bacon Man hurrying to complete his personal mission. He's popping thick slices of bread in the toaster, removing the lid from the butter dish, and extracting a jar from a hiding place. I know exactly what he's doing. There's no time for a sneaky bacon sandwich, so he's going for a palatable alternative, toast with guerrilla marmalade from his secret stash. Home-made, of course, in the middle of the night, when Daisy was away with the fairies, and concealed in the bottom drawer of the kitchen chest, behind a rubber mallet and an electric drill.

"Come on, Bubsie, that's enough. Let's go for a walk."

My tongue is working overtime, polishing the bowl shinier than ever and shoving it around the tiled floor like a dodgem car. What's that Winter Olympic Sport where they push a metal kettle along the ice, and use a broom to sweep a track in front of it? Curling. Why don't they do a canine equivalent and put coq au vin along the kettle's path? With my tongue, I'd be a dead cert for a gold medal.

"Come on, let's go."

Hang on, Bacon Man, I've just missed a bit.

"Bjørn, that's enough."

Uh oh. He called me Bjørn. Bacon Man lassos me with the collar. He's not using the harness, because he must be in a hurry. He attaches the lead and pulls me through the front door, I look back up at him as he closes it as quietly as possible. Bacon Man's face is betrayed by a triumphant smirk. He's managed to leave the house with toast and guerrilla marmalade intact.

But Bacon Man can't sink his teeth in until we get off the island. We're trying to be good citizens by complying with the

Galahad Island Covenant protocols on dog pee and poo. Any transgressions witnessed and reported merit an automatic yellow card. Two yellows are punishable by humiliation in the Residents' Committee weekly newsletter. Three yellows are social death. Invitations to the Coronation Day anniversary Bank Holiday barbecue are rescinded. No appeals allowed. No wonder Bacon Man is striding briskly towards the pedestrian gate. After ten seconds or so, he's puffing like a traction engine. Once or twice, both feet almost make it off the ground at the same time. It's close, but no cigar.

Erratic tugs on the lead during Bacon Man's hundred-yard waddle to the pedestrian gate prevent me from stopping for pee. But once we're through, Bacon Man pauses to get his breath back, and I can finally let go after restraining myself for at least eight hours, a new record.

Bacon Man bends down and unclips the lead. Freedom! That's something Daisy never does. She's far too uptight to let me off the leash yet. Bacon Man is relaxed to the point of being, dare I say it, cool. At first, I suspected he had ulterior motives, such as hoping I might chase a vole down the riverbank and not come back. That was unworthy of me. Bacon Man's not that malicious, although it's possible he lets me follow my nose so that he can walk at his own pace and take a break when he likes.

What's interesting is that he doesn't dig into the toast and marmalade until we're through the creaking wooden barred gate. Although we're both out of Daisy's line of sight, her powers of observation are such that she probably has a superpower of being able to see around corners.

I head towards the ivy behind some trees and squat down.

For some reason I like the feel of ivy on my butt. I'm told there's a place called The Ivy on the High Street in Henlow, the nearest town, that's got several stars attached to its name. As I wonder whether the stars indicate that The Ivy is an upmarket Public Convenience, Bacon Man catches my eye and I feel myself grimace. Go away, Bacon Man, I don't spy on you in the loo. Not all of us are as body confident as Daisy.

Bacon Man looks away and munches his toast. I finish up and trot over, conjuring up a look that suggests I'm in imminent danger of fainting. My performance is interrupted by the coq au vin repeating on me. Bacon Man extends a crust moistened by melted butter and marmalade. Wow. He's surpassed himself, especially when the clandestine nature of its production is considered. I savour a chunk of honey-sweetened navalina orange, with overtones of Sicilian lemon and lime zest. The addition of ginger doesn't agree with me, although I recognise its appeal for a human palate as well as the health benefits.

Normally at this point in the proceedings, with the morning's bathroom break done and dusted, Bacon Man would turn for home. But today is taking a curious course.

"Come on, Bubsie, let's find a good stick."

Now you're talking, Bacon Man. He stamps on a fallen branch with a satisfying crack, leans it against a stump and snaps it in two with his right foot. The path ahead is clear, and my eyes follow the stick as it arcs in an almost straight line. I'm impressed. He's got a good arm.

I'll get it, Bacon Man.

I race down the track, grab the stick in the middle, lie down and wrap my right paw around it in a firm grip. Chewing the bark helps to clean my teeth and remove the ginger after-taste from the marmalade. There's also something satisfying about stripping bark and getting down to the bare wood. In terms of pleasures, it's on a par with hole digging.

I hear wheezing behind me, look around and see Bacon Man bending down. He's managed to grab hold of the end protruding from my mouth.

"We're not here to lie down, Bubsie. Let's crack on. It's a lovely day, let's make the most of it. Come on, let's go."

We begin a tug of war over with the stick. I've got powerful jaws and for a while I manage to keep hold of it. My agility is more than a match for his brawn. As we dance around each other, the angles momentarily favour Bacon Man. He gets some leverage and rips the stick from my mouth, almost taking one of my baby teeth with it, and I yelp.

"Sorry, Bubsie. I didn't mean to hurt you. I don't know my own strength sometimes."

That's alright, Bacon Man. You're forgiven.

"Do you want to play some more?"

Bacon Man teases me with the stick and hurls it into the tunnel. I love this game and chase after it into the darkness. I conquered my fear weeks ago. Now, I'm embarrassed that I once imagined the tunnel was a portal to the Underworld when it's nothing more than a pedestrian thoroughfare beneath a private road leading to a multi-millionaire's riverside mansion.

At least I thought it was safe. I suddenly think I can hear a ghost and feel the fur on my head shaping into a Mohawk. I look around and realise it's just Bacon Man. His wheezing is reverberating off the tunnel's curved ceiling. We have another tug of war contest over the stick, and I concede more easily. I don't fancy a trip to the dog dentist.

This time Bacon Man uses a different technique to throw the stick. He can't hurl it from the shoulder because the tunnel is too low. Instead, he employs a sideways motion, almost like a squash shot. Wow, I'm impressed, he's got a tremendously powerful wrist. I wonder what sort of exercise he does for that.

The stick flies out of the tunnel's exit into the shins of a lean, ruddy-faced man in his mid-seventies, wearing an ensemble of a checked flannel shirt, sensible V-necked sweater, corduroy trousers, stout walking shoes, topped off with a tweed cap.

"Oi, you bloody hooligan. Do that again and I'll give you what for with my twelve-bore," he roars.

Then he grins.

"Don't worry," he says. "I'm just joking. That's Bjørn isn't it? I see him every day with a lady that I presume is your wife. Normally she's a lot further down the track by this time of the morning."

"Yes, this is Bjørn and yes, that was my wife, or still is, the last time I looked."

"Tony Bisham," chuckles the country gent.

"Morgan Somerville. Good to meet you," smiles Bacon Man as they shake hands.

Now I'm really confused. How many names does Bacon Man have? I wonder why Daisy calls him *Skatter* and not Morgan.

"Ah, you're the farmer who lost everything in the fire, and are now renting on Galahad Island. Astrid told me about you."

"That's right. And you're that bloke off the telly, aren't you?"

"Not anymore."

"Why not?"

"Oh, the usual. Being pale, male and stale. I plead guilty to the first two charges. Not guilty to the third."

I sense Bacon Man doesn't want to elaborate and he changes the subject as he so often does.

"I'm surprised that I haven't seen you on the island."

"I try not to spend much time there," replies Bisham. "Awful bloody people."

"What do you mean?"

"One of the first things I did was to put up a low fence on the water's edge to stop the dog falling in the river and drowning. Straight away several anonymous letters came through the mailbox saying I was in breach of the Covenant. The next day a committee member told me that if I didn't take the fence down immediately, my landlord would be asked to evict me."

"Par for the course, I'm afraid."

"They had a more liberal regime in Colditz."

OK, Bacon Man. I've heard enough and so have you. I start barking and nipping at his trouser bottoms.

"I think we'd better get going."

Damn right, Bacon Man. Get a move on.

"I'm glad we've had this conversation, Tony. See you next time."

"Good to meet you too," replies Tony. Enjoy your walk."

Bacon Man and I resume playing stick and walk along a private paved road for about five minutes. Goodness, he's slow and nothing like Daisy. With her long legs, she maintains a cracking pace. Bacon Man would pass out if we walked at her speed. He spies a bench and sits down, wheezing again. Come on, Bacon Man, I bark. We've still got some way to go. Daisy and I always reach the river. We need to go into the big field, turn right down another narrow path and then we can see the boats.

Cor. What's that smell? It's a squillion times better than bacon. I turn around and spot a lithe runner in shorts and singlet, loping along at a cracking pace. Her ponytail is bobbing, well, like a pony's tail. And she's being pursued by a very fit cockapoo, who shoots past me. Now the wind is in the right direction, the scent is even more intense. Why isn't she stopping so I can get a better sniff?

Hey, wait for me.

I manage to catch up with her and bury my snout in her lady parts. Oh, my this is divine. All my senses are zoning in on this aroma, although I can vaguely hear Bacon Man bellowing at the top of his voice.

"Bjørn. Stop. Come back here this minute."

You must be joking, Bacon Man. It smells like I'm on a promise. Whatever that is. Cor, this is a real challenge. She must be playing hard to get. She's off sprinting again, trying to catch up with her owner. In the distance I can hear Bacon Man yelling

"Is your dog on heat?"

It's all to no avail. The runner keeps on pounding the footpath along the river. The cockapoo follows and so do I. Bacon Man's voice is fading into the distance.

"Oh, for fuck's sake. Daisy will kill me if I lose him."

After two minutes or so of the best game of chase I've ever had, the runner stops and sees that I'm stuck like glue to the cockapoo. She looks back along the riverbank and decides to walk back the way she came. She's also trying, without much success, to stop me from mounting the cockapoo. Eventually she and Bacon Man converge. Bacon Man is drenched in sweat and wheezing.

"Is your dog on heat?" gasps Bacon Man.

The woman ignores him. A look of exasperation crosses his face, and he manages to catch her eye.

"Is your dog on heat?" he bellows.

I bet they could hear him in Henley. The woman pulls out her ear pods.

"What did you say?" she inquires.

"Is your dog on heat?"

"Yes, I suppose so," she replies nonchalantly.

Without further ado, she puts the earphones back in, turns towards Henley and resumes her run, pursued by the cockapoo. I'm a bit slow off the mark. Bacon Man catches me by the collar and lassos me with the lead.

"That's it, you little bugger. We're going home."

By the time we reach 69, Galahad Island, Bacon Man's clothes are as fetid as the Everglades. I bound into the kitchen where Daisy is standing by the washing machine, squirting some unpleasant looking garments with a pink spray bottle.

"Oh, there you are. I was just about to send out a search party."

Bacon Man doesn't respond. He goes straight to the fridge,

opens a large bottle of sparkling water, necks it in one go, belches, and collapses onto a wooden kitchen chair.

"Look at the state of you," exclaims Daisy. "What happened?"

"Bloody unbelievable. I've been halfway to Henley and back trying to get Bjørn under control. He was chasing a dog on heat."

"Was it difficult?"

"Almost impossible. I'm knackered. The dog's owner was a runner and didn't stop when I shouted. She had bloody headphones in and couldn't hear me."

Daisy snorts.

"So how many steps have you done this morning?"

Bacon Man looks at his Apple Watch.

"About twelve thousand."

"Excellent. Hopefully, you'll meet up again tomorrow. At this rate you'll lose weight in no time at all."

"Very funny."

In an instant, Daisy's tone changes. If I was Bacon Man, I'd take cover.

"While you've been out schmoozing the locals, I've spent the past half hour trying to get shit off your boxers. It's caked in and almost impossible to remove, despite using a whole bottle of Vanish."

"Well, er, I don't know how that happened," Bacon Man stumbles.

"I'll tell you exactly how and why it happened," says Daisy.

Uh oh. A storm is coming. She's uncurled her bottom lip, and she's got her feet in the boxer's position. I don't like it when she does that. Her bottom teeth are crooked, and her face becomes less attractive.

"You're so morbidly obese that you can no longer wipe properly. Your T-Rex arms aren't long enough anymore. Do I need to spell it out? You can no longer reach your fucking arse because there's too much fat in the way. How sad is that?"

I agree with Daisy. It is sad. The fur around my butthole never gets poo on it because of the way I squat, and because I've got super powerful muscles in my lower abdomen from running after balls and sticks. So, I'm able to expel the turds some distance. Ta da! On the odd occasion when my fur might get some splash back, I simply lick it off. Why can't Bacon Man do that? No need to answer.

The uncomfortable truth is that humans haven't been taught to be that flexible. I've only ever heard the issue being discussed in the context of a nuclear strike. Have I lost you? It's the answer to this question. What do you do if you're about to get hit by a nuclear bomb? Bend over and kiss your arse goodbye. Maybe ending the Cold War wasn't such a good thing after all. Bomb drills are good for you. Better than bloody Pilates, that's for certain. Good Lord, Daisy's still banging on.

"Do you know what? I think I'm going to take a photograph of your boxers and post it on Facebook. I may not be able to get you to lose weight, but maybe if I publicly shame you, that will work."

"Oh, Daisy. Please. I know you're capable of doing it but please don't."

I haven't seen Bacon Man looking this scared before and I don't blame him. I'm coming to realise that you become complacent around Daisy at your peril. She's completely unpredictable.

"Ok. But do you realise how serious this is?" she asks.

You should see Bacon Man right now. He's sweating buckets and looking crestfallen. The lecture isn't over.

"Did you see that story online the other day, about the thirty-five stone bedridden woman who needs a special machine with a spray gun to wash her arse because she can longer manage to do it herself?"

Maybe she got an old fire hose on eBay. Lots of room for collateral damage with a machine like that. Gosh, Daisy's on a roll this morning.

"You're heading that way. What are you? Twenty-one stones? Twenty-three? Probably more like twenty-three or four. I don't know what that is in kilos, but you're soon going to be in her ballpark. Let's find out how much you weigh. This minute. When was the last time you went on the scales? Don't bother answering. Just wait there. We don't want you passing out from over exertion on the stairs, I'll go and get them."

"Stop, Daisy, just stop. This is ridiculous. You know you're the smartest woman I've ever met, and somehow you are incredibly stupid."

Oh dear. I'm all in favour of Bacon Man arguing back, but he should have learned by now, that he won't get Daisy to retreat by insulting her.

"You think you know how to handle people, but the psychology you're using is all wrong. You're all stick and no carrot."

What is it you humans say? When you're in a hole, stop

digging. But Bacon Man's just exchanged his spade for an excavator.

"You're not using persuasion. You're wielding a very blunt instrument. Every time you attack me in this way, I just dig my heels in even deeper just to spite you. You'd be much better off using reverse psychology or at least offering some encouragement. Like how about a shag? Sex is exercise, it's good for the heart and the cardiovascular system."

"Sex? Sex? What planet are you on?"

Daisy is a couple of notches away from screaming. It's suddenly gone quiet outside. I bet the neighbours are holding glasses against the wall.

"If that's your attitude, I'm going to cook myself a full English. Fuck your Danish oatmeal."

"You're unbelievable, Morgan."

Uh Oh. She's called him by his first name. That means double trouble.

"You want to get all romantic? You must be joking. How much of a turn on do you think your soiled boxers are?"

There are websites for that sort of thing. It's a strange world. Who knows, there might be a niche market for Bacon Man's handiwork. Sorry. Handiwork is the wrong word, because his hands can't reach. Crumbs, Daisy's still going full throttle.

"I can't believe my life has come to this. I used to have a glamorous existence before I met you. I had a great job. Six figure salary, unlimited expenses, a fabulous apartment. I turned down a marriage proposal from a property magnate who used to take me to the south of France on his yacht. It had a crew of ten and was more than a hundred feet long."

It's a good job Daisy doesn't have it now, because Maurice Oxford wouldn't let her park it in the Galahad Island marina.

"I've partied with princes and rock stars. I never used to have any regrets. But now I'm not so sure."

I look over at Bacon Man. He seems to be shrinking. I don't think I've ever seen him look so short.

"I've always told you I'm not going to die curious. Unfortunately, that's truer than ever. I've encountered a mystery I thought I'd never have to deal with. I now know what it's like to scrape the shit off your boxers. Well, this is the last time I'll ever do it. Believe me. From now on, you can do your own fucking laundry, or you can buy up Marks and Spencer's worldwide stock of tent sized underpants and use a new pair every day. How dare you treat me like the maid. Come on, Bjørn, let's go for a walk. You're the only joy in my life."

CHAPTER FIFTEEN

PURPLE HEARTS AND BODY BAGS

Now I realise why humans love their cars. The people and dog watching are such great entertainment. I've spotted some serious babes strolling down the High Street on leads. Stop it. I know what you're thinking. I've watched *Fifty Shades of Grey* as well. You all have such dirty minds.

I'm talking about other puppies. With four legs and tails. Well, not just puppies. There was one young bitch who was definitely putting out. I had to muster all my reserves of restraint not to leap out of the car.

Now, just to be crystal clear, I'm referring to humans. People are so friendly. Every other person who's spotted me sticking my head out of the rear nearside window has smiled and waved. They have such great taste. Yes, I'm so sweet. I'm so cute. Just kidding, I'm not that vain. But this new experience is making me genuinely happy. I feel like I'm making the world a better place, one person at a time. I'm sure I'm improving everyone's day with a brief glimpse of me. If I look them in the eye, they're getting a dose of oxytocin, the love hormone. Yes, I'm talking to you, sir. Feel those stress levels go down and your mood improve. You're very welcome. Have a nice day. Here's another golden retriever smile. It costs me nothing. I learned a new word this morning. Cruising. I think it means driving slowly down a busy street and showing off. After our post breakfast walk this morning, Bacon Man asked me if I wanted to come cruising. Being in Bacon Man's company means there's always the possibility of a mystery snack, so of course, I was game. I love the feel of the wind blowing my ears back. And I don't feel the slightest bit sick. When you've got something to look at, it distracts you from worrying about motion sickness.

Uh oh. There are the syncopated string stabs. It's the intro to Barry White's greatest hit. Daisy wants to give Bacon Man a bollocking. Again. He pushes a button and Daisy appears to be talking in Sensurround. She's everywhere in the car.

"Where are you?" she demands. "And more importantly, where's the dog?"

"He's with me," replies Bacon Man.

"I bloody well hope you're not on the motorway and dog-napping him again."

"Of course not. Didn't you check your spying gear before calling? And shame on you for thinking such a thing. I gave you my word that he could stay. Besides, Bubsie and I are getting along just fine."

"So where are you?"

"Just driving back from town. We just went to the pharmacy to pick up Lillian's heart medication. Also, we had nothing in, so I went to the baker for some croissants and fresh bread. I'm looking in the wing mirror right now. Bubsie is leaning out of the back window."

"Is he strapped in?"

"No. He's fine."

"Isn't there a risk of him falling out?"

"Stop worrying. He's taking in the sights and having a blast. He's got a big smile on his face. Oooh. There's a head turn. He's just checking out another puppy. We'll be back in ten minutes. Could you make some coffee please?"

"Will do. See you shortly, *Skatter*."

Bacon Man's right, I'm really enjoying myself. I feel sorry for all these dogs in town, being restricted on leads, whereas I am free to roam when Bacon Man takes me out.

We're now crossing the river. Rowers are performing 180 degree turns on the left-hand side of the bridge to avoid getting caught in the tow effect of the water speeding up and dropping over what I think is called a weir. I'm looking back now and studying a beautiful church with a tall sharp steeple. A graveyard runs down to the water's edge. What a glorious place to spend eternity.

Now, I've lost sight of the river, and nothing is grabbing my attention. We're passing through a village of small red brick cottages. No one is out on the pavement. It's not as interesting, so I duck back inside, lie down on the rear leather seat, and watch Bacon Man steering.

"Did you enjoy that, Bubsie? We'll be home soon and maybe you can have a piece of croissant."

Above the throb of the Mercedes engine, I hear the higher frequencies of the river flowing to the right of us. I stand up and try to see what I can see but the window is closed. Then it starts to open by itself, and I poke my head out.

"There you go, Bubsie, electric windows, especially for you."

More proof, if needed, that dogs rule and humans are the servant class. We're driving parallel to the river. The view is blocked by hedgerows, although I get the odd glimpse through gaps and over wooden gates.

Bacon Man slows down as we approach a cluster of cottages whose gardens back on to the creek opposite our part of Galahad Island. I scan the road ahead and spot Genevieve, a singer who performs in musicals in London's theatre district. We see her several times a week during our walks. Bacon Man and Daisy are always talking about what a great social catalyst and influencer I am. They're meeting people they would never normally approach. I break the ice because people want to talk about me.

I bark a greeting, and Genevieve waves back. Bacon Man slows down and opens his electric window.

"Hello, Gen, how are you?"

"Hello, Bjørn. My goodness, you're growing," she says.

Glad to see Genevieve has her priorities right. Addressing me first.

"How old is he now, Morgan?"

Who's Morgan? Oh yes, it's Bacon Man. I wonder if he's in trouble with Genevieve as well as Daisy.

"I'm not too sure precisely, but I think he's about eight months now, give or take a week or two. Astrid will know. She's got all the paperwork."

"And you look a little slimmer. Are you losing weight? Is that the Bjørn effect?"

"Thanks very much. That's very kind. I don't know whether I'm losing weight. I'm reluctant to go on the scales. But I feel much better. Walking is such a painless way to improve your health. Anyway, how are things with you."

"All good, thanks. We're playing to packed audiences, and bookings are solid for months. Anyway, I'm glad I've caught you. An old friend of mine is in a spot of trouble and could do with your skill set."

"Oh really. Anyone I might know? Andrew Lloyd Webber?"

"Tommy Bentwaters."

"Not *The* Tommy Bentwaters, the rock singer."

"That's the one. I was one of his backing singers when I was starting out, and we've stayed friends."

"The only global superstar Suffolk has ever produced."

"You're forgetting Ed Sheeran," says Genevieve.

"Ed who?"

Genevieve chuckles.

"I think you'll find that Ed Sheeran is more famous these days. But if you're a Tommy Bentwaters fan, I can see why he wouldn't have crossed your radar."

"I saw Tommy in Ipswich in the 1970s. At the Gaumont cinema if I remember correctly. It was when protests against the Vietnam War were really gaining traction and he had that massive hit. What was it called?"

"Purple Hearts and Body Bags."

"Thanks. It was on the tip of my tongue."

"Well, Tommy's in danger of being cancelled because of

that very song. He could lose a fortune and needs some specialist help. That's where you come in. I've told him all about you two and he wanted me to connect you as soon as possible. It's urgent."

"Have you had breakfast?"

Typical Bacon Man. Thinking about food before anything else.

"No, I haven't."

"Well, jump in and join us. We can discuss it with Astrid."

"I'll get in the back with Bjørn. And we can have a cuddle."

Genevieve climbs in beside me. For some strange reason, I find myself being irritated. The back seat is my territory, and I don't like sharing. I want to be able to move between both left and right windows at will. Genevieve is in the way. I stick my head out of the right-hand window and pout.

"He doesn't look very happy," says Genevieve.

But as soon as I hang out of the window I feel better. I do some of my best thinking with the wind in my fur.

I'm so lucky that I'm a dog. I have no filters, while you humans are terrified of making a careless remark and being labelled racist, or phobic and being cancelled, like Tommy Bentwaters. I have a big bone to pick with the sanctimonious crusaders doing the cancelling. Why are they so sloppy with their language? Especially when they're so swift to condemn people and eviscerate careers and livelihoods, sometimes because of a single word.

Do they know what a phobia really is?

Phobia comes from the Greek and means having irrational fear. Just in case that isn't clear enough, let me give you a few synonyms for irrational. Unreasonable, illogical, groundless, baseless, unfounded, unjustifiable, unsound, absurd, ridiculous, stupid. Need I go on?

When I go for walkies, I'm petrified that another male dog with a penchant for the beast with two backs is going to jump me. Does that make me homophobic? No, it doesn't. My fear is **rational** because most hounds around here swing both ways.

Let's put this in a human context. How would you categorise a pretty boy who goes to jail and is desperately trying not to drop the soap in the shower? Would you say his fear is irrational? Of course not. He's not homophobic. He's just covering his arse from convicted predators. Like the former BBC presenter Huw Edwards. Sorry. My mistake. Edwards preferred them younger.

Anyway, I have a similar issue with the term Islamophobia. As British traditions fade away, I'm genuinely worried that Ramadan will catch on and I'll die of starvation after fasting for a month.

That was just a joke, by the way. Not a Danish cartoon. So, keep your beard on.

But Islamist terrorists who slaughter others while invoking their God are no laughing matter. If my fears are irrational and what the ill-educated term "Islamophobic", let's put it to the test. Scrap all security at every single airport on the planet. Then we'll see who's laughing.

We're living in an age when intelligent people are being silenced so that stupid people won't be offended.

As an aspirational world leader, I've a duty to spread the message that cancel culture is destructive. Not only does it stamp on free expression and prevent a healthy exchange of ideas, but it also perpetuates the cycle of hatred. I urge you to follow my lead by forgiving those who've learned from their mistakes.

Take Daisy's picture-perfect homeland, Denmark. Until recently, animal brothels were totally legal there. I'm sure you find that hard to believe, but it's true. Where do you think the phrase "all fur coat and no knickers" came from?

Finally, in 2015, those bestial bordellos were outlawed. No more Roger the Rabbit, Deep Stoat, Pop goes the Weasel, Mountain Goats, or Pigs in Blankets. The Danes redeemed themselves. Unreservedly, I grant them absolution.

But, I hear you ask, what about the Koreans and their doggie diet?

Well, the South Korean parliament has passed a law banning the distribution and sale of dog meat. It won't come into effect until 2027. Therefore, in the spirit of reconciliation, I won't cancel South Korea, because the country is on the path of righteousness.

But North Koreans? They still regard the Battersea Dogs' Home as an all-you-can eat buffet.

Bloody cannibals.

No wonder their country belongs to the Axis of Evil.

Oooh, look, we're home.

Bacon Man puts me on the lead, and I trot beside him as we head towards the front door. He reaches for the key, but the door opens and there's Daisy standing in just a long shirt. None of the buttons are done up. She opens the shirt in a flash, exposing her breasts. She's not wearing her usual waist high comfort knickers either.

"A little reward for being so kind to my puppy," she grins.

"Perfect timing, Daisy. Put them away, we've got company. Genevieve is joining us for breakfast."

"Fuck. You might have told me. Sorry, Gen, I didn't spot you there behind Morgan."

"Don't worry, Astrid, nothing I haven't seen in a dressing room."

"Come in, excuse the mess. There's dog hair everywhere. I haven't hoovered yet. I'll just go and put some clothes on......"

"For a change," cracks Bacon Man.

"Let's have breakfast on the balcony. It's a lovely morning."

"Gen, do you want to take Bjørn on to the deck, and I'll fix breakfast. What would you like to drink? Cappuccino, expresso, green tea, English breakfast, or tea with lemon and honey to keep those vocal cords in shape?"

"Ooh, tea with lemon and honey please."

"Coming right up."

I trot behind Genevieve as she heads outside. I've forgiven her for invading my space in the car. I pick up a chewy stick that I've been working on for weeks. Perhaps she'd like a tug of war. Genevieve is a sport. She grabs hold of the end that I swivel in her direction and doesn't wince when I pretend to growl fiercely.

Before I know it, Bacon Man shuffles on to the balcony carrying a tray laden with plates, cutlery, baskets of golden pastries, and fist-sized cylinders of an artisan baguette. The aroma is divine. Drool is fermenting in the back of my mouth and here comes Daisy, now fully dressed, carrying beverages on a smaller tray.

Mmm. There's something different about her. She's wearing lip gloss. Maybe Genevieve's presence has activated her competitive instincts and prompted her to up her game.

"This is from the new bakery in town," says Bacon Man. "They're as good as any patisserie in Paris. The taste is almost identical. There's home-made marmalade, goat's cheese, brie, cheddar, and I'll just get some strawberries."

Daisy's face is a picture as she computes the words marmalade and cheddar. Her eyebrows arch violently and almost touch her hairline. If Genevieve wasn't here, Daisy would have snatched the outlawed foodstuffs and dumped them in the waste bin. But she's too well-mannered to humiliate Bacon Man in front of their guest.

"What a great view you have," says Genevieve.

"Yes, the cottages next to you are so much more attractive to look at than the monstrosities on Galahad Island," says Daisy.

"I'm just grateful to have a roof over my head," says Genevieve. "The music business is really precarious and every day, I thank my lucky stars my aunt left me the cottage in her will."

I'm glad she did. Genevieve is a major upgrade on our neighbours.

"My aunt hated Galahad Island with a vengeance," says Genevieve.

"She used to have a great view right across the river. She and other cottage owners tried to stop the construction but failed."

I told you Galahad Island was a blot on the landscape."

"My aunt thought someone got a backhander. She died a bitter and angry woman."

"I'm not surprised, Gen. Now come on, tuck in," says Bacon Man, plonking a chunk of cheddar and dollop of guerrilla marmalade on his plate.

He's looking sideways at Daisy, and now he's winking at me.

"I'll just have a croissant, please. I've got dance rehearsals this afternoon and can work it off."

"Yes, you'd better follow Bacon Man's rules of the road," says Daisy with a look that says I've lost this skirmish, but I'll win the war.

"Eat when you can, drink when you can, sleep when you can, pee and poo when you can, because you never know when you'll next have an opportunity."

"Bacon Man?" asks Genevieve.

"It's the name we use for Morgan in this house because he used bacon to win Bjørn's affections. It was the only way he could do it. Bribery."

"That's slander," he replies. "Now tell us all about Tommy Bentwaters' predicament. I'd love to help. It'd make a welcome change from dealing with corporate suits."

"Do you mean Tommy Bentwaters, the singer who just got divorced from tall, blonde wife number four?" asks Daisy.

"Didn't he lose a castle as part of the settlement? Good for her. Tall blondes should stick together. I'm sick of us getting a bad rap. Oh, and short blondes as well, Genevieve."

"Well, the divorce hasn't helped. But it's nothing compared to the problems he's facing over *Purple Hearts and Body Bags*."

"What problems?" asks Daisy.

"An online campaign accusing Tommy of glorifying prostitution. It's gaining momentum."

This part of the conversation is way over my head, so I walk over to Bacon Man and put my head on his lap. He knows what I really, really want. A piece of bread or a croissant. He's not playing ball. Maybe I should try Genevieve, she's not eating. She's talking.

"People are demanding that Tommy drops the song from his set. There's also an online petition aimed at forcing venues on his upcoming tour to cancel his gigs, if he insists on performing it."

"So is Tommy going to comply?" asks Daisy.

"His manager and the record label are applying enormous pressure. They want him to give in. But he's looking for a way out. I can get him on the phone now if you like."

"Hang on a minute," says Daisy. "Let's look at the lyrics first. I want to see if the words are totally indefensible."

"No need. I've got the song on a playlist," says Bacon Man.

"Of course you have," says Daisy. "I bet it's just like the rest of your sad old man's music."

"Just listen before you pass judgement."

Bacon Man scrolls through his phone, looking for the song.

"Oh, this marmalade is to die for," says Genevieve with her mouth full. "So many different flavours and I love the touch of ginger."

"Home-made," says Bacon Man, as he hits play and we're assailed by raunchy power chords and a driving bass line.

"Just like the rest of your sad old man's music," quips Daisy.

"Give it a rest. You wanted to hear the lyrics."

Tommy Bentwaters' gravelly voice kicks in.

We weren't put on this earth,
To fight the Vietcong.
Marching on Saigon,
To our swan song.
My drafted platoon
Honoured the flag.
I lost count
Of purple hearts and body bags,
Chopper me out,
Of the Mekong Delta
Got my discharge papers,
And I'm going to take shelter,
Where there's beer,
Bar girls and Chinese molasses.
And the only firefight, all night long
Is an artillery duel
Of Thai ping pong.
I'm gonna banish
The memories in Old Patpong.

"Well, I think the lyrics are crap," says Daisy. "But I can't hear the problem although there are some phrases I don't understand, maybe because I'm Danish."

"Like what?" asks Bacon Man.

"Chinese molasses. Thai ping pong. Old Patpong."

"Well, I can help you out on a couple of those," says Bacon Man. "But let me first just check the urban slang for Chinese molasses."

Bacon Man does a quick Google search on his mobile.

"Chinese molasses is the street term for opium. Opium dens were commonplace in Vietnam, Laos, Cambodia, and Thailand during the Vietnam war. Besides weed, opium was the drug of choice for those seeking a kind of euphoric release."

"But Tommy's not under attack for glorifying drug use," says Genevieve. "It's prostitution."

Daisy's eyes widen and a thin smile spreads across her face as she addresses Bacon Man.

"So please enlighten me about Old Patpong and Thai ping-pong, dear."

Bacon Man clears his throat and goes red in the face.

"Er, well, er I don't know if Patpong Road exists any more. It is, or was, a street in Bangkok, lined with girly bars, massage parlours, and brothels. So, there's the prostitution element."

"You're forgetting Thai ping-pong, dear," says Daisy gently, maintaining that smile.

"Er, er, er, it's difficult to describe in polite company."

"Oh, don't feel embarrassed in front of me," smiles Genevieve.

"Right. Um. Well, in some of the bars, there are, or were, performers who insert ping pong balls into their lady bits, and then use the, er, muscles, to, er, shoot them out again."

I'm tempted to make a comment here, but for once, I'll refrain.

"Er, and er, some, er go, er, quite some distance. So, I suppose, that in the bar Tommy was writing about, two girls were firing ping-pong balls at each like machine guns."

"It's sad isn't it," says Daisy "and degrading, that women are forced to make a living by performing tricks like that. Although I have to say, they must have marvellous Kegel muscles."

"We could do with them down in the nets, at the cricket club," says Bacon Man with a grin. "It might improve the batsmen's averages."

"What did you say?" snarls Daisy.

"Just joking, dear."

"Well, that's just not funny. If you're not careful, I'll cancel you."

Genevieve intervenes to save Bacon Man's bacon.

"Sorry to interrupt, Astrid, but do you think Tommy's position is a lost cause?"

"No. It can be fixed," says Daisy. "But time is of the essence. We need a strategy that first stops the damage, then flips, and ultimately boosts Tommy both as an artist and a brand."

"Won't that be difficult?" asks Genevieve.

"That's where we work our magic."

"Shall we get Tommy on the phone now, Gen?" suggests Bacon Man.

Within seconds the old rocker's up on FaceTime. I can't make out the precise contours of his face, but he seems to resemble a walnut, pitted with deep fissures, where collagen has been eroded by years of hard living. Piercing blue eyes are his saving graces, along with a piratical cackle.

"Hello, Gen, babe. Is that the cavalry that's gonna save me from the woke brigade?"

"Hi, Tommy, yes. I'm with Morgan and Astrid now."

"Hi, Tommy, good to talk to you," says Bacon Man.

Daisy finishes his sentence for him. After bickering over the cricket joke, they become totally professional.

"Gen has briefed us. And we're sure we can help."

"Thank Christ for that. I need some serious lateral thinking. My tour's in real jeopardy. I won't trouble you with the numbers. All you need to know is that I can't afford to take the financial hit and neither can the band."

What kind of world is it where even a famous rock star doesn't have financial security? I realise that having four ex-wives is rather careless. But is it only Russian oligarchs and hedge fund managers who're rolling in it? I wonder why Tommy is digging his heels in.

"I won a Grammy for the song for fuck's sake, and it became an anthem for the anti-war movement. So, it's historic. But I'm locked in a stand-off with my manager and the PR 'consultants.' Unless they all sign off on a solution, the tour's fucked."

"When do you need to get this sorted by?" asks Daisy.

"Yesterday afternoon," he smiles. "In all honesty, by close of play today."

"That's tight."

"I know. I've got a meeting with my manager, the record label and their PR people this afternoon at two. Can you be here by then?"

"Where are you?"

A place called Bawdsey on the Suffolk coast."

"I know roughly where it is." says Bacon Man. "Across the Deben from Felixstowe. That's quite a schlepp. I reckon we could make it in time, if we set off in the next half an hour or so."

"We'll be there," says Daisy.

"That's brilliant. Thanks so much, I'll ping you the address. Thanks a lot, Gen, you're a lifesaver, I'll be in touch. Ciao."

"Right, I'd better be going," says Genevieve. "Don't worry, I'll see myself out. Thanks for breakfast, and I must get the recipe for that marmalade. Bye."

Bacon Man and Daisy load the tray with the remains of breakfast and head towards the kitchen.

"Right," says Bacon Man. "What the fuck are we going to do with the dog?"

CHAPTER SIXTEEN
STAR WARS

I'M HAVING A PANIC ATTACK of an intensity I've never experienced before. Machine-gun spasms of utter terror overwhelm my attempts to be rational. Maybe this is the separation anxiety the breeder was talking about. Daisy and Bacon Man have abandoned me. I can't believe it. I haven't been left alone since I arrived on Galahad Island. One of them has always been there. They're my emotional crutches, and without them, even for just a couple of minutes, I've collapsed. Frankly, I'm surprised at my own frailty.

I'm in the backseat of the car in the middle of a lunar landscape, outside a weird circular structure resembling a spaceship. The rear left passenger window is open. The air is surprisingly fresh, and I can hear running water nearby. I haven't a clue where on earth I am.

Since breakfast on the balcony, the day has gone from bad to worse. Daisy and Bacon Man have been at loggerheads after failing to find a dog-sitter.

"I told you this would happen," said Bacon Man. "You're going to have to stay behind. I'll handle this myself."

"You can't do that," replied Daisy. "Your misogynistic crack about the cricket nets proves you're not equipped to deal with a sensitive issue like prostitution."

"I'm not a misogynist. It was just a bloody gag, for Christ's sake. Where's your sense of humour?"

"Not everyone appreciates your jokes. We don't know who's going to be at this meeting. There's a real risk you could wreck things with one of your inappropriate cracks."

"Of course, I won't. I'm not a complete idiot."

"Look, we're a team, we always have been. So, I'm coming. That's final. And so is Bjørn. Come on, Bubba, let's go cruising."

I thought I was in for a little light posing in the back window, checking out bitches on the High Street. But we turned right, instead of left at the roundabout at the end of the country lane, and Bacon Man floored it. The dual carriageway was like a racetrack. My ears shot back and developed so much lift, I almost took off. The wind battered my eyes into submission, and I ducked back in and lay down for most of the journey.

Daisy allowed me to stretch my legs in a lay-by somewhere south of Ipswich. I had a leisurely pee as Bacon Man waddled behind a tree at warp speed. He emerged looking mightily relieved. However, he was in trouble again after Woodbridge as he followed road signs to Bawdsey and ignored the Google Maps' woman. Daisy berated him while we went off-piste for fifteen minutes and strayed into a disused Cold War military testing site. But after Bacon Man was re-educated about the need to follow Google Maps' instructions to the letter, we finally arrived at this spaceship a few minutes behind schedule.

Hello. There they are, on the top deck. The man with the

walnut face is opening one of the cockpit windows. Are they all about to take off? I suddenly find my voice and start howling. Please don't leave me. I can't live without you. Ground Control to Major Tommy. I don't care if there's life on Mars. You've got to remain on earth with me.

"Hello, little fellow. No need to be so upset. You don't have to stay in the car. Come inside the Martello Tower, and we'll get you some water and biscuits."

It's the man with the walnut face, Tommy Bentwaters, and Daisy is with him.

We head up to the roof terrace of what I quickly learn is a converted Victorian coastal fortress and not the Starship Enterprise. Despite Bacon Man's navigational misstep, we're the first ones here. Over the course of half an hour, the other stakeholders, which I think is the current vogue term, rock up. Punctuality is important to me. These people need an inner body clock like mine.

I've instantly taken to Tommy. I can tell he's a dog person by the way he strokes me. Not only that, he's got a great biscuit tin and fabulous taste. Not a platinum record in sight. Perhaps his ex-wives took them all. His glass-walled orangery on top of the tower is filled with comfortable sofas and exotic plants thriving in the sunlight. However, I'm wary of the others hanging around the grand piano. One of them looks at Bacon Man and whispers to a colleague,

"I wasn't expecting to meet the eponymous star of *Free Willy.*"

The other guy doesn't attempt to disguise his sniggers. I

have to say Bacon Man isn't doing himself any favours in the style wars. The music biz people are decked out in expensive black textiles and leather. Bacon Man is wearing his trademark red empire builder shorts, and a black t-shirt that just about covers his gut.

I hate it when people are unkind and judge him on his size alone. They've no idea just how smart, decent, and witty he is. But that's what happens to fat people. They're perceived as weak in both body and mind and unworthy of consideration. Bacon Man's qualities do eventually shine through once people look beyond the blubber, although sometimes it can take a while.

As for Daisy, she doesn't look out of place at all. Her face is subtly made up, applied as we sped up the A12. Her hair is swept into an elegant bun, accentuated by pearl earrings, reserved for special occasions. Her black silk shirt, unbuttoned to reveal a hint of cleavage, is paired with black jeans and trendy Chelsea boots. I'm so proud of my Mama.

Tommy stands up.

"Right, we all know why we're here. But we don't all know each other. This is Morgan and Astrid. They do crisis management and come highly recommended. This is Jim Spiegel, my manager, from back in the day. Ronnie Truss is from Trajectus Records. They're planning to release a remastered greatest hits album to coincide with the Fifty Big Ones tour, if it ever gets off the ground. The production deadline is imminent and that's why we have to make a decision today. Bridget, over there is our brief, or legal counsel. Her nickname is Not U2 because she ain't pro-Bono. Finally, that's Lucian, a media consultant with the record company. I'm forgetting Bjørn, Astrid's golden retriever, the fiercest guard dog on the planet. He'll lick you to death if you're not careful."

That sounds like an introduction to make myself at home. I start to climb onto a leather sofa. Daisy clears her throat, an unmistakable warning that I'd better behave. I back off and settle on a sheepskin in a corner, an acceptable alternative.

Lucian uncrosses his legs, looks down his nose towards Bacon Man.

"Can I just ask, besides being a body double for Meatloaf, what the fuck do you know about the music business?"

What a rude, presumptuous man. Bacon Man doesn't rise to the bait.

"We're here because of our expertise in managing crises and predicting how news stories will play out. It doesn't matter what the business is."

"I tried to check you out, but you don't even have a website."

Daisy intervenes.

"We operate on word of mouth alone because we don't need to flaunt our clients."

Daisy strides to the middle of the room. She seems taller than usual and somehow more intimidating. She's using a tried and tested dog tactic, dominating the pack.

"Right. We're going to work this problem and do it fast. We have one chance to get it right. Here's what we suggest."

That makes me smile. I know Daisy isn't making a suggestion. She's telling them how it's going to be.

"Tommy, you're the key to this. We need to talk to you

alone. So, the rest of you, would you mind leaving the room please? We don't need long. Half an hour max."

"Yes, I do fucking mind," harrumphs the manager, Spiegel. "Who the fuck do you think you are?"

Everyone else chimes in. It's pandemonium. They're all throwing teething rings out of their carry cots. Watching adults regress is bewildering. Maybe it's nap time.

Daisy stands there impassively, surveying the scene. Although I admire her coolness under fire, I decide she needs back up. Perhaps I can mollify some tempers. I walk over to Bridget, the lawyer. She might not be pro-Bono. but who knows, perhaps she's pro-Bonio. Her shrill voice is hurting my sensitive ears. I try the gentle approach by putting my snout in her hand. She ignores me. I nudge harder. Nothing. She's still yapping. So, I bang into her legs with my body and do some canine twerking, to the rhythm of that old chestnut: *If you're happy and you know it, wag your tail.*

She looks down straight into my eyes. Bingo. Oxytocin exchange. I conjure up my cutest look, the one that says, of all the people here, you're the one I like the most. Cynical? *Moi?* She stops whining and bends down to pet me. But there's still work to do.

Record Label Ronnie shouts.

"Why the secrecy?"

Lucian, the public relations executive does what comes naturally. He sucks up on cue.

"Yeah. Why can't we all stay in the room? What is it we're not allowed to see or hear?"

I stop flirting with the lawyer and amble over to Lucian,

brushing against his expensive trousers, somehow depositing a chunk of saliva at calf level. Whoopsie.

"Oh, for God's sake. Bloody dog. I've got his disgusting drool all over my trousers."

"Send us the dry cleaning bill," says Bacon Man.

I realise Bacon Man's been quiet for the past few minutes. He's spent a lifetime observing people and events, and I guess, he knows that sometimes doing nothing is the best course of action.

He's been content to leave the floor to Daisy, standing sphinx-like in the eye of the storm.

"Bjørn, go and lie down."

It's not a request. I sneak over to the leather sofa and climb up without her noticing. Daisy claps her hands. The voices dim. I wonder whether she was a headmistress in another life

"Thank you. You're all wasting Tommy's time and money by bickering. Now, please leave."

"Yeah. Do as the lady says," yells Tommy.

Dissent is silenced. They disappear onto the roof terrace like sheep. I don't even have to round them up. Tommy's entourage may dress like society's rebels. But the real mavericks are Daisy and Bacon Man. They shake shit up.

Now Bacon Man assumes the driver's seat.

"Okay, Tommy, tell us what's the ideal outcome for you. What are your red lines? What are you willing to do and what is totally beyond the pale?"

Daisy realises I'm on the sofa but turns a blind eye. Oh, this is so much more comfortable than the one at home. Berliss.

***

Loud voices wake me up. I've had a wonderful snooze and dreamed about having an Access All Areas pass to Tommy's biscuit tin. I raise my head and notice a patch of drool on the silk pillow which soothed me to sleep. I'll just slip off quietly and lie down elsewhere.

Daisy is arranging chairs in a circle and ignoring fevered conversations taking place around her. Bacon Man is in a corner talking quietly to Tommy. My super hearing picks up the conversation.

"Trust us and let us lead, okay? It'll be fine."

Tommy gets up and leaves the room. I hope he's gone to fetch the biscuit tin.

"Please take a seat everyone." says Daisy calmly.

She doesn't need to raise her voice. They comply, although resentment is writ large across their faces. They're keeping their thoughts to themselves for the time being. All except Lucian, the public relations guy. I recognise his type. Or rather I've heard Bacon Man talk about a raft of incompetents at the BBC. It doesn't matter whether they achieve anything. The sole purpose of their existence is to shine at meetings.

Lucian stands up to steal the floor from Daisy. While he preens himself, I visualise him wearing chaps, (I mean the cowboy leg thingies, not multiple blokes, although he probably does) clenching a butt plug decorated with a fluttering fan of peacock feathers. I really don't know where that image comes from. Maybe it's because online porn is everywhere. I glance over at Daisy sitting down, totally at ease. Her eyes twinkle as her mouth summons an enigmatic smile.

"Right," says Lucian. "I've been on the phone to some well plugged-in contacts….."

Oh yeah? You mean butt plugged.

"……taking the temperature of this shit storm. The hashtag #cancelTommy is growing on Instagram and TikTok. So, we've devised a strategy. We're convinced this is the only course of action that will save the tour, the album and Tommy's reputation."

Bacon Man shoots Daisy a glance. She looks back, the smile is still there. Bacon Man grins and looks back up at Lucian.

"Tommy will issue an apology on all social media platforms and will promise never to play *Purple Hearts and Body Bags* in public again. Trajectus Records has agreed to remove the song from all streaming services. That way we limit the damage already done and show that Tommy takes his audiences' concerns seriously. Tommy will also donate a percentage of the profits from the Greatest Hits album to various charities working to help sex-workers."

A chorus of agreement rises from Tommy's entourage, which is silenced by some dripping sarcasm.

"Thank God, you weren't the Ukrainian President when the Russians invaded."

It's Bacon Man. His deep voice is smooth and immaculately modulated. His intervention has thrown Lucian completely off his stride. Bridget the lawyer has just licked her lips. And Daisy is looking at him just like she did in the honeymoon pictures at home.

"What are you talking about?" stutters Lucian. "What's Ukraine got to do with rock music?"

"With that sort of defeatism, Russia would have won the war on the first day."

"I'm not being defeatist. I'm being realistic, you fat prick."

Bacon Man just smiles away the insult.

"You just don't get it, do you, Lucian?"

Lucian looks bemused as Bacon Man gets into his stride.

"You're giving a blank cheque to any disaffected individual or group that's 'offended ', in quotes, by the lyrics of any artist from any era. You could end up helping to cancel scores, if not hundreds of musicians. What else do you want? Tommy joining a monastery? Having his balls cut off in Trafalgar Square in front of a baying crowd?"

The image of castration has just sent a cold shiver shooting through my balls. I'd better give them a good lick to make sure they're still there. And I've got an audience. Bliss. Here we go, let's give them a big slurp. Marvellous. And now the perineum. Boy, have I got a brilliant tongue. I could do that all day. I love being a dog. Who'd be a human? They just can't reach. Well, despite his age, Mick Jagger's extremely flexible. Maybe he could. What was that line he wrote? *How come you taste so good?*

"Er, er. What about the Rolling Stones?" stutters Lucian.

Christ. I think about the Rolling Stones, and instantly, the humans start talking about them. I can bend them to my will. Another superpower to add to the list.

"What about the Rolling Stones?" replies Bacon Man.

"Well, they retired *Brown Sugar* and no longer play it at

concerts because of black sensitivities over slavery. And the lyrics offend some people."

"Was that a unanimous decision of the entire Stones band, Lucian?"

"Yeah, of course."

"No, you're completely wrong. Keith Richards was pissed off about it. He doesn't understand why 'the sisters' as he calls them, have a beef. *Brown Sugar* is essentially a protest song about the horrors of slavery. The Stones are speaking up for the slaves in *Brown Sugar*. Not the slavers."

"Then why did the Stones cancel it then?" asks Lucian, finding his feet.

Bacon Man answers without hesitation.

"Keef didn't put up a fight over retiring the song because he didn't want to get drawn into a battle. He says he'd like to play *Brown Sugar* again in the future. But it's difficult to come back from a decision like that. So, one of the best classic rock songs of all time, may never be heard in public again."

"Yeah, but look at all the money the Stones are making," says Lucian, looking over at his music colleagues, appealing with his eyes for support.

From the side of the room, Daisy intervenes.

"But they've surrendered control over their own art, what's good about that, Lucian?"

Lucian's mouth is opening and closing. But no sound is coming out. The silence is broken by Bacon Man.

"Do you know who Cold Chisel are?"

"No."

"Have you heard of a song called *Khe Sanh*?"

"No."

"Cold Chisel are an Australian rock band. *Khe Sanh* is probably their greatest hit. It's a protest song about Australia's involvement in the Vietnam War and has become Australia's unofficial national anthem. It deals with precisely the same issues that Tommy sings about in *Purple Hearts and Body Bags*. How prostitutes provided comfort for soldiers traumatized on the battlefield. Notice the tense, Lucian. It's the past tense. Fifty years in the past. When the situation was totally different. Cold Chisel haven't been cancelled. They're still performing *Khe Sanh*. So why should Tommy be cancelled, just because his lyrics aren't as subtle as the ones by Cold Chisel?"

"Careful, Morgan," says Tommy in mock outrage. "Great argument. But leave my fucking Grammy-winning lyrics alone. Remember. You ain't Bernie Taupin."

I didn't see Tommy re-enter the room. Bugger. He's forgotten the biscuits. His entourage is laughing and encouraged by Tommy's intervention. Lucian grabs his chance to bite back.

"So what if you were a hot shot BBC correspondent back in the day. You may know all about obscure wars, but you know fuck all about how to communicate with younger generations. You're totally out of your league."

Bacon Man is about to respond but holds back as Daisy clears her throat and ignores the PR dude.

"Ronnie, I'm sure Trajectus Records has done extensive market research on Tommy's brand before deciding to launch his Greatest Hits album. What are the demographics? Which age groups does he appeal to most?"

"Off the top of my head, it's an older crowd."

"How old?"

"Tommy's age. You know, Baby Boomers. Perhaps a bit younger."

"You mean grandparents, people with money."

"Yup, that's right."

"What percentage of his audience is aged seventeen to twenty five? The age group with the lowest disposable income and virtually no financial clout."

"Er, er. None."

"Are you sure about that?"

"Absolutely."

"What about social media? Which platforms do Tommy's fans use? Instagram, Face book, TikTok X or Twitter, or whatever it's called these days?"

"Er, we haven't actually looked into that?"

"Right." says Daisy.

The way she pronounces that single word tells me all I need to know. Daisy thinks Record Label Ronnie is an imbecile.

"The latest research, Ronnie, shows that Facebook is predominantly used by grey helmets. Most young people wouldn't be seen dead on Facebook. X is also the platform of choice for the more mature, while the under-thirties favour Instagram and TikTok."

"Has the penny dropped yet, folks?" asks Bacon Man, affably. "Tommy's core fan base couldn't give a rat's arse about your little storm in a teacup. If anything, his popularity would be boosted if he stood up to the woke brigade."

"Still not convinced?" asks Daisy. "Lucian, the hashtag

#cancelTommy is not trending on Facebook or X. I've just checked."

The PR guy looks at Daisy with contempt.

"So what? It's the big mainstream media we need to worry about. If just one of them picks up on this hashtag the album and the tour is dead."

"That's a big if, isn't it?"

"Not really. It just takes one major celebrity to post that hashtag and Tommy goes down in flames."

Lucian is smirking as he finishes his speech.

"That's why we need to get ahead of this."

"I totally agree," says Bacon Man, pausing for dramatic effect.

The room falls silent. The music people wear puzzled expressions, as they scan the room, looking at each other, trying to work out what just happened. They think they've won, but they're not too sure.

"We do need to get ahead of the story and dictate the narrative," says Bacon Man. "That's exactly what we're going to do. But it's not going to happen by cancelling Tommy and killing his career at the same time."

Daisy jumps in.

"Tommy, what social media platforms are you on? Instagram, X, Facebook, TikTok."

"Just Facebook as far as I know."

"Is that right? Are there any other platforms Tommy doesn't know about?"

The entourage mumbles.

"So just Facebook then," says Daisy. "Tommy, do you know what the password is?"

"I haven't a clue. I don't control the account. They do."

"What's the password please?" asks Daisy.

"What do you want that for?" asks Jim Spiegel, Tommy's manager.

"We need access to the account, so we can control the content, and get the album and the tour back on track," says Bacon Man.

"I'm not telling you that," says Spiegel. "It's confidential and commercially sensitive."

"Give her the fucking password, Spiegs," says Tommy with steel in his voice.

"No way. They're going to wreck your career, Tommy. I can't let them do that."

"Give her the fucking password or I'll sack you on the spot."

"You'd do that after all these years, Tommy? After everything I've done for you. After all the millions I've made for you. You've known these people for less than twenty-four hours, and you're prepared to nuke a relationship that's lasted nearly half a century? Unfuckingbelievable."

"Spare me, Spiegs. I've made you a mint, especially when I was starting out. That first contract was a fucking disgrace. You had me hog-tied like a gimp for seven years. Seven long years. You paid me a pittance."

"That was a standard industry contract," protests Spiegel.

"I've just worked out what you were in a previous life," snarls Tommy. "A fucking slave owner. While you were getting stinking rich, I was playing stadiums and living on baked beans. Now, if you want to open that can of worms, go ahead. It won't be pretty. Give her the password. It's your last chance. I mean it."

"Patpong69."

"How very politically correct," smirks Bacon Man. "And who's idea was that?"

"Mine, actually," says the manager, meekly.

"Right, Tommy," says Bacon Man, grinning. "We need to get down to some serious work. We don't need anyone else. They're all free to leave."

"Ok, everyone, the party's over. Off you go," says Tommy.

"You must be joking," says Spiegel. "I'm your manager, I insist on staying."

"Spiegs. Just leave. And that goes for the rest of you too."

"Just so you know," says Daisy, tapping away on her mobile. "That Facebook password is no longer valid. We've changed it."

The only participant heading towards the exit and not complaining is the lawyer, Bridget.

"That was very educational, Mr. and Mrs. Somerville. Let me give you some advice, pro-bono. Be very, very careful. This is a highly litigious business."

"She's right, you know," says Tommy. "Your plan had better fucking work, or we'll all be flipping burgers."

Nothing wrong with flipping burgers, as long as some flip my way. Keep the faith, Tommy, it'll all be fine. Trust me.

CHAPTER SEVENTEEN

THE FAT MAN'S KAMA SUTRA

YOU WON'T BELIEVE THE NIGHT I've had. The past few hours have been the worst of my life. We almost lost Bacon Man. I don't mean that he went missing. I mean he almost died. Yes, that's right. I'm not exaggerating. He came within a few seconds of breathing his last. The difference between life and death is miniscule. Maybe it just wasn't his time. Maybe the stars were in perfect alignment. Or perhaps he's just lucky to have a dog. *Moi.*

To coin an old rocker's phrase, I'm all shook up. It's approaching breakfast time, just over a whole day since we got back from Tommy's Martello Tower. Or as another golden oldie might say, twenty-four hours from Bawdsey, the Suffolk equivalent of Tulsa because it's in the middle of nowhere.

Normally, I'd be pestering Bacon Man or Daisy to feed me. But they're both sleeping. I suspect they're as traumatised as I am. It's possible Daisy might have a headache this morning. She was having a Prosecco party before Bacon Man had his nasty turn. Thankfully she's not one of those people who drink themselves into a stupor. Otherwise, her husband might be on a slab right now, waiting to be dissected by the pathologist's scalpel.

I'm grateful to be lying next to Bacon Man, as I often do these days. He's on his right side, with his butt hanging over the edge of his bed. I've got my back towards him, and my head is facing the pillows. His left hand is cuddling my magnificent furry chest. Daisy calls it my Simba chest after the hero in the *Lion King*. Occasionally, in his sleep, he strokes my ear.

I hope my presence comforts him. Although he's not snoring, his breathing is laboured. He's wheezing and it sounds as though something is rattling in his chest. The important thing is that he is breathing, although I'm concerned about the violent cough he's developed overnight.

Life never fails to surprise me. For my own peace of mind, I need to deconstruct what happened. I'm trying to plot the timeline of how triumph flipped so quickly to come within a whisker of total disaster. I've got a lot to tell you, unless, of course, you're not interested.

I'll pick up the story after Tommy Bentwaters' business associates left.

As you might imagine, after spending so much time on the road, and then indoors, I was desperate for a pee. Bacon Man couldn't take me because he had to write the script for Tommy's make or break video message and set up the camera gear. So, Daisy took me for a romp. Tommy was keen to stretch his legs and joined us. I welcomed the chance to read a different newspaper. As I explored new smells among the reeds along the riverbank, I could hear the pair of them talking.

"What a fabulous place you have, Tommy. Not what I expected from a rock n' roller. Where are all the gold records?"

"Divorce settlements," said Tommy.

I knew it.

"It feels really remote here," said Daisy.

"That's the whole point, Astrid. Being out here is cathartic. There's virtually nothing between me and the rest of Europe. Just the North Sea in all its wildness. It's a sanctuary from the big city bullshit. I love it."

"No neighbours to upset when you crank up the volume."

"I don't do that very often these days. I was outrageous when I was younger, but now I'm happy with a cup of tea and an early night. I try to be a good neighbour. All I want is peace and quiet."

"This isn't your only property is it?"

"Matter of fact it is. As you might have read, I just parted company with wife number four and a fifteenth century moated castle. My ex-wives aren't housekeepers, they're bloody castle keepers. I'm down to my last fortress, and I don't want to lose it. That's one of the reasons why I've sought your help."

"Don't worry, Tommy. You'll keep your home. I promise. We ought to head back to shoot the video. The light's going to disappear soon."

"That's a pity. Bjørn's having a blast out here. He's such a beautiful dog."

"Thanks. I love him to pieces."

My heart suddenly felt too big for my Simba chest. I love you to pieces too, Daisy. As we walked back to the Martello Tower, I learned some more about the old rocker. Bentwaters is his stage name. He took it from the former US Air Force base ten miles away, where his father, an American pilot, was stationed, flying F-4 Phantoms. During the late 1960s, at barbecues and other family gatherings, Tommy met helicopter crews assigned to air-sea rescue. Some of them had served in Vietnam and their harrowing stories of wounded GIs rescued from the battlefield were the inspiration for *Purple Hearts and Body Bags*.

"It's golden hour," said Bacon Man, as we entered the orangery. "The light on Tommy's face will be terrific."

"Why have you set up the proper camera?" asked Daisy.

"Because we're going to shoot it on the Canon, in 4k with some decent prime glass. It'll look tremendous."

"No. We're using the iPhone."

"Oh, for fuck's sake, Daisy. What's the point in having a top of the range camera if you don't use it? The iPhone quality is shite in comparison."

"Boys and their toys," said Tommy with a knowing grin.

"We're using the phone because it looks more authentic. It needs to appear as though Tommy shot it himself. The message is more important than the equipment you shoot it on."

"OK. Fair point."

"I'm useless at doing selfies," said Tommy.

"You won't have to," said Bacon Man. "I'll mount the phone on the camera and we'll mic you up properly."

"Make sure you set it up in portrait mode."

"Don't be daft, Daisy. I'm going to shoot it in landscape, because the TV stations all use 16:9 and prefer it."

"Don't you ever listen to me, darling? I said the message is the most important thing here. Most people look at Facebook on their phones. So that's how we're going to shoot it. In portrait."

Uh, oh. Daisy called him darling. Bacon Man's in trouble. Or he would have been if he didn't do as he was told. But he'd been in this situation many times before and knew that sometimes, the best way to fight another day is to beat an orderly retreat.

"Actually, Tommy. Daisy's right. It has to look authentic. The key thing is that you manage to do it in one take, so we don't have to make any edits."

Well, blow me. Tommy is a natural. He got it word-perfect the first time and sounded as if he was speaking from the heart, not memorising a script.

He said that he would never have written the song with those lyrics today. The world had changed completely since the Vietnam war era. Today, everyone was more aware of the scandals of people-trafficking and criminal gangs forcing the desperate to become sex slaves. Tommy unreservedly condemned those practices. But he wouldn't criticise any consenting adult of any gender who decided of their own free will to use their bodies to make money.

"I respect their choices," he said.

Despite growing pressure, and the example of the Rolling Stones, Tommy refused to retire *Purple Hearts and Body Bags*.

"I could change the lyrics. But that would be a cop out. I'm an artist and artistic freedom is very important to me. It's my right and I'll fight for it. I'm not going to cancel my own work. My song might offend some people, but I refuse to apologise.

I'm going to play it on stage every night of my upcoming tour. For this very reason: if you don't grapple with the mindset of the past, you can't learn the lessons of history, and you're doomed to repeat the mistakes. This is my final word on the subject. Except to say that from now on I'm only going to be posting dog videos on social media."

At that moment, I looked up from between Tommy's legs, put my right paw on his thigh and was rewarded with a biscuit. I think it was a plain Hobnob. Scrumptious.

"I think that's a wrap," said Daisy.

"Let me just check to make sure we've got it all. Yup that's fine. Bloody hell, Bjørn's a rock star, isn't he? Well done, Tommy. That was brilliant. Well spoken. You're right as well. If you'd tweaked the lyrics, it would have been much easier. You could have used wrong or song, instead of Ping Pong and Patpong."

"Fuck off, Morgan. How many Grammys have you got?"

"None, Tommy, but I've got a couple of gongs for my reporting. I'm a wordsmith by profession. And I have to get the language right first time and fast. Actually, you could have used gong as well."

"Oooh, listen to Marc Bolan. Watch out for that tree."

"I apologise for my husband, Tommy. He can't help himself. He's always wanted to be in a rock band."

"Never been in a band, Morgan?"

"Not a rock band. But I was press ganged into my dad's dance band when I was a schoolboy in Ipswich. I played the clarinet."

"The clarinet? You must be joking."

"I wish I was. It was like my Saturday job. I was about fourteen and my dad made me wear my school uniform. We used to play at weddings and office parties. One day, as I stood up to play my solo, the coolest guy at my school, a handsome bastard called Peter Thorpe, laughed at me."

"So what happened?"

"I never played the clarinet again. If my dad had bought me a tenor sax, it might have been all so different."

Tommy snorted with laughter. Not the other rock star stuff.

"Do you know what, Morgan? I've got a tenor sax downstairs. It once belonged to Alto Reed, who played the solo in *Old Fashioned Rock and Roll* with Bob Seeger and the Silver Bullet band."

"No way, that's one of the best tenor solos in rock history."

"That's right. I'll tell you what I'll do. I'll trade you that sax for Bjørn."

"Sounds like a great deal to me. What do you think, Daisy?"

I couldn't believe my ears. My future was up in the air once again.

"Absolutely no way, Tommy. He's not for sale. I wish I could recommend Bjørn's breeder. But I can't. Her setup was rather shabby. But I belong to a golden retrievers' group on Facebook. I'll ask around for someone more reputable and let you know."

"Sounds like a plan. Thanks."

I fixed Bacon Man with a look that said I was sad and disappointed with him. He got the message.

"Sorry, Bubsie, I was only joking."

I hope he was. But I'm not a hundred percent certain.

As it was getting late, Tommy offered to let us stay the night in his guest suite. But Daisy said we ought to get back home to handle the video release.

This time, Bacon Man set Google Maps for Galahad Island, to avoid getting lost in the wilds of East Suffolk. Once we hit the A12 he turned it off.

"I used to commute to London on my motorbike along this road when I was twenty-two. I know where I'm going," said Bacon Man, as Daisy told him to switch Google Maps back on.

We made pretty good progress until just south of Colchester when Bacon Man said he was hungry. Only fast-food joints were open. What a shame.

French fries. They're something else, aren't they? And flame-grilled Bacon Double Cheeseburgers. Woohoo. My question is: are they legal? Is some South American cartel smuggling them into the country? Because one bite and you're hooked. No wonder Britain has the highest rate of obesity in Europe.

Neither Bacon Man nor Daisy was generous enough to give me a whole one, although I managed to scrounge three substantial mouthfuls, which briefly played tonsil hockey with my taste buds before zipping down my oesophagus. They lay like bricks on the lining of my stomach. I didn't wake up until I heard the metal gates creak open.

I had an illicit wazz in the driveway after Bacon Man parked.

"Good boy, Bjørn." said Daisy. "Let's hope you weren't spotted."

Fast forward to morning. All manner of alarms on phones,

watches and computers in both Daisy and Bacon Man's bedrooms went off at virtually the same time. How infuriating. I was in the middle of a fantastic dream, sitting behind the wheel of the Mercedes, turning into a drive-thru and ordering a Triple Bacon Cheeseburger with extra-large fries on the side. Now that's what I call a Happy Meal. The server was about to place it in a specially adapted dog bowl when I woke up. I didn't get to taste it.

"Good morning, Bubsie. Time to get up. We've got work to do."

Bacon Man was stroking my ears. Pity about the dream. But a morning hygge isn't a bad way to start the day. Bacon Man doesn't just tolerate me sleeping on his bed, he actively encourages it. Somehow, I manage to zone out when the farmyard noises start. It's a small price to pay for luxury. Another mission accomplished.

I pootled into Daisy's room. She was standing beneath the power shower with her head back and eyes closed until she heard my claws on the tiles.

"Hello, Bubba. Good morning. We're up earlier than usual today. Don't worry, you'll soon have your breakfast. Go and lie down, there's a good boy."

Everything seemed so normal, apart from the hour. But something in my gut, and it wasn't the burger, was telling me that today was going to be significant. The atmosphere changed when we went downstairs.

An air of military efficiency overwhelmed the rustic kitchen of our townhouse. It crackled with a sense of determination, tension, and anticipation.

Alternately sipping warm fresh lemon water and cappuccinos, Daisy and Bacon Man were hunched over their laptops. A couple of iPads were on the table, displaying muted TV news channels with captions. A morning radio show burbled away at low volume.

"It looks like a quiet news day," said Daisy. "That's perfect."

"Oh bugger," exclaimed Bacon Man.

"What's wrong?"

"Arsenal lost again."

"Stop reading the sports pages and check on celebrity and royal news."

"I haven't seen any significant royal stories, but the Sun has got a page lead about a Premier League Footballer being charged with sexual assault. He's out on bail. He's not being named by the police. The only clues to his identity are that he's an international player who lives in the North-West. I'll just check X. There are a few memes identifying him. But I doubt the papers will take it further. Have you seen anything?"

"The Mirror has an exclusive with the toy boy lover of a radio presenter who dumped him after he was found cheating. He's having a self-pity party, saying he loves her and wants to be forgiven."

"You mean he wants his nice, pampered lifestyle back and is afraid of being homeless?"

"Exactly."

"Right. I'll just check my horoscope to see if it's an auspicious day to boost a rock star's career. It says Uranus is in retrograde. How can they tell? You're sitting still, Daisy."

"Stop pratting around."

"What it really says, Daisy, is that I could get my hands on some hidden assets today. I have to make sure I can rise to the occasion, to maximise opportunities. But I should listen out for alarm bells and beware of overeating because I don't want to embarrass myself."

"You don't need an astrologer to tell you to stop over-eating."

"Who knows, maybe Tommy Bentwaters is our hidden asset. Let's rise to the occasion and get that video out there."

"I can't believe you're taking the horoscope that seriously."

"Daisy, are you turning Swedish on me and losing your sense of humour? Of course, I'm not relying on the bloody horoscope. I've scanned the news websites as rigorously as you have. It's not going to get much quieter. The Mail Online front page is so old, rigor mortis has set in. They're in dire need of a big new story. What do you think? Shall we push the button?"

"Yes, let's. I'll give Bjørn breakfast, and we'll go for a quick toilet trip. You post the video on Facebook, and when I come back, we'll make that call to Keith Dudley."

It may have been a landmark day for Daisy and Bacon Man, but there was no celebratory breakfast for me. Three scoops of cat litter without the trimmings. Yup. Kibble. But I'll give Daisy her due. Although she was preoccupied with managing the news about Tommy Bentwaters, she didn't short-change me on the post-breakfast walk. It was the usual length. She was also as fastidious as ever about studying the contents of my poo. It still just looks like shit to me, but she identified the remains of the cheeseburger and its bun. I wonder if she checks Bacon Man's loo to discover what he's been scoffing in secret.

"So have you posted it?"

Bacon Man pulled up Facebook and went to Tommy Bentwaters' page. He pushed the play button. I wasn't listening to Tommy. I was watching me, looking angelic between his thighs as he addressed the camera. Wow. A star is born. The camera really likes me.

"Let's call him," said Daisy.

"It's a bit early. But I'm sure he'll be up and about."

Bacon Man dialled and put the phone on speaker so Daisy could hear. The person at the other end picked up after two rings. Bacon Man put on a stern voice.

"Is that Keith Dudley, the News Editor of MailOnline?"

"Yes it is."

The Lancastrian voice at the other end sounded concerned.

"Morgan Somerville, troublemaker at large."

The Lancastrian chuckled and cheered up considerably.

"Somers, you daft bugger. What a surprise. How are you?"

"Hello, Dudders, I'm fine. Sorry about the uncivilised hour."

"That's OK, Somers. I didn't recognise the number."

"It's a new one, Dudders. Put this one in your contacts for future use. You'll be needing it later. Apologies for calling out of the blue."

"No problem, Somers. So why will I be needing it?"

"I've got a good story for you, exclusive. Nobody else knows about it."

"I'm all ears. You never let us down. That last tale about the

BBC presenter moonlighting for a Chinese bank went down a storm."

"This is much better. Have you been following the story about Tommy Bentwaters?"

"The rocker who's running out of castles?"

"Yes. But it's not the divorce angle. Did you see that he was in danger of being cancelled over one of his greatest hits?"

"Yeah, I spotted a par or two in the Guardian."

"Fuck me, Dudders, you're not turning into a Guardian reader are you?"

"We see everything, Somers. So, what's the story?"

"Well, he's fighting back. He's issued a defiant video statement saying he's standing up for artistic freedom. It's basically a rallying cry for resistance against Britain's growing cancel culture?"

"How do you know about this, Somers?"

"How do you think, Dudders? The video was posted about fifteen minutes ago. Nobody else knows about it. So, you've got a head start. It's on his Facebook page."

"Hang on a minute, Somers. Let me take a quick look."

We sat quietly in the kitchen as we listened to Tommy's voice coming back through the phone speaker.

"So what do you think, Dudders?"

"It's a bloody good story. Leave it with me, I'll get on to our showbiz editor straight away. Oh, before I go. Have you got Tommy's number? Will he give us an interview?"

"Sorry, Dudders. He won't talk to anyone. Believe me. And he's gone off the grid. Everything he wants to say is in the video."

"Ok, understood. It's a cracker. Thanks a lot. I'll put you down for the usual tip fee,"

"No need, Dudders. This one's on me. You can buy me a pint and curry next time we see each other."

"OK, Somers. Thanks a lot. Ciao."

Daisy looked at Bacon Man, raised her eyebrows and smiled.

"Well, we've lit the touch paper. I just hope it won't turn out to be a dud."

"Stop being negative, Daisy, it'll take off, believe me."

"Either way, there's nothing we can do now but wait. It's a lovely day, and Bjørn deserves a long walk after being cooped up for so long yesterday. Let's make the most of it. Are you coming?"

"Of course. I could do with a screen break."

Hurray. I love it when Bacon Man comes walking. There's always the prospect of naughtiness. For once, he had a small rucksack on his back. I wondered what surprises it contained.

As we headed for the main gate, I spotted two swans in the creek. Four smaller brown river birds followed in the swans' wake, treating them like parents. Curious, because apart from having long necks, the kids were nothing like the pristine white adults. I'm wary of using the word mongrel these days, but I wondered if the brown birds had mixed heritage, like cockapoos, and labradoodles. Or, come to think of it, French Bulldogs, the result of congress between genuine bulldogs and gas masks, and that's why they can't breathe properly.

Maybe the mummy swan had been pleasant to a pheasant. Alternatively, she could have been Canada Goosed. No. I know why the male swan was aggressive. He'd been duckolded. Daisy said he's a Mute Swan. I'm not so sure. He was pretty gobby. Judging by his language, he was definitely English. I can't beak read, but I could swear he was saying in swan,

"What the fuck are you looking at?"

I wasn't in the mood to turn the other cheek.

As Daisy says, "If you behave like a doormat, people will walk all over you."

So, I adapted an insult I'd heard on Sky Sports when football fans target players with protruding teeth, or bulging eyes like Luis Suarez and Mesut Özil.

"Oi, your beak is offside."

I realised my voice is breaking. My bark is getting deeper. Not quite Barry White, but it's getting there.

The instant we left the confines of the island, Bacon Man unhitched my lead, which Daisy never does. Off I bounded towards the springy wooden gate. I squeezed underneath so I could start reading the news headlines in the ivy. I was so distracted, I failed to detect the menace in the air.

I was snuffling stoat droppings when, out of the blue, my legs gave way. I wheezed like a Scottish piper as my lungs were crushed. I might even have passed out as my head slammed into the ground. By the time I regained spatial awareness, I was on my back. My paws were scrambling to stop the canine doppelganger of Mike Tyson from ripping out my jugular.

"Ooh, have you found a friend, Woody?"

A friend? You're delusional, pal.

As the dog pinned me to the ground, I caught a glimpse of

his owner. A dippy looking hipster in his forties with a weasel face lift. That's street dog slang for a bloke with a man bun.

"What breed is it?"

I heard concern in Bacon Man's voice.

"A Serbian mastiff. He's just a puppy. He loves playing with other dogs."

"He's not playing. He's trying to ethnically cleanse my retriever. Get him off."

"You're being hysterical, he's only playing."

Bacon Man was right to be worried. My right ear had gone numb. Maybe that's how Evander Holyfield felt when Tyson bit off part of his ear during a fight in Las Vegas. I was waiting for the pain to kick in. As we rolled around, I couldn't determine whether the fluid flying around was blood or slobber from the mastiff's powerful jaws.

"Get him off now or he'll kill my dog," shouted Bacon Man.

"Hey. Are you filming Woody and me?" snarled Weasel Face. "You fucking bitch."

"Don't you dare talk to my wife like that," shouted Bacon Man, sounding angrier than I'd heard before.

"What are you going to do about it, Mr. Blobby? Sit on me?"

"Yes, I am filming you," screamed Daisy. "For evidence. Your dog attacked mine for no reason at all. That's illegal. If my dog has so much as a scratch. I'll prosecute you. You've got no control over him."

"Put that phone down."

"Or what," said Daisy.

"Oi, Mr Blobby. You need to control your wife," sneered Weasel Face.

"She's impossible to control," said Bacon Man. "Just like your evil dog. Now put him on a lead, you moron."

As I grappled with the mastiff, I caught a glimpse of Daisy standing toe to toe with Weasel Face. Her nose was an inch away from his, as she stared him down. Weasel Face clenched his fists.

"Go on," she said. "Hit me. You know you want to."

As she spoke, I somehow got some purchase. One of my paws caught the mastiff in the eye. He yelped and sprinted away. I rolled upright and ran to Daisy for reassurance and protection.

"Here," said Weasel Face. "Your dog is fucking aggressive. He started it."

"Don't be ridiculous," said Bacon Man. "He's a golden retriever. He hasn't got a vicious bone in his body."

"Don't waste your breath on this IDIOT," shouted Daisy, using the Danish pronunciation. It sounded like IDYOATE and spewed more contempt than any English obscenity.

"Oh, fuck off, you pair of weirdos."

"Stay away from us in future, or there'll be trouble," Daisy snarled.

"That's enough, Daisy," said Bacon Man. "Let's go. You've got to be more careful, or you'll get seriously hurt one of these days."

"I can look after myself," she replied tremulously. "I'm not scared of anyone. Come here, Bjørn, let's check you over. Yes, you can have a tummy scrub. Mama's brave boy. We love you."

What is with the British? You criticise their dogs and they take it as a declaration of war. What an angry nation. I'm the innocent victim here. I'm never aggressive. Ever. Daisy knelt next to me and carefully rolled my ears between her fingers.

"I can see where the mastiff nipped him. There are indentations but no puncture wounds. There's no blood either. You were so lucky, Bjørn. We could have lost you."

My thoughts were for Daisy. She placed herself in harm's way and got away with it. Just. As she comforted me, I wondered whether Bacon Man appreciated his wife's extraordinary character. Could she be the reincarnation of an Ancient Greek Amazon? Or Boadicea, the bellicose Queen of the Iceni, an Ancient British tribe? Whatever Daisy was in a previous existence, she's a warrior in this life, battling for Bacon Man's health and for me. She's the embodiment of love, if only Bacon Man could ignore the nagging.

"Don't worry, Bjørn," said Bacon Man. "You're safe now. Do you want to play?"

I was too shell-shocked to respond. I was having an existential crisis. Would every bimble by the Thames involve paw-to-paw combat with a psychopath?

Bacon Man picked up a broken branch and hurled it down the path.

A Stick. My favourite thing. I thundered in pursuit with all my might. What a morning! And we hadn't yet reached the tunnel.

We played fetch all the way to the river, only stopping when a wooden Victorian steamboat hoved into view with a ragtime jazz band riffing at the sharp end. The steamer's whistle hurt my ears. My protest barks solicited waves from burly lads and their WAGs practising the sport in which Britain leads the world. Speed drinking just after breakfast.

"Hopefully we'll have something to celebrate tonight," said Bacon Man.

"That's you in a nutshell," said Daisy. "Always optimistic. I want to see some results before I think about opening a bottle."

They sat on a bench memorialising a rambler who loved the sunsets here. Daisy filled a collapsible plastic dog bowl with water. I'm an elite athlete. Rehydration after stick chasing is essential. I was gasping and virtually swallow-dived into the bowl. Bacon man pulled out his mobile.

"Just checking MailOnline," he said. "Nothing yet."

"It's been less than an hour. Give them time."

"They've got another ninety minutes max. If there's nothing online by then, we need to place it elsewhere. I want to see the broadcasters following up by six o'clock tonight at the latest."

"You're not this tense when we do normal corporate stuff."

"True but most companies make money no matter how deep the shit they're in. This is different. Tommy's the underdog and that pushes all my buttons."

"I can tell you're a lot happier these days and it's not just the gig with Tommy."

"Stop fishing Daisy. You know it's the dog. By the end of the day my facial muscles are almost aching from smiling more and so are you. When we go cruising, I get a genuine buzz from watching faces light up as he hangs out the window."

"I've noticed."

"Now here's another admission. I feel so much better for getting off my fat arse and taking him out. rain or shine. Bjørn's the best personal trainer we could ever have. I'm enjoying the river more than ever. My shorts are a tad looser. But I still don't dare go on the scales."

"Don't worry. You'll get there. Come on. Why don't we head to the lock and have a cup of tea at the café?"

Bacon Man was puffing as his short legs tried to match Daisy's longer stride. Good. He was getting some cardio.

"Hang on Daisy," he shouted, as we reached a footbridge over a spur of the river leading to a boatyard specialising in classic wooden launches.

I did what I always do on the bridge. I spied on the boats going to and from the lock. Then I raced down the ramp to a small sandy beach and went for a swim. I was reluctant to enter the water at first, but Bacon Man encouraged me to go deeper by throwing sticks further and further. Now I'm as proficient as Freya the Walrus.

"I've got shorts, water shoes and a towel in the rucksack," I heard Bacon Man say. "I fancy going for a swim with Bjørn."

"Please don't," pleaded Daisy. "If you get into trouble, I won't be able to save you."

"Oh stop, for heaven's sake. It's perfectly safe and don't forget I've got natural buoyancy. This is the best place I've seen for wild swimming. It's normally packed with families, especially at weekends. There's no one here right now, so I'm not embarrassed to go in."

If I was Bacon Man, I'd listen to Daisy. The water companies have dumped record levels of sewage in the rivers. Every time I go in, I'm worried I might swallow something brown and sticky. And I'm not talking about a stick. I'll tell you what sticks in my throat. Bonuses for water company executives. The only growth they're responsible for is the number of turds in the Thames. They could ruin my immune system and weaken my superpowers.

As I finished my thought, Bacon Man's phone went.

"Dudders."

"Somers. It's up. It's the lead."

"Fantastic. I'll take a look and call you back if there's a problem."

"I'm sure you'll be happy, Somers."

"Thanks so much, Dudders, you're a star. Ciao."

I was doggy paddling, as you do, about thirty yards offshore and willing Bacon Man to throw a stick, but he was glued to his phone.

"Look at the headline, Daisy. 'Veteran rocker Tommy Bentwaters declares war on the woke brigade.' That's a bit strong. But I have to say, whatever you think of the Mail and its politics, if you want to create a shit storm, it's the best place to plant a story."

"I totally agree. But you're wrong about the headline. It's perfect. Just what we need. It sends exactly the right message to the people we want to reach. Unless there's a plane crash or royal death, this will definitely stir things up."

"Let's just hope the Queen doesn't come back from the dead, and prove that resurrection is possible," said Bacon Man. "Because then we'll be royally fucked."

I thought we were about to go straight back home. But

there was nothing Daisy and Bacon Man could do except sit back and watch their handiwork unfold. We headed to the café next to the lock. I lay on the grass at Daisy's feet while she scanned her phone. The tray Bacon Man carried back from the serving hatch was lighter than usual. There was only one slice of carrot cake next to the teapot, cups, and saucers.

"Aren't I having cake today?" asked Daisy.

"No, that's yours. I don't want any."

"Good for you. Keep it up."

He reached into his pocket, pulled out some headphones and dialled a number.

"Hey, Tommy. Hope you pick up this message. Check the MailOnline. We've got a result. I'm sure it's going to take off now. You'll probably be inundated with calls. Just don't talk to anyone. The video message speaks for itself. If you need me, just shout. Bye."

Bacon Man then called Tommy's manager.

"Hi, Jim, I just tried to call Tommy, but it went straight to voicemail. I'll repeat what I told him. MailOnline has done us proud. The story is about to seriously lift off. Every major outlet is going to be nagging you and the PR guy for interviews once they realise Tommy's keeping schtum. It's crucial you don't say anything. Just refer all the hacks to the Facebook video. That's it. Please make sure your people know there's a three-line whip on this. You're welcome. We're around if you need us. Best of luck. See you."

I don't know where the rest of the day went. I caught up on my beauty sleep. Mid-afternoon, Bacon Man took me cruising. We went to the posh supermarket just across the M40. As he parked the car, all the windows closed automatically. Bacon Man lowered mine an inch or so.

"Sorry about this, Bubsie. You've got some air. But I daren't open it any further. You're a prime target for dognappers."

It takes a dognapper to know one, Bacon Man. I might have forgiven you, but I haven't forgotten.

"Lie down, there's a good boy. I'm just going to pick up some sushi. I'll be back in a minute."

The look in Bacon Man's eyes said I trust you to be a big boy. Dig down and find the courage to fight the separation anxiety. You'll be safe. Don't worry. I contemplated barking but caught sight of myself in the rear-view mirror and gave myself a good talking to. I'm not one of those irritating midgets that are constantly yapping. I'm the strong, silent type. When I speak, people listen. Every word matters. I resolved to dog up.

As ever, Bacon Man was true to his word. He was back within ten minutes. His shopping bag was clinking. I didn't know sushi came in bottles.

My mistake. It doesn't. I'm happy to issue a correction after watching Bacon Man unpack and put his purchases in the fridge. The kitchen resembled a newsroom again. Daisy and Bacon Man sipped tea, while monitoring laptops, iPads, and phones, occasionally wandering into the sitting room to check the television and compare notes.

Previously, I thought of Daisy and Bacon Man as bickering adoptive parents whose main purpose was to feed me and keep me entertained.

The past few days changed my perspective in that I started

to appreciate the professional components of their characters. I'd witnessed a masterclass in manipulating the media and public opinion. I never thought I'd say this, but Bacon Man is genuinely cool. I know how much he's derided because of his size. I wish his detractors could see his genius at work as I've done. He made one astute phone call and within hours most of Britain was talking about Tommy Bentwaters, and word was spreading abroad.

As Bacon Man predicted, all the tabloids followed up the Mail's exclusive. More elegant versions surfaced in the broadsheets. Rolling news channels were repeating the story every hour. Daisy checked the international networks, and sure enough, there I was between Tommy Bentwaters' thighs on CNN, France 24, Deutsche Welle, Turkish Television, and even Chinese State TV's English language service.

What was my reward? You've guessed it. Bloody kibble. I was banking on someone losing their grip on the chopsticks later, preferably with a California roll. A controlled pop from the kitchen raised my hopes.

"Aren't you having one?" Daisy asked, as Bacon Man served a goblet of Prosecco in the sitting room to accompany an artistic sushi installation.

"No. I want to keep a clear head, just in case there are complications. Although I'm sure it's going to be fine."

As evening took hold, the sense of adrenaline evaporating was almost tangible. I fell asleep to the sound of Bacon Man loading the dishwasher, aided by the sedative of water lapping against boat hulls. Normally my body clock tells me when it's time for the last pee of the day, and I have to nudge one of them into action. Last night I was pleasantly surprised to be woken by Bacon Man with his shoes on, and the slip lead in his hand.

"Just you and me tonight, Bubsie, Daisy's having a bath. Let's leave her in peace. Come on."

When we returned, there was a distinct change in mood. Looking up the stairs, I saw soft twinkling lights, and heard the rhythmic clang of a cowbell, accompanied by a man squealing with pleasure. I looked quizzically at Bacon Man, and hoped he got the message. What on earth was happening up there?

"Oooooh. Sounds like Daisy is having a party."

My bones throbbed from the vibrations of a bass guitar and kick drum as I followed Bacon Man.

"Wow, I can smell her perfume from here," he said quietly to himself, as we climbed the stairs.

"She hasn't worn that in years. Bloody hell! Candles!"

Daisy's door was wide open. The bedroom was dark yet inviting as dozens of tea-lights shimmered. Then she appeared, swaying softly from side to side, clutching a glass in her right hand. It took me a moment to work out what she was doing. Then I remembered watching Strictly Come Dancing. She was flicking her hips and shaking her Simba chest in a manner that would have disqualified her from the foxtrot.

What a transformation from the stern woman in stout walking boots who was an inch from head-butting the Serbian Mastiff's owner.

I lay down on the landing behind Bacon Man as he stood in the doorway. I could just see past his silhouette. Daisy's hair was teased out. Her eyelids had been painted the same turd colour as our front door, although in the golden light, the combination was stunning. A moist coating on her lips glistened. Was that drool? She wore an identical black blouse to the one she had on the day before, except all the buttons apart from one were undone. Her tight, short skirt rode up towards the danger zone, as her Sepp Piontek thighs swayed.

This was a celebration of voluptuousness in all its glory, with all its flaws. Daisy knew she didn't conform to stereotypes of female beauty and didn't care. Her self-confidence generated power and magnetism. For a moment, I felt as though for once, out of kindness, time had taken a break from its relentless march forward and had turned back twenty years, just to give Bacon Man a taste of his happiest time on this planet.

Daisy was barefoot, apart from blue beaded laces wrapped around her ankles with strands attached to her second toes to keep them in place. I hoped they weren't about to fall off. That would mean she's got type two diabetes, just like Bacon Man.

I was mesmerised. Daisy kept looking at Bacon Man, occasionally sipping from her glass. Although I could only see the back of Bacon Man's head, he appeared to be staring back. Neither of them said a word. Despite everything I'd absorbed from the television, I couldn't identify what was happening. I just hoped Bacon Man wasn't in trouble. Again.

"For a man who's never lost for words," said Daisy, hitching her skirt a couple of degrees higher, "you're awfully quiet."

"Thank goodness I didn't have a drink, although I can see you've had one or two."

"I've got a nice buzz going, thank you."

"I love the barefoot sandals."

Ah, the ankle stringy things. Thank God Daisy's second toes weren't about to fall off.

"Yes, I bought them for our honeymoon, do you remember?"

"I do. I'd forgotten that they're so much sexier than stockings. Especially when you're still so light on your feet."

Daisy smiled and swivelled her hips as Bacon Man posed a question.

"Just out of interest, where did you get the snakeskin skirt from?"

"I found it tucked into an old tennis racquet cover in your bedroom."

"Really?"

Bacon Man swallowed hard.

"Yes really. Such a small piece of stretchy polyester. It must have cost you a fortune."

"Er, six quid in a sale from the curvy section of Dorothy Perkins."

"I didn't realise I was so high maintenance."

"Ummmmmmmmmmm,"

"When did you buy it?"

Daisy gyrated and lifted one side of the skirt up to the top of her thigh.

"Er, about two years ago."

"Why?"

"Er, because I had this fantasy about you dressing up like a slut."

"Why didn't you give it to me?"

"I didn't dare."

Daisy didn't respond. She just stared at Bacon Man, as the music became increasingly steamy.

"Well, you're in luck. I feel like being a slut tonight."

Bacon Man swallowed even harder.

"Do you know what else I found in the racquet cover?"

"Er, I have a rough idea."

"This bra from Playful Promises. At least it wasn't from Dorothy Perkins."

As she spoke, Daisy undid the remaining buttons of her blouse and slipped it off her shoulders. The black bra was more revealing than the leopard skin one she'd hung on the washing line.

"And then I found these. Nipplicious Baby!"

Skilfully, Daisy shook her shoulders and her breasts popped out of the cups. Strings of beads and tiny bells dangled from erect nipples. Daisy jiggled gently and was beginning to sound a lot like Christmas.

"Finally, this. Ta da!"

Daisy pirouetted, lifted her skirt, showing off her back bottom. Just like dogs do.

"A peachy g-string from Playful Promises."

Bacon Man gulped again. He was completely dry. If I could, I'd have dashed downstairs to get him my water bowl.

The music changed and became even raunchier, if that were possible.

"Do you know what this song is?"

"What is this? A pop quiz?" asked Bacon Man.

"It's *Do Me Baby* by Prince."

"Oh yeah."

"Do you remember the property developer with the yacht in the South of France? I used to play this song when I stripped for him."

"In a skirt like that?" asked Bacon Man.

"I had a short leather one, with a zip."

She pretended to unzip the front of the skirt and wiggled.

"That'd work for me."

"I kept the skirt on while he fucked me on the rear deck."

"We should try that the next time we catch the ferry to the Isle of Wight," said Bacon Man.

Daisy moved her head from side to side. Her hair took a wild ride in the candlelight. She raised her arms and shimmied. Bacon Man breathed deeply and seemed to squeak.

"I put on a hell of a show, because I knew the captain and his female first mate were watching from the shadows…"

"Daisy, we should have…"

"..and they both wanted to fuck me."

"…more conversations like this."

"Especially the first mate, who was black and drop dead gorgeous."

"Because you only talk dirty to me when we take rubbish to the council dump."

"Oh shut up, for fuck's sake."

Daisy pulled Bacon Man towards her and kicked the door shut. I rolled over and listened. I could just about discern what was happening, although everything was muffled by music. The soundscape behind the door was a medley of licking lips, sliding tongues, and approving grunts. They were obviously eating something tasty.

"Do you know what? You've still got the sexiest kiss in the world," whispered Daisy.

"Do you remember that first kiss in Sarajevo?"

Why was Bacon Man prolonging the conversation? What on earth was he doing? Preparing a risk assessment?

"Of course," whispered Daisy. "When I close my eyes I can still picture us sitting on that sofa in your hotel room. I was wearing my big winter coat. There was no heating because of the siege. We were drinking wine. Suddenly you leaned in, found my lips with yours and kissed me in a way that I'd never been kissed before."

"That's because I knew that I only had one chance. For some reason, George Michael's *Careless Whisper* came to mind. And I kissed you with all the passion and desire in the saxophone intro to that song."

"Your lips are made for playing the sax, and for kissing."

"You're the most exciting woman I've ever known." said Bacon Man "I love you so much."

"And I love you too."

"I love you even more with those nipple bells."

There was some more lip-smacking and Rudolph the Red-Nosed reindeer's sleigh slowly accelerated. Then I heard Bacon Man.

"Oooooh Baby. You've shaved your pussy."

I was gobsmacked. There was a cat in there. And it was bald? How did I miss that?

"Do you want to see if those golden paws can make my pussy talk?"

I was confused. Was she addressing Bacon Man or me?

I started barking. Hey let me in. Let me get at the talking cat. Come on. Open up. What's going on?

They ignored me and stopped talking. Bacon Man was giving Daisy a super-fast tummy scrub. He must have hit the sweet spot, because she suddenly screamed at the top of her voice.

"Oooooo Babeeeeee....."

Outside all the ducks started laughing.

"You haven't lost your touch," she moaned. "Come on, Baby. Fuck me."

Then the negotiations started. From the sounds of things, Britain leaving the European Union was a squillion times easier.

"How are we going to do this?"

"You can't lie on top because your stomach's in the way," said Daisy.

"Let's try spooning."

Aha. They were eating.

The spooning also failed because of Bacon Man's gut. As did other permutations of the fat man's Kama Sutra. The Randy Rider, the Leg Glider, the Standing Pretzel. The mattress was too high. Bacon Man's legs were too short. When they finally attempted the Modified Doggy, whatever that is, Bacon Man announced

"Woody has disappeared."

So what? Who cares? That Serbian thug had it coming. But Bacon Man did not.

"This is what happens when you don't use it," he said. "You lose it."

When they emerged from the bedroom, Bacon Man was naked. Daisy's skirt was around her waist. She was half in and half out of the bra. It sounded as if Santa's sleigh had hit speed bumps as I dashed past them to search for the cat. But the sneaky bastard had escaped. When I came out, they'd shut themselves into Bacon Man's room with its lower mattress.

I could go on, but I don't wish to humiliate Bacon Man any further. He was distraught as they lay in *my* bed talking. After ten minutes or so Daisy appeared,

"Good night, Bubsie. See you in the morning. I love you."

She patted me on the head, returned to her room, emptied her glass and poured herself another large one.

Bacon Man ignored me as he headed to the kitchen. Reading the runes, I trotted behind. Bacon Man made a massive bacon sandwich. Although he wasn't in a sharing mood, I was confident there'd be spillage. He shouldn't have done it naked. Hot oil from the frying pan spat on his damaged pride. Well, at least something did.

He carried a plate into the sitting room, rested it on his gut, gazed at the river, and took a huge bite. Almost instantly, he stood up and started staggering backwards and forwards, moaning airlessly, and clutching his throat. Colour drained from his face. He was turning blue. Bacon Man opened a door and stumbled onto the balcony. His eyes rolled upwards. He was gasping for breath, but none came. I started barking as loudly as I could.

Daisy must have heard the commotion. She burst onto the balcony like President George Bush Senior's all-time favourite joke. How do you titillate an ocelot? You oscillate her tits a lot.

"Will you be quiet," she hissed at Bacon Man, as he rasped and struggled to trigger the reflex that ordinarily would expel a blockage and draw oxygen into his constricted airways. But the requisite muscle couldn't muster sufficient power. A familiar Bacon Man problem.

"You'll wake up the neighbours."

Fear spread across Bacon Man's face. I heard a death rattle and so did he.

"Oh my God. Are you choking?"

It was extraordinary how soft tissue in the throat mimicked the metallic grinding of a seizing car engine. Daisy stood behind Bacon Man, reached around his chest and tried to squeeze.

Just then, our neighbour, The Silver Fox, appeared on his deck and I heard him mutter.

"She's pegging the lucky bugger. Is this a private party? Or can I gate-crash?"

Bacon Man was fading fast.

"You're too fat for me to do the Heimlich manoeuvre. I can't get my arms around you."

Daisy didn't panic. She stepped back and swung a right-handed haymaker that caught Bacon Man square in the back. He coughed violently. Thank God. The blockage was out. His chest heaved as he greedily sucked in fresh air. Then he wilted over the balcony, hacking like a life-long smoker.

Neighbours switched on their lights, twitched their curtains and expanded my vocabulary.

"Debauched."

"Trollop."

"Perverts."

"Dogging on Galahad Island. Whatever next?"

Was that comment directed at me?

"This is insane," cried Daisy, and she rumbaed back inside. It was Rudolf's last hurrah. Daisy unpeeled the nipple bells and threw them in a bin. Still coughing, Bacon Man followed behind.

"Thank God you came down, Daisy. I just couldn't get it up. A couple more seconds and I'd have been dead."

"I'm fully aware you couldn't get it up. In more ways than one. Now will you lose weight? The reason you almost choked is that you've got so much fat in that double chin. I'm so angry with you for wrecking your health."

Daisy disappeared upstairs and slammed her bedroom door. She never does that. It's normally open so I can wander in and out. I hope she comes out soon. I'm getting hungry. But that's of secondary importance right now. I'm just counting my blessings that Bacon Man is still breathing. That cough isn't getting any better. I wonder if some of the sandwich is still stuck in his lungs. I'm worried he might start choking again. Do you know another thing I've thought of?

Bacon Man should have paid more attention to that horoscope.

CHAPTER EIGHTEEN
A WORD TO THE WISE

Well, we're finally up and at them. Bacon Man and I have passed the springy gate and are heading towards the tunnel. We're running seriously late this morning, and that's because I allowed them to have a lie in after last night's shenanigans. There are limits, however, even for a considerate golden retriever. I had no alternative but to give Bacon Man a wake-up lick when my early warning system indicated that reactor number two was about to melt down and go nuclear. Yes, I know that's a euphemism. After yesterday's F-bomb fest, I think we could all do with some moderation.

I don't know whether I'm Arthur or Martha right now. I'm not having an identity crisis, but ever since Tommy Bentwaters appeared on the scene, my routine has been shot to pieces and it's disturbing my equilibrium. I like to have a clear plan for the day, every single day, and the way things are going, I fear Daisy might miss my spa for the second time in a week. She was still in bed when we left, and I don't know when she's going to surface. While Bacon Man is multifaceted, a beautician he is not.

My spa is scheduled immediately following Daisy's breakfast, after walk number two, the long one. I'm fed treats while she combs the mud, drool, and fox poo out of my fur, brushes my Simba chest and inquires,

"Do I know a golden who deserves a chewy stick?"

What a daft question. Of course, I deserve it. Only the best is good enough for me. My point is, I don't know when I'm going to get the chewy stick. How would you feel if you couldn't remove cat litter from your teeth? Right now, I'm having to prise the kibble out of my fangs with tree bark.

To his credit, Bacon Man is keeping up a steady supply of sticks. hurling them down the track. His aim is true, despite the occasional cough. This morning he's got a good length going. Hang on, I'll try to rephrase that description, if I can think of something more appropriate.

Bacon Man's now in the tunnel, where he can't throw an overarm. I'm just outside, preparing to catch the meaty branch he's lining up in his right hand. Catching is the latest addition to my quiver of tricks. Here he goes, and it's a great one off the wrist. It flies over my head, and I'm confident that's a new Bacon Man long distance record. Without doubt, the superfast tummy scrub he administered to Daisy last night was responsible for this explosive improvement. I'll insist he gives me one several times a day as part of his new fitness regime.

Hello, here comes Farmer Tony Bisham. He's still got his angry Jack Russell cross with him. Despite not having a fence at the end of his lawn, the pooch hasn't drowned yet. For once, I side entirely with members of the island's Residents' Committee. They were completely right to insist on Farmer

Bisham dismantling the fence, not least because they have more confidence in dogs' intelligence than he does. We're not in the habit of hurling ourselves to our deaths. What does the farmer think we are? Bloody lemmings? Whoops, that's another dog biscuit in the swear box.

The farmer's dog and I indulge in a little mutual butt-sniffing. To be frank, I don't know why we do it. I haven't a clue what I'm looking for. Perhaps, that'll become clearer when I'm older. My only take away from the experience is that he really needs a bath. We head to the newsstand in the ivy and peruse our separate publications. But I can listen in to the humans' conversation.

"Good morning, Morgan,"

"Hi, Tony. Glorious day."

Bacon Man is keen to press on, but the farmer is determined to engage him.

"A word to the wise. It's none of my business, but I feel obliged to warn you that you're the subject of a lot of gossip circulating on the island,"

"So what, Tony? They're always gossiping about something. It's Gossip Central. I couldn't care less what they say about us."

"The reason I mention it is because it could turn serious. It sounds like trouble's brewing."

"Well, that's very kind of you, but I can assure you we've got nothing to worry about."

"I'm not so sure. It's about last night."

"What about last night?"

"On your balcony."

"Oh that. So what have you heard?"

"Remember, these are a neighbour's words, not mine."

"Go on, spit it out. Don't be shy. I'm a grown up. Besides, I could do with a laugh."

"How should I put this? He described seeing some very intimate activity taking place. And he also said some of the other older residents…"

"That's virtually everyone on the island."

"…are talking about witnessing indecent exposure and offensive behaviour."

"That's absurd."

"Yes, but that's the reason I'm warning you, because those are potentially criminal offences, and you could end up getting kicked off the island."

"I'll tell you precisely what happened."

"I'd rather not know, but I think you need to nip this in the bud."

"It's a fart in a phone booth."

"Don't be so sure."

"Well, Tony, thanks for letting me know."

"I'd better be going."

Bacon Man picks up a stick and launches it into the tree line. A pheasant minding its own business in the hedgerow shrieks and takes off. I'm caught in two minds. Bird or stick. Stick or bird. And miss both.

"Come on, Bubsie, let's head home."

Bugger. I mean, blast. I was hoping to go for a swim. It's not fair. This is me time.

***

As I bounce through the front door, I can tell that Daisy is steaming. Her bad moods never fail to infect the entire house. I glance up at Bacon Man. He knows he's in for a bollocking. Whoopsie. The swear box is doing well today.

"Hello, Bubsie, there you are."

Daisy greets me in her usual cheerful manner. In her dealings with me, she's a model of consistency. With the rest of the world, especially Bacon Man, she's completely unpredictable. Even I can recognise that the kitchen is a mess. Bacon Man failed to clear up after his duel with the killer bacon sandwich. I do what I can to help the poor man by hoovering up breadcrumbs still soaked in bacon fat along with a few dollops of butter. I then slink into a neutral corner.

"Good morning," says Bacon Man. "I just met Tony Bisham. I think we could be in trouble after last night."

"No. You're in trouble," snarls Daisy. "How dare you leave the kitchen like this? It's a pigsty. You didn't even bother to put the bacon back in the fridge after your little food orgy. I'll have to chuck it out. It's a complete waste. On second thoughts, that's a good thing. You shouldn't be eating bacon. And how did you manage to smear butter all over the place? On second thoughts. Don't answer that. I don't want to know."

"I'm sorry I'll clean it up."

"Your apologies are worthless. Nothing ever changes, does it? I'm sick of you treating me like a servant."

"That's not true."

"You have absolutely no respect for me or the work I do in this house."

"I do respect your work. I just forgot."

"You forgot?"

"Give it a rest, Daisy. I think you've forgotten what happened last night."

"Last night is indelibly printed on my brain. I'm never going to forget it, more's the pity."

"Me too. But I'm not talking about the sex. Or the lack of it. I nearly bloody died."

"I know. I was there. Remember? I saved your life. You could at least have shown some gratitude by cleaning up the kitchen."

"Do you have any sense of perspective? You were a couple of seconds from being a widow."

"I am not your maid."

"It's like arguing with a lamp post. I've got the picture. I've apologised. I will clean up the kitchen up but for fuck's sake listen to me. I think we might be in trouble."

I can't stand their shouting. I've had enough. I leave my corner and jump up at Daisy. My front paws almost reach her chest. I get down and try to get Bacon Man's attention in the same way and reach slightly further up his front. They think I'm seeking reassurance. But I'm not. I'm cross and I start barking and I don't stop.

Shut up. The pair of you. You're both as bad as each other. I'm sick to death of all this unnecessary conflict. I want peace and quiet and I know that you do too. I can't abide the constant fighting. It's so destructive. It's not just Daisy who insists on having the last word. You won't back down either, will you Bacon Man? You're both intelligent people. Can't you resolve your differences in a more reasonable manner? I love you both to pieces, but really, this is insufferable. I can't stand it any longer. I need some space. So, I'm going for a lie down on Bacon Man's bed. Try to keep it down, will you? I'll be back in time for my daily spa. Please have the chewy stick ready. With that, I turn and as I head upstairs, I can hear their post-performance analysis.

"Wow," says Daisy. "He's really upset with us.."

"Yes,. I've never heard him express himself like that before. I felt like he was trying to communicate with us. He hates it when we fight."

Well done, Bacon Man. You're learning to speak golden retriever. Now be quiet and let me sleep. There's a nice sunbeam in your room. I mean my room. But I'm too restless. My head is spinning with all the drama of the past day, and I recognise that trouble's looming. I hear footsteps outside the front door. Beyond a shadow of doubt, something's up. The post person has already completed their daily delivery. I hope I got the right personal pronoun there. I hate offending people.

I spring off the bed and head downstairs. I reach the door just as a letter slips through the letterbox. I unleash a medium level bark, designed to scare off the slightly nervous and to attract the attention of either Daisy or Bacon Man. I don't know how Google would translate it into English. Probably Oi.

Daisy gets to the door first and opens the letter.

"You were right," she says "We could be in real trouble."

CHAPTER NINETEEN

PENALTY SHOOT OUT

It must be serious. This is the first time I've seen Bacon Man in long trousers. Even during winter's last temper tantrum, when the marina froze over, he was challenging the wind to whistle up his red shorts and give him a urinary tract infection. I don't understand why he's changed into chinos. Black makes some people appear slimmer, but not those with the profile of a tugboat.

I'm concerned that he's lacking confidence about this evening's kangaroo court, I mean the Residents' Committee emergency meeting. He's not being true to himself. The shorts aren't simply an integral part of his personality, they're also a weapon of reverse psychology. I've heard him tell Daisy that the shorts lull people into a false sense of security, because they underestimate him. Then he floors them with a killer question or an unexpected display of intelligence.

Daisy isn't dressing up. Nor is she putting on make-up as she sometimes does.

"Why should I make an effort for that bunch of sanctimonious nobodies? The last thing I want to do is to let them think I take them seriously. Come on Bjørn, let's go."

I'm coming along as well. That's a surprise. It's one of those occasions when I wish I could speak Human. Such a pity I can't, because I could tell Daisy and Bacon Man what the others are whispering.

We amble past the marina to the western tip of the island. The foamy waters of the weir behave like a disco ball, firing tracer rounds from a purple and gold sunset towards a wooden pagoda, where the residents are gathering.

"You can't bring that dog in here," says Colin, a retired solicitor from Number 4, Galahad Island, who doubles as the committee's minutes' secretary.

"Aren't you a lawyer, Colin?" asks Daisy,

"Yes, that's right."

"Then you'll know what precedent is?"

"Of course I do?"

"Well, here's a copy of the last island newsletter. Would you care to look at the front page?"

"What are you talking about?"

"Let me show you. There's a photograph of the committee chairman presiding over the meeting and sitting next to him is his Scottish Terrier. That's precedent. If the chairman can bring his dog in, then so can we."

Colin steps aside, doing goldfish impressions.

"Come on, Bjørn. There's a good boy."

My, this looks very formal. A long table straddles a low stage. There are places for five committee members. I spot Janet, who's married to our neighbour, the Silver Fox. She's sitting right of centre and sipping from a blue Ikea pint glass, like the ones we have at home. I'll just do a long-range sniff test.

Just as I thought, Chardonnay. Janet's bleached perm is especially electric tonight. Every strand is horizontal, as if she's attached to the mains. I adjust the sniff filter in my left nostril. Dogs can do that, you know. Yup. My snout never fails me. Janet's overdone the hairspray. If someone lights a cigarette, she'll napalm Henley-on-Thames.

Janet is sitting next to Lillian Tremonti, the Spitfire pilot from Number 64, the island's oldest resident. Lillian's hearing has declined in recent years, especially since her husband, a former Italian prisoner of war, passed away.

I catch Janet watching us take our seats. She whispers to Lillian.

"There's that strumpet."

"Love crumpets. Are we having them tonight?"

"No, Lillian. Our neighbour. The hussy who Reginald saw naked on the balcony. Having some sort of orgy."

"They don't have a corgi. They've got a lovely golden retriever."

"That harlot was naked."

"Naked you say? Nothing wrong with that. Used to sunbathe naked when I was a gal. Still do on a hot day. Like to wave to the coxed fours. Their times have really improved this year."

"Look at her. She's dressed like a Polish cleaner."

"Got a lot of time for the Poles. Brilliant pilots during the Battle of Britain. Fearless, even reckless. More kills than any other squadron. Didn't get the credit they deserved at the time. Shameful. My district nurse? Polish. Couldn't be kinder."

Janet raises her eyebrows as she swigs some more "let's pretend it's water" water.

"Order. Order."

With the fervour of the French Revolutionary Judge, Maxmillian Robespierre, Maurice Oxford strikes the table with a gavel. The room is hushed.

"Good evening Ladies and Gentlemen. I presume you're all in possession of this evening's agenda. For those unfamiliar with the rules, or those who need a reminder, and yes, I'm addressing you Mr. and Mrs. Somerville, this is a democratic assembly. Everyone has the right to speak. But only members of the committee, sitting either side of me, have the right to vote on the relevant motions."

Doesn't sound very democratic to me. But to give Mr. Tickety-boo his dues, he's doing his best to explain how the process works. He's mansplaining. Or as I'd call it, dogsplaining.

"If there's a tie, I have the casting vote. According to the Covenant, there's no appeal process. But if any complainant feels suitably aggrieved, they can seek redress through the High Courts. However, I would strongly recommend acceptance of the residents' committee's rulings. We have a proud record of upholding our byelaws and traditions. This is not a threat. But we are litigious, and our legal contingency fund currently stands at over three hundred thousand pounds. That's accurate isn't it, Madam Treasurer?"

"Yesh. Thatsh correct."

Ah, so Janet is the treasurer.

"Right, we have three items on the agenda this evening. The parking status of a commercial vehicle bearing a company logo. Adjudication on the mooring dimensions of a new vessel at Number 23. And thirdly, the, ahem, incident last night at Number 69."

"Scandinavian sodomite."

The female whisper came from behind me, just to the left, at the eight o'clock position. It threw me. What's a sodomite? The woman's husband was equally confused.

"Do you mean she was tackled from behind on the balcony?"

"No, she was tackling him."

"What with?"

"Reginald said it was a peg."

"I'm so glad we complained about their washing."

Maurice rapped his gavel. A barely perceptible smile of pleasure shuffled his moustache.

"I'm sure you'll all agree with me, when I say that the third item, concerning the residents at Number 69, is the most egregious issue on the agenda. I trust there's no one here under the age of eighteen. If so, could I ask you to please take your leave because this subject will no doubt involve some sensitive themes.

"So let's begin. The new occupants of Number 17 have a Mercedes shooting brake. For those of you under seventy, that's an estate car. The vehicle is dual purpose in that it is used commercially for Number 17's business, and privately, so they can travel between work and home. However, the matter is complicated because the lower left-hand side of the vehicle is adorned with a logo belonging to their company, Chiltern

Chainsaws. I should hasten to add that the registered office of Chiltern Chainsaws is not on Galahad Island, and therefore does not breach the byelaws. But the presence of a logo explicitly contravenes paragraph seven of the byelaws. This paragraph states that no commercial vehicle shall be parked anywhere on the estate apart from the temporary purposes of loading or unloading."

"May I speak, Mr. Oxford?"

I assume that is Mr. Chiltern Chainsaws from Number 17.

"Can I propose a compromise, Sir?"

"You may."

"Would it be acceptable if we were to enclose the vehicle in a protective cover overnight?"

"I'm afraid not. That would contravene the Amenity paragraph of the Covenant which unequivocally states that in accordance with the majority view of a residents' survey conducted in 2011, and further endorsed at the Annual General Meeting in 2022, vehicle covers are not permitted. So, that's clear cut. I don't think we need a vote."

"But Mr. Chairman, may I make an alternative suggestion?"

"And that is?"

"That for the duration of our occupation of Number 17, Galahad Island, we provide a stipend for an annual celebration of the ascent to the throne of King Charles III. How does a thousand pounds a year sound?"

"That's a very generous offer, and in that spirit, I recommend we attempt to be flexible. I'm doing some blue sky thinking here. As a compromise, why don't we allow you to park your vehicle on the lot furthest away from the main body of the properties. But the vehicle must be facing towards the river so that the logo will not be seen by, and therefore offend, most residents."

"That's extremely kind of you, Mr. Chairman."

Maurice Oxford looks either side of him.

"Are we all agreed?"

Everyone nods, apart from Lillian. She appears to be asleep. Yes, I can hear her gently snoring.

"Passed unanimously. Now, the cruiser belonging to Number 23. We appointed specialist marine engineers to double, and triple check the dimensions of the said vessel. The findings were consistent. The vessel is three inches too long. We are prepared to revisit this issue should Number 23 agree to the necessary hull modifications to shorten it to the requisite length. If not, then only one lawful remedy is available to us."

Maurice turns to his fellow committee members. Colin the lawyer mumbles that the chairman has interpreted the rules correctly. The others nod in agreement.

"So that's settled. The owners of Number 23 are required to moor the vessel elsewhere."

"Mr. Chairman, may I address the bench please?"

It's Captain Twenty-Three.

"Certainly."

"With all due respect, your suggestion about remodelling the hull is totally impractical. It could cost at least two hundred thousand pounds and throw the hydrodynamics out of kilter. The boat is top of the range. It cost me three hundred thousand pounds."

"That is not the committee's problem," replied Maurice.

"We bought a house here because of the free mooring. The nearest marina with vacant spaces is fifteen miles away."

"Well, you should have measured the vessel properly before purchase."

"Oh please. Be reasonable. Three inches here or there doesn't matter."

"Who says?" whispers Daisy.

"I heard that," says Bacon Man.

"Case rejected," says Maurice. "Please vacate the mooring by this time next week. If you fail to do so, after the grace period, there'll be a weekly fine which will increase incrementally."

"You bastard," shouts Captain Number 23.

"There's no need for offensive language," says Maurice calmly. "This is an important message for all newcomers. You all move here for the views. Of that, I'm sure. But none of you bother to check the small print. If you don't like the rules here, you're at liberty to move elsewhere. Now. Item number three. The incident at Number 69."

"Ooooh I'm looking forward to thish," slurs Janet.

"What did you say?" says Lillian, waking from her slumber.

"There are multiple allegations of breaches of the byelaws," reads Maurice, from what I assume must be a charge sheet.

"Some are of a potentially criminal nature, such as sexual activity taking place outside the closed walls of a property. The way it stands, there is a *prime facie* case of outraging public decency through lewd or obscene behaviour. And that, if I'm not mistaken, is a sexual offence under British law. Am I right, Colin?"

"Yes, Mr. Chairman. Furthermore, defendants who are convicted are required to sign the Register of Sex Offenders, which I must emphasise, is highly damaging to the reputation of the person or persons concerned."

"Thank you, Mr. Secretary. The other alleged breach concerns the noise created during this disturbance. That contravenes the overarching rule about doing nothing that upsets the general enjoyment of the island."

"Mr. Chairman," says Colin. "Given the gravity of these allegations, I think it's only correct that we call upon the residents of Number 69 to give an account of themselves."

"Point of order, Mr. Secretary," interrupts Maurice, "Just in case anyone is in doubt about the seriousness, let me just reiterate the potential consequences. The ultimate sanction could be that the occupants of Number 69 would be expelled from the Island Association, and that would result in a compulsory sale order."

My attention diverts to Daisy who's inhaling deeply. She whispers to Bacon Man.

"Bloody hell, they are serious. I'd better start looking at estate agents."

"Don't be so negative, Daisy," Bacon Man whispers. "The worst case scenario doesn't always happen."

"One further point, Mr. Chairman."

Colin, the secretary, has resumed speaking.

"I'm firmly of the view that we should grant anonymity to the complainants. We want to ensure there's no harassment of, or retribution towards, potential witnesses."

"Don't be ridiculous," shouts Bacon Man. "You make it

sound like they need to get plastic surgery and go into witness protection. What do you think we're going to do? Cut off horses' heads and put them in their beds? We've got a pretty good idea who it is anyway, don't we, Janet?"

"Kindly refrain from heckling Mr. Somerville." says Maurice at his most authoritative.

"I will not tolerate verbal attacks on members of the committee. This is a civilised chamber. Not the House of Commons. If you can't behave, I'll expel you and we'll take a decision behind closed doors."

"Let's not get too carried away, shall we?"

It's Daisy, taking control.

She shoots Bacon Man a warning glance as she stands up and walks to the middle of the floor. She stands tall with her legs slightly apart.

"Watch this, Bubsie," Bacon Man whispers. "It's going to be wild."

"Yes, it's absolutely true that my husband and I were on our balcony last night. We had just had rampant sex upstairs in our bedroom with the windows closed, so as not to disturb the neighbours, because I can be seriously noisy when I get going."

"Oh Lord," whispered Bacon Man. "Here we go."

"It was really, really good sex. I came twice. The first time it was my husband's golden paws that……."

"Mrs. Somerville, please spare us," pleads Maurice Oxford.

"No, I insist on giving you the full story. In my country, Denmark,….."

"But this is the Home Counties, Mrs. Somerville. Please. How about some decorum?"

"There's nothing to be ashamed of Maurice, we Danes are very open about sex."

Suddenly Janet, the treasurer, puts down her drink.

"That's one of the reasons we voted for Brexit," she shouted. "To put an end to all of those obnoxious European practices."

"What obnoxious practices, Janet? Do you mean sex?"

"No, of course not. I mean prostitutes posing in windows in the red-light districts by canals. We don't want brothels along the banks of the Thames. This is a respectable neighbourhood."

"What you're describing is Amsterdam in Holland, not Denmark. I hope you're not accusing me of being a prostitute. If you are, I'll sue you for slander. All I was doing was enjoying conjugal sex with my husband. As I was saying….."

"Ladies, please. Stop."

Maurice Oxford is bright red and puffing hard. Brexit does that to people. Here's my considered opinion on the matter.

There's no doubt that immigration was the trigger for most voters in the Brexit referendum. I entirely agree that Britain is overcrowded. But a quarter of the population are morbidly obese. That's more than fifteen million people. If they all lost weight, there'd be more room. Simples.

Brexiteers obviously want to be surrounded by their own kind of people. But statistics show that the British birth rate is constantly declining. Maybe that's because of all the spare tyres out there. Your little tadpoles can't get to the end of the diving board, let alone do the doggie paddle upstream. Bacon Man is just the tip of that particular iceberg. Yes. The tip. A quarter of all British bedrooms resemble the dodgems at the end of the pier. You're all bouncing off each other.

Maurice Oxford is bouncing off the walls of the committee room for other reasons.

"Mrs. Somerville. Please. I beg you. We don't need to know every detail of your bedroom activities."

"Oh yes we do. Vital part of her evidence."

It's Lillian, the former Spitfire pilot.

"Mrs. Somerville has every right to give her side of the story in whatever manner she chooses. Free speech is a fundamental freedom. Liberty. That's what we fought for and why we sacrificed so much."

On the far side of the committee table, a stout woman on the cusp of seventy leans into the secretary and whispers.

"Can't we get rid of her, Colin? She's pushing a hundred, for heaven's sake."

"Impossible, Stephanie. You can't be removed from the committee on the grounds of age. Only if your mental faculties are impaired. And as we all know, Lillian's marbles are still very much intact."

Maurice isn't happy either.

"Lillian this is beyond the pale."

"Stop being so prudish, Maurice. We've all had sex in this room. Well, not in this room. But you know what I mean. Let the lady speak. I insist."

"Now where was I?"

Daisy resumes her position and ploughs on.

"So, after my first orgasm I had a sip of water, climbed on top of my husband and rode him hard. Reverse cowgirl. He had his hands full and was yelling 'more cowbell' as he tried to replicate the intro to *Honky Tonk Woman* with my nipple bells."

Wait a minute. That's anatomically impossible. With his huge gut, Bacon Man can't reach that far. Daisy says she never fakes it. But she's fibbing, I'm sure of it. I glance up at Bacon Man. He's staring at his feet.

"If you ask my husband, he'll tell you he had a really powerful orgasm."

I don't think he will. Bacon Man also originates from the Home Counties. And as far as I recall, he was virtually crying from frustration.

"My husband was so turned on, that we went at it again almost immediately."

"I bet he was, the old dog," said the Silver Fox underneath his breath.

I smelled our neighbour entering the pagoda once the first two items on the agenda had been rubber stamped. But what I want to know is what happened to the bald cat. Where did he end up?

"Have you quite finished, Mrs. Somerville?" begs Maurice.

"I'm now getting to the climax of the story. Bear with me,"

"Oooh, I can't wait," chuckles Lillian.

"After my second orgasm, my husband went downstairs….."

Second orgasm? Really, Daisy! You're telling Porkies.

"……..made himself a bacon sandwich, choked on a piece of bacon and ran onto the balcony gasping for fresh air. Bjørn alerted me to his predicament, and I raced down the stairs, tried the Heimlich manoeuvre, unsuccessfully, as it turns out. I slammed him on his back which dislodged the offending piece of bacon from his throat.

"So, Maurice, I admit being almost naked on the balcony. But in the rush to save my husband's life, I didn't have time to get out of the lingerie I bought from Copenhagen's finest sex shop. What's more, the rubber nooses were super-tight around my nipples, just the way I like it. And I completely forgot how much noise the bells make when my boobs bounce up and down. I see you're taking notes, Colin. For the record, they're 44 double F."

"Ding Dong. That's my jam. *Jiggle Bells*," muttered the Silver Fox.

"Hang on. Wait a minute. There was something else."

Janet, the Silver Fox's wife, has found her voice.

"My husband was certain he saw you pegging your husband. This choking story is nothing but a pack of lies. There you are, Reginald. Come on, back me up. You tell them."

The Silver Fox's confidence melts like Greenland's ice cap.

"Well, er, er. It was very dark and I, er, might have been mistaken."

"What's pegging?" asks Lillian.

Her hearing seems to have improved over the course of the evening.

"Yes, what is pegging?" asks Maurice. "I'm only asking for the sake of justice."

"You tell them, Reginald. I insist."

Janet's tone clearly indicates she rules the roost at home.

"You're obviously an expert."

"Yes, please tell us, Reginald. I'm dying to know," says Lillian.

"I agree, Reginald," says Maurice. "The minutes will record you as a technical witness."

"Er well, I'm led to believe that this an increasingly popular practice, whereby the male partner is the stooper and the female is the stabber. The female partner wears something like a carpenter's tool belt, and attaches a prosthetic penis, or dildo."

"Is that pleasurable?" asks Lillian. "In 1944, I once had two fuckers up my arse between Southampton and the Needles. Stimulating certainly, but not in a good way."

I scan the committee table, and Stephanie is whispering to Colin.

"What is that woman talking about?"

"She's fibbing," replies Colin. "Those Fokkers were Messerschmitts."

After an uncomfortable pause, the Silver Fox starts to answer Lillian's question.

"Well, not it's not pleasurable for the woman obviously, because….."

"How do you know, Reginald?" demands Janet. "Is there something you want to tell me?"

"That's enough technical evidence for the time being," rules Maurice. "We haven't heard from Mr. Somerville yet. Do you have anything to add?"

"Not really. My wife's description is accurate. Yes, I was naked when I dashed onto the balcony. I was within an inch of losing my life and was desperate for fresh air. Reginald's description is wrong, I promise you. If I'm being kind, I'd say he was confused by the darkness. After my throat was cleared, I checked up on methods for dealing with choking and pegging isn't one of them. When the Queen Mother got a fish bone stuck in her throat, her staff rushed her to hospital for an emergency operation. They didn't reach for a strap-on."

"Mr. Somerville! Really." exclaims Maurice. "There's no need to drag the Royal Family into this scenario, In fact, I don't believe there's any need for more witness statements, do you Colin?"

"No. We have enough information to make a judgement."

"The committee will adjourn to consider its decision. Would you all mind stepping outside until we do?"

Five minutes later, Maurice's gavel summons everyone back inside.

"Very well. I'm obliged to inform you that we have a split decision. The issue at stake is whether Mr. and Mrs. Somerville should be expelled from the Island Association. The implication of such a decision would be that they would be obliged to sell their property and be barred in perpetuity from holding the deeds of any other unit on the estate. These may sound like draconian measures, but they have been tested in law before. I will now ask the committee members to tell us how they stand and why. Madam Treasurer?"

"I vote for expulsion. I've explained my reasons. That's all I have to say."

Just what I expected from Janet. It's like a penalty shoot-out. We're behind.

"And let's hear from Stephanie Board-Tilley, my predecessor as chairman, I mean chairwoman, who has been uncharacteristically quiet this evening."

"I'm with Janet. Expulsion."

"Any further comments?"

"None needed."

Woooh. Now we're really up against it. One more vote and we're out.

"Mr. Secretary. Colin, what's your verdict?"

"I'm against expulsion. Such a decision would be legally unsafe. Although some witness statements indicate that a breach of the byelaws did take place, the forensic evidence is weak, as we have no pictures or other technical documentation to support these claims. If we were to expel Mr. and Mrs. Somerville from the island association, they would have solid grounds for legal action. In all probability, they would be successful. So, although the committee normally speaks with one voice, on this occasion, Janet and Stephanie, I'm afraid it doesn't."

Two to one. We've got a fighting chance. I'm sure we can count on the next vote.

"Lillian. Lillian."

"Thank you, Maurice. I heard you the first time. It's outrageous that poor Mr. and Mrs. Somerville have been dragged here and put through this ordeal. I have no hesitation in rejecting the diabolical proposal that they should be forced to abandon their home when all they were trying to do was to save Mr. Somerville's life. You all ought to be ashamed of yourselves?"

Wow, thank you, Lillian. We're level pegging, if that's the right word.

"Very well," says Maurice, pulling himself up to his full height. "I have the casting vote. Thank you for that impassioned speech, Lillian. We'll have to agree to disagree about some of your remarks."

Oh no. We're doomed. Where on earth will we go? Apart from the swans, I really love my walks along the river.

"However......"

Maurice pauses for dramatic effect. Hold that previous thought.

"I shall vote to reject the proposal. That is to say, I line up alongside Lillian, and the Secretary, Colin, because I'm cognisant of the risks that he has outlined. So, that brings proceedings to a close. One word of advice, Mr. and Mrs. Somerville. Could you possibly invest in dressing gowns before you next venture on to the balcony."

CHAPTER TWENTY
LENTIL MAN

You won't be surprised to learn that Daisy and Bacon Man haven't bought dressing gowns. On principle, they would never acquiesce to Maurice Oxford, although they have listened to the mood music from the emergency meeting. Personally, I'm relieved that life has been less dramatic these past few months. Adopting a lower profile was a wise strategy because they'd lost a key ally.

Lillian the Spitfire pilot, I'm sad to say, is no longer a member of the Residents' Committee. Stephanie Board-Tilly, the silent but deadly member who voted against us on the big night, got her wish.

Lillian has a different set of wings. She's a celestial pilot and has flown to a place ruled by someone that humans worship. His name is Dog. No, sorry, I spelt it wrongly. It's God. Bloody half-palindromes. Allow me to clarify in case I've upset someone. Her name is God. Alternatively, if you're Swedish or a member of the Scottish National Party, their name is God. Pick whichever one you like, I don't care. Live and let live. Just leave my dog bowl alone.

In the new spirit of non-confrontation, avoiding offence or just being plain vanilla, I should point out that while I might sound frivolous about Lillian's passing, I'm not being disrespectful. I'm not mourning her loss; I'm celebrating her life. She was a grand old lady who had a good innings. One year short of the royal telegram. Not too shabby. Moreover, she died with a smile on her face.

How do I know? Well, first thing in the morning after the emergency committee, Lillian's eldest son Carlo knocked on the door to break the news. Bacon Man made genuine Italian espresso in his Bialetti Moka Express coffee maker, while Carlo sat in the kitchen and described her final moments. Lillian had been on the phone to her son, regaling him with details of the committee meeting, roaring with laughter, when suddenly, there was a thump and the line went dead.

An hour later, Carlo and his wife found Lillian lying on the floor, clutching the phone, going cold, with her mouth wide open, and a twinkle gently fading from her eyes.

"Why didn't you call an ambulance?" asked Daisy.

"Because Mama signed a DNR."

"What's that?" asked Bacon Man.

"A Do Not Resuscitate document," said Daisy. "Don't worry, I won't ask you to sign one."

"Oh, I assure you, Mama signed it of her own free will," said Carlo, a little too vehemently.

Daisy was standing behind Carlo. He didn't see that she put her finger just below her right eye and pushed her cheek down as if to say, 'pull the other one.' She didn't believe Carlo because she thought he coveted the E-type Jag and Lillian's waterfront property. Well, he's in luck, thanks to a bacon sandwich.

"What did the doctor say?" asked Bacon Man.

"Death by natural causes. Her heart gave out."

I suppose that was the kindest option because it meant the coroner wasn't troubled, and her body was spared a postmortem.

Carlo said his mother was ecstatic at thwarting the hardliners on the committee.

"Bloody busybodies. They're beyond the pale. I can't abide them. They got what was coming to them. You should have seen their faces as Mrs. Somerville described the lead up to the choking incident. What's more, that idiot Reginald thought that she was pegging her husband."

Then Lillian guffawed with laughter and spoke her last words.

"Do you know what pegging is?"

As final words go, they're not in the same league as Caesar's "Et tu, Brute," or Admiral Nelson's "Kiss me Hardy."

It's one of Dog's little jokes. I mean God. You just don't know when he/she/they is/are going to push the stop button on your heart. Actually, in an age of gender fluidity, you have to accept the possibility that God identifies as a Dog. That's fine by me. Although I doubt the residents of Galahad Island are ready for acceptance.

In keeping with their traditions, our neighbours lined the access road to the main gate as Lillian's hearse headed for the crematorium. Maurice Oxford stood sentinel by the twin flag poles and lowered the Union Jack to half-staff, along with a pennant depicting a Knight of the Round Table, the emblem of Galahad Island.

Just as the gates were opening Bacon Man looked up.

"Listen, Daisy. A Merlin engine. Unmistakeable."

"The Wizard? What are you talking about?"

"No, it's a Spitfire, the plane Lillian used to fly. It's got a Merlin engine."

As he spoke, the pilot performed a low-level barrel roll before climbing steeply to starboard.

"Have you got a hard on?" murmured Daisy. "I know what you're like. You used to get one every time there was a thunderstorm, because it reminded you of Sarajevo."

"Actually, Daisy, something's stirring."

"Don't even think about playing *The Battle of Britain* soundtrack in the bedroom."

As Daisy whispered in Bacon Man's ear, I had a vision of Lillian's ghost floating above her coffin, chuckling at their private joke and laughing at the island's residents tracking the hearse with their rheumy eyes, wondering if they'd be next for the bespoke oak suit. Russet leaves were floating to the ground. Would they make it to Christmas?

Although he grinned at being teased, Bacon Man's characteristic spare tyre of good humour had lost its tread over recent weeks. He was tetchier than I'd ever seen him.

Our honour guard duties finished, we embarked on my main event of the day, a four-mile ramble along the Thames Path, starting as always, with the ritual handbags at dawn duel with the gobby swan. He hissed and swore at me. I barked back fearlessly. If I wasn't on a lead, I'd have sprinted over there and given him a good talking to, face to face. He was so lucky that Daisy was holding me back.

Companionable silences often punctuate our morning constitutionals. But on the day of Lillian's funeral, Bacon Man was positively garrulous. The choking episode had put flesh on the spectre of his mortality.

"Do you know something, Daisy, that's the closest I've ever come to death. Can you imagine the full story being revealed at a memorial service? Killed by a bacon sandwich."

"Well, you've only got yourself to blame."

"Stop it, Daisy. The truth is I still can't believe it. During my time as a war correspondent I had so many close calls that I managed to laugh it off. But I'm struggling to find anything funny about choking on the balcony. I honestly don't think I've been more terrified in my life. I seriously thought I was about to croak."

"You probably bit off more than you could chew," said Daisy. There's so much fat around your airways from your double chins. It's playing havoc with your breathing."

Years of appeasing his appetite had reached a tipping point. Bacon Man's body was taking revenge. Longer, more vigorous walks with Daisy and me were invariably pleasant and the routine of reaching ten thousand steps each morning had enabled Bacon Man to tighten his belt by one notch, but no further. However, if he was to undo decades of damage, significantly more drastic action was required and he knew it, despite his flippant mask.

Bacon Man was no longer able to ignore doctors as he had done in the past, or keep Daisy in the dark. She'd gained access to his NHS account which detailed all his medical appointments and test results.

For the first time, the annual diabetes-related eye examination showed that his vision was being affected by the disease. Other tests revealed his blood sugar levels were more elevated than ever. His blood pressure was sky high. And his resting heart rate was around ninety beats per minute.

"You're killing yourself. Is that what you secretly want?" asked Daisy.

"Of course not. I've got so much more to do. For a start, I'd like to see my dick before I die."

"Well, attach some wing mirrors to your gut then," quipped Daisy.

"Very funny. Remarks like that do nothing for my self-esteem. I'm starting to question whether you ever enjoyed sex with me."

"My God, you're needy at the moment."

"Maybe I am."

"After all these years, you surely ought to know that I never fake anything. We had a fabulous sex life in the early years. When I fell in love with you, I used to cry afterwards."

"Probably out of frustration."

"Stop fishing. Those were tears of happiness. Yes, I had lots of rampant sex before I met you. But much of it was mindless and animalistic."

Daisy was interrupted as a vicar walked out of a riverside parsonage, leading a poodle with her butt in the air and that musky better-than-bacon scent. I burrowed my snout into her tightly wound perm and went deeper than a nit nurse.

"Come here, Bjørn, leave her alone," insisted Daisy.

I couldn't believe Daisy was interfering. I'd just found the highway to heaven.

"I do apologise, Vicar. I'll put him on a lead."

"Thank you."

"Is she in season?"

"Not as far as I know," replied the clergyman.

Daisy dragged me off. Infuriating. I was beginning to understand how Bacon Man felt. Once we'd put distance between us and the vicar, it was obvious that Bacon Man was still on heat.

"I wish I'd met you when I was younger and when you were wilder."

"Yes, I bet you do. But only because my boobs hadn't gone south then."

"Well there might be some truth in that. And if you want them lifted, we can always sell the dog, although I don't think we'll get five grand for him."

"Don't say things like that. Look at Bjørn, he's crestfallen."

Daisy was right. Bacon Man can be a prize dick sometimes.

"Anyway, I'm not having surgery. Ever. You'll just have to live with the stretch marks. They're my battle honours. Besides, I wouldn't have looked at you twice when you were younger."

"Why not?"

"You know why. You just weren't my type."

"So why was I suddenly your type?"

"You know the reason why. This self-pitying is so out of character."

"My self-esteem is shot to shit."

"How many times do I have to tell you? I was ready to settle down. Yes, there were men who were taller, richer, more muscular and more handsome than you, but none of them made me feel as complete as you or could meet me at eye level as you do."

"I feel the same way. Although sometimes I wish I was taller."

Daisy was kind enough not to respond and we walked in relative silence while Bacon Man hurled sticks as far as he could.

When we got home, Bacon Man still had sex on the brain and began talking about discovering an old diary.

"Even back then, you were telling me to lose weight," he said. "Once, after we'd had sex, you said it was difficult to concentrate when it looked like I was about to have a heart attack."

"That's true. It's a real passion killer."

"Reading it was excruciating. My performances were shocking. I couldn't last as long as I used to. No wonder you were frustrated. If I'm honest, my weight and lack of fitness were to blame."

"That's true. When we got married, you were much fitter and stronger and could go on for longer."

"But Daisy, in the diary, I also wrote that the menopause kicked in earlier than expected. And you lost interest in sex. Also, the kids got in the way. The only time we had a chance to fool around was just before picking them up from school."

"You never seemed to resent those afternoons," she replied. "As a matter of fact I remember you being far more energetic and aroused than when we had sex in the evenings."

"You know why I didn't resent it? Because from a bloke's point of view, there's no such thing as bad sex and bad sex is better than no sex."

Daisy chuckled.

"I can assure you that no one has ever had bad sex with me."

"Oh really?" said Bacon Man with a grin. "What about that guy who once fell asleep on top of you?"

"What about him? I'd exhausted him. Back in the day, sex with me was pretty vigorous and the way I remember it he wasn't particularly fit."

"Lucky bastard," sighed Bacon Man.

"Look, I recognise that my libido has completely dropped off since the menopause kicked in. Maybe I ought to reconsider Hormone Replacement Therapy."

"Do you mean that, Daisy?"

"Yes, I'm serious."

"You're not teasing me?"

"No. If you're serious about losing weight, I'll definitely look into HRT."

"But I thought you were completely against it because of the cancer risk?"

"Well, some studies show a link between HRT and breast cancer. But this is also about quality of life, and I'd like my libido back."

"That cheers me up no end. But if you start taking hormones, regular breast checks are essential. Why don't we start now?"

"We'll leave mammograms to the professionals," said Daisy, smiling.

"I can be professional about it," said Bacon Man. "I'll give them a thorough once over, and you can pay me fifty quid."

Much as though I love Bacon Man, sometimes I despair. He just keeps pushing. It really can be tiresome. I gave him a look that said do yourself a favour, pal. Take some advice from a golden retriever and stop while you're ahead.

"Come on, why don't we see how bad it is?"

"What do you mean?" asked Bacon Man.

"If I'm prepared to have HRT, the least you can do is get on the scales."

"There's no need," replied Bacon Man, "I've got a rough idea, and I'd rather not know."

"You can't continue burying your head in the sand. Isn't it better to know the truth?"

"Ok, I suppose so."

Daisy led the way upstairs, followed by Bacon Man, who, for all the world, looked as if he was heading to the gallows. I tiptoed behind them.

"Take off all your clothes, including your socks. And your watch. We might as well get an accurate reading."

I won't embarrass Bacon Man with a full description, except to say he should never consider a career in pole dancing unless it was in a fetish club.

He stood with his toes next to the scales as if he was about to plunge to his death from a great height.

"Stop hesitating," commanded Daisy.

"I don't want to do it," said Bacon Man.

"You're being ridiculous."

Bacon Man took a deep breath, wheezed and stepped up.

The scales suffered whiplash as the numbers accelerated from nought to beyond a hundred.

"Bloody hell," said Daisy. "A hundred and forty seven kilos."

"A hundred and forty six point nine, to be precise," said Bacon Man, stepping off quickly and reaching for his boxer shorts.

"That's terrible," said Daisy.

"I know, I'm so embarrassed," said Bacon Man.

He was crestfallen almost to the point of tears.

"To be honest, I thought it was going to be worse. I thought you were around a hundred and fifty," said Daisy.

"I think I was that heavy when I last went to the doctor. But walking with Bjørn has really helped. I do feel a bit lighter."

"But it's still terrible."

"I know. I wonder what that is in stones?"

Bacon Man finished dressing and went in search of his phone.

"Oh my God, it's more than twenty three stones. That's awful. I've got to do something."

"What about one of those amazing new weight loss drugs?" said Daisy. "Everybody's on them."

"I have been looking at them. But the side-effects scare me. I've seen pictures of people who've lost so much weight, their faces have turned long and droopy. They look like bloodhounds."

I'd look like a bloodhound if I relied on Daisy to feed me. All that bloody kibble.

"The medication you're already on has side-effects, but you've been ok so far," said Daisy.

"I saw a story the other day where researchers were warned that one of those slimming jabs could cause blindness," said Bacon Man.

"They said the same thing about masturbation," said Daisy. "But your eyesight seems alright to me."

"I'd have twenty-twenty vision if you called off your sex strike."

"Oh, grow up."

And on they bickered.

That choking incident changed everything. Bacon Man no longer tip-toed downstairs for a snack in the middle of the night. As usual, I was lying next to him in bed on top of the duvet, with my back against his chest, when I heard him wake up. I rolled over and waved my legs in the air, inviting a tummy scrub. Bacon Man obliged as he always does. And just in case you're wondering, it wasn't one of those special high-speed scrubs he gave to Daisy on the night that we no longer talk about.

"I'm starving, Bubsie. What about you? But, I'm afraid you're going to have to wait until breakfast time. No more midnight snacks for me. I'm terrified I'll choke again, and that I'll die alone on the kitchen floor. I know it sounds stupid, but I no longer trust myself to eat properly."

Two days after stepping on the scales, over morning coffee in the kitchen, Bacon Man cleared his throat.

"I've got an announcement to make."

"Do you mind, I'm reading my news sites," said Daisy, not looking up from her screen.

"Can't it wait?"

"No. It's important."

"It had better be. You know I like peace and quiet in the morning," said Daisy as she removed her headphones.

"I'm going cold turkey," declared Bacon Man.

"Is that it? Can I go back to *The Times* now please?"

"Give me a break, Daisy. I mean I'm going to change my lifestyle completely. I'm going to start eating healthily and I'm going to step up the exercise."

"Oh yeah? I'll believe it when I see it. What about the jabs we talked about? The ones used for treating diabetes and helps suppress your appetite."

"I agree, Daisy, that does look like a good option. But I'm sick of all the bloody medication I'm on and I'm worried about potential side-effects."

"But *Skatter*, isn't death the ultimate side-effect of obesity?"

"Look, Daisy, I don't want to have another unnecessary

pharmaceutical product foisted on me. You talked about me having discipline in other areas of my life. Well, it's time for me to dig deep. I want my body back."

"That's what I want too, but you know what that means, don't you?" said Daisy.

"Yes, it's going to be tough, but I can't take this anymore."

Blimey. I was witnessing Bacon Man's Revolution Day. Was this the start of a potential renaissance? Could the Cavalier really flip and become a puritanical Roundhead? Did Bacon Man the bon vivant possess the fortitude to become Lentil Man the ascetic?

"I'll tell you the first thing that's going, Daisy," he said.

"What's that?"

"Bacon."

FUCCCCCCCKKKKKKKK.

CHAPTER TWENTY ONE

LIQUORICE MICHELIN MAN

I TOOK UP MY SPYING position in the kitchen after they'd returned from a major shopping expedition to the posh supermarket across the motorway. Lying in front of the dishwasher, I monitored every single purchase to determine whether Bacon Man's pledge was genuine or a big fat fib.

This was the first time they'd been for groceries since his big announcement and unless I'd blinked, I didn't spot any bacon being squirrelled away in the fridge. I didn't see any squirrel meat either. The Lord Dog knows I'd like to give it a try. Throughout autumn I chased a squillion squirrels. Although my sprinting rivalled that of Usain Bolt, the critters never failed to get away. I resolved to become a better stalker. I mean in a hunting sense. Not in a lurking-outside-the-parsonage-with-the-perfumed-poodle sense.

I also needed to expand my palate to include all the new ingredients that had transformed the kitchen into an outlet of a health food chain. At least Bacon Man hadn't suddenly gone all vegetarian on me. He might have loaded up on vegetables. quinoa, pulses, nuts, oatmeal, kefir, and kimchi, abandoning carbs and replacing red meat with fish and chicken. But after the best part of a year in his company, I was confident Bacon Man could combine his cookery skills and love of good food into dishes that would still make me drool.

The natural extension of living in the moment means embracing change, going with the flow even if it means living without bacon.

My only concern was that to stave off hunger, Bacon Man would husband the contents of his plates and not share.

"Portion control is everything," said Daisy, adding lifestyle coach to the many hats she wore as the Regimental Sergeant-Major of Number 69, Galahad Island.

Bacon Man couldn't have chosen a worse time to try to shed weight. Christmas was rapidly approaching. Throughout their marriage, the Somervilles had always celebrated twice. Daisy insisted on marking Danish Christmas on December 24th, to keep her traditions alive while Bacon Man refused to surrender the British excesses of Christmas Day itself.

Like me, Bacon Man sets himself targets and he had told Daisy that he wanted to lose seven kilos before Christmas. That would take him down to a hundred and forty kilos, or a tad over twenty-two stone, which for him, was something of a psychological landmark. It was a tall order. He had less than two months to achieve his goal. But to his credit, he knuckled down with a steely determination, from some secret reserve, deep within his core.

Daisy persuaded him to start the day with her favourite Danish breakfast. Full English platters were replaced by oatmeal, soaked in semi-skimmed milk, and garnished with walnuts, protein-rich chia seeds, dried cranberries and other berries. Bacon Man needed to cut back on carbohydrates that turned into fat. Oatmeal represented good carbs because it was unprocessed, slow burning, containing vital minerals and vitamins. Occasionally he'd ring the changes with smoked haddock, poached eggs, spinach, and homemade kimchi to improve his gut health.

Abstaining from carbs was a wrench. Sometimes, as we were cruising down through Henlow, I'd see him glancing wistfully at the fish and chip shop, and the Jaipur Palace. Under the new regime there were no more chips, no rice, no noodles, and at the bakery, the baskets containing white bread and pastries became zero tolerance exclusion zones. But fibre rich rye bread was acceptable because he had to keep his bowels in order, although thank heavens, I didn't have to clear up after him with a Bacon Man bag. There are limits to devotion. Not only that, but I don't want to throw a spoke in the wheel of evolution's progress, do we? Humans need to know their place.

Surprisingly I've developed a taste for rye bread. Bacon Man toasts a couple of slices for his mid-afternoon snack and opens a tin of pilchards, full of Omega-3 fats and a high protein, low-calorific way of combating heart disease.

"A taste of my childhood," he always says.

Or a jar of dill pickled herring for a taste of Daisy's childhood with the same physiological benefits. Then I get to do a pre-wash.

This may upset some of the more sensitive among you. But we've got into this routine whereby I lick the plates clean before they're subjected to programme three of the dishwasher. This has two benefits. I get a fishy amuse-bouche and the kitchen sink doesn't get bunged up.

I know some of you will be disgusted. But it's perfectly hygienic. Yes, I know my quality time is spent sniffing other dogs' butts, however, I assure you, I'm not transmitting germs to the crockery and cutlery. All the bacteria get killed by the hot water. Stop being so squeamish. You do understand science, don't you? Now where was I?

Oh yes. I've been doing my bit to make Bacon Man's exercise regime tickety-boo, to coin a Maurice Oxfordism. I've perfected a technique to get his attention when it's time for our constitutionals. I nudge him in some soft tissue, which basically means any part of his body. It's akin to a head butt, but not the full Glasgow kiss. So, I've been walking him a lot. Yes, you read that correctly. I've been exercising him. Not the other way round.

We've been stepping it up gradually, moving at a faster pace and going further. We probably cover about five miles during the main post-breakfast effort. Daisy comes along too to ensure there's no slacking. I'm starting to see the results. He's less breathless than he used to be, and in a mild breeze and favourable light, I can just discern where his jawline is buried.

The only disruption to our routine takes place when Bacon Man has to earn a crust. Sometimes it means giving guest lectures at journalism colleges. Those gigs don't pay particularly well, and some of the students make him despair.

"They're so bloody sensitive," he complained to Daisy after one jaunt up country.

"They just hide behind their screens. Many of them don't

even dare talk to people. They'll only communicate by email or text. Do you know what, Daisy? We should rent out Bjørn as an anxiety dog to keep them company when they leave the safety of their screens."

What a cheek. For a start, Bacon Man spends half his life in front of a screen. And secondly, I already earn my keep by bringing happiness into the Somerville residence.

In monetary terms, Bacon Man prefers doing corporate crisis management. Bigger crises mean better bank deposits. Although this line of work plays havoc with his conscience, he needs to keep me in organic dog treats, chewy sticks, and other luxuries.

But I seriously worry just how much longer he can keep on working. Karma had come hammering on his door again, inflicting more penalties for the visceral fat encasing his organs.

A routine visit to the senior nurse at the surgery in Henlow ended with Bacon Man being compelled to add another blister pack of tablets to his rapidly growing prescription drug stash.

I wasn't present, but the story came out as Daisy unboxed a blood pressure testing kit. Bacon Man had gone for an annual type two diabetes health check. The nurse had checked the blood circulation in his feet to ensure they weren't in danger of falling off or requiring amputation. I'm not exaggerating. According to the latest statistics, British surgeons were more productive than the axe men in Riyadh's Chop Chop Square, amputating a diabetic's toe, foot or leg, every hour in Britain. Sometimes all three. Extremities are most at risk from the disease, but being good sports, the Brits draw the line at heads. Unlike the Saudis.

Using a pin, the nurse pricked several places on the soles of Bacon Man's feet. He reacted positively to each sensation, which meant the nerves were alive.

Bacon Man was reassured to learn that, for the foreseeable future, he could dance the full Hokey Cokey with legs that didn't end at the ankles. In fact, his luck was rather Hokey Cokey these days, in that it was in, out, in, out, and shaken all about. Which was more than you could say for his sex life.

The nurse wouldn't let him leave the surgery until he'd been seen by the duty doctor because his blood pressure was in the danger zone.

"You were lucky to get away with medication," said Daisy. "I thought you were going to be admitted to hospital."

Given Bacon Man's ostrich tendencies with his health, it was fortunate that Daisy had accompanied him to the appointment, otherwise he might have glossed over the latest diagnosis, or even defied it.

For the first time since I took over the house, Bacon Man's nonchalance had been replaced by genuine fear. There was no self-deprecating joke. His veneer of flippancy vanished. His face seemed redder than ever. I'd never seen Bacon Man looking so melancholy.

"I'm terrified of having a stroke," he told Daisy. "My dad had a whole series of mini strokes. He was locked inside his mind for five years or so. He couldn't speak. He became incontinent and incapable of doing anything for himself. It was such an awful, undignified end. I couldn't bear that happening to me."

"Hopefully the tablets will help bring down your blood pressure, and we've caught it in time," said Daisy.

I sat on the big sofa as Daisy unwrapped the kit. Bacon Man looked tense, so I climbed on to the smaller sofa next to him and lay my head on his lap.

"Look at Bjørn's face," said Daisy. "He's frowning and looks really worried. He senses that you're anxious."

"Stop fussing."

"Now relax, breathe deeply, uncross your legs and don't move or talk."

"Anything else, nurse?"

"I wasn't put on this planet to be your nurse."

"What about our marriage vows? You know, the one about 'in sickness and health?'"

"I got the wrong end of that deal, didn't I? Now stop talking, otherwise we won't get a proper reading."

Bacon Man did as he was told, and gently stroked the furrow on my forehead. I registered his breathing easing even as Daisy slid the cuff over his left arm. I could hear his arteries protesting as the tourniquet filled with air and tightened, but the chambers in his heart seemed to be straining less than I feared. Yes, my hearing is that good.

When the machine switched itself off and the tourniquet deflated, Daisy exclaimed,

"Wow, that's so much lower than the numbers in the surgery. It's a hundred and seventy-three over eighty-six. It's still pretty bad, but the medication must be working and then there's the Bjørn effect."

Daisy's right. According to the latest science, stroking a

dog lowers your blood pressure by up to ten percent. Bacon Man needed me more than ever. We looked at each other for a moment. He smiled gratefully and said thank you with his eyes. That was progress. He was communicating like a dog. I really fancied a tummy scrub but realised this moment wasn't all about me, so I held my position while Daisy went through the process a second time.

"That's amazing," she said. "A hundred and fifty nine over eighty five. It's still too high. We're aiming for a hundred and thirty over eighty. We'll get there. You just have to keep on doing what you're doing. Eating sensibly, losing weight, and stepping up the exercise."

We repeated the routine twice a day for the rest of the week and Daisy recorded the numbers to give the doctor the data he needed to assess Bacon Man's condition. After seven days, his blood pressure had consistently improved, although it was still some distance from the healthy range.

A couple of days later, I was walking through the pedestrian gate of Galahad Island on the lead with Daisy when I caught Bacon Man's scent about two to three hundred yards away. He was swiftly closing on us. I could tell he wasn't driving because I could see the car parked in its usual spot. The main gates creaked open, and Bacon Man appeared astride a sturdy bicycle with fat tyres and a motorised crank. He was clad head to toe in black Lycra and his head was encased in a lime green helmet. Imagine the Michelin Man as a Liquorice Allsort.

"How much was it?" asked Daisy.

"Just over three grand," replied Bacon Man.

"More expensive than Bjørn."

"Aren't you forgetting that we paid five thousand for him?"

"And whose fault was that?"

"Fair point, Daisy."

I wondered whether Bacon Man would be too enamoured with his electric bike to come walking. But no. Our morning yomp along the river path was now as much a part of his routine cleaning his teeth. Whenever possible, he rode his bike in the afternoons, and the rides seemed to take longer as the days became shorter and darker. Although Daisy encouraged Bacon Man to cycle, she couldn't disguise her Danish pessimism. She fretted that he would either have an accident on the slick country lanes or that his body would give up on him, so the house was always tense until he walked through the door looking pleased with himself.

He was also pleased to see me. I'm not being boastful, but I think I've earned my stripes as his friend. I've now assumed another responsibility, which I will faithfully undertake with all the powers at my disposal. I'm his healer. Maybe this is why I'm here.

CHAPTER TWENTY TWO
MIRROR, MIRROR

THE DOORBELL RINGS. I CAN'T see who's outside. But I know the visitors are two young women. One is trying to hide her anxiety behind a chimera of over-excitement. The other is completely terrified. Their secretions are so powerful that the scent has rocketed through wood, brick and mortar straight into my olfactory bulb. If you've been paying attention, you'll remember what that is.

Bacon Man opens the door and tries to hold me back. But I'm not having it. Here are two new friends and I'm obliged to make them feel welcome to my home. So, I leap up at the tall blonde woman first.

"Oh you're much more beautiful than your photographs aren't you?" she yells through my big wet kiss.

What impeccable taste she has. This must be Sarah, Bacon Man and Daisy's daughter. She's taller than she appears in her photographs, if just a tad shorter than Daisy. I land back down on all fours and this time I spring up even higher towards the chin of the other woman, the one who's terrified. I want to prove that I'm amazeballs friendly and she's got absolutely nothing to worry about. Her screams are loud enough to be heard in Henlow High Street, two miles up the river.

"It's OK, Mira," says Sarah, "He's harmless. I promise you. There's no need to be frightened."

"Bjørn, get down, now."

Uh oh. Bacon Man just called me Bjørn. I'm in trouble. Not only that. Mira's scream elicits an immediate response from the neighbours. I can hear several of them individually complaining about more drama at the Somerville residence. Some things never change. I also pick up the familiar sound of curtains twitching.

"I'm so sorry about the dog. Is it Mira? I thought your name was Mirembe," inquires Bacon Man gently.

"No, Mr. Somerville. I should apologise to you. I'm sorry for my reaction. But I'm really scared of dogs. We don't keep them as pets in Uganda."

I really want to give the woman called Mira another kiss. But Bacon Man grabs the fur behind my head to hold me back. I'm shocked. It hurts. By Bacon Man's standards that almost counts as violence. I know my mama, I mean my dog mama, used to pick me up by the scruff of the neck, but that was different. Although the pain swiftly disappears, my pride is hurt, and I jump up at Bacon Man to seek reassurance.

"Get down, Bjørn, for heaven's sake."

He's called me Bjørn twice in less than a minute. That's not good.

"There's no need to apologise," says Bacon Man. "And there's no need to be so formal. It's not Mr. Somerville. It's Morgan."

"Actually, Dad, Mum said you've got a new name these days. Bacon Man."

"That's true. I can't remember the last time your Mum called me by my first name."

"Well, let's get the introductions properly out of the way," says Sarah. "Mira, this is my Dad. And wow, there's a lot less of you. Well done."

"Thanks, Sarah. And you can thank Bubsie for that. He's been a great personal trainer."

Phew. He's calling me Bubsie. I'm back in Bacon Man's good books.

"Who's Bubsie?" asks Mira.

"The dog," says Sarah.

"I thought his name was Bjørn," replies Mira.

"It is, but that's the English for you," says Sarah with a smile. "They never use your proper name. You don't belong unless you have a nickname. Dad, this is Mirembe, but I call her Mira."

"You mean like, mirror, mirror on the wall?"

"Yes Dad."

"Not Myra Myra, as in Myra Hindley?"

"Dad, that's so not funny."

"Who's Myra Hindley?" asks Mira.

"A notorious child killer." replies Sarah. "She died in prison a few years back. I told you that my father has a warped sense of humour. If he's started this early, it's going to be a long Christmas. Stop it, Dad."

"Typical. I'm in doo doo with my daughter already. So, do you mind if we call you Mira?"

"That's fine by me," says Mira. "It's a lot easier than my proper name."

"Mirembe means peace, Dad,"

"Actually, Sarah, Mira also sounds like peace in more than one language. In Bosnia, the word for peace is mir. Mira. It's a nice name. I like it."

Both women smile.

"So what shall I call you, Mr. Somerville?" asks Mira.

"Call him Bacon Man," says Sarah. "I think it suits him. But call my Mum Astrid. Only my dad calls her Daisy. Come to think of it, Dad. Why do you call her Daisy?"

"Well her proper name is Daisy Drop Drawers. Because she dropped them on our second date."

"Daaaaad. Way too much information!"

"I'm going to help your mother bring in your suitcases before I get into any more trouble."

"Oh, thanks, Dad. We've only got one suitcase. Mum said she could manage."

I look at Bacon Man and I can tell that his brain has just ingested some information it can't compute. He scurries off towards the car and Daisy.

"What was that joke about the child killer?" asks Mira.

"One thing you have to learn about the English is that they joke around all the time, especially if they like you. The fact that Dad made that joke means he likes you. What you have to watch for is the moment the English stop joking and no longer take the piss. That's when you know they don't like you. In fact, when they talk normally to you, it means they can't stand you. Does that make sense?"

"No, not at all. It sounds like the English are two faced."

"They can be. But Dad is very straight forward. He lets people know when he doesn't like them."

Although the door is closed, I can hear Bacon Man outside speaking *sotto voce* to Daisy.

"I'll take the suitcase. Strange, isn't it, Daisy?"

"What's strange?"

"They've only got one suitcase. But I suppose it means there's less to haul around at the station."

"It's not strange."

"Next you'll be telling me they're sharing a bed."

"Well, they are."

"But we've got four bedrooms. You don't mean….?"

"Mean what?"

"That they're sharing a bed."

"That's exactly what I mean?"

"I thought they were just friends."

Even though I'm inside the house, I can hear the cogs in Bacon Man's brain are finally joining the dots.

"They are. Special friends."

"Are you saying that Sarah is gay, or whatever the correct initial is these days?"

"What do you think?"

I can just discern the sound of Bacon Man's mouth making goldfish impressions. It's times like these when I pay thanks to the Lord Dog for giving my canine brothers, sisters and me extra powerful hearing. I get so much more of an overview of what's really happening. I see the full picture. You poor humans. You don't have a clue what's really going on. You just have to guess. And that's why you make so many bad decisions."

Bacon Man is lost for words. But then he rallies.

"I just thought she was too busy with work in Paris to have a steady boyfriend. Are you sure she's gay? She had loads of boyfriends when she was younger."

"I know, but I think that was just a phase. For the past five years I'm quite certain she's only had girlfriends."

"Why didn't you tell me?"

"I wasn't a hundred percent sure and we never really talked about it. But the main reason I didn't tell you was that it's up to Sarah to decide what she wants to share with us. She only confided in me a few months ago, when Mira moved into her flat and she specifically told me to keep it to myself for the time being."

"You're not going to cause a scene are you, *Skatter*? Mira is really sweet, and this is a big deal for her."

"What do you take me for? Of course, I'm not going to create a scene. If Sarah's happy, then I'm happy. I just don't want her to be hurt, that's all. But I do object to being the last one to know, as usual."

"Don't blame me. You just aren't as observant as you think you are."

"So what about Alex? Are there any secrets that I'm missing out on, Daisy? Is he identifying as an octopus or a unicorn? Nothing would surprise me."

"That's exactly the kind of unhelpful remark we don't need right now."

"As long as he hasn't tattooed his face. That would be beyond the pale."

"No, there are no secrets as far as I know. And yes, I can't bear those kinds of tattoos either. Come on, let's go inside and make them welcome. I just want this to be a nice, calm, family Christmas."

"Well, it's going to be a pretty lean one for me," says Bacon Man.

"And who's fault was that? But you can still cook up a storm. I know it's your way of showing love."

I never thought of it like that before. But of course, it's true. Bacon Man is showing his love for me when he cooks. How wonderful. I think I adore him more than ever, if that's possible.

Sarah and Mira are out on the balcony, holding hands and admiring the view. I sense that Bacon Man is not deliriously happy but he's trying to put a brave face on this relationship. I'm also rather puzzled. I've never come across a human being who didn't instantly think that I was the most glorious creature on earth, and I'm not too sure how to try to win Mira round. It took time to get Bacon Man on side, so maybe I should be patient with Mira and not be too pushy. It's not in my nature. But I'll try.

Bacon Man comes on to the balcony.

"Can I just ask a simple question please?"

"Of course you can, Dad. Fire away."

"What are your preferences?"

"What on earth do you mean, Dad?"

"I mean in terms of food, of course. The supermarkets are

going to close this evening and won't reopen till Boxing Day, so I want to make sure I've got enough to cater for you. You're not vegan now are you, Sarah? Last time you were home for Christmas, I seem to remember you eating duck and turkey."

"No, Dad, I'm not vegan. But I have changed my diet. Like Mira, I'm now a pescatarian slash vegetarian."

Mmm, somebody had better explain that pesky thing to me. I want to know what kind of scraps I might be able to scrounge. I'm certainly not interested in vegetarian stuff.

"Let me take a stab at that," says Bacon Man. "Does it mean you supplement a vegetarian diet with fish?"

"Well done, Dad. You didn't need to phone a friend. That is, if you've got any left."

"I'll ignore that, Sarah. Just so I've got it absolutely right, the term fish doesn't extend to any waterborne creature, does it?"

I'm looking at Mira. My finely tuned instincts detect that this exchange is putting her on edge. I'm sure that historically, Bacon Man has always had these types of droll conversations with his daughter. But times have changed. Mira is not in on their private joke, and is wearing a poker face, nevertheless, Bacon Man presses on.

"So, I'd be right in assuming that duck is no longer acceptable?"

"That's right, Dad. No duck."

"Are you sure?"

"Absolutely."

"You won't object if your mother, brother and I have duck tomorrow night will you?"

"Of course not, as long as anything we eat is not tainted by duck."

"Fine, I can live with that. I promise not to put any duck feathers in your salmon en croute." says Bacon Man. "What if I fancied going all Henry the eighth on you and cooked roast swan?"

"Even though you could fit into Henry the eighth's tights, that's never going to happen."

It's fine by me, Bacon Man. As long as it's the gobby swan in the creek. You can go down there and throttle him right now if you want, and I'll happily supplement my kibble with roast swan for the next few months.

"Final question and I'll leave you in peace," says Bacon Man. "Are eggs, cheese and shellfish allowed?"

"Absolutely."

"Thank goodness for that. We got there in the end."

Yes, I thought he was never going to stop.

"I'm just going to shoot out and get some supplies. I'll be gone for about an hour or so."

I look up hopefully at Bacon Man. I fancy going cruising. It'll give me a chance to pose in the back window and get some more fans. Bacon Man looks me in the eye and reads me straight away. His golden retriever skills are improving all the time.

"No, Bjørn. You're not coming. You stay here with Sarah and Mira. See you later."

The minute Bacon Man is out the door, Daisy starts rustling up cups and saucers and makes tea. I saunter into the living room and take pole position on the big sofa. Sure enough, there's the rattle of biscuit tin. Daisy keeps it hidden on top of a kitchen cabinet beyond Bacon Man's reach and only brings it out when she's alone. When it comes to sharing, she's certainly not as generous as Bacon Man, although she usually capitulates after I've deposited sufficient drool on her clothes or the sofa.

"Mum," says Sarah as she sits down on *my* sofa. "While Mira is upstairs unpacking, I want to tell you something".

I scamper over to the other sofa and put my head on Daisy's Sepp Pionteks. She pours tea and passes a plate of Danish ginger snaps that she baked recently, while Bacon Man was out on his bike. She obviously learned guerrilla cooking from him. Oh goodie. Sarah puts the plate down without taking any biscuits. More for me.

"Mira and I are engaged."

I'm puzzled. I've heard the expression engaged before but only in relation to the toilet. They can't both be in the bathroom because Sarah is here in the sitting room. Then I realise the word has another significance. Lying with my head on Daisy's thighs I feel the happy hormone dopamine surging through her body, like a sledgehammer of joy.

"*Søde lille skat.* Sarah, that's wonderful."

Allow me to translate. Yes, I'm bi-lingual. Are you surprised? I hope not. Daisy called Sarah a precious little sweetheart. It's like the nickname she gives Bacon Man. Just not as working class. Daisy often uses Danish words when she wants to express herself more accurately. When I was a puppy, she used to call me *søde*. Literally, it translates as sweet, although in Danish, it's ripe with more affection and without the slightly ironic connotations it sometimes has in English.

Daisy has tears in her eyes as she leans across the table and hugs her daughter.

"Thank you, Mum. She's the one. I am so happy."

"How about her family? Have you told them?"

"Good God no. As you know, Mira had to flee Uganda because she's gay. Her father is an ultra-conservative Christian minister. He was talking about performing an exorcism when she made a run for it."

"God, how awful. Thank goodness she got away."

"That's how I feel. She's so adorable, Mum. She's kind and sweet and smart. I really hope you'll love her like another daughter."

"I'm sure I will, *lille skat.*"

"I know it sounds like we're in a hurry, but we're hoping to get married in London this summer."

"If you're so much in love and you're sure she's the one, then why wait? Your father and I didn't. I don't believe in never-ending engagements. I'm so happy for you, Sarah. But what on earth are you going to do about her parents?"

"They'll be invited out of courtesy, but they've disowned her and Mira doesn't expect them to come. It's really painful for her, because she still loves them, despite the way they treated her."

"I can understand that," says Daisy, sipping green tea and munching a ginger snap.

I look Daisy in the eye, sit right in front of her and put my right paw in her lap.

"Oh, Mum, he's so lovely. What a great dog."

I snaffle the biscuit and crumbs go flying.

"We're so glad we got him."

Yes Sarah, and your Mum paid five thousand pounds for me, that's how much she wanted me. I'm worth it and I'm worth another biscuit. Go on. Be a sport. But she's not paying attention.

"Anyway, Mum, I wanted to talk to you alone because I am a bit worried about how dad will react."

"Crack a bad joke as usual. That's how he always deals with situations outside his comfort zone."

"I don't want Mira to feel uncomfortable or awkward."

"Your dad would never intentionally do any such thing. He's far better than that."

"I know, but sometimes he just goes off on one."

"That's a bit unfair, Sarah."

"Maybe, but I was thinking if you could tell him, please?"

"Why? You shouldn't be timid about this, Sarah. If you truly believe in what you're doing, you must find the courage to tell him yourself. This is such brilliant news. He'll be fine. You'll see."

"But I'm afraid he's not going to react like you've done. Don't you think he would rather see me married to a bloke?"

"Of course, but then, if I'm being totally honest, so would I."

"That's a bit old fashioned isn't it?"

"Although society is much more liberal these days, it can still be difficult to be gay, get married and have a family."

"What do you mean, Mum?"

"You'll definitely face more obstacles and challenges than a heterosexual couple. You do realise that don't you?"

Sarah grabs one of Daisy's gingersnaps. I raise my head, look her in the eye and deliver an unequivocal message that sharing is permissible, desirable, and if I had my way, obligatory. But either she doesn't understand golden retriever, or she's just plain greedy and swallows it in one bite.

"Look Mum, I'm not frightened of Dad. Not at all, but I'm asking for Mira's sake. It's taken a lot of courage to come out as gay and to come here."

"I get that, Sarah and I hope she knows that this is also her home while she's here?"

"Thanks Mum, You know as well as anyone that meeting the in-laws for the first time is an ordeal, but imagine what it's like for someone like Mira with her background. She doesn't need Dad making bad jokes or saying something inappropriate."

I'm starting to bristle. I feel like Sarah is maligning Bacon Man. As his daughter, she ought to know how kind he is. Good old Daisy for putting her straight.

"I get that. But beneath that cynical exterior, your dad is really empathetic. Remember he covered the war in Bosnia from start to finish. He's probably seen more refugees than you have."

"I hadn't thought of it that way. But that war was ages ago."

"Yes I know. But, Sarah, it was his experiences in Bosnia that made him the man he is today. Not physically of course, but inside."

They both chuckle and Sarah gives me half of a biscuit.

Maybe the joke about Bacon Man's weight has given her paws for thought.

"Actually, Mum, I think Dad is one of those people who's doomed to be fat. He's got bad genes. I mean, look at grandma, rest her soul."

"And his sister. The one we don't talk about," says Daisy.

They both throw back their heads and roar hysterically.

"Dad once told me that he put on weight during the Ethiopian famine. And he was only there for three days."

Their laughter is contagious. I find myself smiling as well and direct a look at Sarah which says another biscuit wouldn't go amiss.

"Look Sarah, you've got nothing to worry about. Your dad's bottom line is and will always be that he just wants you and your brother to be happy. That's it. Nothing more. Nothing less. If Mira makes you happy, then he's as happy as I am."

"Are you sure Mum?"

"Absolutely, *lille skat*. As a parent, it really is that simple. If you and Mira have children, you'll know what I am talking about. Have you discussed having children?"

"Yes, we've talked about it but we haven't made any firm decisions."

"Well, you'd better be prepared to talk about children because your dad will have some questions. You know what he's like."

Yes. I know what he's like. But if Bacon Man and Daisy are happy. Then I'm happy too. I'd better get my head down. The next few days are going to be an emotional rollercoaster. I'm going to need my beauty sleep

CHAPTER TWENTY THREE
THE OTHER WOMAN

Christmas Eve is finally here. This time last year I was languishing at the breeder's farm. Back then, every day was Groundhog Day. But this is the first family Christmas I'll be celebrating. We're just waiting for the arrival of Alex, the underachiever. He's leaving it to the last minute and giving his mother kittens as a result. Metaphorically speaking of course. Apart from the bald cat, wherever that went, ours is strictly a dog household.

Boy, last night's supper was a doozy. That pescatarian vegetarianism in Bacon Man's culinary hands is pretty damn good. In dietary terms, the meal conformed to his new regime. There were no carbs. He went Greek and dished up something unpronounceably delicious as a starter. *Kolokothokeftedes*. Wow. I did it. Don't ask me to say it a second time. It's like a big meatball except the main ingredient is a shredded courgette. Served with homemade tzatziki, it slipped down a treat. Not as good as bacon. But then nothing is.

For the main course, he grilled sea bream, and dressed it with a mixture of olive oil and lemon juice. I had the fish heads.

All four of them. For the first time in my life, I felt like a cat. But please don't tell any of my dog chums. Bacon Man also made a Greek village salad. The less said about that the better. Tomatoes. Terrible things. I know I'm repeating myself. But I really can't stand them.

Conversation more than compensated for the veggies. It was fascinating. Mira told the story of her escape from Uganda and her rescue at sea. I've spent much of today trying to work out how someone as brave as Mira can fear me. As dogs go, I'm a pussy cat. Again, please keep that little nugget to yourself. I still identify as a golden retriever, whatever you may think.

While we're waiting for Alex to rock up, shall I give you the headlines of Mira's back story? You don't have a choice. I'm going to do it anyway.

Mira lived with her parents in a town called Entebbe on Lake Victoria. Almost all her fundamentalist Christian extended family turned against her when they discovered she was gay. Not very Christian behaviour if you ask me. Yes, I have watched *Songs of Praise* and that's because there was nothing else on at the time. What was it Jesus said?

"Let the children come to me, and do not hinder them, for the Kingdom of Heaven belongs to such as these."

That's pretty clear isn't it. JC was talking about every child. So how do fundamentalist Christian preachers twist his words, so they come out, if you'll pardon the expression, as saying, "Sorry disciples, I meant to say, 'Let the children come to me, all except the gay ones.'"

I have no truck with religion. It's the Chinese molasses of the masses. For the life of me, I can't understand why sophisticated twenty-first century humans beings still swallow myths written more than two thousand years ago. You might as well believe in the tooth fairy.

I'm sure people back then were gullible, but let's take this to its logical conclusion. If a so-called disciple had spun a yarn about an anti-Roman rabble rouser who was a golden retriever, then who knows, perhaps today I'd be living in luxury, somewhere "spiritual", pontificating to a quarter of the world's population about the "sin" of contraception and taking an unholy interest in choir boys.

I'm just going to wrap up this thought, not least because I'm starving and want my Christmas Eve supper. Yes, I know that's a religious festival and you're thinking I'm a hypocrite, but it's a feast day and golden retrievers can't survive on oxygen alone.

I think it's eminently possible that you humans have got religion all wrong. They didn't have spell check for speaking in tongues, when Moses supposedly came down from Mount Sinai. He thought he was carrying the Ten Commandments on iPads, which you and I know as tablets. Maybe the key word in those alleged Commandments wasn't God, but Dog. It's an easy mistake to make.

In which case, the First Commandment should read, "I am the Lord thy Dog. Thou shalt have no other Dogs but Me."

And the Second translates as, "Thou shalt not take the name of the Lord thy Dog in vain."

Given that some communities in Britain are keen to reinstate blasphemy as a crime, I'm clearly on contentious ground. But as free expression is a pillar of our democracy, I'm going to pursue this theme without fear or favour. According to the Bible, and some other books it's safer not to mention, the world was created in six days. To those who believe the claim in Genesis that God pulled almost a week of all nighters six millenia ago, I have one word to say.

Triceratops.

Please give me the creationists' theory on dinosaurs, wiped out sixty-five million years ago. On second thoughts, don't. It's crazy that so many wars have been carried out in the name of religion, and "Prophets," people who were little more than storytellers when time is supposed to have begun. Or as we call them, influencers.

I suppose it's possible they might have been employed by the mainstream media three thousand years before Christ. By then, of course, fact-checking had come on leaps and bounds since Adam took a chunk out of a Golden Delicious in the Garden of Eden. Not. As they were fond of carrying tablets, these influencers might possibly have been tabloid journalists. How can you judge? It's impossible to fact check.

Who can tell whether Abraham worked for the ancient equivalent of *The Sun,* or *The Wall Street Journal?* Or maybe he just vented in the desert to gossips around an oasis. And like all gossips, they embellished the story with Chinese whispers. Before Abraham croaked three thousand years ago, his big scoop was predicting that Israel was the Promised Land.

I'd call that an early example of Gotcha journalism. Why? Gotcha a country didn't he?

Let me be clear. I'm not an atheist. But I am a fundamentalist agnostic and that's because I can't say with one hundred percent certainty that God, or the Lord Dog, doesn't exist. But if he/she/it is real, then for heaven's sake, prove it. Until then, I put my faith in science.

Now, let's get back to Mira's odyssey, an epic true story of courage and resilience. Mira's only ally was her brother, who worked as a deckhand on a rust bucket that carried all manner of cargoes between Uganda and Kenya. On the night before her father was due to conduct the exorcism, her brother helped her stow away on a ship heading for the Kenyan port of Kisumu.

Even then she wasn't completely safe, because in Kenya, there's widespread discrimination against people who aren't straight. Mira had to keep moving. From Kisumu, she made her way to the Sudanese capital Khartoum, where she sought out people smugglers whose underlings led would-be asylum seekers across the Sahara Desert to the Libyan coast.

Mira was in tears as she described how some of her companions collapsed and died in the desert. But somehow, she survived. She spent three months locked up and effectively held hostage in Libya.

"Mira doesn't need to go into details," said Sarah. "But the guards were brutal. You can guess what happened. Mira would still be in that hellhole if her brother hadn't managed to raise three thousand dollars and get it to the traffickers. He's a real hero."

Bacon Man and Daisy both winced as Mira sipped a glass of wine and continued recounting her ordeal.

Eventually, Mira and about fifty other refugees and economic migrants were taken to a beach in the middle of the night. The smugglers pulled out pistols and ordered them to climb into a flimsy rubber dinghy, powered by a weak outboard engine and pointed them in the direction of Italy.

After about three hours, a hole developed in the bottom of the raft and the engine cut out. There was panic and the people tried to get away from the leak, even though they had nowhere to go. The weaker ones, mostly women, were trampled underfoot. In all, twenty-two women and one man drowned in just a few inches of water. Some of the survivors were burned by a dangerous mix of leaking diesel and salt water.

They were saved by the Aurora, a rescue ship belonging to Braving the Waves, a pan-European humanitarian charity. Sarah is employed in their Paris headquarters as a press officer and fundraiser.

When the Aurora's rescue teams reached the dinghy, it was still floating. Just. The survivors were all looking outwards, desperately avoiding the bodies floating face down behind them.

"I'm haunted by the memory of standing on one of the corpses as I climbed out of the raft to get to the rescuers' boat," said Mira.

"I tried to step on the edge of the raft but slipped. If I close my eyes, I can remember how the body felt and moved beneath the soles of my foot as I was helped out. I have nightmares about it."

Tears were flowing down Daisy's cheeks by this point. Bacon Man was equally captivated. He managed to listen without cracking a single joke. Thank goodness.

Sarah then picked up the story. After the drama of the rescue had receded, Mira recounted her ordeal to specialists from Braving the Waves who were gathering information to support asylum claims.

"They were hugely impressed with Mira's intelligence and the forensic detail she provided about the trafficking operation from Khartoum to Libya," said Sarah.

The clarity of Mira's testimony wasn't surprising because she was on the verge of graduating with a law degree when she was forced to flee Entebbe.

Braving the Waves was always looking for new talent and offered her a position at the charity's headquarters in Paris as a human rights researcher. Having the promise of a job helped fast track her asylum claim. Within two months of stepping foot on European soil, Mira was living in Paris.

"And that's where we met," said Sarah, beaming at Mira.

Right now, they're at home with Bacon Man, who, I assume, is in the kitchen juggling the various dietary requirements for this evening's Danish Christmas supper. I'm in the pick-up zone of Henlow railway station, sitting in the back seat of the Mercedes with Daisy at the wheel. She's anxious. The last train from London was cancelled. Alex is late and he's not responding to her text messages.

"Oh, there he is. At last," exclaims Daisy.

I stick my head out the window and spot Alex immediately. Tall, gawky, and looking for all the world as if he doesn't want to be seen. He's hiding his face beneath a baseball cap, beneath a hoodie, and a scarf is covering the bottom half of his face. Only his eyes and nose are visible. He's dragging a huge holdall behind him and struggling to manoeuvre it. What's he got in there? A corpse?

"Where have you been, Alex? I've been frantic. Why haven't you answered my texts?"

"Merry Christmas to you too, Mum," says Alex.

His tone is offhand. I can tell he's here under sufferance. He'd rather be anywhere else in the world than home right now.

"Sorry about the texts. But my phone died."

"Don't you have a charger?"

"I forgot it."

"Never mind. We've got spares at home. How long are you staying for? That bag is massive. It looks like you've got enough gear for a week or more."

"Oh, that's my laundry. I'm leaving on Boxing Day."

"Merry Christmas to you too," says Daisy.

She sounds disappointed.

"I was rather hoping I could avoid the washing machine for the next few days. Obviously not."

"Don't worry, Mum, I'll do my own laundry."

"Oh really? Anyway, aren't you going to say hello to Bjørn? Don't you think he's grown?"

Yes, Alex hasn't even acknowledged me. I have to say I'm disappointed by his indifference. Of our three houseguests, only Sarah has shown any enthusiasm towards me. One out of three, that's a terrible hit rate. It's going to be a tough few days if it continues like this.

New restrictions are already in place after Sarah's intervention last night. There's to be no more pre-washing until they've left.

"Oh that's disgusting," Sarah declared as I licked the fish plates before they went in the dishwasher.

"Please don't do it in front of Mira. It'll completely turn her stomach and put her off dogs even more."

"OK, I hear what you're saying," said Bacon Man.

What a blow. I thought Bacon Man was made of sterner stuff. But I guessed that Sarah was still Daddy's little princess, and he'd do anything to please her.

"I promise Bjørn won't be allowed to do pre-washes for the duration of your stay."

Then Bacon Man caught my eye, winked and grinned. I know what that means. He'll just close the kitchen door and we'll carry on as normal. Good old Bacon Man. He's the king of secret eating. Or maybe he's not anymore. Let's wait and see.

At last, Alex warms up as we head down the country lanes towards home. I give him no option. I nudge him in the neck. He turns round and pats me.

"Yes, Mum, he has grown. He's really handsome."

That's better. You're absolutely right, Alex. I am handsome. Then, just as we enter the gates of Galahad Island, Alex turns to Daisy.

"Mum, can you lend me five hundred pounds please?"

"What for? Have you lost your job?"

"That's what it cost me to come home for Christmas. I persuaded someone to take over my shifts for Christmas Eve and Christmas Day. You don't know how difficult that was. And the guy said he'd do it for seven hundred and fifty. But I got him down to five hundred."

"That's robbery, Alex."

"It's real life, Mum. Almost everyone in my age range is trying to make ends meet the best way they can. You wanted me to come back for Christmas. So, I did what I had to do."

"Your father is going to go nuts if he finds out. And he will find out."

"Well, I don't want you to get into trouble, Mum."

"I'm never in trouble for long. He'll get over it. He always does. Anyway, I'm glad you're here. Your dad's probably busy in the kitchen. If he is, I'll transfer the money straight away, and with any luck he'll be too busy to notice when a bank notification flashes up on his phone."

Daisy opens my door and I'm my usual helpful self as I bounce out. I pick up the end of my lead and carry it to the house while she and Alex follow behind me.

Bacon Man opens the door. He's red in the face and he's clutching a big wine glass that's half empty. He seems to be swaying slightly.

"Hello, Alex. Late as usual. What's the excuse this time?"

Uh oh, Bacon Man seems to be in a provocative mood.

"Blimey, look at that bag. It's massive. How long are you planning on staying for? A month?"

"No, Dad. It contains my laundry."

"It's Christmas for Christ's sake. Do you expect your mother to clean your skivvies while you're getting hammered?"

"Well, if that's the way you feel about it, Dad, I can always turn around straight away and get a train back home."

"You can't actually, because the trains stop running across the country in about half an hour's time."

"Well I'll take a taxi then."

"Oh yes, and who'll pay for that? The bank of Mum and Dad as usual?"

"Stop it you two," says Daisy.

It's an order not a plea.

"What are you doing, drinking?" she demands.

"It's Christmas. I fancy a drink. I always have one when I cook Christmas dinner."

"But you've been off the booze for nearly three months now. You've been doing so well."

"Well I decided to treat myself. I deserve it."

"How many glasses have you had?"

"Two. That's all."

"But they've been big ones, haven't they. I can tell. Are you pissed already?"

There's some real needle in the air. My instincts tell me a domestic storm is brewing.

"Of course, I'm not pissed," says Bacon Man. "But I've got a nice little glow going."

"Hadn't you better go back to the kitchen, and slow down with the drinking, please. After being dry for so long, your system isn't used to it."

I follow Bacon Man into the kitchen where he opens the dual ovens to check on the progress of the main courses. Satisfied, he tops up his glass with a generous splodge of Malbec. He's on a roll. We'd better take cover.

I head into the sitting room. Daisy is on her mobile, tapping the screen as fast as she can. She stops as Bacon Man heads towards her, clutching a fat glass full of golden bubbles.

"Prosecco, Daisy. Sorry we haven't got any ice. I completely forgot to buy some. But it's been in the freezer, so it's nice and cold."

"I think I'm going to need this," says Daisy.

Having dumped his bag upstairs, Alex walks into the room.

"If we're drinking, I'll have a beer."

"They're in the fridge," says Bacon Man. "And please use a glass. I can't bear it when you neck it from the bottle."

"Stop being an old fart, Dad."

Sarah and Mira skip into the sitting room looking a little flushed.

"We'll have some bubbles, Dad," says Sarah.

"I'm in the mood to celebrate. Aren't you, Mira?"

"I'll be happy with just water thank you," replies Mira.

"If I was you, Mira," says Alex, "I'd have a drink. I can see which way this evening is going to go, and it'd be better not to be sober."

Maybe there's some dog in that boy Alex. He's got good instincts. I sense trouble too. I have to say, Alex's beer looks enticing. I wonder if I can persuade him to let me try it.

Bacon Man's cooking is reaching a crescendo and he asks for a hand to make sure all the dishes are served hot and on time. Sarah, Mira, and Daisy carry steaming bowls of vegetables and sauces into the dining room. Alex disappears into the sitting room, and I hear the television being switched on.

"Right, can everyone take a seat, and I'll serve the main courses," says Bacon Man.

He's in his element, trying to be the perfect host. The aromas emanating from the kitchen are mouthwatering. Who'd have thought those chubby chatty little critters with green heads could smell so wonderful when cooked in their own fat.

A strange notion just entered my mind. I wonder what Bacon Man would smell like if cooked in his own fat. Would he smell as good as a duck? Oh dear, I wish I hadn't had that thought. I can't unthink it. Or unsee that image. It's wrecking my appetite. That's got to be a first. I must distract myself. I just hope the meat eaters round here save a few slithers of duck for me. Thank goodness Sarah and Mira are having a fish dish. There'll be more duck for me. That's it. Think duck. Duck. Duck. Duck.

Bacon Man serves Mira and Sarah first, with a pink fish cooked in what looks like a golden basket.

"Salmon en croute," declares Bacon Man. "It's not a traditional Danish Christmas dish, but perhaps it will be from now on."

Personally, I'd prefer steak en croute from Greggs, although I think that delicacy is marketed under a different name. What is it? Steak bake?

However, now that Bacon Man is counting the calories, pastry is firmly off the menu.

He returns to the kitchen and brings out three plates of roast duck meat. I feel two strands of drool form on either side of my mouth, that just keep on going and hit the floor in seconds. I've never salivated so prodigiously. Well, perhaps I did when I got a whiff of the parson's poodle the other week.

"Please tuck in," says Bacon Man. "Mira, just help yourself to whatever you like. Everything on the table is vegetarian, except for this sauce, which goes with the duck."

"Let's have a toast before we eat," says Daisy.

"To Sarah and Mira!"

I notice that neither Daisy nor Bacon Man take polite sips. They're knocking the wine back as if Prohibition is just hours away.

"Where are the caramelized potatoes?" asks Alex. "We always have those with duck at Danish Christmas."

"I didn't do any," says Bacon Man. I'm trying to cut back on sugar, and also those potatoes don't really go with the salmon. That's why I've done new potatoes with butter and parsley."

"It's not the same," complains Alex. "I need another beer. Anyone else want one?"

Yes, I could murder one. Could you pour it into my dog bowl please?

"So, Mira, would I be right in thinking that you celebrate Christmas in Uganda?" asks Daisy.

"Yes, it's a very important festival for us."

"What sort of food would you have to celebrate?"

"It varies. It could be chicken, beef, or goat. I found goat meat hard to stomach and that's what led me to becoming a vegetarian. But to answer your question, a Ugandan favourite is a dish called Luwombo."

"Do you know what the recipe is?" asks Bacon Man.

It's early days in his attempt to lose weight and that question is a sign he's desperate to keep the diet interesting.

"I'm not too sure about all the spices that go into it," says Mira, "But essentially it's made by wrapping meat, fish or chicken in banana leaves with groundnut paste, which is like peanut butter. The dish takes a while to prepare, and it has to steam for about an hour and a half. But it's delicious."

I'll take Mira's word for it. I'm not so sure. I've tried bananas and they came straight back up. The only time I eat leaves is when I'm constipated. Just so you know, I'm regular most of the time. Thanks for asking.

"And we serve Luwombo with Matooke," says Mira.

"What's Matooke?" asks Daisy.

"It's like a green banana that's steamed and then mashed."

Sounds like hot guacamole without the interesting bits. I could think of nothing worse.

"I've never really tried African food," says Daisy.

"Really, Daisy?" asks Bacon Man, just as she puts a slither of duck leg in her mouth.

"You told me you'd eaten African before, actually on more than one occasion."

Daisy's face contorts into a shape I haven't seen before. Simultaneously, she's swallowing, grinning and frowning at Bacon Man.

"Whoops, that nearly went down the wrong way," she says.

"That's what you said at the time, Daisy," smirks Bacon Man.

"Stop it, *Skatter*. Now Mira, if we found the ingredients for the Matooke, perhaps you could cook it for us, next time you visit."

"Alright. I'd love to," says Mira.

"I don't mind a little competition in the kitchen," says Bacon Man.

As Bacon Man finishes the sentence, his phone vibrates. I

peer up at him and can tell instantly that he's about to blow a gasket. He reaches for the red wine bottle, pours himself a big one and takes a hefty slug. He looks intently at Daisy and then at Alex. I can tell that he's debating whether to say something. He also looks as though he's imagining an argument with someone.

Razor sharp as ever, Daisy notices that his demeanour has changed. She pours more Prosecco and matches Bacon Man by knocking back half a glass in one go. They're now staring at each other. I've seen this type of interaction before. Although they're not saying anything, it's potentially explosive. She's sending him a visual message which translates as, 'don't you dare say anything'. He's responding with a look that says, 'don't tell me what to do' A fuse has been lit. The only question is whether Bacon Man will have the common sense to restrain himself. Self-restraint is not one of his virtues. Uh oh, here he goes.

"Why have you just given Alex five hundred pounds, Daisy?"

"What are you doing with your phone at the table?" asks Daisy.

She shoots Bacon Man a look that says, 'quit while you're ahead.' He responds with a scowl that says, 'don't tell me what to do.'

"I was using the timer to make sure the sour cherry sauce wasn't burned."

"It's far too early to put the cherry sauce on. We usually do that after we've finished the duck and removed the plates because we all need time to digest the main course."

Bacon Man and Daisy are talking in normal voices, but I can tell they're both getting angry. I can hear the blood vessels in their temples throbbing. Sarah and Alex exchange knowing glances. They know how it's going to play out.

"Dad," says Sarah. "This salmon is divine. How did you manage to get the pastry so light and fluffy?"

"Actually, Dad. It was the right call to stiff the caramelized potatoes this year. The new potatoes are so much better."

Blimey, the situation must be serious if Alex has broken his silence and joined the conversation.

"Well, Alex," says Bacon Man. "Why don't you go and buy yourself five hundred pounds worth of new potatoes? They should last you for about two years."

"Morgan," says Daisy in a low, calm, firm voice.

She might as well have used a megaphone because I know from experience that when Daisy uses Bacon Man's real name, it's about to go pear shaped.

"Very funny, Dad. You're always the first to pass judgement when you don't know what the fuck you're talking about."

"Don't you swear at me."

"Calm down, the pair of you."

Daisy is almost shouting.

"Yes, I gave Alex the money. He needed it to bribe someone to do his Christmas shifts. Without that money he wouldn't have been here."

"So why didn't you ask me, Daisy?"

The words in Bacon Man's sentences seemed to be joined together. I've never heard his speech that slurred before.

"Oh, so I have to ask you now before I spend money, do I?" she replies. "I thought we were equal partners."

"Doing it behind my back is downright deceitful."

Bacon Man has got a dangerous rhythm going. He's shouting then drinking. Shouting and drinking. Mira looks bewildered and Sarah decides she needs to step in.

"Dad, please. Can you and Mum discuss this later?"

"I wish we didn't have to discuss it at all, Sarah, but while we're on the subject of deceit, why was I the last one to know you are gay?"

Sarah gasps, Mira drops her knife and fork in shock, poor thing. From the look on Mira's face, I'd say that Sarah hasn't prepared her for the volatility of the Somerville household. Daisy slams her fist on the table. Her glass of Prosecco totters and just about stays upright.

"I'll tell you what's deceitful. It's you sneaking off to see your fancy woman every Wednesday for the past month."

"What the hell are you talking about?" says Bacon Man, looking baffled.

"Don't tell me you're screwing around, Dad? How do you manage when you're so bloody fat? It's a bit late to have a mid-life crisis, isn't it? What a bloody cliche," snarls Alex.

"Do we really have to talk about this now?" says Sarah.

"So, Sarah, you think it's ok that Dad's cheating on Mum as long as we don't have to talk about it now?" asks Alex.

"I'm not cheating on your Mother, for Christ's sake."

I believe Bacon Man is telling the truth. He's devoted to Daisy, even though she can be a battle axe on occasions. I wish

I could help him out. But I can't. I just hope there's a simple explanation.

"As far as I'm concerned," says Daisy, "the evidence is pretty clear. Every Wednesday you disappear on your new bike for two hours, and every time you take out a hundred pounds in cash. You're not having a pedicure for that kind of money, are you? I've seen your toenails and they're not pretty."

"Do we really have to talk about this now? I will tell you, Daisy, but later."

"No, Dad, you fess up now," insists Alex. "That's the least you can do for Mum."

"So who is this woman then?" says Daisy.

She scrolls through photographs on her mobile, until she finds the right one. And she thrusts the phone in Bacon Man's face.

"Have you been following me?" shouts Bacon Man.

"Mum, really? Have you been following Dad?" asks Sarah.

"I just want to know one thing," says Daisy. "Who is she? I didn't realise you preferred older women. But she's blonde and has got big boobs, so she's definitely your type. I have to say though, she's a bit mumsy for a hooker."

"She's not a hooker for Christ's sake. And she's not my fancy woman. Wait a minute. I'll get her card."

"Is it one of those cards you find in telephone boxes?" taunts Alex.

"Shut up, Alex. You're so useless, you couldn't organise a fuck in a phone booth," shouts Bacon Man.

Wow. That was a very cruel thing to say. And in front of Mira as well. That's terrible behaviour. I didn't realise Bacon

Man has such a nasty streak. I wonder if it's got anything to do with the amount of wine he's been drinking.

"That's it. Fuck you, Dad. I'm going to the pub."

Alex stands up from the table. Half of his meal remains on the plate. I wouldn't be too unhappy if he stormed out, because I'm sure Bacon Man will give me the leftovers. But I'm conflicted, because I know Daisy will be really upset if the meal ends in chaos.

"Stop it. You bunch of over-privileged moppets. Most people in my country can't afford to put a meal like this on the table, yet all you do is bicker and fight. Shame on you. All of you."

Wow, that was a showstopper. Alex slides back into his chair as Mira sits back down. Sarah shoots Daisy and Bacon Man a murderous look and gives Mira a hug. This is unprecedented. For once, everyone in the Somerville household is lost for words, until Bacon Man roars with laughter.

"Actually, Mira, I think you'll find the word is pronounced muppet. Where did you learn that expression?"

"Sarah taught me."

Daisy giggles and reaches for her glass of Prosecco. But it's empty, as is the bottle.

Alex catches his mother's eye, goes to the kitchen and returns with more beer and wine. He walks around the table refilling everybody's glasses and stops at Mira, bends down and plants a kiss on top of her head.".

"You're absolutely right. We're all a bunch of muppets. Welcome to the family."

Sarah shoots daggers at Alex. I wonder if the look has

something to do with that engagement-thingy that Bacon Man is not supposed to know about.

"I'll drink to that," roars Bacon Man. "Here's to you Mira. It took a lot of courage to speak out like that."

"I agree," says Daisy. "I admire your courage, I really do."

"Now is everybody ready for dessert?"

Bacon Man levers himself up from the table and staggers towards the kitchen.

I trot behind him as Daisy carries the dinner plates. The potential for pre-washing is enormous. I just hope Sarah doesn't come in. I have to say I'm hugely impressed with Mira. Her intervention has completely distracted Bacon Man and Daisy from the five hundred pounds given to Alex and the mystery woman that Bacon Man has been visiting on his bike. Uh oh. Premature articulation.

"So who's your fancy woman?" asks Daisy.

"She's not my fancy woman," insists Bacon Man.

"Have you been on some dating site? Or is she one of those Only Fans performers, in inverted commas, who appeals to blokes your age and provides a full service for the right amount?"

"Of course not. I've told you I'm not interested in screwing someone else."

"Then who is she?"

"Her name's Brenda."

"Brenda. How suburban. So, if she's not giving you an executive massage, what service does she offer precisely."

"She's a sex therapist."

"You're kidding."

Daisy starts laughing hysterically. I don't understand why. Nor does Bacon Man.

"What's so funny, Daisy?"

"That's hilarious."

"No it's not."

"You don't need to see a sex therapist. You just need to lose some bloody weight And, until tonight you were doing really well."

"Actually, I think you're wrong. There are some issues I want to sort out. But I'm not going to do it now. Let's get dessert out of the way first and then I'll tell you more. I promise."

CHAPTER TWENTY FOUR
NO MERCY SHAGS

What a day. I'm lying in my dog beddie in Daisy's bedroom. I'm trying to get some shut eye, but Bacon Man is doing farmyard impressions. Daisy has allowed him back into the marital bed for the duration of Christmas to make room for the children and Mira. Daisy is in the bathroom cleaning her teeth. I don't think I'm going to be getting much sleep because of Bacon Man's snoring, as well as the unfinished business hanging over us.

After the big argument and Mira's intervention, the tension dissipated, and the atmosphere improved immeasurably. Bacon Man served the traditional Danish Christmas dessert of rice pudding and sour cherry sauce. You have to eat the dessert carefully to make sure you don't swallow the hidden almond. The person who finds the almond wins a prize, a marzipan pig. How quintessentially Danish. I wonder if they make marzipan bacon.

Normally after a Danish Christmas supper, presents are distributed, and guests dance around the tree. But Bacon Man was wearing his stumbling slippers instead of his dancing shoes, so that didn't happen. There weren't any presents either. This was a very modern Christmas. In lieu of buying gifts, Daisy and Bacon Man donated to Sarah's charity, Breaking the Waves.

"And we're also making a donation to the charity called Alex," said Bacon Man.

He just can't help himself. I wish he'd leave the poor lad alone.

That was Alex's cue to head to a medieval pub in the next village, a one mile walk in total darkness along a well-worn track. Sarah and Mira joined him, while Daisy cleared up the kitchen. Bacon Man had left it in quite a state, and he was packed off to bed because he was deemed to be a health and safety hazard.

Ooh. He's stirring and swinging his legs out of bed. For a moment he can't work out where he is. But I can tell he's just regained his bearings. And he's heading to the en-suite bathroom.

"Here he is, the chief muppet," says Daisy.

"Guilty as charged. Do you mind if I have a slash?"

"Be my guest, just make sure you hit the target. This bathroom has been spick and span since you moved out."

"You mean since you kicked me out."

"Ooh well done. You got it all in the bowl. That's good, it means I won't go paddling on the tiles in the middle of the night."

"Come on, Daisy. Ceasefire."

"OK. Are you still drunk?"

"I wasn't drunk, just a bit squiffy."

"That was way over the top at dinner. I'm really embarrassed."

"Me too, Daisy. I know I went too far. I blame the drink. Pathetic excuse, but I'm just not used to it anymore. I'll go and sleep on the couch in the office if you like."

"No, it's too cramped. You can stay here. I'll just have to put two pillows over my head."

"That'll be an improvement. You're definitely a two pillows girl."

Bacon Man climbs back into the left-hand side of the bed, and Daisy takes the right.

"Ooh, you're so wonderfully warm," says Daisy. "I've missed your body heat."

"How do you think I feel?"

"Right, now tell me all about Brenda the sex therapist."

Uh oh. The argument has just gone into extra time. I wonder if there'll be a clear winner, or we'll have to go to penalties.

"Well, there's not much to tell. It was a very frustrating experience."

"Is that because you didn't or couldn't shag her?"

"She isn't that kind of sex therapist. I don't know what the correct term is. But she deals with the underlying problems that couples have in their sex lives."

"Well, the problem isn't underlying. It's on top of you. It's your weight."

"If you're just going to take cheap shots at me, I'm not going to tell you about it."

"OK, I'm all ears."

This is going to be interesting. Let's see if Bacon Man can make any progress or whether he's just going to dig himself deeper into trouble. I'm rooting for him, if that's the right word. But I'm not optimistic on his behalf.

"Well, Daisy, as I said, it was frustrating. The reason I started sessions with her was because I was hoping to reboot our sexual relationship while I was losing weight. You might think that was cheating."

"You got that right. There are no shortcuts."

"Do you want to know what happened or not?"

"Yes. Of course."

"Ok. I was hoping to get some answers and Brenda just kept asking me questions. In fact, I stopped going a week or so ago, because I wasn't really getting anywhere."

"So, what happened then?"

"At first she wouldn't take me on as a client because she said she only dealt with couples. But when I said there was no way you'd participate in the sessions, she relented and said she'd give it a try."

"You're spot on there. I don't need Brenda to tell me how to behave in bed."

I could give Bacon Man some advice on how to behave in bed. Stop snoring.

"So for two sessions," he says, "she kept asking me questions about our relationship and before I knew it, she said, 'Time's up. We'll pick up the conversation next time. So, at the start of the third session, I said 'Look, I've come here to get some answers.' And she said, 'That's not the way the process works. I ask you questions, and you try to find the answers within yourself.'"

"So have you found any answers?"

"Not really. If that's therapy, then I'm just not interested. You could go on forever answering questions and never get anywhere."

"So, is that it then?"

"No. I was insistent that she give me some guidance. Brenda didn't like the tables being turned, but I managed to extract some half-baked answers."

"I just can't wait to hear Brenda's insight," says Daisy.

Uh oh. Batten down the hatches. Here comes a truth bomb. I'm tempted to slip out of the bedroom onto the landing. But this is compelling stuff. Maybe I can pick up a tip or two for next time I meet the parson's poodle.

"So I explained that we'd drifted apart and that sex began to dry up when the menopause kicked in early and also when the kids came on the scene."

Even though it's dark, I can tell Daisy is getting riled.

"Our sex life didn't dry up because of the kids or my menopause. It dried up largely because of your gut. Sex shouldn't be an obstacle course. I wanted to get laid, not join the bloody army. Your obesity is and has been a complete passion killer. You're still in total denial about the damage it's inflicted on both of us."

"I'm sorry, but you're not being honest, Daisy. The menopause had a serious impact. You were exhausted, and in pain. You lost your desire. And don't forget that I was completely understanding. I never put any pressure on you at all."

"That's so not true. You've never stopped applying pressure. Right up until the day I declared a sex strike because of your size. You're also forgetting that you started gaining weight long before my menopause kicked in. So, it wasn't my fault. You've got to stop blaming me for something you've done to yourself."

Oh gawd. They're going around in circles. I've heard these same arguments countless times before. To be honest, it's boring. I hope they come up with something original, otherwise I'm going to fall asleep.

"What Brenda did say is that you should never withhold sex. But that's what you've been doing. You've just admitted it. You're on sex strike. It's worse than being married to Arthur Scargill of the miners' union. The only difference is the miners eventually caved in and you've got better tits than our Arthur."

"I take great exception to you comparing my pussy to a coal mine."

She's talking about that cat again. Where the hell is she hiding it?

"Well actually, Daisy, there are similarities. If you don't use a pit, it closes down. And becomes almost impossible to open again. The last thing you want is for it to become a museum piece."

"Well, the strike is as solid as ever. One out, all out, and that includes you."

"Look, Daisy, it's really destructive to use sex as a punishment and as a weapon against me. Brenda and I also talked about your refusal to have sex while the children were in the house. And she said that suggested you had some sensitivity about sex."

"I must say, Brenda has been a complete waste of our money."

Here we go. I knew Bacon Man was never going to win this one. And he's not going to get a word in edgeways.

"I wonder if that Brenda has ever had children. ANY mum will tell you that having sex while your children are sleeping next door is difficult, at best. The maternal instinct kicks in when you know your kids are nearby, because you listen out for them, even when you're having sex. I remember Alex walking in on us on a few occasions because he needed a pee at night, and you were so pissed off. However, Brenda is right in one respect. I have weaponized sex. Lots of women do. But it was simply the last ammunition in my battle to get you to lose weight. It didn't work, of course."

That's not true. Bacon Man has been losing weight recently.

"But you might just have lowered the drawbridge once or twice as an incentive. Besides sex is good exercise," says Bacon Man.

Somehow, I don't think that argument is going to win the day.

"I'm your wife. Not a charity. I don't dish out mercy shags just because you think I should. Or because I take pity on you. I'll tell you what really pisses me off about Brenda's analysis."

Oh Lord. Daisy is really hitting her stride here.

"It's about my sensitivity. What a lot of nonsense. My only sensitivity issue is about your stomach. It's so big that I can no longer feel you."

I hope for Bacon Man's sake he doesn't mention that Daisy has got a bit of a tummy herself. It won't end well. I think we've reached a stalemate here. I hope so, then maybe I can get some sleep. I can't see Bacon Man bouncing back from that. But here he goes again. He just can't let Daisy have the last word. They're both the same in that respect.

"Listen, Daisy. The other main thing that came out of these Brenda sessions, is something I wasn't aware of. And that's about the nature of our relationship. Besides being husband and wife, we're also best friends. According to Brenda's relationship theory, couples who are very good friends find it difficult to have the sexual polarity that enables them to maintain sex through a long marriage."

"Those who manage to keep the sex going, flounce off and dramatise everything. They're the ones that are always packing up and leaving. The reason they fuck more is because they're always having making-up sex. And that's never happened with us. Maybe I should start having hissy fits and storm off every now and again."

"But you do have hissy fits. Don't you see that? And you do storm off occasionally. And when you do, you go to the curry house and fill your face."

Please make this argument end. It's so tedious. And repetitive. I really need to sleep. I'm thinking about a nice female golden retriever in the next village and trying to imagine she smells like the parson's poodle. Does that make me a perv? I'm not going to find out because the dream won't gel while these two are bickering.

"That's unfair, Daisy. I can't remember the last time I had a curry blow-out. And I am losing weight."

"That's true, to be fair. And that's why I've made an

appointment with a hormone doctor in London to try HRT. Maybe that will boost my libido, so we are making progress."

"Ok, Daisy, let's leave it there for Christ's sake, I'm boring myself stupid."

"Ok. *Glædelig Jul*, and good night."

"Merry Christmas to you too. I love you, Daisy."

"I love you too."

Thank goodness. They've stopped. I can get some shut eye now.

"Get your hands off my tits."

"I'm sorry, I thought they were Arthur Scargill's. Come on. One out. All out."

Daisy's giggling. But I don't think Bacon Man's going to prevail.

"Stop it."

"Come on comrade, let the flying pickets in, they want to reverse the pit closure."

"Stop it."

"Oh, go on. Be a sport. It's Christmas."

"And what did we decide this Christmas?"

"What was that?"

"No presents. So, keep your hands to yourself and stay on your own side. And please try not to snore."

In your dreams, Daisy.

CHAPTER TWENTY FIVE

ROUND TWO

The good thing about having two Christmases is that if you don't get it right the first time, you have a second opportunity to make amends. Hopefully, the Somervilles' English Christmas will be conducted with the dignity, stateliness, kindness, and generosity you would associate with a golden retriever. Quite frankly, yesterday was a disgrace.

Daisy and Bacon Man conducted themselves no better than the most inconsiderate, ill-mannered dogs. You all know the type to which I'm referring. The ones that yap constantly for no apparent reason and won't button it when instructed, even when offered treats.

Perhaps Bacon Man and Daisy haven't been properly trained. Despite their middle-class appearances, they can't shake off a feral element that they both possess. I don't know if they'd even wish to. I'm not sure whether either of them has the self-awareness to realise that although they're mature in age terms, they still have this untamed characteristic. Is it because of their original profession as journalists? The concept of deference is one they've completely banished from their lives. They don't share the same boundaries as other people. Maybe that's because for so many years, they had free reign to ask difficult or impertinent questions of the high and mighty and the low and shitey. Did that give them a sense of entitlement that's impossible to erase or even tone down? They laud untrammelled free speech, yet they seem to think that gives them the freedom to be offensive.

How have they managed to get to this stage of their lives without being sent to the pound? I suppose it's entirely possible that they're human rescues, mistakenly released from the Battersea Home for Badly Behaved Journalists. That's the trouble with rescues. You never can be sure about their pasts and whether they might suddenly turn.

On the other hand, the good thing about yesterday was that Bacon Man and Daisy showed some of the darker shades from their emotional spectra. There was none of that British reserve, which gives the impression of gentility, but can often be a smokescreen for profound contempt. That's probably Daisy's influence. Although she hasn't lived in Denmark for years, she retains the national trait of bluntness. As she's often said, if you ask a Dane for an opinion, they won't hold back or sugar coat it. At least you know where you stand. Whereas if a British person says, 'you must come round for dinner,' what they really mean is, 'I'll set the dogs on you if you knock on my door.' And I'm not talking about golden retrievers here.

So, I hope Mira realises she was given an accurate glimpse into the characters of her future in-laws. That is, if she doesn't bolt. Today's Christmas lunch is a potential minefield because that's when Sarah intends to announce their plans to get married. Bacon Man can't bear being the last to know. No doubt because as a journalist, he hated being scooped. With any luck, he'll manage to contain himself. If I was Daisy, I'd keep him away from the red wine and she should lay off the Prosecco.

I'll just go into the kitchen to see how preparations for this grand English feast are progressing. Oh dear, Bacon Man is putting two bottles of Prosecco in the freezer. He's already brought out half a case of Malbec, along with some Belgian beer that's even stronger than the brews Alex was slugging yesterday. Won't they ever learn?

Do you know why Buddhism isn't Britain's main religion? Because one of its main precepts is the prohibition of intoxication. How would that work over here? Imagine the horror of having to down coffee before an early morning package holiday flight instead of seven pints of lager? How peaceful family Christmases would be, if fuelled by coconut water or lactose-free Rudolph the Red-Nosed Reindeer milk? There would be no arguments or embarrassing revelations. It just wouldn't be Christmas would it?

Er, hang on. I just need to re-arrange the biology of that previous remark. I mean Rudolph the Trans-Sexual Red-Nosed Reindeer with added pro-lactin, the hormone that helps lactation. As do the herbs, fenugreek and fennel seeds. Mmmmm. Interesting.

So, there's no need to leave out a carrot along with Santa's glass of coconut water. Just let Rudolph attack your spice rack.

Now where was I?

I think I'll slip upstairs and lie on the landing outside Sarah and Mira's room to see if I can pick up any intelligence. It's always best to be prepared.

They're awake and whispering. But I can hear what they're saying.

"I do hope they're better behaved today," says Sarah. "They weren't just bad. They were appalling."

"Stop troubling yourself, *Cherie*. Today is a new day. And besides, they were both a little intoxicated."

"A little?"

Sarah and Mira are giggling quietly.

"Well, maybe more than a little."

Absolutely. As pissed as Christmas puddings, I'd say. The pair of them.

"I really wanted you to like them," says Sarah. "And they let themselves down so badly."

"This is a completely new experience for me. And after everything I've been through, I'm much more wary than I used to be about strangers. So, I'm still making up my mind. I don't think I've seen what they're really like."

"Oh you have, and that's a good thing. And I think they like you, because if they didn't, they would have been immaculately polite at the table. The fact that they felt able to go full throttle in front of you means that they're cool with you."

"That's good to know. Thank you. That makes me happy. I hope it means that they will be cool with the announcement."

"Don't bank on it, Mira. I do worry about my dad's reaction. My mum is usually the unpredictable one, but on this occasion, I know she will be fine."

"Well, if it becomes unbearable we can always make an excuse and catch an earlier train back to Paris."

"We can't, I'm afraid," says Sarah. "I've checked the Eurostar app. They're all fully booked."

"Well, *Cherie*, we could always go back to bed."

Suddenly I hear a deep intake of breath and a suppressed squeal of pleasure. Time to invoke that old journalistic fall back. I'm making my excuses and leaving.

Besides, I need to keep an eye on Bacon Man and Daisy. I can hear faint brush strokes coming from the en-suite bathroom. She's making an effort today and applying make-up. She doesn't need to. Our chilly five-mile romp along the river this morning painted some colour on her cheeks and expunged any lingering Prosecco fogginess.

Bacon Man's also pretty chipper. If he's feeling any pain, he's not letting on. He's far too busy getting to grips with the challenge of creating a nut roast, something he's never done before. But I see he's got a tall fat glass on the go, full to the brim with a transparent bubbly liquid, ice and a slice of lime. I take a deep sniff. I'm trying to isolate the aroma of juniper that always accompanies the sundowners of Reginald, the Silver Fox who lives next door. No, there's no gin in that glass. I'm sure it's sparkling water.

Right, everything's tickety-boo. I love that word. Thank you, Maurice Oxford. I can tell the sun is about to emerge from behind a cloud. By my calculations, it should warm up my favourite sofa for an hour or so and then it'll be time for turkey and all the trimmings. You can stick the nut roast when the sun shineth not. My, that was a big yawn. I'm going to have a little lie down and sharpen my appetite by licking my balls. They're really swinging these days. Just thought I'd remind you. I'm a dog. And I'm keeping it real.

* * *

"So what's the story with Dad's floozy? Where are we at?"

"Alex, are you determined to cause trouble?" asks Daisy.

That's some greeting. We haven't even started eating yet.

"It's a fair question, Mum," says Sarah. "I think we all deserve to know whether you're going to get divorced."

"Of course not," replies Daisy. "I might want to kill your father occasionally, but I would never divorce him?"

"Even if he went off with a prostitute?" asks Alex.

Mira has put down her knife and fork and is looking down at her plate. I think she needs some sympathy, so I walk around the table and put my head in her lap. She starts shaking jerkily. I don't think that's what they call a lap dance.

"Get him off," she whispers to Sarah. "Get him off me."

"Dad, Bjørn's bothering Mira, can you put him outside please?"

That's a bit much. I don't want to be exiled in the cold, so I go and lie by Daisy's feet.

"Will someone please tell me what's going on with Dad's fancy woman," demands Alex.

"Oh, for heaven's sake," says Bacon Man. "She's a therapist. I went to see her about some personal issues."

"What issues, Mum?" asks Alex, still not satisfied.

"None of your business, Alex. The issue is closed. And just

so that there's no doubt about it, I apologise for making accusations against your father yesterday. I jumped to the wrong conclusion. My description of her was also unkind. There's nothing wrong with looking Mumsy."

"Thank you, Daisy, apology accepted," says Bacon Man. "And Alex, I'd like to say sorry for calling you useless yesterday. I didn't mean it. It was deeply hurtful and if I could I'd like to withdraw the remark. Please forgive me."

"Yes, it was hurtful," replied Alex. "It completely undermined my self-confidence."

"That's the last thing I want to do," says Bacon Man. "What I said has been playing on my conscience all night."

"So what about the five hundred quid Mum gave me yesterday, are you still pissed off about that."

"No, not at all, Alex."

"Christ. Really?"

"Yes, really, Alex."

I glance over at Mira and Sarah, who seem to be conversing through facial expressions. Mira is nodding. And Sarah is mouthing the words ok.

"Well," says Sarah, "as it seems that peace has broken out, this feels like a good time to make an announcement."

She gulps and pauses as everyone lays down their knives and forks.

"Mira and I have decided to get married. We're engaged."

"Congratulations, *lille Skat*. I'm so happy for you both."

Daisy beams broadly as she stands up and hugs them in turn. Bacon Man's face is sphinx-like. For two seconds he says nothing. Sarah looks at him anxiously.

"That's wonderful news. I'm delighted for both of you."

Both Sarah and Mira look surprised.

"Let's have a toast," says Bacon Man. "To Sarah and Mira, may you live happily ever after."

Sarah rushes over to Bacon Man and crushes him in a bear hug.

"Are you sure you're happy, Daddy?"

"Absolutely," replies Bacon Man. "As long as I can walk you down the aisle, or whatever you decide to do, I'm more than happy."

"Have either of you got engagement rings?" asks Daisy. "I can't see them."

"Yes, we do," says Mira. "They're upstairs in our room. We didn't dare wear them until we'd told you."

"There's no need to be afraid, Mira," says Bacon Man. "Why don't you go upstairs and get them."

The girls leave the table and sprint upstairs. Daisy has bewilderment in her eyes as she looks over at Bacon Man. I'm guessing she's completely surprised by his response.

"Blimey, Dad," says Alex. "I thought you were going to go ballistic. And so did the girls, they were both terrified."

"That shows just how little you really know me, doesn't it, Alex."

I must confess; I'm puzzled as well. I would have bet a roast duck that Bacon Man would have reacted badly, because he was taken unawares by the announcement. The other thing I notice is that nobody seems to have touched their smoked salmon starter. I hope they've all lost their appetites in the excitement over the engagement, because I'm in the mood to gorge myself.

A couple of minutes later, the couple return, both self-consciously touching thin matching bands of gold.

"Let me take a look at the rings, *lille Skat*," says Daisy.

"We bought them from a jeweller in Barbes, in Paris. They're engraved with African symbols."

"They're beautiful," says Daisy.

"So what about children?" asks Bacon Man.

Both gulp. They look at each other and Mira speaks up first.

"We've talked about it."

"Not straight away, Dad," says Sarah. "But sooner or later, yes, we'd love to have a family."

"Well, there's no rush," says Bacon Man. "You're both young and you've got lots of time left, you lucky people. Now come on, let's eat. You didn't have breakfast. You must be starving."

Thanks a lot for reminding them, Bacon Man. There goes my smoked salmon. Sarah and Mira seem giddy with excitement. They shrug their shoulders nervously and start drinking Prosecco. Not sipping. Drinking. English style. Yes. That's what I mean. Speed drinking. The national sport. Alex is no slouch either, he's on his third Belgian beer.

"We need another bottle of Prosecco," says Daisy.

I follow Bacon Man into the kitchen because there's always a chance of a snack. I'm not going to get anything from this table in this mood.

"Hello, . Are you coming to keep me company? Or are you just peckish and on the scrounge?"

Well, that question has put me on the spot. And I suddenly realise that maybe Bacon Man is lonely, despite being surrounded by the people he loves most of all. As he opens the bottle of Prosecco, I catch his eye. And we stare at each other for a full five seconds.

He doesn't have to say a word. I know what he's thinking. He's not a man to wallow in self-pity, but he's thinking about his own mortality. His daughter's engagement is a mile marker closer to the end of his journey. Death is the ultimate lonely planet destination. No matter how many of our kind surround us, we all die alone. I understand why Bacon Man is so wistful. He doesn't begrudge Sarah her happiness. But he's suddenly missing the carefree happiness of his youth. From now on he'll be careworn and he's wondering whether he and Daisy will ever again share a fraction of the joy his daughter is experiencing right now. Time is so precious, and it travels so fast. Then Bacon Man smiles at me. He recognises the depth of our bond. I can tell he loves me. Then he looks away, strokes me gently on the forehead, and takes the bottle into the dining room.

Everyone has finished their salmon apart from Bacon Man.

"I'll just go and carve," he says, walking around the table, collecting the plates.

He leaves his plate till last and puts it on top of the file and winks at me. I know what that means. And I trot into the kitchen behind him. Bacon Man lowers the dishwasher door and puts the top plate down on what they call my workstation.

"There you go, Bubsie. Enjoy."

"Daaaaaaad."

The shout is so loud, I stop eating. That doesn't happen

often, believe me. Sarah has come into the kitchen unexpectedly. I thought she was welded to Mira.

"That's just disgusting. Stop it, Bjørn."

You must be joking. I'd better finish the salmon before she takes the plate away. I somehow manage to get the biggest slice into my mouth, toss my head up to realign my jaws and swallow it in one. I don't like bolting my food, because I don't get to taste it properly. I was looking forward to savouring the fish, but I've been denied the chance by her hysteria. So, I dive back down again and lick off the remaining slithers. That's better. Now I can taste it.

"Oh for heaven's sake, Sarah, get over yourself."

"No I won't. Do you know how dirty dog's mouths are? He's getting his germs all over the plates."

"What's all the shouting about?"

Daisy has stormed into the kitchen.

"Dad's letting Bjørn lick the plates, and he promised he'd stop."

"Well your dad shouldn't make promises he can't keep. In this house, Bjørn always does the pre-wash."

"Mum, I can't believe that you of all people let that happen. His tongue is covered in bacteria. He's always licking his balls. Urrggghh."

Huh. One of life's great pleasures. Believe me, I'm never gonna give that up. Did you hear that? I sounded just like Rick Astley. *We're no strangers to lurrrrvvve......*

"Well none of us have been sick so far," says Daisy, her voice rising up the scale.

"That's a bloody miracle," snarls Sarah.

"No, it's not a miracle. We run the dishwasher at seventy degrees, so everything gets thoroughly clean."

"What? You run the dishwasher at seventy degrees. You should do a cold wash. Don't you care about the planet? And you're Danish. What a hypocrite."

Daisy's face looks like thunder.

"The last thing I am is a hypocrite."

"Yes you are. You're always banging on about how the Danes are the world's green leaders, but you really don't give a shit about your own carbon footprint do you? And that's because it's more important that your little doggie gets his treaty wheaty."

"I wouldn't get all high and mighty about carbon footprints, Sarah."

Now Bacon Man is wading in. I'm not too sure that the environment is his strong point. He could be in for another battering.

"Coming from you, that's pretty rich, Dad."

"What do you mean?"

"I'm so embarrassed that you drive a diesel car. And it's ancient."

"Not too embarrassed to be chauffeur driven around in it. And do you want to know why we haven't got a new car? We can't afford one, because most of our spare cash goes on subsidising you and Alex."

Uh oh, it's getting personal. And none of them are not particularly squiffy yet.

"No you don't. I pay my own way."

"Who paid for your Venice cruise? If you were so environmentally friendly, Sarah, you'd have gone sailing somewhere else instead of Instagramming from the Grand Canal on a floating skyscraper," says Daisy.

Bacon Man finishes her thought.

"Do you have any idea of the damage cruise liners cause to Venice? Besides the pollution from running their engines all day long, they're wrecking the lagoon. So get off your high horse."

"Yeah, Dad. Let's get back to animals. The bloody dog rules this house, not you or Mum."

You're damn right I do. That's why it's such a happy home. Well, not at the moment obviously.

"What's wrong with you, Dad? He's just a dog. But you treat him like a child. It's ridiculous. He's not human. Mira's right. Dogs should be kept outside and stay there."

That sounds like fighting talk to me.

"Is Mira still scared of Bjørn?" asks Bacon Man gently.

"She's scared she's going to pick up a disease from him. He sleeps in your bed; he lies on the sofa. And he licks the plates. She was brought up to fear dogs because they have rabies, and one bite could kill."

"There's no rabies in Britain, and certainly not on Galahad Island. Bjørn only needed a rabies jab to get a doggie passport. This is the Thames Valley, not Mogadishu."

"What did you say, Dad?"

Wow. Sarah is almost screaming.

"I said Bjørn has got a doggie passport."

"No, you said this is the Thames Valley, not Mogadishu."

"And...?"

"And do you have any idea how that sounds?"

"It's a statement of fact. We live by the River Thames not in Somalia."

"No, it just shows your levels of unconscious racism. Mira is from Entebbe not Mogadishu. There's a huge difference."

"What is wrong with you, Sarah? It was the first African city that came to my mind. That's all. Are you looking for offence in everything we say or do?"

Bacon Man seems genuinely bewildered.

"How dare you, Sarah. I will not stand for it."

Daisy is furious. She's like a battleship with all her big guns trained on one target.

"How can you possibly accuse your father of racism after all the kindness he has shown you and Mira these past couple of days?"

"Are you supporting him, Mum? If so, that makes you a racist too."

I wonder if Sarah realises what she has just unleashed. Daisy is more than capable of defending herself, but she cannot abide anyone being unkind to Bacon Man, and always goes into battle on his behalf, without exception.

"Sometimes, I wonder what colour your older brother would have been."

"What are you talking about, Mum? What older brother?"

After blowing herself up into a balloon of righteous indignation, Sarah has just suffered a catastrophic puncture. I never fail to be impressed by Daisy's ability to deflate and confuse people by doing the totally unexpected. But I have to say, Sarah is asking the right question. I'm as intrigued as she is.

I look over at Bacon Man in the hope that he can offer some enlightenment. For once, I can't decipher what he's thinking. His face is completely impassive as he stands quietly next to the island in the centre of the kitchen, observing the scene, waiting to carve the steaming nut roast and turkey. What I do sense though, is the unspoken bond between Bacon Man and Daisy. When conflict looms, they close ranks and are indivisible.

Daisy's face is more revealing. She's livid, but like Bacon Man, she's saying nothing. More than anyone, Daisy understands the value of silence. She's controlling it and increasing the tension with every passing second. I glance at Sarah, who's desperate for someone to speak. She knows she's losing ground. In the end, she can't bear the silence.

"Mum, what are you talking about? Please tell me. Do we have an older brother?"

Sarah is shaking and on the verge of tears. Daisy takes her time before replying.

"After that outburst I'm sure that Mira is feeling very awkward right now And it's your fault. Now I suggest you calm down and behave in a civilised manner."

Sarah turns and leaves the kitchen with a big sigh.

I look at Bacon Man. He winks at me, carves a slither of turkey, and tosses it over to me. I catch it with ease. It's a tad hot, but perfectly succulent.

"Happy Families," says Bacon Man with a chuckle. "How do you want to play this, Daisy?"

"I haven't made my mind up yet," says Daisy.

"Are you going to tell them?"

Tell them what? I'm dying to know. I'd better not eat too much in case I fall asleep and miss the big revelation.

"I never intended to tell them. They don't need to know everything about my past."

"That's true, Daisy," says Bacon Man. "Maybe we should behave like the Royal Family? Reveal nothing, shroud ourselves in mystery and preserve our power."

"*Skatter*, no one, especially our daughter, gets away with calling us racists. I'm still making up my mind whether to tell them."

"Well, it's up to you, Daisy. I don't think Sarah meant it. I think she's just hyper-emotional for obvious reasons."

"But it's still unacceptable. It was the worst kind of insult. It's also wrong. And if we don't address it, the issue will fester."

"It's your call, Daisy."

"Let's put the food on the table before they drink themselves stupid," says Daisy. "But let's also make them sweat."

Bacon Man chuckles.

"Okay, Daisy, you lead, I'll follow. As usual."

Daisy looks Bacon Man in the eye and gives him a conspiratorial grin.

CHAPTER TWENTY SIX
TWATS

I'M GOING WHERE THE FOOD is so I trot behind Daisy as she and Bacon Man enter the dining room with platters of nut roast and turkey.

"So, what's up, Mum? Do I have a black older brother or what?"

Bravo, Alex. As subtle as a breeze block.

"Would you like turkey or nut roast, Alex?" asks Daisy.

"I'll take any explanation you dish up."

"The turkey came from Norfolk and I made the nut roast myself," says Bacon Man. "It's all organic. The Brazil nuts and pecans are quite spectacular."

"Don't you think you owe us an explanation, Mum?" says Sarah. "You can't just say things like that."

"But you clearly think you can say whatever you like, Sarah. You just called us racists," says Daisy.

"I'm sorry, Mum, I was out of order."

"You certainly were. What about Dad? He deserves an apology too."

"Sorry, Dad, I didn't mean it."

"Are you sure about that, Sarah?" asks Daisy.

"Yes, Mum. I really am sorry, Dad."

"Apology accepted," says Bacon Man.

"For fuck's sake, stop tap dancing," says Alex banging his beer glass on the table. "Tell us the truth. Do we have a black sibling?"

"Calm down, Alex and stop issuing orders," says Daisy. "I won't tolerate it. You know better than that."

"But, Mum, we have a right to know," insists Alex.

"What makes you think that, Alex? You don't have an automatic right to anything, and neither does Sarah, especially after insulting your father and me just now."

I glance up at Bacon Man. He's sitting there scanning the table, trying to suppress a grin. I've seen him like this many times before, glowing in the reflected glory of Daisy's dominant aura. Sarah and Alex's crestfallen expressions are signs of defeat, acknowledging that the power balance in the Somerville family is some years from passing to the younger generation. Sarah looks like she's going to burst into tears. Mira reaches for her hand under the table.

"Sorry, Mum," mumbles Alex.

"And apologise to your father," insists Daisy.

"Sorry, Dad." he whispers.

"What did you say?" asks Daisy. "I didn't hear it."

"Sorry, Dad," says Alex, a little more forcefully.

"Right," says Daisy, "I want to knock this idea of racism on the head once and for all. This is important for all of you, especially Mira. Because, darling, I don't want you to feel uncomfortable in our home."

"I'm not uncomfortable, Mrs. Somerville," says Mira sweetly.

"The fact that you're calling me Mrs. Somerville tells me you *are* uncomfortable, Mira. It's Astrid, OK? I know it's a bit confusing in this house because Morgan calls me Daisy. That's the Brits for you. They have two or three names for everyone. Call me Astrid. I insist."

"Ok, Astrid, I will," says Mira.

"Thank you, Mira. I can assure you that Sarah's father is one of the kindest people you'll ever meet, and I can assure you that he doesn't have a racist bone in his body."

"Actually, Mira," interrupts Bacon Man. "Daisy is exaggerating, I'm not that kind, and like everyone else I've got a dark side. There are some people I do discriminate against."

"What type of people, Dad?" asks Sarah.

"Twats."

Chuckles ripple around the table, from Daisy to Alex and then Sarah. With one word Bacon Man has defused the tension.

"What's a twat, Mr. Somerville?" asks Mira, wide-eyed.

"Just call me Bacon Man, Mira. It's a lot easier. Now, a real twat is someone who lets the hot food that I've lovingly prepared go cold."

This time Mira joins in the laughter around the table.

"Now dig in, please," implores Bacon Man. "And I'll explain who qualifies as a twat."

"Anybody who eats Brussels sprouts is a twat," shouts Alex.

"In that case, I'm a twat. Pass the sprouts," says Bacon Man. "They're part of my Keto diet."

"Such strength," says Daisy. "But can you resist the roast potatoes?"

"Yes I can," replies Bacon Man. "Actually, Alex is partially right about sprouts. Anyone whose signature dish is a Brussels sprouts quiche is a twat."

Daisy giggles.

"What's so funny about that, Mum?" asks Sarah.

"When I was dating your mum," says Bacon Man, "We spent a few exquisite days getting to know each other in Cannes, in the villa of one of her best friends. AnneMette? Remember her? One of the other house guests was a Danish guy called Mogens, who had the serious hots for your mum. One night, Mogens insisted on cooking supper and served up a Brussels sprout quiche. In France, of all places. The land of great cuisine! Extraordinary! Believe me, Brussels sprouts quiche is not the highway into your mother's underwear. What a twat."

"Daaad, too much information," wails Sarah.

"It takes more than a quiche," says Daisy with an infectious smile.

"An African dish might do it," says Bacon Man.

I scan the table, trying to catch someone's eye in the hope that they'll throw me a morsel, but they're all ignoring me and filling their faces at the same time. I'm the best-looking creature in the room and putting on my biggest smile. It's just not working. I can't believe that I'm being ghosted. This has never happened before.

"This nut roast is fantastic, Mr. Somerville, I mean Bacon Man."

"Thanks, Mira, better than Mogens' quiche any day of the week."

"You're being unkind, *Skatter*," says Daisy. "Mogens was a nice guy."

"Maybe he had hidden qualities, Daisy, but I thought he was terminally dull. If there's one thing that's worse than being a twat, it's being boring."

"So, what exactly is a twat, Bacon Man?" asks Mira.

"Strictly speaking, Mira, it's a very vulgar term for a vagina."

Mira's eyebrows almost hit the ceiling. I bet this is the only Christmas lunch conversation on Galahad Island about vaginas.

"But most Brits don't use the word in that way," says Bacon Man. "A twat is mainly someone who's done something foolish, like making a sprouts quiche. But the term can also apply to someone who's evil."

Like the ginger cat at Number 23.

"Can you give me an example, Bacon Man?" grins Mira.

"Well, I've been a twat on multiple occasions," says Bacon Man.

"Nooooooh. Not you," says Daisy, slugging another glass of Prosecco. She really is knocking it back.

"It's true. I was a twat for losing my gig at the BBC. I picked all the wrong battles, made enemies of senior managers and in the end, they kicked me out of a job I really loved."

"But at least you stood up for what you believed in," says Daisy.

"So, Dad, are you saying that twats are mainly white?" asks Sarah.

"Now there's a question. I'd say that on balance, yes, twattery is predominantly a white preserve, but there are also black twats, brown twats, and yellow twats."

"What about my dad, Bacon Man?" asks Mira. "Is he a twat?"

"Do you want an honest answer, Mira?"

"Yes, Bacon Man."

"Careful, Dad," says Alex munching on a roast parsnip. "This is dangerous territory. Don't be a twat now."

"Well, I don't know your dad, Mira, but I'd say on balance, yes, he's a twat."

"Why?" asks Mira.

Sarah is pursing her lips and waiting to pounce.

"He professes to be a man of God. But then he banishes you into the wilderness for how you choose to love. There's no greater force for good in this world than love, and he, as a preacher, should recognise that."

Sarah rushes round to Bacon Man and smothers him in a bear hug and kisses, while snot streams from her nose.

"Don't be daft, Sarah. I love you too. Now please put me down before my sprouts go cold."

I look around the table to see how everyone is reacting. Daisy pours herself another substantial glass of Prosecco and is almost gargling.

"Right," she says, "I want to tell an anecdote about your father."

"He once refused a free meal." snipes Alex.

I'm sure Bacon Man did no such thing. I certainly wouldn't. I could do with a free meal right now. I've taken my head off Bacon Man's thigh because he's not getting the message. Most unlike him. I wish they'd all hurry up and finish lunch so I can do the mother of all pre-washes.

"Dad was Slimmer of the Year?"

"Actually, Alex, your father was much trimmer when I met him, and I've got every faith that he can get back close to his fighting weight. He's certainly on the right track. Now here's a pub quiz question. Who was America's President before Barack Obama?"

"George W. Bush."

"Exactly, Sarah," says Daisy. "Glad to see that degree in International Relations wasn't wasted."

"International Relations clearly are her forte, aren't they, Mira?"

Alex titters at his own remark.

"You really are a twat, aren't you, Alex? Is it any wonder you're still single?" barks Sarah.

"So, Astrid, was George Bush a twat as well?" asks Mira.

"Yes, and not because he mispronounced verds, I mean words," says Daisy. "I do that all the time."

Especially when she's on the Prosecco.

"And no one in their right mind would dare call your mother a twat," says Bacon Man.

"Especially if they want to carry on breathing."

Come on people. Bacon Man's making you laugh. The least you can do is to share the love and throw me a slice of turkey, or a chunk of sausage meat. I've got two strands of drool hanging from my mouth. They're virtually reaching the floor. How much of a hint do you need?

"George W's election in 2000 was one of the high points of your dad's career," says Daisy.

"How is that possible, Mum?" asks Sarah "I thought Bush's victory was a disaster?"

"It wasn't America's finest moment, but it was one of your father's. We were living in Florida at the time and your dad was covering the election result from Nashville, where Bush's opponent was based."

"Al Gore," says Bacon Man.

"Anyway, around midnight, most of the American television networks started calling the election for Bush. The BBC crossed live to dad, and he was under enormous pressure to report that Gore had lost. But your dad didn't. And that's because he's a truly independent spirit and never afraid to swim against the tide. That takes nuts."

"You mean balls, Daisy."

"So what happened, Dad?"

"Well, Sarah, the numbers didn't add up. There were still some precincts in Florida which hadn't been called, especially in the African American districts. I told my audience on BBC World that something unusual was happening, because Gore wasn't conceding. Normally, the defeated candidate would have done so if the outcome was clear. It obviously wasn't over, despite the fact that all the American networks were calling the election for Bush."

"And your Dad was spot on the money."

"You mean right on the money, Daisy."

"Don't interrupt, *Skatter*. Gore refused to accept the result in Florida and there was an enormous effort to recount all the votes. It took weeks to sort out."

"Why should I be interested in this?" whines Alex. "I hate politics. It's so boring. It's Christmas Day, we're supposed to be having fun."

"Stop being a rude twat, Alex," says Sarah. "I want to know the end of the story."

"Thank you, Sarah," says Daisy.

Daisy's slurring has stepped up a notch.

"If you're not interested, Alex, you're free to leave the table."

"Ok, Mum. I'm sorry."

"May I continue?"

"Yes, Mum."

"Thank you, Alex."

Daisy takes another sip. Her cheeks are glowing. Not quite Rudolph the Red Nosed Reindeer, but she's heading in that direction.

"The reason I'm telling you all this is to demonstrate to Mira, and to remind you, Alex and Sarah, that not only is your dad a brilliant journalist……"

"Not any more, Daisy."

Bacon Man looks genuinely sad.

"But he always stands up for the underdog and provides a voice for the weakest in society, no matter what their nationality or colour. And that's why Sarah's racist accusation pissed me off."

"So, what happened next, Astrid?" asks Mira.

Daisy glugs more Prosecco.

"After the election result was put on hold because of the stalemate, your dad started digging and was one of the first journalists to uncover a campaign to stop black Floridians from voting."

Both Sarah and Mira are now listening intently. Even Alex shows an interest as Bacon Man picks up the story. I love the way he and Daisy seem to finish each other's sentences. Despite their differences, it shows just how much in harmony they are, deep down.

"I headed up to Northern Florida and interviewed scores of African American voters who said they'd been intimidated by Highway Patrolmen as they headed to the polling stations. Some officers were suspected of being members of the Ku Klux Klan. The African-American voters were told in no uncertain terms to turn around and go home. They were really scared."

"That's terrible," says Mira. "I thought all that kind of stuff had stopped fifty years ago."

"No, not at all," says Bacon Man.

Daisy jumps back in.

"To cut a long story short, the result of the election was decided by America's Supreme Court, which ruled that Bush had won. And the complaints of the African-Americans about being stopped from voting were largely ignored."

"They were clearly disenfranchised. It was criminal." says Bacon Man.

"I see," says Sarah.

"Do you, Sarah?" asks Daisy. "Do you see how that demonstrates your father isn't a racist?"

"Yes, Mum."

"Do I need to tell you any more stories about your Dad to prove my point? Because I've got loads."

"No, Mum," says Sarah. "We get it. Don't we Alex? But what we'd like to know now is whether we've got a black sibling?"

That's a showstopper of a question. The tension has just killed off my hunger pangs. Trust me. That's never happened before.

Daisy tops up her Prosecco glass and knocks back half.

"No you don't."

"Then why did you mention it, Mum?" says Sarah.

"Because you almost did."

"What do you mean?"

"I had an abortion?"

"Is that because you were unfaithful to Dad?"

"No, it happened a little while before I met your father. And just so you know, I've never even looked at another man since I married your dad. I love him to pieces."

"So what happened then, Mum?"

Yes. Come on Daisy. I'm dying to know what happened.

"One of the last boyfriends I had before I met your father, was a Congolese session musician in Copenhagen. He played bass with a lot of top funk bands."

"Was he famous, Mum?" asks Alex.

"Don't tell him, Daisy for Christ's sake!" pleads Bacon Man, "Otherwise, Alex will be playing the guy's records on his radio show, saying 'great track and guess what, the bass player shagged my Mum.'"

"Stop it, Dad," snaps Sarah. "Mum, why did you have an abortion?"

"Well, Sarah, it was a tough decision. I really wanted to have children and this guy was lots of fun. But he wasn't a good long-term prospect, let's put it that way."

"Because he was black?" asks Sarah.

"Of course, not, Sarah. He made a decent living and was as sexy as hell."

"Just rub it in, why don't you," whispers Bacon Man.

"Stop it, Dad. Were you in love with him, Mum?" asks Sarah.

"In lust, if I'm honest. He was a seriously naughty man. Very well equipped. I needed to apply an ice pack after a night with him."

"And you wonder why I'm seeing a sex therapist? Jesus!" exclaims Bacon Man.

"Or a packet of frozen peas," sighs Daisy.

"That's enough detail thank you, Daisy," snaps Bacon Man.

"Pass the peas," says Alex. "On second thoughts, maybe not."

"He was an animal in bed, and not just in bed."

Crumbs, Daisy is on a roll. She's stroking the Prosecco glass so vigorously, I'm afraid it's going to break.

"Against the wall…. on the kitchen table…in the back of taxis…on the dance floor at a James Brown concert. Or maybe that was someone else? Possibly the basketball player from Burkino Faso, I can't remember."

"Mum, I never knew you had such a wild side."

Sarah obviously hasn't seen her mother's washing line recently.

"*Get up offa that thing*, a James Brown classic."

"Very funny Alex! Perhaps you should ease off the bubbles, Daisy." snarls Bacon Man.

The Prosecco has really loosened Daisy's tongue. Normally, she never, ever, humiliates Bacon Man in public. Poor guy.

"I can't imagine dad being an animal in bed," says Alex, "unless he was a manatee."

"Thank you so much, Alex," says Bacon Man, "for that prime example of man's inhumanity to manatees."

That's Bacon Man to a T. Self-deprecation is one of his great qualities. So, what if he's not an animal on the kitchen table? That's still where he does some of his best work.

"But we're getting off the point here. Please tell us, Mum, why did you have the abortion?"

"I could have raised a child by myself, Sarah. I was certainly well-established in my career back then and could have managed financially. I didn't expect anything of the bass player. He was one of those bad boys that some women get hooked on. And I was hooked for a while."

"How bad was he, Mum?"

"Well, he was hugely charming, but a serial womanizer, and an absentee father. He had children dotted around all over the place that he never saw. I wanted my baby to have a daddy."

"Please don't take this the wrong way, Mum, but wasn't that a rather callous reason to have an abortion?"

"My body, my choice, Sarah. It just didn't feel right. I mean, I always wanted my children to have the kind of loving father that I had. Someone who was a permanent presence in their lives."

Well, they couldn't have a better dad than Bacon Man. Oh my, Daisy's got tears in her eyes.

"But without fail, every year when my due date comes around, I get a twinge in my stomach and I wonder what the baby would have looked like."

"Aww Mum. It's ok. I understand, but what puzzles me is why you didn't use contraception?"

"I did, Sarah. I was on the coil."

"So how did you become pregnant then?"

"I don't know, he was just so powerful."

"That's enough, Daisy," shouts Bacon Man. "Stop drinking this minute."

Well, that killed the conversation stone dead. Daisy has got a faraway look in her eyes that I've never seen before, and I don't think it's just because she's squiffy. Bacon Man has laid down his knife and fork. There's no clearer sign that he's upset. Mind you, I do understand his inferiority complex. I feel the same way whenever a bitch rejects me and plays nice with a Rottweiler.

"So, how did you two meet, Astrid?"

Well done, Mira, for coming to the rescue. Alex and Sarah have obviously heard the story so many times before because they start telling it like a game of table tennis.

"Mum and Dad met in Sarajevo, during the siege." says Sarah.

"At the end of the Bosnian War," says Alex.

"Dad was a war correspondent,"

"Not a very brave one,"

"Mum went to shoot a documentary for Danish television."

"Dad didn't think he stood a chance,"

"Because he was so short and Mum was so tall,"

And a bit of a chubster. I bet.

"But Dad made her laugh."

I can believe that.

"And he fucked me in Sniper Alley, during a NATO bombing raid," says Daisy.

"Muuum. Too much information," groans Sarah.

"Yes, it was the most memorable shag I've ever had," says Bacon Man.

"Daaaaadddd. Please stop or I'll gag on my sprouts," says Alex.

"She was the most remarkable woman I'd ever met. And I just had to make her mine. Anyone for Christmas pudding?"

CHAPTER TWENTY-SEVEN
BACK IN THE SACK

I ADORE THE COLOURS SIGNALLING the rebirth of nature; purple and gold crocuses with their saffron stigmas, the first green buds on the trees, bumblebee yellow daffodils shining like miniature mirrors of the sun along the Thames pathway and beyond. I know their purpose is to bring joy to the world, and I have a pang of conscience whenever I trample a daffodil while chasing a stick, or my latest favourite thing, a hard orange rubber ball. It fits into a cup at the end of a long blue plastic handle. Bacon Man cracks the launcher like a whip.

His *Flexor Carpi Ulnaris* has grown and developed some serious explosive power in recent weeks. Didn't you have a classical education? Fear not, I'll enlighten you. I'm talking about his wrist muscle. I know the reason why it's been getting stronger, and it's not what you think. Bacon Man has taken up racketball, completely against medical advice. He didn't die of a heart attack during the first session and so he's been stepping it up.

I'm getting the benefit of his strong right arm. Sometimes, as he gets fitter, the ball flies sixty or seventy yards. I go hurtling after it like a whippet. Well, a forty-kilo whippet, wearing a heavy fur coat. Nothing, including daffodils, gets in my way. The other colour that's on my mind is the snow white gobby swan in the creek. He's even more aggressive than usual. His bird is spending a lot of time on the nest after their four kids flew the coop.

Which brings me conveniently back to Christmas. I have to say, I was relieved when our guests left on Boxing Day and I'm sure Bacon Man and Daisy were as well. We could all breathe once more, and they were able to talk freely, without fear of triggering the latest cultural trip wire.

But I know what you're dying to find out. Were there any more dramas, or dark secrets that came bounding to the surface? And the answer is, nothing to trouble the scorers. I think the only thing worth mentioning is that Bacon Man is back in the marital sack. He's been there since Christmas. Daisy relished both his body heat and his company. As far as I can tell there hasn't been any coitus restartus yet. I'm sure Bacon Man is building up to it. And Daisy is taking hormones every morning.

To his credit, Bacon Man hasn't touched alcohol since Boxing Day and consequently his snoring has ameliorated, although occasionally the marital bedroom resembles Old MacDonald's Farm with an oink oink here and a moo moo there.

Both of them seem to have had a good night's sleep and are sounding pretty jaunty as we pass a field full of sheep and lambs skipping behind a barbed wire fence. Yes, they're lovely, aren't they? But they'd look even better in a roasting tin, especially that plump little fellow by the weeping willow.

"So how do you feel about neutering?" asks Daisy.

"If you're talking about me, then I'm a thousand percent against it," replies Bacon Man. "Despite what you may think, there's still life in the old dog yet."

"I meant Bjørn. Do you think we should have him done?"

What? They're talking about me. The word whose name shall not be spoken. The C word. Castration. I mean, I'm just entering puberty. I can't believe they're even asking the question. This is the Thames Valley, not the Tavistock Clinic. When was the last time you saw a happy eunuch outside of Brighton?

I'll tell you. During the Ming Dynasty, there was a famous Chinese eunuch called Wei Zhonxian who castrated himself at the age of twenty-one and was able to enter the Forbidden City. Good for him. But I've got no desire to go to Birmingham. However, I am interested in my own Ming Dynasty, just so long as it rhymes with fringe.

"We can't do that to him," says Bacon Man. "I mean, look at him. He's magnificent. We can't neuter him. It would be mutilation."

Thank God. I knew Bacon Man would defend me. My balls have been as cold as a penguin's diving board for the past ten seconds. But they're starting to warm up now. I'm surprised and to be frank, deeply offended that Daisy raised the issue. She's my Mama for heaven's sake.

"I agree," she says.

I could almost faint with relief because we all know who rules the roost in the Somerville residence.

"I've been looking at recent research which shows that neutering can alter a dog's hormonal balance," says Daisy.

One of the reasons Daisy wears the strides at home is because she's the one who applies logic and empirical evidence to the big decisions, whereas Bacon Man relies on his ever-shrinking gut instincts.

"Do you remember why we neutered Dash?" asks Daisy.

"Of course. He was always running away and was totally skittish. But he calmed down after he was done."

"Yes, but his hip joints eventually seized up. It was awful when he sat down that day and couldn't get back up."

"Are you saying the hormonal change was responsible, Daisy?"

"Possibly. He was only ten when he died, and I certainly hope Bjørn will go on for much longer."

Me too. What a double whammy. Having your balls cut off and being subjected to slow euthanasia.

"I'm glad we're on the same page," says Bacon Man.

"So we won't do it then. Besides, I think Bjørn ought to have the chance to have puppies, don't you? They'd be so beautiful."

Thank you. Thank you. Thank you. Woohoo. I'm gonna be a stud. I'm staying intact, I'm gonna make an impact. See if Mabel's able. Canoodle with a poodle. Make a setter wetter. Anoint a pair of pointers. Make a chow chow bow wow. The more the merrier. I'll even schtup a terrier.

"Bjørn!"

Yes, Bacon Man?

"Fetch the ballie."

Yessir. Anything you say sir.

"So, do you think your hormone lozenges are making any difference, Daisy?"

I'm lying down about fifty yards away from them. This is pleasant. I like the feel of the new grass under my stomach. I think I'll just listen to them while I chew on this stick and clean my teeth.

"I feel as though I've got more energy, and I like that. But my breasts are a bit sore. And it feels like I'm about to have a period."

"Christ, you don't think you could get pregnant do you?"

"I don't think so," replies Daisy.

"Unless it was the Immaculate Conception," says Bacon Man wistfully.

"Do you want to play, Bjørn?" asks Daisy.

No, I'm knackered. I just want to lie in the grass.

"He's pooped," says Bacon Man. "Let's go home."

* * *

Gosh. My legs are stiff. Bacon Man really ran me hard this afternoon. I was so thirsty that I drank two whole bowls of water when I got back and then I wolfed down my supper of sardines and kibble. I must have fallen asleep almost straight away. The house is really quiet. I wonder where are they? They're not downstairs. Perhaps they're having an early night. Yes, it sounds like it. I can hear laughing upstairs. I'll just go and see what they're doing.

Ah, they're in bed, having a hygge, watching a movie on

Bacon Man's computer. Intermission time. I need my last outing of the day.

"There you are, Bubsie," says Bacon Man. "We were wondering where you'd got to."

I jump up so my paws are on top of the mattress, although I know better than to climb on the bed in Daisy's room. Whoops. I mean their room. Daisy's looking different. Chainmail is more inviting than her normal nighttime attire of winceyette star-covered pyjamas. Tonight, her shoulders are on display. She's wearing a black number with spaghetti straps. Except it's that thicker pasta, fettuccine. How do I put this delicately? She needs the support.

"Come on, Bubsie," says Bacon Man, sliding out from beneath the duvet. "Let's take you for a pee."

Blimey. The gobby swan is out on manoeuvres. He's climbed out of the water and is heading our way, hissing like a rattlesnake. Now he's beating his wings. I didn't realise they were so powerful. But I suppose it's not surprising when you consider that swans need as long to take off as a B52 bomber. We exchange words as usual. For form's sake, I bark and tell him to wind his neck in, although I understand why he's being so leery. He's just protecting his nest. I have to say, I'm rather partial to raw eggs, but I wouldn't dream of touching his bird's. There'd be blood and feathers everywhere and they would mostly be mine.

"I hope your dog is not going to attack that swan."

Who do you think that grating Midlands' voice belongs to? You only have one attempt to get it right. When I said I had no desire to go to Birmingham, that's because I suspect its citizens will sound equally irritating. I can hear Bacon Man's heart pump harder. The man's tone has opened a lock gate holding back a flood of suppressed anger.

"What is it with you, Maurice? Don't you ever stop poking your nose where it's not needed?"

"Well, there's no need to take that attitude, Morgan. I'm just looking after the interests of the wildlife. They're here for the enjoyment of all the residents."

"Do you really think I'd let Bjørn harm a swan? Get real. The swan's more likely to attack him. And they're not here for the benefit of the residents. They were here first, long before this place was built."

I'm so engrossed in the conversation that I've completely forgotten all about the pressure in my bladder. I won't cock my leg. I'll just squat slightly. Good God. It must have been the two bowls of water. It's like a firehose.

"Now you can see why I need to patrol," says Maurice. "You're in breach of the rules governing dog fouling."

"Get a life, Maurice. Good night."

I hear Maurice grumbling to himself as we head in our different directions. I wonder if Bacon Man is going to resume watching that film on his computer when he gets back to bed. They were having such a nice *hygge*, I think I'll leave them alone and sleep downstairs. Actually, I left my stuffed penguin in my doggie beddie in their bedroom, and I fancy a quiet chew. I'm sure they won't mind my presence. For some reason Bacon Man still uses the main bathroom to clean his teeth. He's doing his standard two minutes on the top row, two minutes on the bottom row then a quick gargle with the anti-gum disease mouthwash.

My claws are clacking on the wooden floor as I head to beddie, but I'm being as quiet as I can. I see Daisy isn't watching the film anymore. Ooh look. That's strange. The duvet seems to be moving. One of the fettuccine straps has fallen down and her left breast is exposed. Daisy is rolling her nipple between her fingers. Maybe she's doing a self-examination. But she's grunting quietly. I hope she's not in pain. I'd better go and check. I leap up onto her side of the bed a bit too enthusiastically.

"Ow, Bjørn. Get down."

Oh Christ, I'm in the doghouse.

"Your claws just scratched me. Go to bed now."

Yes, ma'am. Straight away, Ma'am. I didn't mean to hurt you, Ma'am.

"Shit. I've lost it."

Bacon Man does a double take as he enters the bedroom and sees Daisy leaning on her right-hand side with both fettuccine straps off her shoulders.

"Are you alright?" he asks.

"Come to bed," she says.

That's the fastest I've seen Bacon Man move. Ever.

"Can we see what those golden paws can do," she whispers.

I know she's not talking about mine. Maybe I should sneak out of the room and give them some privacy. But I don't want to disturb them. So, I'd better stay put.

"Kiss me," she says.

Wow, I'm impressed. I've seen far worse big screen kisses on the TV. Bacon Man's quite the smoocher.

"Oooosh," says Daisy "You haven't lost your touch baby."

"Do you want me to talk dirty to you?" asks Bacon Man.

"No, just put those golden paws to work."

"We can take the bins out or go to the dump, if you like."

"Stop it," she says. "See if you can make my pussy talk,"

I'm not falling for that again. I know there's not a cat in there. I know what she's talking about. I've sniffed the parson's poodle. I've put my nose in pussy grass out by the river.

What do you mean you don't know what pussy grass is? Stop interrupting the commentary. Pussy grass is where a bitch on heat has left her mark on a lawn or in a field. For the older ones among you, it's a dog's equivalent of Page Three, before The Sun virtue signalled by scrapping topless pictures from the newspaper. Now can we get back to the action, people?

Go on Bacon Man, make her pussy talk.

Wow, all that racquetball and ball throwing for me have seriously made a difference to his strength. I can see his arm is going like the piston of that Little Engine That Could. The only difference is, he's not saying, 'I think I can, I think I can, I think I can.'

"Ah, just there," moans Daisy.

Those are the last words she says for a while. She seems to be thinking very hard about something. I don't think it's the Hoovering.

Her breathing is now very deep and heavy. Good to see she's getting a cardiovascular workout.

And then she screams.

"Oh baby,"

That was loud enough to wake the dead in the churchyard a mile away. Now what's going to happen. Are they going to start negotiations about how to proceed in the next stage? But Bacon Man has taken decisive action. He's kneeling in front of Daisy, and she lifts her legs onto his shoulders.

"Oh, I'm still a bit dry," she says.

Perhaps I can help out. I'm drooling quite badly. Maybe they'd like some. On second thoughts, better not. I'll stay put.

Now Bacon Man has bent down again, and I can't quite see what's going on, but Daisy's legs seem to have lowered and it sounds like he's eating something. Old habits die hard.

"Ooooh Baby," says Daisy. "That's a surprise, keep going."

Daisy's moaning again. And not like she does when Bacon Man doesn't load the dishwasher properly.

Now he's back on his knees and Daisy's legs are on his shoulders again.

"Wow, you're so much harder than the last time. And so much stronger. I can really feel you."

I'm just going to sneak out of my doggie beddie, so I can get a better angle on the action. Bacon Man has increased the tempo. I can see her toes are curling with pleasure. Daisy makes her breasts stand up by putting her arms by her sides. In this light, they almost look pert, and it's much cheaper than the cosmetic operation that Bacon Man kept wanging on about months ago. Now she's performing a belly dancer's trick of shaking from side to side.

"Don't do that, don't do that," shouts Bacon Man.

Daisy giggles and shakes them even more exuberantly.

"Oh FUCKKKKKKKKKKKK," he shouts.

Then Bacon Man screams in a way that I'm struggling to put into words. I've never been to a Halal abattoir, but I'm sure that's what it must sound like when a goat has its throat cut.

"That was fantastic," says Bacon Man. "I could have gone on longer, but then you did that thing with your tits. Why did you do it?"

Daisy giggles.

"Because I know you like it."

"But is that because you wanted to…..."

"Shut up with the analysis will you? It's not Match of the Day," says Daisy. "Let's just enjoy the moment."

I'd better sneak back into my beddie. Just as I'm about to lay my head on the toy penguin, Bacon Man rolls onto his back, and I hear his facial muscles break into a broad smile.

"That was wonderful, Daisy. I love you. Any chance of an action replay?"

"Yeah, right. Good night. I love you too."

CHAPTER TWENTY EIGHT

BACON MAN DOWN

Bacon Man's in a great mood this morning. He was up with the lark, and he's humming. I don't mean musically. He just hasn't taken a shower yet. He's fed me breakfast, given me a fresh bowl of water and we're now heading out the door for the morning ones and twos. Bacon Man's routine is slightly different to normal. After drinking a small cappuccino, he's put the orange ball in the launcher. Usually, he has coffee after the first walk, and does the ball thing before the second walk of the day. Maybe he's letting Daisy have a lie in.

Blimey, the swan is also up and at them. At least he's not out on the river bank this morning, but he's like a destroyer hunting a submarine, swimming a purposeful figure of eight. Here we go, through the pedestrian gate, into the free world, and I'll just take a quick wazz on the post box. That's my first delivery of the day. Let's trot on a bit further, through the swinging barred gate towards the tunnel and I could do with a quick how's-your-father in the ivy, preferably with a sniff of Page Three to make the time pass by. I'm having a bit of trouble this morning. Normally I'm as regular as clockwork, but my stomach seems to be playing up. I'll just go deeper into the foliage. Maybe that'll loosen things up.

I look behind me, and Bacon Man's following, leaving the footpath, and pushing his way through the foliage like David Attenborough. There's no need for that, Bacon Man. How about some privacy? You don't want to watch me taking a dump, do you? Really. Ah, that's better, here we go. It was one of those movements that's better than sex. I don't have copyright on that expression. It's a Daisy original. If those are her preferences, no wonder Bacon Man's been frustrated for so long.

Bacon Man's trying to extricate the last green poo bag from the small plastic cylinder attached to the lead. I don't know why he's bothering. We're some distance away from the footpath, and so there's no need for him to pick up my doings. They're hidden in the bushes. Nobody's going to notice. He could get away with it without risking a hundred and fifty pound fine. But I know why he wants to pick it up. It's because he can. When we started this malarkey, it was almost as much of an effort for him as running a half marathon. But the new, comparatively slimmer Bacon Man is so much more flexible and can bend down without having a heart attack.

Or can he? Have I spoken too soon? Bacon Man's just fallen over. Oh no. He went down like a sack of hammers. I didn't see him trip over anything. He didn't make a sound.

Bacon Man, get up. Come on.

He's just lying there with his arms outstretched. His face is twisted to the left. He's not moving.

Come on, Bacon Man, stop fooling around.

I bend down and put my nose to his face and lick it. Nothing. I'm starting to panic. But I manage to tell myself to calm down and use my special powers. Panicking will only make matters worse.

Listen, Bjørn. Listen. What can you hear? Think.

I can hear Bacon Man's heart beating, but it doesn't sound quite right. At least he's breathing. But for how long? Maybe I can wake him up if I bark. I reach down into my belly and conjure up the deepest, loudest bark I can muster. Nothing. I bark about ten times in a row. But still, he's not responding, and if there's anyone on the footpath, they're just ignoring me. What am I going to do? I know. I'll get Daisy and bring her back here.

I can find my way home, no problem. I crash through the trees to get back to the path and carry on sprinting towards Galahad Island. I caught myself on a sharp branch as I went through. I'm pretty sure I'm bleeding, but I can't feel any pain. It must be the adrenaline. My heart has never pounded this hard before. I haven't crawled beneath the springy barred gate for months because I've grown. But somehow, I squeeze myself through the gap, get to my feet and reach the Island's iron gates within seconds. They're closed. Damn!

I try to crawl underneath but I'm not a dachshund. It's impossible. I stand at the gate and bark to try to raise attention inside. That's amazing. There's nobody about. Maybe I should wait for a car. It doesn't matter which direction it comes from. I could slip through when the gates open electronically. I can't believe it's as quiet as a grave, and that's where Bacon Man will end up if I don't find a way through. I know what I can do.

I start running as fast as I can along the lane that we take to go cruising and I dash into a driveway. I hope this is the right house. Yes. It's the one that belongs to Genevieve, the singer. The gate to her back garden is open, thank goodness. I cross the small lawn in four or five bounds and get down to the creek. I can see our house over to the left. There's no time to bark. I feel my way into the water between two cabin cruisers and start doggy paddling towards the other side.

Oh Christ, there's the gobby swan. He's about five cabin cruisers up the creek to the left of me. Oh no. He's spotted me and he's closing at a rapid rate of knots. I never thought he was that fast. I reach down to see if my feet will touch the bottom so I can get some purchase on the mud and perhaps move more quickly towards the opposite bank. Shit. I'm out of my depth. The swan's hissing and snorting at the top of his voice. I don't have a clue what he's yelling, but I'm sure he's not asking me whether I want my eggs boiled or scrambled.

Wooooaaaauuuw. That really hurt. Mr. Gobby just battered me with his left wing and now the right. I can't believe the power in his chest muscles. His wings might be covered in feathers and his bones might be hollow, but they're delivering extremely effective headshots. I've got to keep my chin above water. Physically, I should be stronger than him, but I'm not in my natural element.

He's more agile in the water and somehow, he's forcing me under, and away from the bank. I mustn't swallow. I mustn't swallow. I come back up to the surface and gulp in fresh air. I wish the swan would understand that I'm not threatening his nest. But this is no time for negotiation. It's fight or flight and I just want to get away. Leave me alone.

Somehow, I've bounced up ahead of the swan. Suddenly this doesn't seem real. I'm experiencing this weird sensation where my mind seems to have separated from my body. I feel like I'm hovering above the creek watching a golden retriever fighting for survival. I know the psychological term. It's dissociation. My brain is trying to protect me from the mental anguish of what I'm enduring.

I'm watching myself paddling with all my might and I suddenly hear myself crying out in a voice I've never heard before. There's a ghostly echo. Is this real or a dream? It's real, because in a nanosecond I work out that the sound is bouncing back at me off the resin hulls of the cabin cruisers. I'm howling for help in a register that I hope will attract Daisy or someone on Galahad Island. My lungs are hurting from crying as loudly as possible and from the effort of swimming for my life. Out of the corner of my eye, I see Maurice Oxford striding towards the bank. I hope he doesn't think that I'm attacking the swan.

"Come on, Bjørn, you can do it,"

The voice encouraging me belongs to Maurice. What a surprise. Thank the Lord Dog. He's seen what's happening and I'm not in trouble. I must reach the bank before the swan outflanks me and gets ahead of me again. My front paws are within touching distance of the bank and now he's attacking me from the side. First one wing, then the other, then both together. I've gone under and my mouth is open. Oh no. I've swallowed water. I've got to get to the surface.

Suddenly, I feel a change in the water pressure next to me

and human hands are reaching beneath my body to push me up. It gives me new heart, and somehow, I get my head back above water. I'm amazed to see Maurice Oxford neck deep in the River Thames, pushing me with one hand, and trying to repel the swan with the other.

"Hang on, Maurice, I'll help."

Blimey, Reginald, the Silver Fox, is sprinting down to the bank. And behind him I can see Daisy, looking frantic. All the while the swan is battering me, and now he's got hold of my left ear in his beak. It feels like he's tearing it to shreds. I hear myself shrieking in pain. I didn't think swans had teeth, but his beak feels like a saw and he's ripping me to pieces. It's agony.

I'm struggling to breathe. It feels like I'm being strangled. I'm choking. Reginald is pulling on my collar, and now Daisy has got a grip as well and together they're hauling me out of the water. I've never been so relieved to have my feet on terra firma. My first instinct is to shake the river out of my fur. I hear myself whimpering from the pain and then I become conscious of Maurice trying to claw his way on to the bank. He can't manage alone.

Reginald takes one arm, Daisy the other, and together they get the top half of Maurice's body out of the water, before they themselves fall over. Daisy gets to her feet first. She's covered in dirt. She grabs Maurice's right hand and pulls him up far enough so he can use his right leg to lever himself up.

"Thank you, Maurice," she gasps, "that was so brave of you. You saved Bjørn's life."

"It was nothing, Astrid," he says, wheezing. "He's a lovely dog. I couldn't let him drown."

"I'm so grateful," says Daisy. "But where's Morgan? Bjørn, where's Bacon Man? Maurice, have you seen Morgan?"

"No, Astrid. I don't know where he is, and I don't know how Bjørn fell in the water."

"Gen, have you seen Morgan?"

I look across to the other side of the creek and I can see Genevieve standing at the end of her garden. She's obviously been alerted by the kerfuffle.

"No, Astrid. I was upstairs when I saw Bjørn dashing through the garden. He dived straight into the river and was attacked by the swan."

"So where is Morgan? Bjørn, where's Bacon Man? Is he hurt?"

At last, she understands. I start barking and jumping up and down.

"Where's your lead?" asks Daisy. "You've only got your collar. Morgan must have the lead with him. Bjørn, do you know where he is? Let's find Bacon Man."

I bark again and run off in the direction of the main gate.

"Bjørn, stop," Daisy yells.

I do as I'm told because I'm sure Daisy knows what she's doing.

"Sit."

I sit down and wait patiently.

Daisy comes up to me and holds me by the collar.

"Shit," she says, "I don't have a lead."

So, she peels off her long-sleeved sweatshirt and threads one of the arms through my collar and ties it in a knot. She's using the rest of the garment as a lead. Then I look up at her and realise she's just wearing a bra, leggings and a pair of boots.

I look at Reginald, the Silver Fox and he's doing goldfish impressions. That must be his trademark.

"Astrid, hang on, put some clothes on and I'll get a rope," shouts Maurice.

"Sorry there's not time, we've got to find Morgan. Come on, Bjørn, let's find Bacon Man, where is he?"

I start pulling her towards the gate. She's struggling to hold me. But I've got to pull her along. It's amazing isn't it. When I was barking for help about five minutes ago, there seemed to be no one on the island. But now it's bloody rush hour. Every man and woman and their dog seem to be out on the road or pathway leading off the island. They can't believe what they're seeing. Two cars almost collide as Daisy strides across the road towards the pedestrian gate with her bra struggling to contain her breasts. Wooo. The pain is really kicking in. My ears are hurting and so is my left leg.

"I see everything's back to normal at Number 69," I hear one woman say.

"She just can't keep them under cover can she?"

"She's such a slut."

"Reginald. Stop gawking. Where are you going?"

I look back and see that Reginald is following us. Daisy is impervious to the furore she's causing. We're quickly through the pedestrian gate and in no time, we're at the springy barred wooden gate. Bacon Man isn't far away. I can smell him. I'm pulling Daisy along as fast as I can go. It sounds like she's being whipped as she forces her way through the foliage. She's wincing and squealing in pain as the branches dig into her flesh.

"There he is." she screams. "Good boy, Bjørn."

She lets go of the sweatshirt. I race over to Bacon Man and lick his face as vigorously as I can. I feel him stir and he rolls over onto his back and opens his eyes.

Just at that moment Daisy bends down, trips and falls onto Bacon Man. Her décolletage smacks him in the face.

"Ooo, hello, Daisy. You're a bit forward for this time in the morning. But I'm up for it if you are."

Daisy splutters. I can't work out if she's going to laugh or cry.

"I thought you were dead."

"Don't be daft," says Bacon Man. "I'm fine. What's going on? Why are you just wearing a bra?"

"Fuck, I left my phone at home," says Daisy.

"Do you want to take a selfie? Hang on, I'll get mine, it's in my pocket. I'll take a picture."

"I don't want to take a picture, I want to call 999?"

"What on earth for?":

"To call an ambulance. You've had a heart attack, and you could die if we don't get help straight away."

"Oh stop being hysterical. My heart's perfectly fine."

Daisy ignores him and punches away at the keyboard and puts the phone on speaker.

"What's your emergency? Which service do you require?"

"Ambulance please?"

"Daisy stop, this is ridiculous. I'm fine."

Bacon Man tries to stand up but wobbles and sits back down again straight away.

"Wooooo."

"Don't move," says Daisy, "You might damage something."

"This is absurd," protests Bacon Man. "Daisy, put your sweatshirt on, you'll catch your death of cold. Oh God, look at Bjørn's leg. He's bleeding. Give me the sweatshirt."

I look down. Yes, I'm bleeding. I start licking it, but I can't stop the flow. The swan must have cut down to a blood vessel with its sharp beak.

Bacon Man tries in vain to tear the sweatshirt. As he's pulling at the fabric, Daisy gets through to the ambulance controllers. She's having a conversation about our location and Bacon Man's condition, but I'm concentrating on what Bacon Man is doing. He's found a hole in the sweatshirt that I probably made with my teeth when trying to get Daisy's attention in the house. He's working at it with one of his keys. I don't know what on earth he's doing, but I think he's trying to do something to help me. Eventually he manages to rip off a strip of material.

"Ok, ," he says, "Lie still, there's a good boy. We're going to patch you up."

Bacon Man gets hold of my injured paw and starts wrapping material around the wound in my leg. It's really tight. It hurts and I whimper.

"Sorry, I don't mean to hurt you, but it has to be tight to stop the bleeding. Be a good boy. No. Don't bite it. Leave it alone, there's a good boy."

We stare into each other's eyes, and he smiles.

"Don't worry, we'll sort you out."

He ties the rag in a knot. He's made a reasonably efficient bandage, but I can see that the blood stain is spreading through the material.

"Right," says Daisy. "They're sending a helicopter."

"You're joking, Daisy," he says. "That's completely over the top. I'm perfectly fine."

"You're not fine. You're going in the helicopter whether you like it or not."

"But Daisy," protests Bacon Man, "the one who's in bad shape is Bjørn, we need to get him to a vet. I haven't managed to stop the bleeding."

This time he works at the remaining sleeve and separates from the body of the shirt. He unties the first tourniquet, wraps the sleeve around my wound even tighter, and knots it. And then he clamps his hand over the top of the wound and applies extra pressure. I can feel the blood bubbling away and I have this weird sensation of the cells trying to knit themselves together. It really hurts. But I'm not going to whimper.

In the distance I hear the rotors of a helicopter banging the air hard as it flies in our direction.

"Won't be long now," says Daisy.

"Do they know where to come," asks Bacon Man."

"Yes, of course they do," says Daisy, "I pinned our location and they'll find us using GPS."

"This is so embarrassing," says Bacon Man.

"Don't be silly. We've got to get you to hospital, and because there are no access roads here, they've decided to send a chopper."

"That's nuts," says Bacon Man. "Completely over the top."

I'm feeling tired, and I'm starting to get sleepy.

"There you are, Astrid," says a voice.

I look up and see the Silver Fox forcing his way through the bushes.

"What can I do to help," he asks. "Have you called an ambulance?"

"Yes, Reginald,"

"Call me Reggie,"

"Yes, Reggie, I'm sure that chopper you can hear is for us. They decided not to send an ambulance. I think it's going to land somewhere near, probably in a field, and the crew are going to get here on foot."

"Is there anything I can do?" he asks.

"I'm really worried about Bjørn," says Bacon Man. "He's got a bad leg wound and is losing blood. I'm trying to staunch the flow and as long as I apply pressure, I think it's working. But he needs to get to a vet. His ear is torn to shreds as well."

"Ok, I'll take him," says Reggie. "Which vet do you use?"

"It's the big one in Henlow," says Daisy. "On the right, on the main road out of town."

"Going east or west?"

"East."

"I know the one you mean. Opposite the Rule Britannia pub?"

"Yup, that's the one."

"Here take my shirt," says Reggie. "You don't want to get cold."

"Thanks. That's very kind of you."

Reggie peels off his shirt and reveals a trim, tanned, muscular physique. Daisy just about manages to squeeze into the shirt, which is a couple of sizes too small. She hands the lead to Reggie, and I start limping back towards the path. I look back and Bacon Man is sitting up. Daisy is texting furiously.

"Go on, Bjørn, off you go, there's a good boy, everything'll be fine," says Bacon Man.

I hope so. He's always so optimistic. But what about him? Will he be alright?

The pain is getting worse, and I'm struggling to get through the hedgerow. I limp along the path towards the springy gate. I can hardly bear to put my front left leg on the ground. I'm staggering on three legs, completely off balance. Every time I put my left foot down, pain shoots along the whole bone structure and seems to strike me behind the eyes.

"Come on, Bjørn, you can do it," encourages Reggie.

He seems like a kind man after all. Here we are, at the entrance to Galahad Island. I thought we were going to the vet. What's happening to me? I feel faint. Everything's going blurry. Is this it? Am I dying? If I've saved Bacon Man, then it's been worth it.

CHAPTER TWENTY NINE

THE RECKONING

I'm lying down in a strange enclosure. I've never felt this woozy before. Is this what a hangover is like, or coming down from a drug binge? I don't feel as though I'm connected to my body. Am I alive or dead? I've got strange sensations in my left leg and my ears. It's a dull pain, as if it's been numbed. I look down at my left leg and see it's wrapped in a big bandage. I don't like that at all. I want to rip it off. I try to reach it with my mouth, but there's a transparent plastic thingy around my neck, that's stopping me from reaching.

"Hello, Bjørn, are you awake?"

Is that an angel? Quite possibly. My eyes are struggling to focus, but now the face in front of me is sharp. It's the nurse who's looked after me before when I've been to the vet for my injections. She's a babe.

"You sweet boy. You brave boy. How are you feeling?"

Like a swan has tried to kill me. That's how I'm feeling. But I guess I'm alive. Hurray.

"Well, you're going to be alright. You'll be fine in a few

days. Your mummy's coming to get you. She'll be here in a few minutes. Ah, here she is now. Hello, Mrs. Somerville."

"Hi, sorry I'm later than I said I'd be. How's he doing?"

"He's fine. We had to sedate him quite heavily, but he's coming round. He looks a bit wobbly. It's going to take a while to wear off. But he's ok. You'll be able to take him home. I'll just get the vet."

I look up and Daisy is smiling down at me. She crouches down and rubs my tummy.

"Hello, Bubsie. How are you doing? Who's Mama's brave boy? You brave, brave boy. You're a real hero. Do you know that? You deserve a medal. Oh dear, look at your eye. It's really bloodshot."

But what about Bacon Man? What's happened to Bacon Man?

"Hello, Mrs. Somerville, I'm the duty vet."

"Hi, looks like you've done a good job on him. How's he doing?"

"He's in good shape. He's going to make a full recovery."

"What happened to his eye?" Daisy asks.

Yes, I'd like to know what happened. But that might explain why I'm having trouble focusing.

"I think the swan must have caught him with one of his wings. He was lucky not to be blinded. But it's worse than it looks. It should heal up in a couple of days. And his vision will be fine. He won't have to wear glasses."

The vet laughs at her own joke. She's got that nervous tic that lots of British people seem to have. They laugh for no reason at things that aren't funny. It's a sign of insecurity. Why am I even thinking like that? I want to know what happened to Bacon Man.

"I can see that you've patched up his ear," says Daisy.

Yes, I'm wearing a bandage. My ears are my best feature. They're now deformed. It's so embarrassing.

"What about the bandage on his leg?"

"We had to remove the dew claw?"

"What's that?"

"It's the claw on the back of the leg attached to what looks like a bulb. It looks like the swan managed to split the claw, so we had to remove it. But it'll grow back. It needs to be bandaged."

"Any lasting damage?"

"No, but swan bites can be complicated. They carry a lot of bacteria in their mouths, and there's a real danger that wounds can become infected. So, we've taken the precaution of giving him a big dose of antibiotics. That needs to be topped up to keep infection at bay. And he's going to have to continue wearing the cone of shame."

"Ok, so I can take him home?"

"Yes you can. Mr. Hobbs told us that Bjørn is something of a hero?"

"Mr Hobbs?"

"Reggie?"

"Oh now, I know who you are talking about. I didn't know his surname."

"He's quite the flirt."

"I wouldn't know," says Daisy, "but he was very kind to my husband and me. I'm so grateful that he brought Bjørn here."

"How is your husband doing?"

"Not too sure. But better than expected, I think."

Oh fantastic. That's great news. I'm so relieved. I wonder when I can see Bacon Man to check up on him.

"So what happened to him?" asks the vet.

"Well, it seems he had something called syncope? He basically fainted in the woods. He was lucky he collapsed on soft ground, because he didn't hit his head, or suffer neck trauma. He's stable in hospital right now. I was going to stay with him, but the doctors said he was fine and needed some bed rest. They've got to conduct a whole batch of tests to check his heart and other functions."

"Syncope can be just a one off, or it could be a sign of some more serious underlying condition," says the vet. "It can happen in animals as well. The important thing is he's in the right place."

"Yes. I'll settle up with you," says Daisy. "And I'll take him home."

"Have you got someone else at home to help out?"

"No, but my son lives in London. And he should be on the train now. He's promised to help."

"That's good. I'm afraid, Mrs Somerville, the bill's going to be rather steep."

"What can you do? Anyway, every penny is worth it. Bjørn's a hero. He saved my husband's life."

The staff at the vets line up to see me out. I'm stroked and petted and given a few treats on my way to the car. Daisy opens the back door of the Merc. Normally, I can leap up with ease. But I'm so stiff, and I daren't put any weight on my front legs. I put my front paws on the back seat, and Daisy gets behind me, puts her hands either side of my tail and pushes me up.

She starts the engine and hits the button to make my window go down. I try to stick my head out, but the plastic thingy around my neck gets stuck on the door pillar. I wriggle around and eventually I manage to manoeuvre in such a way that my whole head is outside the car, and my shoulders are up against the door. I hope that a little light people watching as we cruise home will distract me from my suffering.

Daisy's still got a heavy right foot, and I think we're going a few miles an hour above the speed limit. It's not very comfortable, because the plastic hood is acting like a sail. It's catching the wind and forcing my head back. I seem to be attracting a lot of attention from people on the pavement. There are so many "aaaaaahs", it sounds like a bloody choir out there. The last thing I want to do is to be an object of pity or sympathy. Luckily, the hood is tapered, and so it's easier to duck back inside the car, than to try to peer out. I decide I'm going to lie down out of sight until we get home.

Daisy goes to the sink and fills my bowl full of fresh water. But I don't feel like drinking. I head into the sitting room and climb on to my favourite sofa. The sun is shining brightly. Daisy opens the French window to the balcony, and I'm going to grab a few zeds in the sunbeam, which feels a lot warmer than usual. Then Daisy's phone rings, and as usual, she puts it on speaker.

"Hello?" she inquires.

"Hi, Daisy, it's Tommy."

"Sorry. Tommy who?"

"Tommy Bentwaters, how are you doing?"

"Oh, hi, Tommy, sorry I didn't recognise your voice. How lovely to hear from you, how are you?"

"Everything's good this end, but I hear that you've had a few dramas."

"How did you find out?"

"I was talking to Gen, and she filled me in. Sounds pretty dramatic."

"Yes, it's been an interesting few hours, but things are settling down."

"How's Morgan doing?"

"He's fine, I think. He collapsed, as Gen may have told you. He's having some heart tests done, and the doctors at the hospital told me it's quite likely he may need surgery. Possibly a bypass of some sort."

"Which hospital is he at?"

"He's at Wexford Park, about ten miles from here."

"What's it like?" Tommy asks.

"Typical NHS. Fairly ancient, pretty run down. But the care seems good enough. They're really looking after him."

"Look, Astrid, I'd like to help."

"That's really kind, Tommy, but honestly, there's no need. We'll be fine."

"Listen, Astrid. I mean it. I had a few heart issues a few years back. I kept it quiet. I didn't want it getting out. But I've got a fantastic heart surgeon. And I'll ask him to sort Morgan out. I went to a private hospital not far from where you live. I'll book Morgan in and ask the doc to do the necessary."

"We couldn't possibly, Tommy. It's so generous of you, but Morgan hates the idea of charity and so do I."

"It's not charity, Astrid. It's the least I can do. You and Morgan have saved my career and given me a new lease of life. The tour is going brilliantly. We're sold out. More dates are being added. We're going to Europe after we've done the UK and Dublin. And there's the possibility of a US tour."

"That's fantastic, Tommy. I'm so pleased for you."

"Not only that, but the greatest hits album is hovering around the top of the rock charts, and I've got a new single coming out. I'm back in the big time. Who knows? I might be able to buy myself another castle. Please let me help."

"Well, you're pretty persuasive, Tommy. Let me talk to Morgan and see what he says."

"Yeah, do that. But the other good thing about going into a private hospital is that you'll be able to take Bjørn in. You couldn't do that at an NHS place. And that might help Morgan's recovery time."

That's right, Tommy, you tell her. That sounds like a great idea to me. I'm suddenly not feeling so sorry for myself.

* * *

I've been allowed into the hospital. Let me tell you it's a lot better than the vet's surgery. It's more like a hotel. Much more upscale than the places I've stayed in when I've been taken on the road. We're being led down a very swish looking corridor. I know where we're going. I can smell Bacon Man, he's not far away. From here, I can tell he's not humming as much as he did when he collapsed. He's showered away Daisy's scent and now he smells just like frustrated Bacon Man.

"There he is. Hello, Bubsie. How are you doing, you brave boy?"

Daisy lets the lead go. I dash into the room and leap on the bed. The cone of shame bangs him in the face, and his laptop goes flying. Bacon Man manages to catch it with his left hand. Not bad reactions for a guy of his age, and in bed with a possible heart condition. I'm so disappointed that I can't lick Bacon Man.

"So what do the doctors say?" asks Daisy.

"The verdict's not that bad. The cholesterol tablets haven't been as effective as they should have been, and one of my arteries is a bit furred up, and so they want to put in a stent. It's a routine operation. I should be out of hospital in a couple of days. And within a few days I should be right as rain."

Just then Daisy's phone rings. For once, she doesn't put it on speaker. So, we just hear her side of the conversation.

"Yes, that's me. Oh really. Hello. I didn't expect to hear from you again. Oh, that's interesting. I understand that. Let me talk to my husband. I've got your number in my phone. I'll call you back in five minutes. Yes, I promise to let you know."

I'm virtually cross eyed. My eyes have been switching backwards and forwards between Daisy and Bacon Man during her conversation. What on earth was that all about?

"Come on, Daisy," says Bacon Man, "Don't keep us in suspense. Who was that?"

"It was the breeder in Hampshire," says Daisy.

"What did she want?" asks Bacon Man.

"She's got a two year old female golden that she needs to find a home for straight away."

Ooooooh. My ears prick up.

"She belonged to a widow who died. And the widow's only daughter is allergic to dogs and so she's letting her go."

"Does she want another two and a half grand?" asks Bacon Man.

"No, not at all. The breeder isn't asking for any money."

"Really?"

"Yes. That was one of the conditions imposed by the widow's daughter. She just wants the dog to go to a good home. And because we paid double for Bjørn, the breeder thought of us first."

"But that means puppies. You know what a hound dog he's become recently," says Bacon Man. "I don't think that's a good idea."

"No. She's been neutered. So, there won't be any puppies."

"Well, think of the positives. They would keep each other company, and that might reduce the strain on both of us, while I try to regain my strength. It would probably mean more walks and longer ones."

"But that's a good thing for both of us," says Daisy.

"I got the impression the breeder wants a quick decision. Is that right, Daisy?"

"Yes. We agreed that I call her back in a couple of minutes or she'll ask someone else to take the Golden."

Bacon Man sighs. We look into each other's eyes and lock on. I know I'm just a dog. But every fibre of my being signals that we're transcending our differences as creatures and are communicating on a higher plane that exists beyond the grasp of human discovery. Just as plasma in blood delivers nutrients to our cells, oxytocin, the love hormone that we're producing, allows us to reach each other's souls. We've exchanged meaningful looks before, but this moment feels like a re-dedication of the bond between us.

We're both in the wars and I feel ridiculous peering at him through the blinkers of the cone of shame. Appearances aside, I'm confident of my total recovery. In comparative terms, I'm much younger than Bacon Man. Although I'm optimistic about his recuperation, I can't help but worry that it'll take longer than he expects, and he may be somehow diminished.

But I've got his back, and so does Daisy. She may not demonstrate her love in the manner that he craves, but love takes many forms, and her commitment to him is irrefutable. As I look into those kind, grey-green eyes, I'm asking him a simple question. Am I worthy of the same opportunity?

It may seem to you that our ethereal dialogue has lasted for several minutes, or even longer. Perhaps you are wondering whether we've missed the breeder's deadline and that the chance has been lost. On one level, our exchange is timeless, but in terms of the human clock, it's done and dusted in a nanosecond.

"What are you waiting for, Daisy?" says Bacon Man. "Give her a call."

CHAPTER THIRTY

GOOD GOLLY MISS MOLLY

We've just watched the most incredible sunset. The four of us have been on the balcony, mesmerised by the wonders of nature. Yes, you've guessed correctly. Bacon Man is back home. His operation was a success. As with any surgery, the insertion of the stent was invasive, and his body is taking time to heal. We're walking. Not as far or as quickly as we were before he nose-dived into the ivy. However, he's diligent about his exercise regime and is on the right track. The worry lines on Daisy's forehead are no longer as deeply furrowed. Bacon Man is still awaiting the results from some of his blood tests, but the overall prognosis is good to fabulous.

They've just disappeared inside. I think they might be having a *hygge* in bed. Molly and I are curled up together on the decking, gazing up at the most extraordinary palette of violet and purple, blending into velvety-pink low altitude strato-cumulous clouds. I've never seen the sky looking more vibrant.

"God's painting tonight," said Daisy, before she went indoors.

She's right, if there is a Lord Dog, he/she/they has/have

got a wonderful eye. He/she/they has/have painted those colours upside down in the river in front of us as well.

"Is it always this beautiful?" asks Molly.

"No, it's not," I reply. "Sometimes, it's really miserable. It's Britain after all. But maybe, if there's someone up there looking over us, he/she/they is/are making a special effort to celebrate your arrival in your new home."

"Ah thank you, that's so sweet."

"I feel so much better now that I've had the cone of shame removed. Do you now realise, Molly, that I can kiss you properly for the first time?"

"Yes, I do."

"I don't mean to beg, Molly, but I don't suppose there's a chance of a thanks-for-letting-me-move-into-this-marvellous-Thames-side-shag-pad-shag is there?"

"You're absolutely spot on, Bjørn."

"I am?"

"Yes. You shouldn't suppose there's a chance."

"But you've been nibbling my ear. I thought that was a come-on."

"That's what golden retrievers do when they're being friendly."

"I suppose you're right. Can we just have a cuddle and see what happens?"

"Do you think it's Christmas?"

"No I don't, but...."

"There are no buts about it. I'm not in the habit of dishing out I've-had-the-cone-of-shame-removed-celebration shags. There is one thing I've noticed about you though, Bjørn."

"Yes Molly. And what's that?"

"You like your food don't you?"

"Yes, it always cheers me up and Bacon Man is such a great cook."

"Have you seen the size of your stomach recently?"

"From what angle?"

"The angle doesn't matter. I'm pretty sure I wouldn't be able to feel you properly. There's going to be nothing in it for me. So, what's the point?"

"Oh Molly, I'm deflated."

"So I've noticed. But let me ask you this?"

"Yes, Molly. What's that?"

"Do you fancy a shag?"

"Oh yes please."

"Well, lose a few kilos and I'll think about it."

THE END

Printed in Great Britain
by Amazon